Praise for

The Secret Confessions of Anne Shakespeare

"An entertaining and admirable novel that offers a surprising reinterpretation of Will Shakespeare's wife, Anne Hathaway, who shares, and helps shape, his dream."

—Sandra Worth, author of *The King's Daughter:*
A Novel of the First Tudor Queen

"Arliss Ryan knows her Tudor London and the theater of that era. *The Secret Confessions* brings Anne Hathaway out of the shadows into real life, not as the neglected shrew William happily left behind in Stratford, but as a sensual, humorous, talented, and daring woman. This is a compelling novel with unexpected turns in every satisfying chapter."

—Jeane Westin, author of *The Virgin's Daughters*

"Controversial and clever, daring and detailed, *The Secret Confessions of Anne Shakespeare* outshocks any modern-day tell-all. Anne, the feisty and dynamic narrator, gives us an in-depth view of her own life and of Queen Elizabeth's England. The novel is as sweeping and insightful, tragic and comic as some of the Bard's own plays."

—Karen Harper, national bestselling author of *Mistress Shakespeare*
and *The Que   erness*

The Secret Confessions of Anne Shakespeare

ARLISS RYAN

NEW AMERICAN LIBRARY

New American Library
Published by New American Library,
a division of Penguin Group (USA) Inc.,
375 Hudson Street, New York, New York 10014, USA
Penguin Group (Canada), 90 Eglinton Avenue East, Suite 700, Toronto,
Ontario M4P 2Y3, Canada (a division of Pearson Penguin Canada Inc.)
Penguin Books Ltd., 80 Strand, London WC2R 0RL, England
Penguin Ireland, 25 St. Stephen's Green, Dublin 2,
Ireland (a division of Penguin Books Ltd.)
Penguin Group (Australia), 250 Camberwell Road, Camberwell,
Victoria 3124, Australia (a division of Pearson Australia Group Pty. Ltd.)
Penguin Books India Pvt. Ltd., 11 Community Centre,
Panchsheel Park, New Delhi - 110 017, India
Penguin Group (NZ), 67 Apollo Drive, Rosedale, North Shore 0632,
New Zealand (a division of Pearson New Zealand Ltd.)
Penguin Books (South Africa) (Pty.) Ltd., 24 Sturdee Avenue,
Rosebank, Johannesburg 2196, South Africa

Penguin Books Ltd., Registered Offices:
80 Strand, London WC2R 0RL, England

First published by New American Library,
a division of Penguin Group (USA) Inc.

First Printing, June 2010
1   3   5   7   9   10   8   6   4   2

 REGISTERED TRADEMARK—MARCA REGISTRADA

LIBRARY OF CONGRESS CATALOGING-IN-PUBLICATION DATA:

Ryan, Arliss.
The secret confessions of Anne Shakespeare/Arliss Ryan.
p. cm.
ISBN 978-0-451-22995-3
1. Hathaway, Anne, 1556?–1623—Fiction. 2. Shakespeare, William, 1564–1616—Fiction.
3. London (England)—History—16th century—Fiction. 4. Author's spouses—Fiction.
5. Dramatists—Ficiton. I. Title.
PS3568.Y262S43 2010
813'.54—dc22   2010005080

Set in Simoncini Garamond • Designed by Elke Sigal

Printed in the United States of America

For Kira and Dane

The Secret Confessions of Anne Shakespeare

Prologue

"*G*ranny! Gran, look what has come for you!"

With the greatest effort I lift my eyelids; each one seems weighted with a stone. I peer through the rheumy blur to find Lizbeth's face, anxious as always at my fast-failing health. How fortunate I am, as I lie here dying in my second-best bed, to have one sweet soul, this dear granddaughter, to care for and comfort me. It almost makes up for the pain, the gnawing aches in my joints and toothless sockets, the useless hip that confines me to my mattress and piss pot. I lick my chapped lips and twitch my mouth to smile for the pretty child. Oh, to be dead, to be dead. Have I not lived long enough, sixty-seven years in this year of our Lord 1623, to have earned my eternal rest?

Or have I died, and this Lizbeth is a vision that shines like a lamp above me? Fifteen and the freshness of youth upon her, as if dewdrops might spring up where she treads. Her eyes are the color of cinnamon, her hair ripples like sunlit wheat. Never mind that she is small breasted. She has a tender disposition and dancing butterfly hands, and as the only child of Dr. John and Susanna Hall she is, in Stratford terms, a bit of an heiress. Why, she'll have New Place, the Henley Street house and all the plate and household goods, since Will left almost everything to Susanna. We certainly couldn't bequeath the properties to Judith, not after the scandal she brought upon us with that lout Thomas Quiney. A crook, a drunkard, a pox-ridden betrayer. Oh, my poor younger daughter, what a low choice you have made! But neither can I trust the glassy bright excellence of Susanna and John. There is something awry when a healthy man and woman produce but one child in sixteen years of marriage, as I myself can attest.

"Gran, see the package? It is from London—with your name! I'll take off the wrapping. . . . Oh, Gran, look!"

Lizbeth's gasp reaches my ears, and in her excitement she holds a large rectangular shape too close to my face. Then, seeing my confusion, she draws it back inch by inch to catch the point at which my eyes will focus. I force a nod from my stiff neck when the exact distance is reached, and even that mere movement sends a crick of pain down my spine, dispelling the blissful notion that I am indeed deceased and Lizbeth an angel leading me to heaven's gate. I stare hard at the object before me; then it becomes clear. It is the book, the folio, so long awaited. Tears start to my eyes.

"Show me," I rasp.

Eagerly, Lizbeth scrapes up the chair beside my bed, the seat whereon she sits to feed me broth and puddings and other soft stuff. When her mother is not by, she sneaks me spoonfuls of marzipan paste, which I savor and dissolve on my tongue, and tots of spiced wine. I am only two years shy of the age achieved by our great Elizabeth, that old orange-headed lion, and by the time she died her teeth were black stubs and the makeup on her face was a permanent mask of white paint and vermilion a half inch thick. A pretty corpse indeed. I suppose I shan't look much better, but never mind, never fret. The book exists!

"I don't see a note," says Lizbeth. "Maybe the publisher sent it? Did you know it was coming, Gran? Look, gold trim." She settles the book on her lap and opens the leather cover. "The title page reads: 'Mr. William Shakespeares Comedies, Histories, and Tragedies. Published according to the True Originall Copies.' Can you see the picture?"

She shifts it toward me. And there you are, Will. That domey, bald head, the silly snippet of beard, the starched collar and mild, serious mien. Seven years dead.

"Shall I read you the dedication?"

I blink my consent. That Lizbeth is highly literate is due entirely to me, for Susanna barely got beyond the alphabet and paternoster on her hornbook, and Judith's brain proved impervious to even that humble object. Only Hamnet, God rest his innocent soul, showed the propensity for learning one might have expected from a poet's offspring.

"Oh, well, our daughters won't need letters," Will had said, shrugging off the girls' disinclination for schooling. "They will have husbands to take care of them."

As you have taken care of me?

I bite my tongue. I have spent a lifetime biting my tongue; there must be scars thick as stars in the firmament of my mouth from all the secrets I have kept. But at least where I failed my two girls, I have requited myself in Lizbeth, tutoring her in summer on the garden bench here at New Place, in winter reading by the hearth. Thinking a little learning harmless, Susanna did not protest. It never occurred to her I might have more than a little learning to impart. Besides, it kept the child from running loose in John's study, smudging his casebook and breaking the urine bottles of important patients. I sigh that we shall soon become as enamored of education for our daughters as for our sons. God's blood, is this not the seventeenth century?

"Gran, did you hear what I read?"

No, I missed it. I make a disappointed sound, and Lizbeth pats my hand.

"Don't worry. I'll tell it short. First is a dedication to the earls of Pembroke and Montgomery, written by Mr. John Heminge and Mr. Henry Condell. They compare their humble offering of the volume to a leavened cake set out at a temple for the gods." Lizbeth chuckles. "What flattery to the earls!"

"Sticky honey traps best," I croak, hooking my finger toward the mug on the bedside table. Lizbeth braces my shoulders so I can drink. Water—Susanna may return from the market at any moment, so no spiced wine today, alas—but it wets my throat and lets me speak. "Read on."

Lizbeth settles me and resumes. "Next there comes an epistle to the readers, exhorting them to open their purses. 'You wil stand for your priviledges, wee know: to read, and censure. Do so, but buy it first . . . whatever you do, Buy.'"

Lizbeth tilts her head in laughter, and I content myself with an inward smile. Good men, John Heminge and Henry Condell. I am not sure how the project fell to them, but it being the style of dedications to fawn and supplicate, I will not twit them for the great service they have rendered me. Now they call Will "a happie imitator of Nature . . . a most gentle expresser of it. His mind and hand went together: And what he thought, he uttered with that easinesse, that wee have scarce received from him a blot in his papers." Not true, but heartfelt. I like it.

Lizbeth turns the page, scanning. "Here is a tribute from Mr. Jonson. Why, I remember when you had me send him that bundle. . . ." She pauses, her forehead puzzling, but I motion her to go on. "'To the memory of my beloved, The Author Mr. William Shakespeare . . . I confesse thy writings to be such As neither Man, nor Muse, can praise too much. . . .'"

Tears gather in the child's eyes. Her grandpapa was her beloved too. She was but eight years old when he died. When she was even smaller, her hands in ours, we would swing her between us as we walked through town. But what's this, Ben? You only "confesse" to the plays' quality? You couldn't declare, proclaim, announce, pronounce, assert or avow? You had to have it wrung out of you like a sinner in a confession box?

"'Soule of the Age!'" Lizbeth's voice soars. "'The applause! delight! the wonder of our Stage!'"

That's better. Don't tell me words don't mean exactly what they say.

"'And though thou hadst small Latine, and lesse Greeke . . .'"

What? Ben, you know very well that Will's Latin was the equal of yours. He was the star pupil of Stratford grammar school and there had hard masters and Latin drills from sunup till sundown, and anyone who thinks we live as illiterate country bumpkins is an uninformed city snob. As if anyone will stage your plays a hundred years hence! Lizbeth reads on, but my anger has cost me my place. Wait, wait. Was that something about Kit? Damn, I missed it! And shake a spear, shake a stage? No, no, not that old pun again!

Lizbeth reaches the end. "I like this line," she says quietly. " 'For a good Poet's made, as well as borne.' That's very true, isn't it? But of all Mr. Jonson has written, here is the best: 'He was not of an age, but for all time!' "

Really? Ben said that? I want to stop and savor it, but Lizbeth, face aglow, searches on for more. A trio of short and not very good tributes follows. I don't recognize the names of the men who wrote them. So many of those we first knew are gone: Kyd, Peele, Nashe, poor jealous Robert Greene who lives on only for his pathetic pamphlet. Remember when they wouldn't let Will join their club of University Wits? Only Kit was our friend from the start, the muse's and my darling, such a brilliant light extinguished, murdered so treacherously young. Shall I see any of them in the hereafter? Since Her late Majesty officially abolished Purgatory and its attendant buying and selling of indulgences as a greedy popish invention, I tremble to think where my soul must go. Sins do blot my papers—please, God, you will grant me a little mercy and allow it was you who formed me thus? Can I help what you wrought? Oh, please, do not let me burn!

"Gran! You are shivering!"

Lizbeth bustles with my blankets, scolding herself for negligence. I am not supposed to call her Lizbeth, by the way. Susanna has decreed anything else than the full Elizabeth to be undignified. But when my granddaughter comes, she sings up the stairs, "Gra-ann! Your Lizbeth is here!"

"I am all right," I say, and manage to shoo my hand. "Don't fuss over me. Read more."

"The plays come next. Which one?"

"You pick. Dip in."

She wets her lips, a child faced with a tray of delectable treats.

With all the plays now published in one legitimate volume, they will be protected from future piracies and careless copiers, and I expect Will can stop turning in his grave. Or rather, that I can stop twisting on his behalf. Have you seen that bust of him in the church? Hideous, him looking like a provincial burgher, all ruddy and prosperous. But Susanna approved the likeness—it was so respectable—and since I must live under her roof, I went along.

"Am I tiring you, Granny? Is it too much?"

I shake my head, though I haven't heard a word, and Lizbeth does tend to prattle. Still, I taught her not only to read and write but also to appreciate, for they are not one and the same. Anyone can become literate—as Sir Thomas More feared—and perhaps this is not, after all, a good thing. For then many will read and write but few will appreciate, and we shall have no end of hack poets and second-rate playwrights churning out drivel to clog the mind. No, to appreciate is essential, for it requires discernment and sensitivity, qualities often lacking in the mob at the Globe. Though I do not condemn outright our penny groundlings; dullards sit in equal measure on their cushioned bums in the galleries looking down. Whereas my Lizbeth *feels* what she reads. She draws it into her heart, bids it pulse through her veins, lets it quicken and enthrall her, then pass out in a breath of understanding that is both heartbreak and delight.

"Listen, Gran. I remember when you used to read this to me. 'The quality of mercy is not strained; It droppeth as the gentle rain from heaven. . . .'" Lizbeth sighs. "It is true what Ben Jonson said, isn't it? Grandpapa will be remembered as long as time shall last!"

"I hope the plays shall be remembered," I say, but she is too carried away to catch my feeble remark.

"And writers will forever honor and respect him. How I wish I had not been such a child when he died! I rue that I have so few memories of him." She bounds up and walks about the room, pressing the book to her bosom as if she could absorb it through her skin. She is imagining herself Portia, Juliet, Miranda, Rosalind, and she twirls till it seems the room itself must join in her delirious spin. "And you, Granny, how lucky you were to have married the genius of the age! Why do you so rarely talk about him? You should have told me everything, everything, so I may tell my children and they tell theirs. I know it is hard on your throat, and you would never boast, but tell me just one wondrous thing. . . ."

She flits back to my side, eagerly anticipating. She who is my last heartbeat and will be my sole mourner. Shall I, shall I reveal . . . ?

"Your grandfather did not write the plays," I whisper. "Not all of them. Not exactly."

"What?"

She stops, not quite having heard me. I am surprised to hear myself. Her highly fluent Majesty Elizabeth is said to have spoken six languages, or so she once bragged to an ambassador to her court. When he commented that it was a great accomplishment for a princess, the queen replied that the real marvel was to make a woman hold her tongue. Well, I have been that marvel for more than thirty years. And why? Why should a woman hold her tongue? Why should I, any longer?

"He did not write them," I repeat, and it is as if the scars in my mouth, all that bitten flesh, are suddenly opened and raw. But it cleanses as it hurts me, and now my tongue remembers how to work, how to shape and cleave and utter the purging sounds. At last someone will know the truth before I die here in my second-best bed. "William Shakespeare is not who you think."

My granddaughter's eyes open wide. Then she gives a merry laugh. "Don't tease, Granny. You make sport of my silliness. I should behave with more decorum, I know. But if I did, who would bring your marzipan and spiced wine when Mother's back is turned?"

"No, no sport, Lizbeth." I push myself to sit upright.

"Gran, what are you doing? Do you need your chamber pot? Oh, no, what have I done?" She snatches up pillows and props them behind me, but I fend off her ministering hands.

"Lizbeth, listen to me. The plays . . . there was another author."

"But Grandpapa wrote them." She points to the title page. "It is published, right here."

"His name, yes. But that is not how it was."

Lizbeth draws back, doubting my sanity, her curiosity piqued. She tries on several faces to see my reaction: the disapproving look of a mother with an obstinate child, the pout of a skeptic daring to be proven wrong, the bafflement of a young woman trying to make sense of a contention all known evidence declares to be false. I reach for her hand, and she sits beside me, her soft white palm offered in return.

"Granny . . ." She smiles, willing to forgive me, but I shake my head.

"I swear on this my deathbed that what I speak is true."

Lizbeth's face pales. We both know a deathbed is no place for a liar. She leans forward intently, and after so many years, oh, what peace, what relief, what vengeance at last.

I speak each word with utmost clarity and care. "William Shakespeare of Stratford-upon-Avon did not write all the plays that appear in his name."

My granddaughter's reply is a taut whisper, urgent for truth.

"Then if he didn't write them, Gran, who did?"

Chapter 1

$\mathscr{I}$t will be said that I seduced the boy, that I was conniving and desperate. Him but eighteen and me twenty-six, near to being left on the shelf. It will be presumed I was common, a coarse country wench. Once wed, I became nagging and shrewish—doesn't every disaffected husband claim the like?—or worse, I turned plump, unambitious, content. And of course I had no more imagination or intellect than a pudding on a plate. Surely a man would not leave a pretty, spirited wife?

Will did. After only five years of marriage, damn him. Oh, how I wish I had a portrait of myself, a sketch, anything to prove the loveliness I once possessed. Look at my eyes and you would have thought on bluebells—Will did. Imagine arched brows, clear skin, straight nose. If my forehead was a trifle wide, none could deny the fine symmetry of cheekbones tapering to a delicate jaw. I had a long, smooth neck. As to my hair, it tumbled fawn brown almost to my hips. My body was in good proportion, and I stood eye-to-eye with Will, who was not over-tall. In those first months of pleasure I would lie naked in our secret bower by Shottery Brook, and Will would array long strands of my hair over me so that my breasts peeked through and the ends fringed above the patch of my soft woman's parts.

Would Will Shakespeare ever have fallen in love with me if I were ugly?

"You are my doe of the forest," he would proclaim, and I would tease and stretch until greedy desire overcame him, and his fingers explored and roused me. He would not shed his own clothes first. No, it was always I who had to bare myself to him.

I *felt* beautiful.

And I was smart, and I knew it long before Will Shakespeare came along.

~~

I was born in the year 1556 and was two years old when Elizabeth Tudor ascended to the throne. My father, Richard Hathaway, was a well-to-do yeoman farmer and I the second-eldest of his eight living children. My mother, Anne, for whom I was named, gave him the first three. Then she died and he married my stepmother, Joan, a round, kindly woman he nicknamed Duck. She hatched the remaining five, and together we all became his ducklings.

We lived in the hamlet of Shottery, a mile's stroll west of Stratford-upon-Avon. To the north lies the Forest of Arden, verdant with leftover magic. From a city dweller's perspective, it is a rustic place of farms and fields and winding footpaths. To a child, it was idyllic. Our home at Hewlands Farm comprised over ninety acres of tilled and wooded land, orchards, house, barn and outbuildings. Sheep and chickens, pigs and geese bleated and squawked and grunted in the yard, while from the brew house came the aroma of hearty amber ale. Our timbered, thatch-roofed dwelling comprised two generous rooms, and though we had no painted wall hangings as some in Stratford could boast, our home was comfortably furnished and a cupboard displayed our pewter. Every spring we took out all the furniture—our two beds and our goose-feather mattresses, the table, benches and chests—and painted the walls with lime wash to whiten and brighten them.

I especially loved the herb garden. It holds my one sure memory of my mother, at a time when I was perhaps four years old. I had plopped myself down amongst the herbs on a summer afternoon, and a wonderful fragrance arose from the crushed plants beneath my skirt. I began plucking a leaf from each plant and rubbing it between my thumb and a different finger in turn, then sniffing that finger to my nose. Rosemary, lavender, sage, thyme. I switched from the right hand to the left. Parsley, origanum, tarragon, chives. Uh-oh, no more fingers. The next samples, mint and chamomile, I applied to my palms. Then on to my wrists and arms, pushing up my sleeves as I went. Savory, marjoram, rue, lemon balm. So absorbed was I in my perfumery that I never heard my mother approach, until I suddenly looked up and there was her figure, hands on hips, face obscured by the sun in my eyes. I fell over in guilt, my little arms and legs flailing like a beetle. Then out of the sunlight came a laugh, and my mother's body shook with amusement above me. I wish I could remember the sound of her laugh. I wish the sunlight had not blocked out her face.

It must have been the next year that I was sent to the petty school with Bartholomew. This was a small, partitioned area of the grammar school in Stratford, presided over by an assistant to the master. Children of five and six are too young to be helpful at home, too clever to be left to their own mischief, and although I do not believe I was a troublesome child, the petty school kept boys and girls alike occupied. Under the assistant's baleful eye, we learned good manners, our ABCs and the basics of reading. I recall one blond boy who was wont to misbehave. "You will never be admitted to the grammar school," the teacher would threaten. We girls giggled. We would never be admitted to the grammar school at all. By the age of seven at the latest, our mothers would reclaim us and begin our instruction in the vital arts of housewifery. However, my father did expect me as well as Bartholomew to acquire some skill in reading. As staunch Protestants in a region that still harbored many Catholic families, we had a duty to know God's word direct from our Bible.

"Many people have suffered to bring us this," he would say, holding the holy book before our awed faces. "William Tyndale was strangled and burned at the stake for translating the Bible into English, and bloody Queen Mary made martyrs of three hundred brave Protestant souls. Sir Thomas More did not want ordinary folk to read at all lest they go interpreting the Bible for themselves, but we shall show him, eh?"

Bartholomew and I nodded fervently. Strangled and burned at the stake! We made a secret vow to learn the Bible by heart, though our brains soon hurt from trying to decipher the "begats." But there was another reason to keep us two at school and out of our house just then. After me, my mother had suffered a series of stillbirths and miscarriages that left her sick and weakened. When she took to bed, her belly once again growing, Nan the servant girl shooed us out and closed the door. Bartholomew and I rejoiced at the increased playtime—climbing trees in the orchard was our favorite game—and when our mother died, we were as much bewildered as grieved. She was not coming back again, ever? We poked in curiosity at our new baby sister, and the following year our father married Duck. A household must be kept running.

~

Why did God give woman an imagination? Men are not meant to bear children and therefore have no womb. If we females were intended solely to churn butter and darn socks, why endow us with a mind's eye that can rove from lovers to swordplay, from high tragedy to bawdy farce? When traveling players came to Stratford and the citizens flocked to the market square to see them perform, did the girls and women stare at the stage blank faced while the men and boys cheered the show? What a strange sight that would be, half the audience dumb as posts! Oh, no, our hearts and brains raced. We swooned for handsome actors and yearned for adventures in faraway lands. I don't say we expected any such thing to happen. We knew our place and our likely fates. But, God's blood, there was a woman ruling England! And though we granted that Elizabeth was an exception—perhaps even an aberration with a man's organ beneath those jewel-encrusted skirts—what more example did we need? If just one woman could command an army, negotiate treaties, sign laws, speak Latin, compose verses, refuse to marry, and ride like a whirlwind to the hunt, and that woman was God's anointed . . . well, it did stir the mind.

So while the boys romped and played at being knights and kings and pirates, we girls pretended to be ladies, princesses and queens. We welcomed foreign ambassadors and royal suitors. We paraded in our silk gowns. We sent our enemies to the Tower and threw coins to our devoted people as we rode our white horses through the streets. My father's history tales provided much inspiration. Though a poor reader himself, he had acquired a headful of stories, and if the details were not always accurate, the rousing delivery more than acquitted him. Whenever the players or a person of distinction passed through town, we absorbed their dress and speech with greedy eyes and ears. Then we refined our renditions with the latest knowledge.

"A lady would not curtsey to the executioner," scolded Mary, a chubby girl and a stickler for perfection, as we enacted the beheading of Anne Boleyn beside my father's stable. It was the christening day of my newest sibling, the first child of my father and Duck, and all the neighborhood had come to celebrate. I was ten years old.

"I did *not* curtsey," countered Katherine, whose dark hair had cast her as Mistress Boleyn. "I was only about to kneel."

"Try to do it more gracefully," I suggested, "as we saw the boy do on Tuesday last when he played Lady Jane Grey. When you bob halfway down, it appears as a curtsey."

"Well, it is hard to kneel gracefully with all my skirts and robes," Katherine complained. She gestured in a wide circle about her, and though she wore only a homespun dress and her apron was stained from picking strawberries, our eyes saw a flowing velvet cloak and gown. "How am I to hold both my skirts and the coin I must give the executioner?"

"Perhaps we could skip the coin?" offered Margaret, one of the ladies-in-waiting.

"No, I want my coin!" This from Tom, Margaret's younger brother, whom we often collared to play the male roles.

"All right, all right, you'll have your coin," said Margaret, though what we had was only a small, flat stone from the brook.

"Try it like this," I said, stepping into Katherine's role. A handful of other children had gathered, and under their curious and critical gaze I started toward the executioner's block, a bale of hay. Head high, wearing a martyr's gaze, I glided regally toward my fate.

"Your crown'll fall off!" hooted a burly boy as I knelt and bent my head to meet the block.

"She didn't wear a crown!" I jumped erect, hands on hips. "What a numbskull you are! Anne Boleyn had beautiful, long black hair, and for her execution she bound it up to bare her neck and make it easier for the executioner."

"She was a whore!" cried the same boy, and the children laughed with guilty pleasure at the word.

"She was the mother of our Queen Elizabeth!" replied an indignant Mary.

They broke into a squabble, until my voice cut in. "Wait, wait. We have it wrong!" I signaled for quiet as I pieced together my thoughts. "The stories say Anne Boleyn was executed by a swordsman they sent for specially from France. I don't think she would have bowed her head over a block to be sliced by a sword."

A silence fell. Then, "She's right!" cried several voices, including the burly boy's. "You have to bow your head for an ax, but the executioner would swing sideways with a sword."

Now a fresh noise began as everyone debated the bloody details, and those who had been skeptical and scoffing clamored to join the play. The matter of executing a woman, be she queen or whore, seemed of particular interest to the boys. After all had quieted, they looked again to me, and I saw that my superior knowledge of the event had gained me some credit among them.

"All right," I said, though I had a strange feeling that even I did not know what words would issue from my mouth. "Here is how it would have been." I arranged the audience in a half circle before the bale of hay and positioned Tom with his long stick for the sword. "You must stop short on your swing, for if you hit me in the neck, I will break your arm," I whispered in his ear. Tom quailed and nodded and put on the grain sack we had cut with eyeholes for the executioner's hood. Then, with Mary, Margaret and Katherine as my weeping ladies-in-waiting, I walked forward and stood before them with the humiliation and dignity befitting a disgraced queen and abandoned wife.

"My good people," I declared in a clear voice, "I have ever been a true and loyal subject of my husband the king, and I go to meet my God in heaven with a pure heart. He alone shall judge me, for I swear to you I am innocent of these false charges. I have been a faithful wife and loving mother, and I pray you be good to my little daughter, Elizabeth, for she shall be a great queen in her day." I knelt smoothly before the audience, rested my hands on the hay bale in prayer and lifted my face to Tom. I could see his blue eyes and the tip of his freckled nose poking through the loose weave of the bag. I pressed the stone into his grimy palm and patted my hand to the back of my head, hinting at my twined-up locks. "I trust my hair will not impede you?" I asked, and as the executioner's lower lip began to tremble, I sought to console him. "It is a sharp sword, and I have but a little neck."

I closed my eyes to await the blow, and a fear of death so overcame me that a whimper escaped my throat. Oh, kill me. Kill me quickly or I shall faint! And indeed I began to swoon. But the next instant I opened my eyes as a sobbing Tom dropped his sword and ran away and my ladies fell into bawling. In the half circle of onlookers, a few children had gone stark white in the face, and several others stood with their mouths agape.

A shiver came over me. What had just happened? Where did I get that word *impede*? I was sure I had never used it before, but I knew exactly what it meant. And that speech, what had possessed me? Did I say those words? Did I think and utter them?

"Here, you little heathens!" Margaret's father stormed into the play, dragging the blubbering Tom by the scruff of his neck. "What have you done to frighten the boy? What's the commotion? Is it plays again? You, Anne Hathaway, what witchcraft are you up to?"

"Please, sir—"

I was allowed no answer. In one rude movement, I was yanked to my feet and a blow cut across my cheek. I ran for my life, and the other children did likewise. My father calmed our neighbor, who willingly forgot the incident in favor of more mutton and ale, and other than a raised eyebrow from my father, I received no punishment. Yet I was badly shaken. The charge of witchcraft, however loosely spoken, would send a cold stake through anyone's heart, and for several weeks afterward we made no more plays.

But whether it was witchcraft or magic, for one brief moment something inexplicable and undeniable had occurred, and though I dared not court it openly, I wooed it in my brain. Whereas my playmates Katherine, Mary and Margaret gradually gave up their imaginings to marriage and childbirth, my fantasies kept me company as I grew to adulthood. I daydreamed as I kneaded the bread or gathered the eggs and especially as I sat sewing clothes for our expanding household, decorating them with embroidery of flowers, insects and vines. I had an eye for color and design that went beyond the ordinary, and I understood the subtleties of texture and how to enrich without overwhelming a plain dress. Duck would come home from the Thursday market beaming at the compliments my needlework had procured her. But for myself I chose modest garb in muted shades, having no wish to draw attention.

And all the while, my dark mind thought and tumbled and ran.

Chapter 2

*H*e was only a boy when I first met him, a precocious child and even then quite taken with himself. It was the summer of 1575, and in those years Stratford, and indeed all of England, was in good mettle. Crops were abundant, merchants were expanding their ventures, and optimism pervaded our sceptered isle. We lived in peace, weathered the occasional outbreaks of plague, and heard fabulous tales of the savage New World. Though our queen was in her early forties, she was still capable of bearing a child and giving the country an heir. In the running as suitors were François, the Duke of Alençon, and Elizabeth's former horse master and longtime favorite, Robert Dudley, Earl of Leicester. The only fly in our national ointment was the religious and dynastic plots and counterplots that swirled throughout Elizabeth's reign. Spies and conspirators lurked in many corners, and those caught and convicted of treason suffered a gruesome fate. Meanwhile, we rural folk occupied ourselves with the usual births, deaths and marriages, friendships and quarrels, eating and drinking and earning our livelihood. Then, that summer of 1575, for nineteen glorious days, our little world stopped.

"The queen! The queen is coming to Kenilworth Castle!"

Duck hurried the news home from market, and our whole flock gathered around, avid for details. Each summer it was the custom of Elizabeth to go on a great progress through her realm, stopping to visit various noble households on her route. These extended royal outings served several worthy purposes. They provided an escape from the heat and unhealthful conditions of London. They allowed Her Majesty to see and be seen by her provincial subjects, bonding them to her in loyalty and love. The excursions also temporarily transferred the cost of maintaining Elizabeth's huge household from her own account to that of her honored hosts, a commendable savings to the treasury. Finally, since the lucky lord or lady was often bankrupt by the time Her Highness departed, they had no funds left to raise an army against her should the thought ever enter their heads. Clever, that Elizabeth.

Now she was coming to Kenilworth Castle. Fifteen miles to our north, it had been a gift from the queen to Dudley early in her reign, and he transformed the old Norman fortress into a splendid palace to please his generous sovereign. That Elizabeth and Dudley were lovers was widely gossiped; whether they would ever marry was hotly contested. Dudley's influence over Elizabeth so infuriated her other nobles that they roundly opposed him, and his reputation had been seriously blackened by the mysterious death of his wife, dead of a broken neck at the bottom of a flight of stairs. Yet he persisted in proposing, and this visit would surely include a mighty effort to woo her once again. The coming spectacle, Duck reported, would eclipse anything ever seen before.

"She is to arrive the second week of July, and there will be water pageants on the lake, fireworks, plays, music and dancing. They say Kenilworth is crawling with carpenters and workmen, erecting stages and canopies. There might even be an elephant." Duck fluttered her hand before her plump breast. "Oh, Richard, promise we shall go!"

"By all means," said my father, as he and Bartholomew exchanged growing smiles. "Just think, my ducklings. They will need provisions for all those people, food, drink, hay for the horses. Duck, what about the honey from your beekeeping? Anne, you might sell the ladies some of your fine embroidery." He winked and rubbed his hands. "I hear coins clinking!"

For the next weeks we and everyone else for miles around worked in a fever to be ready. Who knew what largesse might befall us when lords and ladies weighted with purses came to town? But more than that, we wanted to impress our queen, to show her our industry and talents. We wanted to make her proud. And what wouldn't we give for a glimpse of Gloriana? They said she wore rubies as large as hen's eggs, that her skin was so milk white it put the fairest ladies in the kingdom to shame. She was like to arrive on a magnificent litter carried by a half dozen handsome young nobles and accompanied by the highest courtiers in the land. I was not quite nineteen, still shy of an age to marry, but if a dashing lord chanced to glance my way, if he paused to purchase an embroidery and his eye lingered on my blushing bosom . . . Giddy girl! Can you be no more creative? Ah, but such light-headed fantasies had us all adream.

On the grand day, we piled into our wagon and left before sunup. As we bumped along, my father regaled us with history tales. It was at Kenilworth, he said, that King Henry V received a great insult from the French dauphin, a chest of tennis balls, implying he was a callow youth not ready to reign.

"Henry said to the ambassadors who brought the gift, 'Tell the dauphin I will take these balls and my racquet and knock the crown right off his father's head!' Then he beat the French to their knees at Agincourt and claimed for wife the fair princess Katherine."

We laughed and jogged on, and by midmorn the road to Kenilworth was swarming with people in carts and on foot. Who would not put aside their daily labor and come? We were an eager hive, buzzing to see its queen. The population of Stratford numbered fifteen hundred souls, and a lame old man who had stayed behind later swore that but for him the town had emptied. Then count the dozens of other villages within a day's journey, merchants and traders from Warwick and Coventry, humble and curious folk from the Forest of Arden, the thronging tenants and household of Kenilworth itself, all converging at the rose-brown sandstone castle during one of the hottest Julys in living memory. What a sight when we saw the battlements rising above the lake and moat that encircled the castle's outer wall.

"The whole world is here," Duck despaired, fanning herself with her hand. "We will never get the wagon close enough. If only I were not so short!"

"Don't fret," said my father, from his calm vantage point a foot taller. "I will pop you on my shoulders if necessary."

While Dudley's men rode about to maintain order, people bumped and jostled to claim a space along the parade route. For the most part, no serious offense was taken, and a scowl followed by a quick apology served to soothe any ruffled feelings. But there will always be those who bluster and try to force themselves forward, and one of these was John Shakespeare. He was arguing with a mounted official; apparently, as a dignitary of Stratford, he felt entitled to preferential treatment. At his side stood a ginger-haired boy of about eleven, a miniature gentleman in an ocher doublet and dark green breeches. The son's pout mimicked the father's as both were ordered back to their places.

I covered the laugh that came to my lips. John Shakespeare and my father were acquainted—who was not in our modest little burg?—and in those days John was in his ascendant. His forefathers had been tenant farmers in the villages to the north, and John came to town intent on bettering himself. He was, to varying degrees, a glover, a corn and wool merchant—my father had sold him fleeces—a moneylender and a dealer in property. A room of the Shakespeare home on Henley Street served as the workshop where he made and sold gloves, purses and other small leather goods. In civic affairs he had risen from ale taster to constable to alderman to mayor and confidently applied to London for a coat of arms. Though he was much chagrined when it was denied, he continued to strut and play the important man. Now, glancing over the crowd, I guessed that even the mayor of Stratford would be only a small fish in this human ocean. Then, just as the multitude began to settle into place, word rippled among us that the queen was delayed and would not arrive until evening.

"Maybe some people will get tired and leave," said Duck, inspired by the groans of disappointment.

"They might," my father agreed, "but let us be busy while we wait."

We had come well provisioned, not only with our own food and drink but with baskets of apples, plums and pears from our orchard, bundles of herbs, pots of honey. While Father and Bartholomew set off to peddle their wares among the crowd, I went my own way, carrying a half dozen embroidered cambric handkerchiefs. I found an area of vendors' stalls bursting with food and merchandise. Fans and gloves, perfumes and ointments, jewelry, wallets, feathers, hats, bolts of fabric, knives and metalwork, ivory carvings and glass beads.

"What'll you buy, what'll you buy?" a woman barked at me from behind her display of lace and trimmings.

"Oh, nothing, I'm sorry. I only meant to look." I dropped the velvet ribbon I had been fondling.

"What's that then?" She pointed at my handkerchiefs, and nervously I held them out. I had stitched them with fruit and flower designs, and I thought the strawberry pattern particularly appealing.

"I made them. I am trying to sell them."

"Not bad, not bad," she barked, shoving them back at me. She had a hatchet face, and her body was all elbows and angles, and beside her huddled a skinny man I took to be her husband. "Look to the customers!" she ordered, pushing him toward a couple who were examining a length of scalloped lace. She began rearranging her wares. "I could take them off you for sixpence."

She hadn't looked up, and it took me a moment to realize she was addressing me. Sixpence? Was she offering to buy my handkerchiefs?

"I . . . I . . ."

"Take it or leave it."

I stepped back—she was too blunt up close—and a customer took my place. I had never sold any of my needlework before. Was sixpence a fair price? And why did she not look me in the eye? I moved off, mulling the encounter, and began to listen more closely to the bargaining around me. A half hour later I returned to the stall.

"Twelve pence," I said.

"What? I'll give eight."

"No, twelve. You can sell them each for three."

"Ten pence for the lot, take it or move on."

I took it. I hadn't much experience in haggling and commerce, and it had required all my courage and a heady sense of the occasion to make my first demand. As I turned to go, the sharp-faced vendor began barking behind me, "Embroidered handkerchiefs, look how fine! Only four pence apiece! Who's buying? Who's buying?" I *tsk*ed at my gullibility, but now I was free to roam, to absorb every sight, odor and sound. I even saw a thief steal a lady's purse; a yelling mob pursued and beat him unconscious. I reveled in the atmosphere and my anonymity and did not return to our wagon until suppertime. Rather than thinning, the crowd had grown steadily throughout the afternoon, but much of the commotion had settled, the children and the drunkards drowsing, the women gossiping as fast as their tongues would go. Father and Bartholomew had sold out their produce and bought a currant cake to sweeten our meal. Duck yawned and cuddled up with her little ones.

"Wake me if the queen ever gets here," she grumbled.

After supper I took another stroll, edging forward until I reached the road. Baggage carts had been rolling toward the castle all afternoon, over three hundred of them, a fat man reported, each laden with chests and drawn by four or six horses. What on earth could they be bringing? Was the whole court on tour? The queen herself had stopped to dine at Itchington, seven miles hence, the fat man continued, and some of her party had gone off hunting.

"But we cannot wait forever!" cried a voice, and there stood young Master Shakespeare, on his face the most plaintive look I had ever seen. The adults laughed at him, and he reddened.

"Don't worry," I said to reassure him. "She will come."

"I know, but I have been standing here three hours and my feet are aching."

"Then go sit down and rest a bit."

"I don't dare. I might miss something." Then he added petulantly, "My father is the mayor of Stratford, and this is not how we should be treated!"

Well, aren't we precious? I had just begun to like Will Shakespeare. Now I chuckled with the others at his posturing. He lowered his head but refused to budge, and again we waited. The heat of the day had cooled somewhat, drying the sweat upon us, but the press of people more than made up for it. Each time I glanced the boy's way, his shoulders had sagged lower, until his knees threatened to buckle, and his face grew tight with fatigue. I was no less resolved to hold my place, and I conceded his determination. Then I forgot the child entirely as a man shouted, "There! Up ahead! I see something!"

"She's coming!" everyone yelled. "Here comes the queen!"

Far up the road, a puff of dust appeared. We craned and stood on tiptoe, peering. The puff became a pale brown cloud that plumed and advanced. Still we waited. What could be taking so long? I felt a strange sensation in the ground beneath my feet. Was that the earth trembling? The dust cloud thickened; it seemed to enclose a muffled din. We craned further, chattering in suspense and anxiety. "Can you see anything?" we each implored our neighbor, and got only a head shake in return. Then a distant fanfare sounded—trumpets!—and a troop of Dudley's horsemen burst out of the dust shouting, "Stand clear! Make way for the queen!" We fell back—up ahead people had begun cheering—and now drums boomed, and the earth shook with marching and hoofbeats as if a great army were approaching.

"I see pennants!" cried a tall man.

The next instant the procession emerged, and suddenly we knew that our pitiful country minds had not begun to grasp the enormity of what we were seeing. Heralds, row upon row, scarlet and gold banners piercing the sky. Ranks of footmen in colorful livery. Bearded officials in ermine-trimmed robes and haughty lady wives competing to show off their gowns. Our heads swiveled right and left, and in our excitement we babbled. "Knights!" someone cried, and forth they rode in flashing armor on massive warhorses, followed by troops of men. Now more officials, moving up in rank, councilors and judges, sober and frowning. Then began the queen's personal retinue, courtiers, ministers and ladies-in-waiting. The clothes grew in richness, the capes flowed longer, and jewels dripped on bosoms, fingers and ears. Around me everyone became an authority, pointing out Lord Burghley, Elizabeth's chief adviser, or Lettice Knollys, Countess of Essex, the queen's beautiful cousin. Half the identifications were doubtless wrong, but not a tongue ceased wagging. Except mine. I stared and stared. Royalty, wealth, power. I felt as if I stood at the center of an empire.

"Here she comes!" a woman shrieked in near ecstasy. "Here comes our queen!"

What a roar went up! What an explosion of anticipation! It was past eight o'clock, and we had been standing another two hours, yet our fatigue fell off like water, and we all sprang forward with the same wild desire. My heart pounded. I would die if I did not see! Then a voice wailed behind me, imperious and despairing, "Let me through, please, oh, please!"

I glanced back and saw Will Shakespeare. Fists outstretched to protect himself, he was trying to punch his way forward. He was far too slight to accomplish it; more likely he would be crushed in the throng. For what reason I cannot tell, I grabbed his wrist and yanked, and given the opening, he leaped nimbly through it. I pulled him in front of me, shielding him with both arms. But rather than thank me, he jerked back his shoulders and broke my embrace. Then, freed of my assistance, he jutted up his chin as if the place had belonged to him all along. Stunned, I allowed several more people to squeeze in front of me. By the time I recovered, I barely glimpsed the Earl of Leicester, riding escort on a snorting black stallion. But even in my confusion, I did not miss Elizabeth. No one could.

There she sat, mounted on a gleaming white palfrey. Of course, her gown was the most splendid of all, snow-white satin studded with jewels. More gems adorned her person, dazzling diamonds and rubies. Her headdress was woven of gold and silver threads garnished with pearls, and as the westering sun caught her red-gold hair it cast up a halo that outshone any crown. Though she was already hoarse from calling, she waved and shouted, "My good people! My loyal subjects!" and we split our throats in reply. From the day she ascended the throne she had proclaimed her love for us and for England, and our hearts swelled to bursting with pride. Many wept, strong men included. Do I exaggerate? Not by a word. Long live Elizabeth! God protect Gloriana! We cheered a full ten minutes after she had passed by.

As the procession neared the castle gate, out of an arbor came a white-clad sibyl who uttered praise of the queen and prophesied a long and prosperous reign. Upon the battlements a great fanfare was performed by six gigantic trumpeters. They were statues, we learned later, with real trumpeters concealed behind them. But the porter was an actual giant, seven feet tall, who delivered an eloquent address and handed Her Majesty the keys to the castle. Then another greeting, by the Lady of the Lake and two nymphs on a movable island blazing with torches. Finally, she entered the inner court where, we heard, she passed between seven pairs of pillars, each attended by a deity offering gifts of birds, fruits, wine, grain and fish to signify the bounty of air, earth and sea. As the queen ascended to her apartments, a grand fireworks display burst over the castle, and the firing of guns could be heard for twenty miles. We outside folk were not neglected. Though there was no elephant, the earl had provided all manner of entertainments: singers, sword swallowers, acrobats, magicians. More to the point, a fountain poured wine, and kegs spurted free beer. I found my family, all beaming. Duck swore the queen had looked right at her.

We slept overnight in our wagon and on the ground, and the following day began the trudge home. For the next three weeks, reports of the wonders at Kenilworth filled our ears. Banquets, bear baitings, running at the quintain, a savage man in moss and ivy who recited verses. The entire visit was said to have cost the earl a thousand pounds a day. But the best tale sprang from a musical water pageant featuring the Greek poet Arion riding on a dolphin. Poor Arion had drunk too much and forgot his oration, and he pulled off his mask and cried, "I am none of Arion, not I, but honest Harry Goldingham." The queen burst out laughing.

Finally, in late July, Elizabeth departed. She left us gratified and sighing, a few richer, many poorer, and all in need of a week's sleep.

Wandering by Shottery Brook, I sorted through my memories. My father had let me keep the money I earned on my handkerchiefs, and with visions of courtiers still bright in my head, I had fresh fuel for my imaginings and new ideas for my sewing. I had witnessed a little of what it takes to be a queen—that it is not enough simply to be a prince; you must constantly act the part. During the queen's stay, the Earl of Leicester had once again urged marriage, and she had once again refused him. Was he desolate, pining? Or was he, as some claimed, already deep in an affair with Lettice Knollys, whom he married three years later? I wished I'd had a better look at him as he rode by. This reminded me of the impudent boy who had deprived me of the sight, but with a snort I banished him from my mind.

After all, what was Will Shakespeare to me?

Chapter 3

*D*id I seduce Will Shakespeare?

Will you even bother to be fair about it?

If so, I confess. But he also seduced me, though not in the way you might expect.

Above all, he seduced himself.

He was just eighteen that day our paths recrossed in April 1582 beside Shottery Brook. Oh, I had seen him once or twice in the interim, though not in any such memorable manner as at Kenilworth. Quite the opposite—John Shakespeare's fortunes had taken a tumble, to the point that the family hardly showed itself for fear of harassment for debt. I don't know exactly what caused it. New restrictions had been imposed on the wool trade, and John was charged as a "brogger" for illegal dealings. His moneylending activities were also suspect—usury, dubious loans, gambling on investments. But many others played those games; perhaps John's luck just ran out. He had even been forced to sell off the property his wife, Mary, had brought to their marriage as her dowry. Her father had been Robert Arden of Wilmcote, a prosperous Catholic landowner whose forebears owned vast tracts in the Forest of Arden; John Shakespeare had definitely married up. Now, with five children to feed, he was in tight straits.

My own father had died the previous September. I missed him, and so did we all. He was a broad-minded man who judged people by their character rather than their religion or the cut of their clothes. I remember once Duck brought a rumor about John Shakespeare home from the market. He had been noted as recusant, skipping church often enough to invite suspicion of his true beliefs. Was he a secret Catholic? Did he sneak off to Masses conducted by the seditious Jesuit priests who had infiltrated England? If so, it was serious business, for the relative tolerance of Elizabeth's early reign had given way to stringent surveillance, steep fines and much worse. One of those recently tried and executed, after grisly tortures, was the Jesuit Edmund Campion, and some of his Warwickshire supporters had ties to Mary Shakespeare's Catholic relatives. But while my father abhorred any whiff of treason against the queen, he clung to a stubborn and perhaps incompatible notion that a man's faith ought to remain a private matter.

"We will not spread rumors," he chastised Duck. "Do not speak of other men's religion and do not give them cause to speak of yours." Then he tapped his temple and added, "It needn't concern us what a man believes, so long as it is all in his head." I am sure he did not intend a humorous interpretation.

In the last year of his life my father was often ill, and as I sat tending him, he urged me to choose a husband. "I would see you happily married before I am gone," he said, but I used his illness to put him off.

"You get better first," I challenged. "I'll not take a husband until you can dance at my wedding." We both lost our bluff.

Thus spring found me walking alone by Shottery Brook. A breath of southern air had enveloped our island kingdom, and the weather was warm as a yellow apple in the sun. Though it was lambing time, we found excuses that afternoon to play truant from our chores. "I'll give you an hour if you will give me one," Duck bargained, and we each took a turn minding the household while the other slipped away. My stepmother returned with a handful of daisies and a regretful sigh. "Oh, Anne, do you remember when I was young and first married your father? Now I am a widow and . . ." Her lip trembled, and she turned it into a crooked smile. "Go on, get out. Go find yourself a lover," she joked, and pushed me through the door.

I admit the thought of a lover, or rather a husband, was on my mind. I would soon be twenty-six, a prime age to wed, and Duck's push had a hint of impatience to it. Having inherited the farm, Bartholomew was enlarging the house, and himself looking to marry, so it required no astrologer to foretell my fate. However amiable my brother's wife, I would be pushed farther and farther into the background, a cumbersome spinster aunt, as a new generation was born into Hewlands Farm. The only solution was a home of my own, and that meant a man near my age who had completed his apprenticeship and had the skills and wherewithal to support a wife. At least in this respect, we ordinary mortals are more fortunate than the nobility. We may choose our own mates, though of course we seek our parents' blessing. In his will my father had left me £6 13s 4d as my dowry, and in his absence I would consult Duck and Bartholomew before I gave my promise to any man.

Yet when my brain played over the likely candidates, my heart remained strangely empty. I did not fancy any of the local bachelors, though one or two had come calling. Even less did I incline toward the widowers and the taking on of their children as my stepmother had done. I knew I did not possess her gifts of patience and nurture. It frightened me to admit I might not make a good mother at all. But whomever I wed, he would expect me to bear him a brood, and the idea of childbirth sent a cold shudder along my spine. My mother had died of it and a dozen more wives I could name. You may call me lily-livered, but I would not have been unhappy to have proven barren.

I had reached the secluded place where the brook pools into a large pond, surrounded by reeds and overhung by willows, dragonflies buzzing above the lily pads. Catching my reflection in the dappled water, I pictured beside it the faces of various eligible men and heaved a glum sigh. Too bad that our late fornicating monarch Henry VIII, in breaking with the Church of Rome, had dissolved the monasteries and religious houses. If we were still Catholic, I would at least have had the option of becoming a nun. It might have well suited me, for in a company of sisters I could have had a brisk and purposeful life, tending the gardens or supervising the kitchen or managing the daily affairs. I could have muttered whatever prayers were required. The more I envisioned it, the greater pity it seemed to have missed out.

I tossed my hand over the water in a commanding arc. "Get thee to a nunnery!" I cried.

"What?"

I whirled around, and there stood Will Shakespeare, chuckling.

"What nunnery?" he demanded, coming closer, pleased at my discomfort.

"No nunnery. It's not important. I—"

"Is there a fish?"

"Where? In the nunnery?"

"No, in the water. You were staring at it as I approached."

"No, there is no fish in the water," I replied.

"But you were fishing, wishing, for something."

"I was only imagining faces." I shrugged, perturbed and hoping to end the conversation. Will's outfit, a blue satin doublet and breeches, seemed a little dandified for a country stroll.

"A strange river that has not fish but faces floating in it," he observed.

"That is not what I meant. There probably are fish in the brook, but I was imagining faces because, well, you can see how the play of sunlight and water and the lily pads might suggest . . . Here, you can see my reflection."

He stepped up beside me, and we both gazed into the pond. While he took the opportunity to study my visage in the water, I found myself contemplating his. Not bad. His hair was close to mine in color but gingery where I was amber brown. His face was well shaped and the forehead prominent. His upper lip was somewhat thin, his mouth and chin fringed with the first appearance of down. Not bad, but far too young for me. Still, I kept looking.

As did he. Glancing up from the brook, he eyed my figure without even pretending to be covert about it, and I thought to myself, *The imp!* He did not introduce himself; he assumed I would know who he was. I wondered if he remembered me from that day at Kenilworth Castle. Probably not; he gave no sign.

"Do you often walk here?" he asked.

"I live nearby," I offered.

"Hewlands Farm," he guessed, his eyes narrowing, and I made a slight nod of assent. "A mysterious lady who walks by a rippling brook . . . and what is thy name?" He bowed like a courtier.

"Anne Hathaway," I replied, half intrigued, half annoyed by his nonsense.

"Then, Mistress Hathaway, shall we walk and talk awhile together?"

"We can talk," I agreed, though Duck would soon be expecting me back.

"Of spring and lilies and larks in the trees?"

"If you wish."

We ambled along the bank, and I saw from the first that he was enamored of words, and his own words in particular. Though his father's reversal had forced him to leave the grammar school before his studies were complete, his love of learning and the good offices of the schoolmaster had obtained him a position as tutor with a prominent Catholic family in Lancashire—until religious intrigues grew, and caution brought him home. Now, full of lofty impressions from that sojourn, he was trying out his tongue and fine clothes on our chance encounter, honing his skills for future conquests among the maidens of Stratford. We walked, and nothing came our way but that he must wrap language around it. A bee was a "buzzing bumbler," the dirt path a "trodden ribbon" beneath our feet.

"I could write a sonnet for you," he bragged.

"Can you write sonnets then?"

"Oh, yes, I excel at it."

"Really? Do you write them for every woman you meet?"

"Only those whose face shoots an arrow into my heart."

What mush! It is a miracle I did not laugh aloud. But perhaps I sensed it was more than vanity, that there was a shiver of desperation in Will, though like me he strove to conceal it. Consider his state: the son of a disgraced former mayor, his hopes of advancement hindered by his family's Catholic leanings, his teaching position gone, no chance to attend a university. And what did his future in Stratford hold? The exciting prospect of glove-making. Will was as trapped as I was, but unlike me he did not yet know it as clearly. Moreover, at eighteen a young man's brain, no matter how much Latin has been crammed into it, is no match for what he carries between his legs. So I stood there on the riverbank and watched Will and his tongue entangle themselves.

"Recite me a poem," I demanded.

"I have to compose it first."

"Well . . . ?"

"I'm thinking. Don't interrupt."

I sat down on the grass and opened the neckline of my dress a little wider. It was a warm day, wasn't it? Will's eyes got caught up in the sight, and I shifted my breasts beneath the fabric. Was it wrong of me to toy with him? He was toying with me. I never expected anything to come of it.

"Well . . . ?" I repeated.

"I'm thinking!" Cross, he dragged away his gaze. "Look, I can't come up with anything just now, but if I wrote it down, I could recite it for you."

"Oh, take another minute," I suggested, and I removed my linen cap. Humming, I began to undo my hair. This would pay him back for catching me off guard, tripping me up about faces and fishes. How long had he been staring at me before I had noticed him anyway? I uncoiled my tresses and let them tumble into my fingers. Will watched hungrily.

"The rays of the sun are dimmed when she unbinds her hair," he began. "Like a white swan her neck joins to the swell of her breasts. . . ."

My ears perked, but suddenly I was afraid to look at him, unsure of what longing I might see in his eyes. And what was happening to my heart? This was not good poetry; believe me, I know. You have no idea how much bad poetry I was to endure until our future bard got the hang of it. But I had no such discernment then and neither did Will, and as he stumbled along I felt my body growing warmer.

". . . still her face in the water mocks me . . ."

Abruptly, his reflection disappeared from beside mine, and I jerked up my head. He was crimson with embarrassment, and I was sorry for my treatment of him. There was no need to have made light of his dreams. At such a moment Will was painfully aware of his predicament—a brain and a passion too bright for a rustic glover— and what could he do about it? Should he spend his whole life trying to outwit his fate, or should he crush futile hope at the start?

"No, no, it was really quite wonderful," I protested.

"Was it?"

"Yes. Why, no one else could have come up with such lines on demand. You have a great talent."

"I've thought so . . . I mean, I try. . . . Which part did you like best?"

"The swan." I smiled and stroked my fingertips down my throat to my collarbone and bosom. "You should write that down."

"Yes, I should." His eyes were on my breasts again, and my annoyance returned.

"Well, I must go," I said. "My stepmother is expecting me."

"Back at Hewlands Farm."

"Yes, it is right over there."

I motioned in the general direction, then I rose and began to walk away along the path. Should I look back? Might he call or was he waving after me? What for? It would be mere coincidence if our paths crossed at the brook again. Yet I knew they would, and the feelings that tickled me were ones I did not want. Stay away, I told myself. He is pampered and pompous and overfond of himself. He is green and carries a headful of nonsense. Stay away, Anne, do you hear me? You must have a man who can give you a home and security, and you will bear him children and be his helpmate till death do you part. That is a woman's lot in the world. There is no way to escape it.

Anne, do you hear?

⁓

We were both at the brook the same time the next day. Neither of us bothered to dissemble it.

"Have you written my sonnet?" I asked, a bit archly.

He gave his courtier's bow and smugly replied, "Sweet lady, I have." From his shirt he produced a scroll of paper and presented it to me with a flourish.

I opened it with an answering sweep of my hand, and my eyes roved down the sheet. "Read it to me," I demanded.

"No, you read it," he countered.

"All right." I wet my lips, playing for time. " 'Tho-those . . . Those l-l-lee . . .' "

"Those lips."

"Yes, that is what I was about to say. 'Those lips . . . th-that Low-vee's . . .' "

"Love's."

"I know that. Don't interrupt." I *tsk*ed at the paper. "It is your handwriting. It's not very good."

He waited.

" 'Those lips . . . that Love's . . . o-o-on . . .' " I made a noise of self-reproach, upset that he should see me struggling. Those two years I had spent at the petty school had been very long ago. " 'Those lips . . . that Love's . . . o-o-own . . .' "

"Let me." He said it gently, not mocking, and held out his hand. On his face was a look of compassion for a creature who could not read. I relinquished the paper, and we seated ourselves on the grassy bank beside the pond, the willows trailing their silvery branches to the water.

> *Those lips that Love's own hand did make*
> *Breath'd forth the sound that said, "I hate,"*
> *To me that languish'd for her sake:*
> *But when she saw my woeful state,*
> *Straight in her heart did mercy come,*
> *Chiding that tongue, that ever sweet*
> *Was used in giving gentle doom;*
> *And taught it thus anew to greet:*
> *"I hate" she alter'd with an end*
> *That follow'd it as gentle day*

Doth follow night, who like a fiend
From heaven to hell is flown away.
"I hate" from hate away she threw,
And sav'd my life, saying "not you."

I will never forget the awe in his voice or in my soul the first time he read me that poem. It silenced us both for a full minute afterward. Could he really be in love with me on such short acquaintance? And I with him? Or was it the words we both fell in love with? How do you separate the poet from the poem?

"I am sorry I cannot read it myself," I said, lowering my head. "I went to school a little, but my skill is rusty."

"That's all right. It isn't hard, you know. I could tutor you."

"I would like that. May I keep the poem?"

I held out my hand for the paper, but he withdrew his, suddenly teasing. "If I give it to you, you could learn to read it by yourself. Then you wouldn't need me."

"Yes, I would."

"Or you would show it off, when it ought to be kept secret."

"No, I promise."

"Besides, I can do better than this first attempt. You shall be my lady love, my inspiration."

For a moment I was too startled by his declaration that I was his lady love to reply.

"Well?" he said, waggling the poem in front of me.

"Teach me to read," I demanded. "Bring books."

"Very well, my pretty pupil, we will begin with the alphabet. Repeat after me: A, B, C . . ."

There are some things I have to thank Will Shakespeare for. A comfortable home. Never experiencing want. And yes, our children. But his first gift to me, teaching me to read and write, is the one I most cherish. Even if it was done mainly to impress me and thereby gain his desires, even if it was to show off his erudition and emphasize his higher station, it was also to bring us together, to create a language between us, to ensphere us in an inviolate lovers' world. Will was right about the poem's quality. Though he never again addressed one to me, many more and better poems were to follow. But those early words are carved on my heart. He loved me, and that sonnet proves it.

As for me, never did any pupil pay stricter attention or study harder. I already knew I was smart. Over the next few weeks I listened, recited and recaptured the elemental workings of letters, words, phrases. At home, I practiced on our Bible; till then, its cover had been more often dusted than opened. I vowed to Will Shakespeare that I would not kiss him until I could read every sentence of our sonnet with fluid ease.

"Then you must learn faster, faster!" Will cried at our next assignation. We did not meet every day. He had to assist his father in the glove-making shop, and I could not always contrive excuses to steal off from the farm, though when I did, Duck never objected. She must have guessed there was an amorous swain from Stratford strolling our way, and, hoping I had attracted a husband at last, she and Bartholomew trusted to my good judgment. What good judgment? It was flying away from me with every X, Y, Z.

" 'S-stre-street . . . street in her heart . . .' No, wait. Don't tell me, Will. 'Straight' . . . that's it . . . 'straight in her heart.' "

"Yes, yes. And the next line? Shall I read it to you?"

"No, no cheating! If you read it to me, I will remember it, and then I won't really be reading, will I?"

"You are too honest and that makes you a cruel mistress!" he moaned. "Shall I never drink a kiss from those claret lips?"

"Be still, you silly poet. I don't think you learned to read in a mere month."

"But of course I did. I was translating Ovid in a fortnight! Then I turned right around and taught the other boys and the master himself. Give me my kiss!"

"No, you wait!"

I pushed back his hands, and he pouted and obeyed, though heaven knows I was ready to unlace my bodice that very minute. I went to bed at night imagining his mouth upon mine, the heat of his panting on my neck. A part of me still protested: Anne, he is a boy, he is not the one, this is not serious. Give up this infatuation and find yourself a real husband. I should have recalled the fate of Anne Boleyn, who held off the lecherous Henry until she was assured a crown, not wanting to bear his bastard as her sister Mary had done. But Mary lived and gained preferment, and Anne lost both her crown and her head. Was it because she promised Henry too much, and the passion could not survive the prelude, the courtship dance? If I had surrendered to Will sooner, would our lust have blown over quickly and both of us escaped with no greater loss than our mutual virginity? Instead, I let the anticipation build and build.

" 'Those lips that Love's own hand did make . . . Breath'd forth the soo . . . the sound that said, "I hate." ' "

"Don't start at the beginning again!" Will moaned. "We will be frost statues beside a frozen pond by the time you reach the end."

I laughed. "Nonsense, it is barely July. Besides, we would be making more progress if you had not skipped the last three days."

"I couldn't sneak away," he confessed, and by this I knew that he too was concealing our meetings. Would his family not have approved of me? The thought was disturbing. But why should he tell them? We were only dallying, weren't we? He was a charming interlude until an appropriate match took my fancy. I was a dress rehearsal for the wife he would woo several years ahead.

"You must get to the end," Will pleaded. "There is a double pun in it."

"Of which you are quite proud?"

"Why shouldn't I be? Besides, it is a pun about you. If I explain it, will you kiss me now?"

"No, you wait."

But by another week, I had prolonged our temptation as long as I could. The tingling, the craving had almost reduced us to quivering jellyfish. Finally, I allowed us to reach the last two lines.

" 'I hate' from hate away she threw, And sav'd my life, saying 'not you.' "

"You see?" said Will. "You see the double pun?"

"No, tell me!" I implored, too heated for our kiss to care anymore about scholarship.

"It is your name, embedded in the lines, or as near as I could make it. 'I hate' from *Hathaway* she threw, *Anne* sav'd my life, saying 'not you.'"

"Then I shall *throw* myself at you with a good *Will*," I rejoined, and did.

I flung myself at his mouth, his lips, his tongue. I grappled my hands into his hair and clutched like a tiger. God help me, I was wanton! And he returned my ardor not like a virgin boy, oh, no, but as a lover who has conquered a thousand women, a man so sure of his power, he sweeps armies before him. Our tongues entwined, his hand plunged into my bodice and I could not get my clothes off fast enough. Naked, I ripped at him, still lean and with no more hair on his chest than a chicken plucked for the pot. We rolled and panted and coupled in the long grass; then we caught our breath and did it again. We ate of each other like famished beggars at a feast; our lust was a banquet ripe and overflowing. How is that for bad poetry?

"Tomorrow?" I begged, my lips bruised from his kisses.

"Tomorrow," he promised, belting up his breeches with a new-found authority.

⁓

There are things you forget to ask at first, critical knowledge you should demand for the record. Why did you fall in love with me? Was it my face, my fortune, my finery? Was it truly all of a moment or had you long admired me from afar? Did you know my age, my parentage, my prospects? Did you have any doubts or did your passion sweep the misgivings aside? But in that first flush we do not question why we are loved. We only rejoice that we are.

"You are my doe of the forest," Will murmured, arraying my long hair about my naked body. "I adore your bluebell eyes."

"I love the taste of your tongue and your kiss in the hollow of my neck," I replied.

"Your coral ears and lyre hips enchant me. I cherish your tender buds and your mysterious dark forest." Here he would tweak my nipples and stroke himself between my legs.

"I love your sturdy lance," I would quip, teasing my fingers along his organ with a feathery touch. "Oh, Will, shake me with your spear!"

What nonsense! Yet we relished every word, and he puffed with pleasure at the too-obvious pun upon his surname. We were rampant and insatiable and dizzy with ecstasy.

Most delicious was the melding of our minds. My head on his shoulder as we sat beneath a willow tree, I drank in his lessons and he coached me to fluency. Sometimes he rewarded my efforts with a long recital of Ovid or Seneca. What other audience did he have? At home his fine learning was no longer an unadulterated source of family pride; it was also a painful reminder how a father's failure had blunted the son's chances. I was as natural a scholar as Will, and he praised my intelligence and encouraged me to love literature as he did.

Would Will Shakespeare ever have fallen in love with me if I were stupid?

One last thing. It is true I never told Will how old I was, but neither did I attempt to deceive him. Everyone else knew my age or could guess closely. He had only to ask around. He never asked me. So it is highly disingenuous of him to pretend he was a naive boy tricked by a scheming older woman. From his sojourn in Lancashire he possessed far more sophistication and experience of the wide world than did I. And don't tell me he didn't have two sturdy legs that could walk away at any time.

Instead he kept walking toward Shottery Brook, and by September I was pregnant.

Chapter 4

$\mathcal{P}$regnant. I had not even seriously considered marrying Will Shakespeare; now I was carrying his child. Oh, God, get me out of this. Let it be some disease that had forestalled my natural cycle. Let me fall ill and miscarry. I stopped eating, and at the brook I pushed Will away, telling him I felt sick. He pouted at the loss of his pleasure and plied me with hugs and kisses. He would make it all better. When I began to cry, he grew alarmed and begged me to confide what ailed me.

"I'm pregnant!" I threw myself down on the bank, sobbing. "I'm pregnant!"

"What?" His voice was blank and puzzled. "No." He leaned over me and roughed my shoulder. "Anne? No."

For several weeks we agonized. The bitter irony was that the pregnancy might easily have been prevented; one of the products crafted and sold on the sly by John Shakespeare in his glover's shop was a soft sheath that fit over a man's organ and kept his seed from spilling out. But Will had not availed himself of this option, and at the time I was ignorant of it. Now what? Could I procure a drug from the apothecary to rid me of the burden? The local quack had poisoned more people with his potions than he had cured. Could I depart for an extended visit to a distant relative and leave the infant to be fostered? Not without revealing my shameful predicament to Duck and

Bartholomew. Perhaps I had mistaken my condition? Give it a few days more.

"Do you think I want to marry *you*?" I rejoined when our anxiety erupted into mutual recriminations. "You're eighteen—you have no trade, no prospects, no employment. You cannot support a wife, let alone a child. We will have to live in your parents' house with your brothers and sister, and they will shun me and fault everything I do. And don't forget you are not the first family of Stratford any longer. If I had meant to ensnare a husband, I could have seduced a man in far better circumstances than you!"

"Maybe it's not mine," said Will.

I went home and told Duck and Bartholomew. My stepmother was distraught, my brother furious. At any other time, they might have shown more understanding, for I was hardly the only bride in Stratford to be preceded by her belly to the altar. But by now it was November, and by church law the wedding season would soon close for the year. Moreover, Bartholomew had recently proposed to Isabella Hancocks, and their nuptials were less than three weeks hence. "How could you disgrace me in front of Isabella and her family?" He pounded his fist into his palm. "Think what you have done to our reputation, Anne."

He gathered two of my father's old friends, and the three grim men went to confront John Shakespeare. They must have been persuasive, for Will quickly capitulated, and all agreed we must be married without delay. An appeal for a special license was made to the consistory court at Worcester, so that instead of the usual church reading of the banns for three Sundays in a row, only one reading was required. In the application for the license, my father's friends swore I was a "maiden." I wonder how many times the bishop had heard that before. I wonder how much they slipped him.

The wedding, held a few days after Bartholomew and Isabella's celebration, was a dismal affair. I had a sick knot in my stomach, and the rain spat on us as we walked to church. At John Shakespeare's insistence, we trekked to the neighboring village of Temple Grafton for the ceremony because the elderly priest there still observed a mildly Catholic form of service. What did it matter? Just get it done. As we reentered Stratford, the people we passed whispered or snickered behind their hands. We had the semblance of a meal at the Shakespeare house, Bartholomew having denied me the traditional bride ale at Hewlands Farm that my father might have given. He did turn over my dowry, which went directly into Will's, or rather his father's, pocket: £6 13s 4d—the price of a dozen good ewes. It behooves a woman to know how much she is worth. Only Duck gave me a present, a silver necklace with a teardrop amber pendant, which she pressed into my palm when no one was looking.

That night Will and I lay in our marriage bed. We didn't touch. We didn't talk. The Shakespeares' house on Henley Street was a step up in size and furnishings from our cottage at Hewlands, and we had been given the middle bedroom of three on the second floor, his sister and brothers having been shuffled to accommodate us. I heard one of them bump against the wall and felt a flash of defiance. If carnal lust was what they were snooping to hear, by God, I would give them a lesson they would not forget. But a glance at my bridegroom doused my intent.

"Will?"

"What?"

"I want to tell you something."

"I'm tired."

"I know, but you need to listen." I waited a moment before continuing. "I am sorry this happened. It is not what either of us foresaw. But we do love each other, and we can have a happy marriage. We have only to surmount this difficult beginning." He gave me no acknowledgment, and after a pause I went on. "I promise to do my part. I will respect and obey your parents and accept their criticisms without complaint. I am proficient at sewing and embroidery. I can clean and cook. I will bear our child and give you more children if you desire them. And we can plan for the future and find you a rewarding position as tutor in another great house. It might even come with a private apartment." I waited, feeling his body an inch apart from mine in the darkness. "Will?"

"I'm tired," he said, and he turned toward the wall.

⁓

So then, he never loved me again from that day forward. End of story.

Not so fast.

It may be true that all things are with more spirit chased than enjoyed, yet love and marriage are far more complicated than any tidy five-act play. I kept my wedding-night promise, and gradually Will came around. Was it so terrible being wed to me, after all? He had not been in love with anyone else when he met me. He was stuck in his father's shop whether he had a wife or no. By the new year, the scandal of our union was stale gossip, and neighbors inquired courteously of my health and the coming baby when I walked in town. We were legitimate now, and the infant would be John Shakespeare's first grandchild, a reason to hold his head up even though his fortunes remained low. Bartholomew had forgiven me also—a hasty temper seldom lasts—and Duck cried and embraced me when I came to visit at Hewlands Farm.

I made the greatest effort to earn a place in Will's family. His youngest brother, Edmund, was two years old and easily won over with affection. Richard, eight, suspected I was a sinful woman and endeavored to scowl at me as his father did, but for the most part he could not spare time from boyish pursuits to hold me in disdain. Will's sister, Joan, thirteen, was the family magpie and found me a useful ear. "Oh? Really? I had no idea," I would say as she exhausted her vocal cords on the latest tattle. The remaining brother, Gilbert, was sixteen, two years Will's junior. He was old enough to see me as an object lesson, yet too generous to maintain a grudge. He esteemed Will openly and desired his approval. If Will stood by me, then Gilbert would stand by Will.

Only my parents-in-law refused to be mollified. John might boast in public of the coming grandchild; in private I was not forgiven for poaching his son from under his nose. Mary smiled smugly each time she rebuked me. I did not eat enough to sustain the baby. I put too many carrots in the stew. "I am sorry," I replied evenly. "I shall try to improve." That I did not snap back irked her the more. "She thinks she is perfect," Mary complained to a neighbor, loud enough to be sure I heard, and when the woman demurred that she never saw me idle or ungracious, Mary huffed, "Only to the unobservant!" It took me a long time to understand Mary Shakespeare, but meanwhile I was obedient, industrious, good-tempered, comely and fruitful. A hefty dowry aside, what other attributes could be required of a daughter-in-law and wife?

Will noticed, and we resumed our bed relations, my belly not yet having reached a size to impede. Indeed, we recovered our former lustiness and once received a hearty pounding on the wall from his parents' side when we thumped and moaned too wildly. When we burst out laughing, John's fist nearly punched through the wall.

We also continued my education. In the gray captivity of winter, it solaced us to sit by the hearth, Will drilling me on my writing or tutoring me in his favorite classical authors. Thanks to a continuing friendship with the schoolmaster, he was able to borrow books. Sometimes Gilbert joined in the lessons, though he insisted he was a dunce. But he had a musical talent, and he played lively tunes for us on his flute.

"A woman has no need of Latin," my father-in-law proclaimed one evening when we three were occupied in study. We looked up and I stiffened. John was right, of course, and I never expected to become a scholar equal to Will. But if my husband took pride in his conjugations, I was happy to be his pupil.

"That's right," Mary seconded, stabbing the needle through her embroidery. "A woman who marries wisely has no need of an education."

"You never filled your head with Latin, did you, Mary?" said John.

"Certainly not. I have devoted my life to a woman's proper sphere, tending my home and raising my children."

"Now, for a man, it is different." John straightened his shoulders importantly. "A man like me has dealings in the world, bills and deeds and correspondence to dispatch. Every man should possess a little literacy."

"Yes," said Mary. "You have stated my opinion exactly."

For several minutes they went back and forth in this vein, John growing ever gruffer, Mary more sanctimonious. Why? My mother-in-law was an intelligent woman. Her father had named her, the youngest of his many daughters, the executor of his will. When a proclamation was posted at the church or in the market, Mary could read it as well as her husband. Was his vanity such that she must ever appease him?

Yet if their intent was to goad me, they should have paused after the first sortie, when my temper was primed. The longer they echoed each other, the less angry and the more fascinated I became. Neither of them regarded me directly, and beads of sweat rose on John's temples, though it was a frigid March night and the crackling hearth barely kept the room warm. I saw that the embroidery pattern on Mary's frame was one I had devised and that two drops of blood spotted the white linen where she had pricked her finger. A mischievous reply formed in my mind: "How is it then, John, if you are so smart, that you cannot sign your own name but must use a glover's mark?" Magpie Joan, Richard and even little Edmund sat riveted in anticipation of just such a sally. But something told me to keep quiet until my in-laws ended their dialogue with a mutually satisfied nod.

Slowly, Will pushed the Latin grammar toward me. "Go on," he said.

I could have kissed him. Later, as we huddled beneath our blankets, I did.

"If only we could get away from here and have a home of our own," he said, snugging me to him.

"Why can't we? As soon as the baby is born, you can seek a schoolmaster's place. You are an excellent teacher."

"But I lack a degree, and that disqualifies me."

"Not from a private position, as you had in Lancashire."

"I might not be able to take you with me."

"Not at first perhaps, but once you were established and invaluable." I shifted to find a comfortable hollow in the mattress. At seven months, my body had become awkward, and to stick an arm or ankle outside the covers in this weather brought instant gooseflesh. It did not help that Will often stole the sheets.

"Who would assist my father in the leather shop? We have but one apprentice."

"He has Gilbert, and whatever he loses in your labor, you can recompense by sending money home."

"And you would let me go?"

I paused. It would mean living under his parents' roof without a friend or ally. "Yes."

"Then after the child is born, we'll make plans."

He caressed his hand over the baby, and in sweet contentment I closed my eyes. I had not planned to play Will off against his parents, and my success illuminated me. Let them taunt and snipe. Henceforth I was proof against their strategies. Best of all, my husband was falling in love with me again.

~

Her "good hour"—that's what they call it when the pains begin. "Her good hour has come upon her." What's good about it?

I had managed to more or less ignore my pregnancy. I was healthy and untroubled by the backaches and swollen ankles that afflict many women. Though my belly could be unwieldy, I had not gained a surfeit of weight and become bloated. The only time I became uneasy was when the baby roiled and curled inside me, like a sea monster churning just below the water's surface. The sight drew a shudder from Will as well, and in those last months he refrained from further lovemaking; he was by nature fastidious. But where I was fortunate in the ease of my pregnancy, the birth pangs were about to put me on the rack.

"Get the midwife!" Mary commanded that May morning at breakfast when I pressed my belly and let out the first surprised gasp. "Get her to bed!"

Everyone jumped up from the table, the boys in particular scattering, fear in their eyes lest they be dragged into some bloody women's mess. Magpie Joan would have stayed—what a good tale it would make!—but Mary ordered her out for being too young. I was not yet in distress and made it to the bedroom on my own feet. Will came with the midwife; then the door was shut in his face. The midwife had large hands and prided herself on her efficiency.

"Has she spilt her water yet?" she asked, and on receiving a negative from Mary, she pushed up my shift and without preamble wedged in her finger. "Let's see what we have here then."

I squeezed my eyes. No one had told me to expect such humiliation.

"She's nowhere near," the midwife announced, examining her mucus-covered finger. "You wouldn't have any breakfast for me, would you? I had to leave my own on the plate when Master Will came running. What a look on his face!" She and Mary chuckled together, and Mary went to fetch her a meal.

"Could my stepmother be sent for?" I asked, the minute my mother-in-law left the room.

"No need to bother her," the midwife replied. "You've hours yet." She slapped me on the knee for good luck.

Mary arrived with a heaping platter of food, and she and the midwife began to chat. The smell of bacon fat and greased eggs made my own breakfast come up.

"The sheets!" Mary *tsk*ed, though they were barely soiled. It was my shift and me that were splattered. "Well, let's get it off."

They stripped me; then all that day they sat there gabbling, their favorite topic being the horrendous labors and deaths of other mothers and infants. I wanted to cry. I was in true fear for my life, but I would not let Mary and her callous cohort see me as weak.

"I have had eight myself, you know," Mary bragged to the midwife, "though three died early, all girls."

"Eleven for me," the woman replied, topping her, "but seven dead, God rest their souls." She pushed up her sleeve and displayed her fat finger. "Let's see how she's doing."

By midafternoon the pains had become both stronger and more frequent. I asked for a drink of water and was forbidden. It would only make me sick again, the midwife said.

"Now we're getting somewhere," she declared as my travail increased and another probe showed up something to her liking. "A beef-and-kidney in thick gravy will suit me fine for supper."

God, I prayed, let me be delivered of this child soon, if only to make this horrid woman disappear!

At twilight, the midwife began to frown.

"What is it? What's wrong?" I demanded, attempting to rise up on my elbow. It had been nigh on twelve hours, and I was tired and sweating, though thus far I had kept my whimpers to myself.

"Nothing," the woman answered, drawing Mary aside. They conferred in whispers, maddening me.

"What's wrong?" I cried, as much as my parched throat allowed.

Mary came and patted my shoulder. "Don't worry, Anne. It will be all right." They were the first kind words she had spoken, and the doubt in her eyes terrified me.

Night fell and now I knew true agony. Demon twists contorted my body and tormented me into a ball. In the candlelight the midwife's face became a leering specter between my legs as Mary paced in the background. She was not so fond of the midwife anymore. She may not have cared how I suffered; she may have enjoyed it for a while. But if the baby should die and she here in the room, accountable . . . She began yelling at the midwife, and the midwife yelled back. Pride and dignity gone, I shrieked loudest of all. Summer nights are short, and day breaks by five of the clock. But my blackness went on past sunup, until the pain made me delirious. Those lusty afternoons with Will nine months before were hardly worth the price I was paying now.

Where is my pregnancy portrait? I wondered in a daze, for it was popular, among those who could afford it, to have a portrait painted of an expectant wife. It proved the woman had done her duty to procreate, and provided a convenient memorial in the quite likely event that she died in the process. All I got was my knees shoved to my chest, and the midwife shouting, "Push, push!" But neither my brain nor my exhausted body could comply, and a fist clawed inside me—God, let me die! The tearing of flesh as the child emerged left me bloody, stinging and raw.

The naked babe they put into my arms was a girl. She was red and slick and squalling and ugly. Within a day she would be pink and beautiful and remain so throughout her life. Susanna—even her name sounds golden. But in those first minutes as I looked around the room, my new daughter at my breast, no pretty sight greeted my eyes. The midwife's hair had come undone about her puffed face, and her arms were crusted with blood. Her body had lost all its bluster. My mother-in-law was a sick gray ghost propped on a chair. My daughter bawled at my breast, unhappy with the milkless fluid leaking from my nipple. I had no brain or body, only a numb wet ache as the afterbirth puddled out of me. I looked at the four of us, and I thought, God hates women. Then I struggled up on the pillow and held the baby's head to suck what she could get.

Chapter 5

$\mathcal{A}$ few weeks after Susanna's birth Will came back to me in bed. My stomach had grown flat again while my breasts, full of milk, were round and alluring. Yet our lovemaking was dispirited, Will overwhelmed by the responsibilities of fatherhood, me tired from awaking two and three times a night to nurse my hungry babe. Moreover, I had yet to feel like a mother. Mary had, of necessity, taken charge of the infant in the days following that arduous labor and now refused to relinquish her care. It may be that Susanna kindled memories of the babies she had lost. Whatever the reason, we had words about it, and to keep peace in the household I was forced to back down.

"We need our own place," I lamented to Will one night as we sat in bed.

He made a hopeless sound. Susanna was asleep in her crib, but through the wall we could hear his parents in the next room. Rutting—it is a crude, goatish word, yet apt to the image I conjured to match John's grunts and heaves as he relieved himself with a gusty spasm. In contrast, Mary was as silent as death in there, and I pictured her with thighs spread and her breasts hanging slack to either side and her arms flung out as if crucified. Did she grit her teeth? Pray for it to be over? I made a bawdy joke of it to Will, thinking it would restore our alliance to laugh together at his parents' foibles. Instead, Will reacted with fury.

"Do not speak of my parents so," he hissed, and I quickly apologized.

Afterward, it dawned on me. Like father, like son. Is that what scared you, Will? Is that what you foresaw? You didn't know yet exactly what you wanted; you only knew it wasn't this. And was I not in much the same position—no pun intended—as my long-suffering mother-in-law? I began to comprehend them better as well. What John Shakespeare craved above all else was to be an Important Man. He believed he deserved it, and during his tenure as mayor of Stratford, he had it in his grasp. So naturally he took it ill when his fortunes fell, and he became curt and disagreeable. What Mary believed she deserved was to be the Wife of an Important Man, and she too had been gratified for a spell. Her punishment for the fall was that she must stoutly maintain her loyalty in case John rose again; no other avenue was open to her. Did she silently and bitterly berate him for his failures and the loss of her inheritance as he thumped upon her? Would this be Will and me a few short years from now?

Yet after a while our optimism returned—sweet youth is ever buoyant. Will took on more duties in the shop, working beside his father and Gilbert. John was one of three glovers in Stratford, and in the yard behind the house, the men worked to turn the lamb, sheep and goat skins he purchased into leather. For ordinary workman's gloves, the skins would be tanned with extract of bark or berries. But for the fine white gloves worn by people of fashion, the far lengthier and more complicated process of whittawing was required. The skins were soaked and rinsed, scraped clean of hair and flesh, then limed for several weeks to remove the grease and soften them. Next they were soaked in urine to make them supple, then rinsed again and steeped in a solution of alum to whiten them. After drying in the sun, more stretching and paring took place. The whiter and softer the leather and the longer the glove fingers, the better; the queen's elegant hands had set the style. No matter if the gloves did not exactly fit. The point was to give them as gifts and carry them for show to church on Sunday.

In the shop, Gilbert became the teacher, a chance to repay Will for the evening lessons by the fire. But though Will tried hard, he never mastered the actual craft of glove making. Cutting out and stitching the intricate parts called for a special skill not resident in his fingers. Where my husband did acquit himself well was in the business end of the leather shop, negotiating prices for skins and other raw goods, enticing customers to buy his wares. Most gloves were plain white, lined with silk, velvet, rabbit skin or fur, but occasionally Will secured an order for something special, a pair of embroidered gloves to complement a lady's or gentleman's fine attire. I gladly put my needle to work on these commissions and earned praise for my artful designs.

I also gradually pried Susanna from her grandmother's protective grip, or rather, Mary and I learned to share. Magpie Joan proved an unexpected help. She seemed to regard Susanna as a delightfully life-like doll and spent hours petting and dressing her. Now that the tainted pregnancy was over and the child disconnected from my body, my status with Will's family improved. Yet while they could not quite deny my contribution to their lineage, they often behaved as if Susanna had sprung miraculously from nowhere, like an infant left on their doorstep by fairies. Susanna blossomed under the attention and was happy as an angel.

From time to time I nudged Will about a teaching position. Was that still what he wanted? Perhaps, but who would hire him now? That same year of Susanna's birth, another religious boil burst open, and among those implicated in the latest Catholic plot to assassinate Eliza-beth was Edward Arden, another of Mary Shakespeare's illustrious relatives. Government agents swarmed into Warwickshire, and suspect houses were searched, quaking citizens interrogated. When they came to Henley Street, I thought I would faint for fear, but John deftly ap-peased them. We Shakespeares attended church regularly, he insisted, glossing over his past recusancy, and after more frowns and warnings, the investigators moved on. But Arden and several others were grue-somely executed in London, and even after the tensions eased, the em-ployment prospects for anyone related to the family remained dim.

"I wish they would all choose one way or the other what we are to believe and let that be an end of it," said Will, as we lay in bed, our voices low. Even at home, everyone remained cautious about being overheard. "Better yet, why doesn't God himself just tell us?"

"My father used to say a person's faith should be his private business," I replied.

"Then he was a smart man, and I wish I had known him."

It was one of the nicest things he could have said, and I patted his hand. "Eventually it must die down. We have only to be patient."

"Maybe. At least there has been no falling off of customers in the shop." Will sighed. "Whatever else their quarrels, all God-fearing people are agreed on the need for gloves."

By Susanna's first birthday I was pregnant again. Will took the news with a jolt.

"What did you expect?" I asked, teasing yet half annoyed. Why do men never make the connection that what they spurt between a woman's legs in April is apt to reemerge in their likeness come January? Will had been happy enough to sport at the time. We even revived our old game. Oh, Will, shake me with your spear! So he did and more than once, and we giggled together. Now he looked at me with shock upon his face. Don't turn churlish on me, Will.

He didn't, and by the next day he had brightened, pointing out that this time it might be a boy. But as the month approached, my worry grew. Another birth, when the first had nearly killed me, and this baby seemed huge. The reason was soon revealed, for although the second delivery supposedly goes easier, mine was a double hell—twins—a boy, then a girl. I was unconscious by the end, and they said I bled a great deal. I was left with a permanent click in my right hip that ached in cold weather ever after. The midwife proclaimed the children healthy, and we named them Hamnet and Judith, after the baker and his wife, good friends of Will's.

Good-bye, books. Farewell, evening lessons by the fire. Oh, both had been dwindling since Susanna anyway. What man has the inclination to recite verses when he has a wife and child—suddenly three children—to support? What woman has the leisure to absorb a bit of Latin after washing dirty linens all day? Get to sleep while you can; you'll have two infants up suckling half the night. My consolation was that I had learned to read and write ably by then, a treasure no one could take away. But that was small comfort when, nursing the twins in the frigid February dark, I fell sick: chills, the ague, a racking cough. I coughed so hard I pulled a muscle in my back, which kept me painfully twisted for weeks.

"You look like a hunchback," Will snapped. "Can't you straighten up?"

"No," I said, fighting back tears as I shouldered a cranky Judith. "No, I can't."

Ah, but wasn't everyone overjoyed at the new grandchildren? Didn't my credit with my in-laws double like yeasted bread? It might have, had Hamnet arrived alone. Him, John and Mary spirited off to be admired; Judith was packaged as an afterthought. And once the excitement of the birth passed, the situation began to add up. Look around. You can count. John and Mary, Gilbert, Joan, Richard, Edmund. Will and me, Susanna and the twins. Eleven in the household, and four of those mouths had come by way of me in a mere two years. Plus, we had to hire a wet nurse—I simply hadn't enough milk for two hungry babes—another expense on my account. Wary frowns were cast toward my belly. Flat for the moment, but was I planning to burden them with another set of twins by December? Could I be a little less fruitful, please? The old criticisms resumed. I let the porridge get too thick. I wasted a candle stub. I apologized and dogged on, a twin on either hip, while my mother-in-law's tongue flicked like a whip at my ankles, and my father-in-law glowered at me behind my back.

Oh, Anne, you exaggerate. The facts, perhaps, but not how I felt. What if my milk dried up completely? How would we feed Hamnet and Judith then? By summer, I was often exhausted; come winter, I fell sick again. Where I had counted on Magpie Joan to provide some relief by adopting the new babies as she had Susanna, they two had become so entwined there was no room for anyone else. My only thought on arising each morn was to get through the day so that I might fall into blessed sleep at night. When the children awoke for some fright or cough or soiling of their clothes, even that little gift of unconsciousness was denied me. I would lie beside Will as he snored, a fretful twin in my arm, and I wanted to hit him, slap him, kick him out of bed.

But poor Will. I could see his side of it. There he was at twenty-one, a reluctant husband and father, a man too highly educated for a simple country life yet still living under his parents' roof and authority. Once, passing the leather shop, I overheard John disparage me and was gladdened when Will retorted in my defense. But that night in bed when I touched him, he shuddered away.

"We cannot afford another child, Anne. Where would we be now but for my parents' charity?"

"It is not charity. You work hard to earn our keep, and so do I." I laid my hand on his shoulder. "It is no use being mad at each other, Will. We must try to set up on our own. A tutoring position for you—"

"—would not feed and house the five of us."

"A headmaster at a grammar school then."

"We have been over that. I lack a degree."

"Then we must cast our net wider. My brother Bartholomew might give us a loan to start our own business in wool or leather."

"I won't take money from your family."

"Then I will work as a seamstress. You can take the money from me."

"And who would mind the children?"

"I would, of course."

"They have worn you to a stick now. Have you looked at yourself lately? Forget it, Anne. We must make the best of this."

He closed his eyes to sleep, and though I let him go, I felt oddly comforted. At least he had noticed how diligently I was working and cared for my state of health. But in the morning when I dragged myself out of bed to answer the twins' cries for milk, I caught my face in the glass, and his comments took on a different light. The lustrous fawn brown hair Will used to spread around me was dull and frayed. My complexion was pallid, my mouth sagged. When I eased my shift off my shoulder to give the twins their suck, my collarbones jutted under my skin like the bony, folded wings of a bat. There was no poetry in my eyes, no music in my hips.

That afternoon while the children napped, I did not churn the butter, as was my task. I washed my face and neck and worked a salve into my chapped lips. I donned my good brown wool dress trimmed in green velvet ribbon. I had not worn it since the twins' christening a year before, and the loose fit was disconcerting. I combed my hair and pinned it neatly under my cap. Then I put on my necklace, the amber pendant on a silver chain that Duck had given me on my wedding day. I had tucked it away after Hamnet and Judith, tired of prying it from sticky fingers, retrieving it from drooling mouths.

"I am going to the market," I informed Mary, and sailed out the door with my cloak. The January day was bright and sunny and the cold air on my face invigorating. My plan was straightforward. I would go to our glove stall, link my arm through my husband's and whisk him off despite his father's protests. Gilbert would back me. "Let them go," he would say, laughing. Then we would stroll past the shops and vendors, exchanging greetings and complimenting their wares. We would pause to buy a sugared bun from Hamnet and Judith Sadler, the twins' godparents. Will was ever fond of sweets.

The market was at the end of Henley Street, and, sidestepping a woman with a flock of geese, I caught sight of Will right away. He was leaning languidly against a wall on the opposite corner, half turned from view. Not so the girl to whom he was speaking . . . Oh, this is so trite. She was simpering and twisting a long lock of hair around her forefinger, pouting and blushing and batting her lashes. She was some farmer's daughter, perhaps fifteen years old. No match for a seasoned wife.

"Will! Here I am! How are the sales today? Oh, and who is this? Do excuse me for interrupting, but I must have a word with my husband. I would have brought the children, dearest, but they are home fast asleep."

Husband? Children? Dearest? You should have seen the look on her face. But at least it was honest, unlike Will's and mine. I sauntered off with him, and he nimbly played the game. We didn't speak of it afterward. What, get upset over a silly little flirt in the marketplace? Yet here is the truth: For all the poetry Will wrote, it was not he but I who possessed the romantic streak, and no matter how foolish my illusions, I could still be hurt when they were wrenched away. Will may not have known yet what he wanted, but what I wanted and believed I deserved was a husband who loved me, because I still loved him.

Once, we had recited couplets together. Now we were coming uncoupled.

~

When the Queen's Men came to Stratford in the summer of 1587, I could not have foreseen what a change it would bring in our lives. I was simply excited like everyone else at the holiday atmosphere and the chance to escape into England's storied past. For that was the prime purpose of these players; they had been founded four years earlier by royal mandate as a touring company to publicize the history and accomplishments of our realm. In Catholic Spain our longtime enemy Philip II was building a great armada to invade our seas. We must unite to defend our nation—huzzah!—and to this end the plays extolled the triumph of the Protestant Reformation and burnished the image of our Virgin Queen. If the plots were often thin as barley porridge when the barley ran short, who cared? That master spy himself, Sir Francis Walsingham, had plucked the best actors from the existing London companies to form the troupe, and they relied upon pomp and pageantry, pantomime and processions to get the message across to the most dull-witted country oaf. England would need him for a solider when the Spanish invasion began.

"They say the clown Richard Tarlton is coming!" reported Magpie Joan, whose affinity for local gossip exceeded even that of my stepmother, Duck. "They say he can change his face in an instant from the hugest grin to the most piteous groan."

"Players are vagabonds." Mary sniffed.

"Oh, Mother, not if they are sent by the queen. But guess what else. One of them murdered another at the last town they stopped in!"

"Murdered?"

"Oh, yes, the news is all about. Two of the players were drinking after the show. They got in a quarrel on leaving the tavern, and one stabbed the other in the neck and killed him dead, dead, dead."

Joan drove an imaginary dagger into her throat in helpful demonstration. I frowned but let the twins continue to watch their chattering aunt. They were sitting side by side on a bench while I adjusted Hamnet's socks. He had a queer fear of them; each morning when I put them on, he would point at his toes, his lower lip would commence to quiver and his fair little face would pucker and collapse in a red bawl. Since he was still short of words, I could only guess that some lump or seam, invisible to my eyes, was distressing his tender toes. Then nothing would do but I must pull off the socks and turn them inside out and pluck any stray wool that might ball into a knot and discomfit His Majesty's digits. This process might bear repeating two or three times before the socks miraculously fit to his pleasure. With the children entranced by Joan's zestful rendition I was able to shoe the boy before he and his dainty toes knew what had transpired.

"And to think," Magpie concluded, "that a young man so full of promise should meet such a cruel and unexpected end. It is a scandal."

"Let's go see the plays," cried Edmund, who was now seven.

"Of course we will," said John, who relished entertainments of whatever sort. "If the queen has sent them to perform for us, it is our duty to attend."

Mary mumbled something more about murderous vagabonds, and indeed, her opinion of the players was a common one. The vagrancy laws classified them as masterless men, and unless a troupe had a noble patron, they were forbidden to travel the roads without permission. Clergymen and scholars railed against actors and the immorality of playgoing, when they weren't themselves sneaking up to listen. Why, actors were no better than charlatans. They took the money out of poor people's pockets—money that should have gone to the church—and gave them only hot air in return. They portrayed—and probably practiced—lewdness, drunkenness and every conceivable sin. They dressed boys as girls, men as women! That audiences loved them only proved their mutual depravity and foreshadowed their eternal damnation. But as usual, Mary followed her husband, and we went to see the Queen's Men.

What fun! In just one week we were dazzled to see *The Famous Victories of Henry V*, *The Troublesome Reign of King John*, *The True Tragedy of Richard III* and *King Leir*, an ancient tale. And what a treat was Richard Tarlton! The curly-haired dwarf scampered about in his baggy pants, playing a pipe and drum and stretching his face into myriad contortions. He had only to pop into view for the audience to burst into laughter. We stood in the crowd, weeping with mirth. Will had hoisted Susanna onto his shoulders, John claimed Hamnet and Gilbert managed Judith. I looked at my empty hands and arms, shoulders and hips, and marveled to feel so unencumbered. In the excitement and noise, what did Will think or feel or say? Not much to me. We had lost the knack of sharing our inmost thoughts, yet on that day I believed we were happy. There stood Will beside me, clapping and cheering the show, passing candies to our children, the picture of contented domesticity. He must have been secretly plotting all the while, craftily gauging the opportunity no one else had seen.

"I will go speak to the actors," he said, as the play ended and other festivities began. "They might need gloves or other goods to add to their costumes."

Over the next few days Will was often gone to confer with the Queen's Men. Twice more I took the children to see them play. But the more they trumpeted England's valor, the more uneasy I became. How could we ever win a war against mighty Spain when here at home we were hardly secure? In February, after decades of intrigue, Mary, Queen of Scots, had been beheaded for scheming to overthrow Elizabeth in the Babington Plot, and none but a fool thought our enemies would cease trying. And though Sir Francis Drake had delayed the Spanish invasion by his daring April raid on Cadiz, how could our fledgling English navy defeat the enormous armada Philip II was building? A shiver ran through me, and I drew the children closer. Even in Stratford we would not be immune, and while the crowd around me clapped for Tarlton, I thanked God for my husband and children, for the roof above us and the food on our table, and I prayed we would be together always.

"I have an announcement," said Will at supper. At first no one paid much heed. It was the end of the week, the Queen's Men were departing Stratford on the morrow, and life was returning to its routine. John was cutting our meat, and Mary and I were serving the children their portions of bread and beans from the garden. As if he realized he had picked the wrong moment, Will let the words lapse. After we were settled, he chose his timing more carefully and spoke again.

"I have an announcement. I am leaving Stratford tomorrow and going on tour with the Queen's Men."

Ah, those words. And even more, the tone of them—serious and formal to begin, growing tickled by the middle, outright delighted by the end.

"What do you mean?" I asked and John demanded, both at the same time. Will must have secured some contract with the players to supply them with leather goods—excellent news!—but why should he have to accompany them? And why didn't John know about it? I looked from my father-in-law's perturbed face back to my husband's.

"I am joining the players," Will said, leaning forward to explain. "You know they lost one of their number before they reached Stratford."

"Lost? He was murdered!" cried Mary. "By one of them!"

"An evil deed." John glared. "But what have you to do with a troupe of ruffians?"

Will chuckled. "They are actors, not ruffians, and highly esteemed in London. Why, the city is full of playhouses, and people pour in to see them. Now they are short a man, and they have offered to take me along. I can easily handle the minor roles, and they'll train me and I will turn it into a living."

"You are going to become an actor?" I said.

Those were the last words I spoke at the table, though there was no dearth of them in my head. *You can't mean this you're not an actor you've never been to London you can't leave me what about the children why are you doing this am I deserted?* The protests bumped and bumbled into one another like a herd of bleating sheep at a crossroads, but I could not seem to voice a single one. I didn't have to.

"The devil you are!" John exploded. "You will stay here and support your family and our business."

"But I can make and send you more money as an actor with the Queen's Men."

"No son of mine will take up that life!"

"In London, it is a respectable career. They play before Elizabeth at her palaces. I can learn as I earn."

"You will do nothing of the sort! You are a glover and a merchant of Stratford."

John thundered to his feet. Mary had begun to cry and the children to blubber. I felt sick and faint, and, glancing across the table, I saw that Gilbert, Richard, Joan and Edmund were likewise starch faced. Will hadn't confided in any of them either.

"The troupe is well compensated for these tours of the country," he persisted, "and generously rewarded when they perform for the queen."

"It is a vagabond life," John retorted. "Your duty is to your family. Quiet, the lot of you!" He rounded on the children, who had begun to bawl, and I crowded them into my arms and ducked my head over them to shelter them from his blast.

"Father," Gilbert began.

"I said, quiet!" John's finger slashed from Gilbert to me to his crying wife. "Can't a man have any peace? You are not going to London. I forbid it." His finger landed on Will.

Will spoke soothingly, though his mouth had tightened. "I know this is unexpected. I wish I could have given you more notice, but they made me the offer only today. And London is not far, scarcely a hundred miles—"

"It's full of thieves and murderers and prostitutes," sobbed Mary.

"—and of perfectly upstanding citizens pursuing respectable occupations," Will continued. "If I don't succeed there, I can always come home."

"You are not leaving in the first place." John resumed his seat and picked up his knife. "Eat."

"I need to make a living."

"Make it here. You got yourself into this." John shot a nasty glance toward me, and my face flamed.

"Don't," said Will, and his hand gripped his own knife. "When I am established in London, I'll send for Anne and the children, and you will never have to feed us again."

It was the most miserable meal of my life. Will kept his tone civil, repeating the advantages, making this new road to wealth sound silky smooth. He fell short once, when Mary interjected a plea that London was rife with plague. The whole Shakespeare family was terrified of the disease, and with good reason: When Will was fifteen, it had killed his seven-year-old sister, Anne. But he rallied. Since there was no escape from plague even in Stratford, he would not let it keep him from London.

John argued and expostulated. "Damn the queen!" he shouted at one point when Will went on too long about his new patron, and in the shocked silence that followed, John threw his mug of ale against the wall. The children burst into fresh wailing, but no one dared speak or leave the table. Wait, I told myself, wait until you have him alone. I hugged and hushed the children, murmuring, "It's all right. Shh, don't be frightened." But my wretchedness was growing. Where will you live? How will you eat? How long will you stay? For every obstacle John threw up, Will had an answer ready, and the tide was turning his way. Later it occurred to me that he had made his announcement before the whole family purposely to constrain me. If he won them over first, my objections would count for nothing. By the time I realized this, he was gone.

"What kind of husband deserts his wife and children to go play at make-believe?" I spat when we were finally in our room. The children were asleep, their faces tear-streaked and puffed from crying, and I had to restrict myself to a furious whisper. The tension from the bedrooms on either side of ours seemed to press against the walls.

"The kind who wants his family to get ahead in the world," Will snapped back. "Are you happy here, Anne? Are you?"

"I'm trying to be."

"Well, I'm not and I won't stay. I am doing this for us."

"You are abandoning us for our sake?"

"Yes, and once I am established in London, I will send for you and the children."

"But it is so far away," I said, torn and yet wanting to believe his promise. "Where would we live in London? We have no family or friends there."

"It is a four-day walk, we can send letters home by the carrier, and we already have new friends, all the players in the Queen's Men and the people at court we'll meet because of them. As for where we would live"—Will laughed and patted the bed for me to come sit beside him— "don't you think a city as big as London is full of houses?"

A home of our own, free of John's scowl and Mary's thumb always pushing me down, an escape from the Catholic Arden connections that limited Will's options, the excitement of London and new companions, the chance to meet the queen . . . It wasn't so far-fetched, was it? To ally yourself with the rich and powerful was how people advanced in the world.

"There are three public playhouses in London already," Will continued, "the Theatre, the Curtain, and a new one, the Rose, that has just opened. And do you remember Edward Alleyn, who used to tour with the provincial players? In London, he has become the principal actor of the Lord Admiral's Men and is feted by the most influential people in town. He acts the lead role in *Tamburlaine*—"

"What is *Tamburlaine*?" I interrupted.

"A new play by Christopher Marlowe that is all the rage."

"Who is Christopher Marlowe?"

"A great new poet, like Thomas Kyd, who wrote *The Spanish Tragedy*, and Robert Greene. In London, actors aren't paupers, begging for applause and coins. They enjoy prestige, wealth and fame."

Will went on and on—what a lot he had learned about the theater in a very short time—and the more enthusiastic he became, the more I seized on the glimmer he offered. He has been unhappy and striven to conceal it, I told myself, and it is our separate discontents that have caused us to become estranged. It is not each other we dislike but our situation, and once that has improved, we shall become a happy family again. Besides, what other avenue was open to me? To disbelieve him would have ended my last illusions about our marriage. Better to pretend I supported my husband's project than to concede I was a rejected wife.

"Come to bed," he coaxed, turning down the sheet, and he made love to me as tenderly as if we were newly wed. Thus did Will Shakespeare seduce me a second time.

The next morning he climbed onto one of the baggage wagons, and with a noisy fanfare the Queen's Men rolled out of town. That night I slept alone. In all my life I had never had a bed to myself; from the earliest age at home there were always two or three or four little brothers and sisters piled in beside me. Susanna and the twins were deep in slumber in their truckle bed, and the rest of the house was silent. Yet I tossed as if the bedbugs were worse than usual, trying to reconstruct how this had come to pass. What had Will been thinking? Was he unhappy all along? Did he still love me or had he left me in spirit long before he walked out the door? Was I that bad a wife?

My mind flinched away from the thought, and I moved into the center of the mattress, usurping both places, commanding myself to enjoy it. To have a bed all one's own, what luxury! What sloth! But those weren't tears of pleasure I fought to hold back. If Will had been deprived without knowing what he wanted, the Queen's Men had opened the sky and showed him a blinding light. He had gone to the other side of the world, and why should he ever come back?

Chapter 6

For weeks after Will's departure, I bore the brunt of my in-laws' displeasure. Since John refused to concede his precious son had disobeyed him, it fell to Mary to do the complaining. At every meal, she harped on what a mistake my husband had made. Your fault, her look implied; if you had kept him happy, he would still be here. Each time I ignored her remarks as long as possible; then I quietly but firmly came to Will's defense, restating the very arguments he had given me. Do you suppose Will was betting on just such loyalty? If I hadn't had to defend him so long to his mother, would I have defended him so long to myself?

Gilbert also spoke up for his brother. From across the table he would cast me a glance that said, Let me try this time. "Don't worry, Mother," he would say. "There are fortunes to be made in London, and if not as an actor, Will will latch onto some other employment. His eye is always to the main chance." Some evenings he was successful in appeasing her, and I privately thanked him.

"It's the truth," he replied, shrugging. "I hope to go to London myself someday."

"I wonder what it is really like there." I dunked a dinner plate in a basin of water and began scrubbing. "I imagine grand houses and palaces and streets teeming with people. How I would love to see the

Tower or St. Paul's Cathedral! Just think, Will might be strolling past them this very minute."

"I expect everything in London is bigger and busier than here in Stratford," said Gilbert, "like the Thames compared to our little Avon. That great stream carries a tide of ships and commerce from faraway ports. Ours is just wide enough to float a few riverboats and flocks of ducklings."

"I always picture the Londoners in fine clothes," I said, "which is rather silly. Even in a great city, you won't find a butcher in a silk doublet or a stonemason in satin breeches."

"Ah, but think of the church bells. Imagine how London sounds on a Sunday morning, all those bells tolling over the rooftops at the same time."

"That is your gift for music speaking."

Gilbert shook his head. "Any gift I have is a very small one."

He left, and I went on washing dishes. Dear Gilbert, he deserved better of life. Because look how things stood for him: never Will's equal at school, never cherished at home, toiling diligently but without hope in his father's business; as second son, Gilbert did not stand to inherit. Whatever dreams he nurtured of going to London, Will had usurped them. John couldn't spare another worker, especially an unpaid one. Will got first choice, and he took it all. Yet Gilbert remained steadfast and kind, and taking heart from his example I strove doubly hard to make up for my husband's absence and the loss of income he had caused the family. I undertook every menial task with a smile. Trading dreams of London with Gilbert became my only pastime.

Thus autumn advanced, the leaves flamed and fell, and gradually my in-laws' attitude softened. John even took to slapping acquaintances on the back and bragging of Will's enterprises in London, a neat trick, since we'd had nary a word from the prodigy.

"Don't worry," said Gilbert. "He will return for Christmas."

He didn't, though after the holiday we finally received a letter addressed to John. He bore it aloft as he strode to the hearth, where the rest of us were gathered in the early dark of the winter evening. A fat candle on the table had dripped a trail of wax onto the boards, and Edmund was stubbing it with his fingernail to make it lift up and peel away. Mary had just slapped Judith's hand for some offense and dumped my child, whining, in the corner. Hamnet had gone to sit by his twin in silent protest and commiseration. They had no comprehension of whom the letter was from. Lately, when I spoke of their father, the word elicited only a blank look in return. Even Susanna, though curious about the letter itself, seemed not to make the connection. But for me that letter carried the first breath of sweet air since Will's departure—until John opened it and passed it to Gilbert to read without so much as looking in my direction.

" 'Dear family,' " Gilbert read; then over the paper's edge he caught my eye.

"Go on," John demanded, flicking an impatient finger toward him.

" 'Dear family,' " Gilbert began again.

Not *Dear Anne* or *Dear wife*. Not *I miss you and long for you daily.* Not *How do our beloved children? I pray for your health and will send for you soon.* Oh, the news itself was excellent, as Will assured us of his rising fame. He had played a half dozen roles already and was fast becoming indispensable to the company. They were to perform at Greenwich Palace before the queen! But while everyone else gasped and exclaimed, my eyes prickled with tears. Damn you, Will. If you had the leisure to write one letter, why not two? Why not something special for me? The extra words would have cost you nothing, a little ink on paper, cheap lies. He didn't even say where he was lodging so I might write back to him. Edmund was still stripping the wax from the table, and for some reason I wanted to reach across and slap him. I bit my lip hard to stop its trembling.

" 'Trusting you are all in good health. Your devoted son, William Shakespeare,' " Gilbert concluded. He held out the letter toward me, and I reached for it with a foolish hope I might find some line he had missed, some fond message. But John intercepted the paper before it could touch my fingers, and he nodded sagely over it as if confirming that Gilbert had read correctly. Damn you all! I could read the best of any of you.

"I'll get it for you later," Gilbert whispered, and that evening he brought it to my room. By candlelight I studied it, but still the words I needed to hear weren't there.

Dear Anne, My heart aches to be with you. I dream of you every night. Love, Will.

"He probably knew we would read it aloud and didn't want to say anything private," said Gilbert with an awkward shrug.

And so began a long, freezing winter. I sat by the hearth and spun or sewed or minded the children. Sometimes I forgot Will entirely, even when looking upon our three offspring. None of them had his face or demeanor. The twins seemed to belong to neither of us, as if they had landed squarely in the middle, blending our features so evenly that my blue eyes and Will's brown had turned hazel in them. Or perhaps they were little chameleons, for at times Hamnet in profile would favor my brother Bartholomew, and Judith would moue her lips in an expression belonging to Magpie Joan. Other days I saw traces of Gilbert in my son—his uncle had bought him a small flute and was teaching him to play—while crosspatch Judith could cut a look in dead imitation of her grandmother Mary. But most of all they resembled one another, and side by side they played without end. I almost believe they could read each other's minds. When Hamnet stood, he would look to Judith as if to say, *Are you coming?*—long before either of them could converse their intentions. And Judith would get to her feet as if it were perfectly understood where they were both bound. I confess it made my mothering of them easier, for once weaned they did not depend on me for affection. They had each other, and their world made perfect sense.

Susanna, now almost four, did resemble me. She had especially my eyes and the contours of my face. How strange it is to look into another visage and see the image of your own imprinted there. Our neighbors often remarked it, and one day at the market a visiting cloth merchant handed her a silver ribbon, deftly commenting that she would grow up to be as pretty as her mother. Susanna curtseyed and piped a thank-you, and I returned him a smile as we moved on. Any mother likes to hear her child praised, nor did I disdain the lingering look the man gave me. I had regained my figure and my color since the twins had ceased to drain me, and it was some slight vindication to know that if Will no longer found me attractive, other men did.

"I wish he would send another letter," I said to Gilbert one spring afternoon. I was kneading bread dough for baking, and he had come in to pilfer a wedge of cheese and an apple.

"He will soon," Gilbert replied. "How many kinds of cheese do you suppose they have in London?"

"Oh, all sorts, I imagine. Cheddar and soft and smoked."

"Cheese from Holland and France." He broke off a chunk of his and popped it into my mouth while my floury hands worked the dough.

"Give me a bite of apple," I begged, and stuck out my tongue. Gilbert picked up a knife and carved a morsel, then held it teasingly away from my lips. "Give it to me." I pouted, and he surrendered the apple from his fingers to my mouth.

"There would be mountains of fruit in the London markets," he said. "Red and yellow apples, brown and green pears, sweet purple plums. Apricots, oranges, pomegranates and figs. A very juicy place, London town."

"A very fishy town, slick with salmon, slippery with oysters and squiggly with eels." I wriggled my fingers at him.

"A very meaty town, full of beef and venison and fat-bellied men." Gilbert puffed his cheeks and thrust his flat stomach forward. "And you could wash down every meal with good English ale and sherry wine from Spain. If they are going to invade, they might at least bring us a cask or two on their armada— I'm sorry, Anne."

Too late, he saw my face crumple, and he waved his hands to erase the air. Our banterings about London were meant to tantalize and cheer us until we could escape there ourselves. By mentioning grimmer news, he had broken the rules of the game.

"Have you heard anything?" I asked. "Please, Gilbert, if there is news, tell me."

"No, only that the mayor says the armada will set sail soon."

We fell silent. Mournful, brooding Philip II had long felt it his duty to return England to the Catholic fold and bring Elizabeth to heel. When his marriage to Mary Tudor ended with her death and no children, he had duly proposed to her heretic half sister. That the most powerful monarch in Christendom should be rejected by the petticoated ruler of a penniless northern island must have galled him. Nor did he appreciate her sending privateers like Sir Francis Drake to plunder his New World settlements and treasure fleet. Her execution of Mary, Queen of Scots, a lawful Catholic queen, was another affront, especially when Elizabeth herself was illegitimate and excommunicated. Finally, consider her audacity in financing the Protestant Netherlands in its ongoing struggle for independence from Spain. She had even sent her lover, the Earl of Leicester, to ally with the Dutch States-General, though the tactless earl had returned in disgrace, his mission a shambles.

Enough! With the pope's blessing, Philip was mobilizing the full might of Spain against us, and rumors of the impending attack churned thicker than mud in a March thaw. Some said the Spanish fleet would bear straight down the Thames for London, others that they would land an army on the west or south coast and advance through the countryside. A few optimists insisted we were safe here in Stratford; the pessimists foresaw rape and pillage throughout the land. Meanwhile, spies and assassins might be anywhere among us, scouting. No one knew for sure.

"Will would return if danger were imminent," said Gilbert, as if he followed my mind.

"Yes, of course," I said. "He would come home."

He didn't, and in May 1588, commanded by the Duke of Medina Sidonia, the armada sailed from Lisbon. A hundred and thirty ships strong, the fleet was to sail up the channel to Calais and there rendezvous with the army of the Duke of Parma, the Spanish general of the Netherlands. Between Parma's troops and the soldiers and sailors carried by the fleet, the combined invasion force topped fifty thousand men. Perhaps the people in London were braver, but if Stratford was any example, most of England was sick with fear. We did not even have a standing army, and our official navy consisted of thirty-odd vessels, augmented by whatever armed merchant ships the cities could provide. Local militias were assembled, and, professing bravado, the men marched and rehearsed for war in the town square. It was not a sight to instill confidence, farmers and tradesmen and gangly apprentices ordered about by a mayor who nicked himself with his own ceremonial sword. If our sea power failed, the Spanish would overrun us, laughing.

Day after day I awoke with my stomach knotted. I cried aloud and rushed to separate Hamnet and Judith when I caught them parrying sticks like soldiers at war. There had been no word from Will, and all unnecessary travel had been curtailed. Prayers were offered daily at the church, and I made it my concern to go there each morning and implore God to keep the Spanish from our shores. What would I do if they landed? Huddled with the children in bed at night, I rehearsed our escape.

If they burst up the stairs while we were sleeping, I would throw the children out the window and leap after them. If they surprised us by daylight near the hearth, I would sweep the children behind my skirt, grab the poker and swing to kill. If a crier rode into town to spread the alarm, we would not dally. Wearing only the clothes on our backs, we would stuff bread and apples into our pockets and flee through the fields. To where? Hewlands Farm would be no sanctuary for long. Warwick and Coventry might already have fallen. Could we fly deep into the Forest of Arden and, with other refugees, form a band of outlaws, as Robin Hood had done? How long before the Spaniards hunted us down one by one? Some said they would show no mercy even to the women and children, that we would be skewered on their bayonets like plump, squealing capons. Night after night I lay down to sleep with my jaw clenched, and in every house in Stratford people felt the same. There was nothing to do but await the enemy's arrival, and our faces grew tight and our nerves frayed.

Delayed by storms, the armada reached English waters in late July. Beacon fires blazed up along the coast, spreading the alarm. The mayor declared a general alert and doubled the night watch. Though our makeshift fleet had swelled to nearly two hundred boats captained by such valiants as Sir Francis Drake and John Hawkins, the situation was desperate.

And then we won. Oh, God, we won! The bells came ringing across the countryside, and a rider dashed into town. He was a young man from a neighboring village, and he was wild with joy. "We won! We won! England has destroyed the armada!" he cried, enthralling us with the tale as we surged around his horse. It was the most narrow of escapes: mistakes and miscommunications between the dukes of Parma and Medina Sidonia, the brazen luck of our knightly pirate Drake, fire ships sent among the Spanish fleet causing it to scatter in confusion, a victorious battle off Gravelines. Gloriana herself had appeared before the troops at Tilbury, a warrior queen mounted on a white charger, a silver cuirass over her white velvet gown.

"I know I have the body but of a weak and feeble woman," she had declared, "but I have the heart and stomach of a king, and of a king of England, too!" Huzzah! Huzzah!

It was a miracle, and in the hubbub that erupted no one heard any more of the young man's breathless details. We cheered and danced in the square, the church bells joined the clamor, and one old widow fainted from excitement. The great knot in my stomach unwrenched itself, and I grabbed my bewildered children and kissed and hugged them.

"Long live Elizabeth! God bless our queen!" we cried. We were saved! We would not die!

An immediate day of celebration was proclaimed by the mayor, a wise decision, since it was already too late to stop it. Kegs of beer and ale were rolled out of homes and taverns. Hams and joints of beef and pies and cakes appeared. Whatever they had in their smokehouses and larders, whatever each family had intended for that day's dinner, was brought forth and added to the feast. Anyone who had a pipe or horn or drum was pressed into service as a musician, songs and toasts were bellowed, and the priest and councilors tried to give speeches to which no one paid any heed. The children romped and shouted together in some nameless tumbling game, and for once their elders forbore to scold. All that fear, coiled like a snake in our bellies, untangled itself and slithered out, and we were limp and giddy with relief. I saw John backslapping among his old friends, and my heart softened to realize how much he had suffered in his isolation. Mary was jubilant, chattering with the other women. Her cheeks grew quite pink—how much had she drunk?—but she was far from the only one. I was beginning to feel a bit dizzy myself when the tavern keeper, who had grabbed me for a jig, spun me out and fell over backward. He lay laughing on the ground as his comrades converged to right him, and I found myself twirling to a stop next to Gilbert, who was playing his flute.

"I can't breathe." I laughed, holding my stomach. "Oh, Gilbert, we're safe! I am so happy!"

"Me too." The grin on his face confirmed he had sampled the free-flowing brews. "Let's get out of here and get some air."

He laced his arm through mine, and we passed through the crowd and headed out of town. It had been months since I had enjoyed a walk free of care. The day was honeyed, the light golden, the scent of flowers mingled in the warm breeze. We sat down by Shottery Brook, near where Will and I had courted, and I felt as if time had unwound and the world was luminous once again.

"You are radiant," said Gilbert.

"Who would not be?" I replied.

Then he reached out and brushed back a lock of hair that had fallen across my cheek.

I know; we should have seen it coming. Yet we were surprised, Gilbert and I. It was not our first touch. At home we might bump shoulders in the doorway or our hands meet as I passed him a plate at the table. More than once he had patted my back when I was discouraged, and I still believe it was done in a brotherly fashion. Gilbert looked up to Will; he would never scheme to betray him. But the instant he stroked my cheek, we knew something more than friendship had ripened between us. We had never so much as planned to be alone together; now we had cast ourselves into peril.

Weakly, we shook our heads at each other, already fabricating excuses for the outcome. Gilbert's fingers traced a slow caress down my cheek, and I let out a moan of breath that should have been heard only by my husband in bed. I caught his fingers and pressed them to my lips. His eyes were bright and sorrowful at the same time.

"Oh, Anne," he said, "let me hold you, let me kiss you, let me know how it feels. Forgive me, forgive me."

But even as he begged forgiveness—and was it of me or of Will?—he pressed himself against me and I welcomed him. All the fear and tension I had carried over the fate of England was only half my anguish, it seemed, for now my whole body released a second time. Yes, kiss me, touch me, love me. You see? I am beautiful, I am desirable, I am alive. It had been a year since Will left, and I was not carved of wood.

"I have tried . . . I have wanted . . . adored you . . . prayed not to . . ." Gilbert's kisses coursed over me, over my face and neck and breasts. He did not pretend to be drunk. He thought he was soberer than he was.

"Hold me," I begged.

We crushed together, and it was as if some sweet, soft fruit burst open between us. We crammed our mouths like greedy, sticky children. We ate with our hands, our legs, our thighs. I was the one who pulled open my bodice and hitched up my tangled skirt. Oh, God, how hot are those flames in hell? Until suddenly Gilbert threw himself off me, protesting and groaning and fumbling at his breeches. "No, no, no," he cried, turning away and grappling between his legs. His hips jerked, and he braced one hand to the ground, his eyes squeezed tight. In grief I watched his spasm as my own ebbed away. I would have, I would have. When Gilbert sat up, his face had the collapsed and purpled look of a man who has suffered a bruising. He sat by Shottery Brook with his head in his hands and wept.

"You are a good and decent man, Gilbert," I pleaded, holding my bodice closed as best I could. "It was the drink, the celebration. Our wits were overcome."

"No, I am wicked. I have loved you almost since the day you set foot in our house. Will should never have left you and gone to London. And all the while you tend the house like the best of wives and raise your children and endure our slights and insults with dignity and patience."

"No, Gilbert, no, I am not half so good as you imagine."

"I would not have left you, Anne! I would not have abandoned you!"

I let him sob, and for some minutes his body heaved and racked as he huddled there. And I, oh, whore, could only rue that his touch was gone and our heat fled and the pleasure stolen from my soul.

"You have been my only friend," I said. "Gilbert, my life would be unbearable without you."

"But what are we to do?" he asked, and there was still some hope in his voice that I might have a solution, as if we could run away from who we were.

"I don't know."

We stared miserably at each other.

"I will have to leave Stratford," he said.

"But I cannot lose you, and your father needs you."

"I dare not stay here. How are we to live in the same house?"

"We must keep to separate rooms. When one comes in, the other goes out."

"Maybe if we both left . . . together?"

I shook my head, tears starting in my eyes. It was impossible—the children—and Gilbert's shoulders sagged in a way that said he had not taken his words seriously.

"He has as good as deserted you," Gilbert said. "You deserve a husband and a home, and he leaves you here like some cast-off coat. . . ." He stopped, his sense of injustice at his brother overridden by remorse at hurting my feelings. "What do we do, Anne?"

"We go back to the house and pretend this did not happen. No one has seen us. No one knows."

"We know."

We sat again, neither moving. I blamed myself. Why not? Everyone else would. I was ten years older than Gilbert—I seemed doomed to attract younger men—and I should have guessed his emotions for me. I was quick enough to notice when that cloth merchant eyed me. Perhaps I did know; a woman is never totally unaware of the effect she has on a man. And what irony that half the reason Gilbert loved me was because he esteemed me a model wife. You should not have left, Will. You set the stage, you cast the roles, too bad if you don't like the play.

"We must return before someone comes along," I said, tying my laces. "I will go first and pretend I have been in the crowd all along. You wait awhile. Your face . . ." I gestured toward him, stopping short of a touch. My linen cap had come off, and I retrieved it from the ground and repinned my hair. "Do I look all right?"

"No." Gilbert motioned toward my shoulder, and my fingers found a blade of grass. "There is another, higher."

I brushed myself and stood up. "It will be all right, Gilbert. We will go back and say nothing, and it will never happen again."

"Forgive me."

I nodded, turned quickly and walked away. I truly believed we could leave desire and guilt behind us on the bank, like two unlabeled parcels for someone else to claim. As I headed homeward, I tried to recover my holiday mood, the better to blend in, but the effect of the beer I had drunk had worn off, and the din from town as I approached clanged off-key and rude. We won! Who cared?

No one had missed me, and I went home to my room. I lay on the bed and stared at the ceiling until the afternoon wore away and the downstairs door opened. I listened for Gilbert's voice among the merry group, and there it was—bold and singing and slurred to incoherency—and I shuddered at what we had nearly done. But what of tomorrow and the day after and all the days forward when I had no husband and Gilbert no wife . . . ?

Incest. No, you'll not pile faggots at my feet for that one.

I collected my sleepy children from their grandparents and tucked them into bed. How innocent they looked, their hair tousled, the twins' mouths red as rosebuds. Judith had scratched her arm, and I bathed and kissed it as she slept, then I took off Hamnet's socks so the lumps would not upset him. Susanna lay between her brother and sister, an arm around each, the pink of her cheeks unfaded even in slumber. I sat by them until the house was dark and the walls were quiet. Then I went down the stairs, filled a satchel with bread and apples and penned a note. It would fall to Gilbert to read it aloud, and as his eyes scanned ahead he would grasp the story he must present and defend.

Dear family, Now that London is safe, it is my duty to join my husband. Anne.

I slipped into the night and walked quickly toward the edge of town. At least Will had the courage to desert us in the broad light of day.

Chapter 7

That first night on the road, I walked with conviction, a gibbous moon lighting the way. Nothing mattered but to get as far as possible from Gilbert and Stratford. An adamant, steady pace but not an exhausting one—I had a hundred miles before me, a sturdy traveler could do twenty-odd a day, and I must not allow my head to trick my legs into wearying by driving them too hard. The summer night would be short enough; by five a.m. the roosters would crow. But given yesterday's revelries and this morning's groggy heads, I hoped to gain a few extra hours before anyone awoke and found me gone.

Please, Gilbert, I prayed, *do not complicate this by coming after me. We have had a near escape. Now you must stick to the fable of the dutiful wife that I have penned.* As for John and Mary, I suspected their anger would quickly evaporate as the advantages began to dawn. *Let her go. She was never one of us anyway. Now we can give our grandchildren a proper upbringing. And should some mischance befall her on the road . . .*

So on I walked, and there is an eerie displacement about traveling at night that dissolves distance and time. By day you cannot help but calculate your progress by the landmarks along the road, the position of the sun overhead. I am halfway there. I have reached the bend. I am almost home. But in the hollow dark, the signposts disappear, and you set aside your expectations and surrender to the blank rhythm of foot-falls with no notion how far you have gone. I ought to have been fright-ened. The farthest I had ever traveled was that trip to Kenilworth, and no virtuous woman set out at night alone. Well, I told myself, you have already forsaken virtue, and if you are set upon by highwaymen you will wake up dead the next morning and that will be the end of it. The idea was curiously refreshing, and I strode on.

At sunup I reached a village and debated leaving the road. To de-part your parish without a legitimate reason or a license from the au-thorities invited trouble; the same vagrancy laws that applied to the players could have you arrested and flogged. I sat down on a grassy clump and ate some bread and one of my apples, reflecting. A few weeks ago I had been planning to stuff my pockets with provisions, grab the children and flee the invading Spaniards. Now I was fleeing my family and had more to fear from my own countrymen. But to skirt the village would cost me time and invite the risk of getting lost. I prac-ticed my line aloud until it sounded not only convincing but joyful, then I walked into town.

"I am going to London to reunite with my brave soldier husband. All praise be to God who has saved us from the armada!"

Armada proved the magic word. In fact, as news of our great En-glish victory had radiated outward from London, I found myself walk-ing deeper and deeper into a circle of celebrations. All the usual laws and suspicions had gone on holiday, and the minute I opened my mouth I was welcomed. "Eat and drink, rest your feet!" the village folk im-plored, and I quickly accepted. I had come away with no money, only my amber necklace from Duck; no one shall accuse me of thievery. On the slight chance anyone had heard of John Shakespeare, former mayor of Stratford, I did lie about my name. Anne Hathaway of Shottery, I said, but no one cared. Did you hear how Drake whipped those cow-ardly Spanish? God is on our side! At noon I fell asleep in a comfort-able bed in a wayside farm. Stars dotted the sky when I awoke, and I slipped out, leaving an apple on the table as my thank-you to the snor-ing family.

That second night on the road, I calculated. If Gilbert were coming after me, he would have borrowed a horse and overtaken me by now. So he had let me go; good, wasn't that what I wanted? My shoulders twitched, shaking off the answer before it could alight. A mile later, another thought landed instead. If Gilbert had not come after me, did that mean he did not love me after all? I stopped, a queasy lump forming in my stomach. Was it possible I had misjudged the incident and my brother-in-law's profession of desire was only the ale-addled speech of an impressionable young man? Had he, on reading my farewell letter, rubbed his stubbled chin, scratched his head and looked up at his family, saying, "What?" My knees buckled, and I folded to the dirt. Oh, God, had I been utterly stupid?

For a minute I sat there, dumbfounded. Anne, you idiot, have you given up everything, children, family, reputation, home, on an ill-conceived whim? You were half-drunk yourself. Then the crush of Gilbert's body on mine rushed back, his taste, his kisses. No, I was not deceived—he said he had loved me from the moment I entered their house—and to stay would have led to sin and damnation. Up, Anne, screw your courage to the sticking-place! I rose and walked on, yet doubts nipped at my heels. Could we not have mastered our temptation and carried on? Even if it was more than mere lust—love shifts and changes, waxes and wanes. A year from now Gilbert and I might have laughed over the incident like old friends.

A soft, heavy whoosh swept over my head, and I jumped inside my skin at the squeal of some poor creature as the owl struck the field beyond me with a muffled thump and took off again. So far the road had remained empty of rogues and murderers, but what about all the other evils that inhabited the night: witches, goblins, vengeful spirits? What about bears and wolves? My glance turned backward, my resolution and my steps faltering. Would it not be better to return and endure those ills I knew than fly to others I knew not of? But what if I had misjudged to the opposite degree? What if Gilbert were so distraught by my departure that he had confessed our passion? If so, the rift with his family would be irreparable. What if they had thrown him out or he had stormed off in another direction? I wavered, then plodded on.

I reached Oxford and took heart at the spires and buildings of honey gold stone, the great university, the bustle of the town. Here too were celebrations, and I gladly accepted an onion tart and a cup of wine. I was halfway now, and at the mention of joining my "brave soldier husband," I was directed to the pack service, where I found a traveling party bound for London. For the next two days I walked in their safe company, my rations of bread and apples generously supplemented from the others' stores in gratitude for my husband's service to our country. By the time we neared London, I half believed my fabrication. But on the last night, camped in a pattering rain, I was forced to face what the morrow might bring.

A joyful reunion? A rush into each other's arms? Unlikely. If I had let my eyes and emotions stray during Will's absence, what had he been doing for a full year in London with no one to censure him? He was probably a favorite at the brothels, a rising actor with a generous purse. He might be keeping a mistress, he was doing so well. Too bad I hadn't disappeared on the road; if I was never heard of again, it would solve everyone's problem, God's included. He most of all could not seem to make up His mind what to do with me. I huddled under a tree, pulling my cloak closer against the rain. You have botched everything, Anne. You don't know if Will wants you or even where he lives in London. Yet a marriage is forever, and whether Will and I liked it or not we were bound. We must find some way to accommodate our differences and restore our family. I rubbed my cheek against the wet bark, knowing full well who would make the concessions.

The next morning we awoke to a signpost that read, LONDON FIVE MILES. I looked at the thickening traffic on the widened road—well-dressed men on horses, merchants, travelers, herds of cattle being driven to market—and my nostrils curled at a strange whiff from ahead. London *smelled*. At the city gate I passed through without a "Halt!"

from anyone. I felt as if I had slipped through a long noose, and taking a deep breath of this pungent new air, I melted into the anonymous flow.

⁓

Oh, London!

Boisterous, stinking, rowdy, resplendent, glorious, enormous, soul-stirring London!

It is hard to recall in what order the sights and sensations assaulted me, they were so rolled up in one great ball of astonishment, repulsion and delight. Almost immediately, there lay St. Paul's Cathedral like a great stone beast recumbent among many smaller buildings. Printers' shops and booksellers' stalls clustered around its base, and I watched a scribe write up a bill for an unemployed servant who wished to post his qualifications among the notices stuck on the church wall. Why, here in London in just one place was more paper than I had seen in a lifetime. As my eyes roved over the stacks of books and pamphlets, treatises and ballads, a peremptory voice issued from one side.

"My good man, do you have Mr. John Lyly's novel *Euphues*?" a distinguished-looking woman inquired of a bookseller. "I want both parts, *The Anatomy of Wit* and *Euphues and His England*."

"Yes, of course, my lady," the bowing man replied. "I carry the latest editions. I am always the best-stocked dealer in London."

I made a note of the woman's inflection. This is how I would order books in the days to come.

But first, I must find Will. Beyond St. Paul's was Cheapside market, and I wandered into it, wondering whom to ask. I passed stalls stocked with everything from leafy turnips to fill the goodwives' baskets to screeching peacocks to decorate the nobles' gardens. On Goldsmiths Row a woman in a pumpkin-colored gown handed over a delicate bracelet for repair, and on Milk Street, Bread Street and Honey Lane customers jostled to buy. Blood and feathers littered Poultry, and an aroma of roast fowl wafted under my nose. I had eaten my last apple the night before, and at the sight and smell of so much food, I pressed my hand to my stomach to still its rumblings.

"Excuse me," I said to a pie seller who had a kind face. "Could you tell me where to find Mr. William Shakespeare, the actor?"

"Hmm, I've never heard of him," the woman replied. "A pie for you, dearie?"

"No, thank you. Mr. Shakespeare is with the Queen's Men and a friend of Richard Tarlton," I explained.

"Oh, poor Tarlton! There was a funny fellow. Used to make me laugh till I cried."

"What do you mean, *poor* Tarlton?"

"Why, don't you know? He just died, God rest him. Ah, well, that's the fate of us all."

I shook my head, remembering how the madcap dwarf had entertained us. "I'm sorry. I didn't know. William Shakespeare is my husband, and I have walked all the way from Stratford-upon-Avon to find him, now that we are safe from the armada."

"Oh, my, yes, praise God! Did you hear how Drake scattered them!" The woman went on at length with the story, though it was now somewhat stale, and I waited for an opening.

"Perhaps you know another actor, Mr. Edward Alleyn," I said, trying the name Will had mentioned. "My husband is probably with him."

"Oh, everyone knows Mr. Alleyn. Why, when I saw him play *Tamburlaine*—"

"Could you tell me where to find him? In which theater does he act?"

"He's across the river at Mr. Henslowe's Rose, across the bridge in Southwark. Buy a pie, dearie?"

"I'm sorry. I have no money," I said, and as if on cue, my stomach gurgled loudly.

Her round face looked me over. "Well," she said, digging deep into her tray, "this one's broken, and I couldn't get a ha'penny for it anyway."

I thanked her repeatedly, vowing to return and repay her when I found Will, but she shooed me on toward the river. I cannot tell you how my heart swelled at this kindness from a stranger. And everywhere, the sights, the people!

Ladies and gentlemen paraded in silk and ribbons. Beggars and pickpockets liberated purses with light-fingered ease. Lawyers strutted in crow-black robes. An angry oysterwife yelled curses at a carter whose swerving wagon had sent her and her wares sprawling. Dirty children ran and stole where they could, their little fingers scuttling out to snatch a sausage or retreat from a blow. Appalled at their thin faces and ragged clothes, I asked one where its mother was and was immediately besieged by a horde clawing at my satchel and clamoring for coins. "Leave off, you filthy maggots, you useless devils!" a man yelled, and set about them with his walking stick, chasing them away. Whether he was some type of officer or merely an indignant passerby I could not tell, but though I pitied the children, I skirted them warily from then on. Yet in a way, London also felt familiar, for many of those I passed had their counterpart in Stratford. The fat baker vending fruit tarts, a seller of eels haggling the price with her customer, young apprentices hurrying on their masters' errands, a shoemaker, a churchman, a bricklayer repairing a wall. Gilbert was right: London was bigger, louder, a magnification of everything I had ever known, and whether you were a knave or a courtier, you could make your fortune here.

Most impressive, the main road of the city was not a road at all but the broad, brown, tide-turbulent Thames. Creaking three-masted ships floated at anchor, unloading cargo, while fleet-footed wherries skimmed passengers to and fro. Taverns and inns jostled for space along the banks, and hundreds of swans bobbed on the water; they were plucked once a year, I later learned, for the queen's bedding and upholstery. Spanning this burgeoning waterway was London Bridge, chockablock with houses and shops up to seven stories tall. In places, the buildings met above the street, forming an arch over the roadway. I gazed at the finery for sale, silks, hosiery, velvet capes, and the stream of people. Breaks between the buildings and at the drawbridge gave glimpses up and down the Thames, and I held my breath to see the watermen shooting their boats beneath the stone arches on the racing tide. Toward the south end of the bridge was Nonsuch House, the lord mayor's magnificent gabled residence. Finally, exiting at the stone gate, I saw a sight that made the last bite of pie come back up my throat: twenty rotting heads on pikes, the traitors' faces still grimacing in their final agony. Flies and crows swarmed around them, feasting on the rancid flesh and pecking out the eyes. I shivered and hurried on.

It took only a few more queries to bring me to the Rose, but in that short distance my surroundings changed. Even in daylight, Southwark had a seamy feel. Poor cottages sat cheek by jowl with alehouses and seedy dwellings where men passed in and out. "You go by the Clink," one man directed me, and when I looked puzzled, he shook his wrists as if they were chained and repeated, "Clink Prison. Then past the Antelope, Hart, and Saracen's Head. Along Maiden Lane to Rose Alley. Come to the bearbaiting and you've gone too far." Though there were still respectable citizens about, there was also an increase of dissolute-looking fellows, insolent women and beggars. A hand pinched my bottom, but before I could recover and spot the offender, he had disappeared, no doubt chuckling to himself. I drew myself in a little, glad I had arrived in the morning with plenty of daylight hours for my search.

Then there was the Rose, a large, splendid building, many sided and oak timbered. A name leaped out from a playbill posted by the entrance: Christopher Marlowe—that was the playwright Will had mentioned. My very first sight of a real theater, and Will would be on the other side of the door. I smoothed my clothes, bit my lip, took a deep breath and stepped inside.

Empty.

My shoulders sagged as I gazed around at the tiered galleries, the painted hangings, the raised stage open to the sky. Any other time I would have deemed it a marvelous structure; even deserted, there was a faint magic in the dust-moted air. But what was I to do now? Why was no one here? Then the loud pounding of a hammer came from under the stage floor.

"Careful, careful!"

A trapdoor in the center of the floor lifted, and a man in carpenter's garb emerged, sawdust in his beard. He climbed out onto the stage and walked around the opening, testing his weight on the boards and calling down instructions to an assistant below. He was too busy to notice me, and as I moved slowly forward, I wondered how it felt to be in the audience at a play. At least it took no great discernment to guess who would sit on the sheltered benches and who would bump in the yard.

"You there! What do you want? The play's not till two o'clock."

The carpenter's voice jolted me, and I quickly returned my eyes to the stage.

"I . . . I am looking for Mr. William Shakespeare," I stammered.

"One of the actors?"

"Yes, yes, that's him!"

"Never heard of him, and if we don't get this trapdoor fixed, there'll be no play anyway, for we'll have actors dropping straight down to hell, and then I'll catch hell from Mr. Henslowe. Be off, trollop!" He gave a rude thrust of his hips, and the assistant poked up his head from under the stage to join in the laughter.

Red faced, I made a hasty exit. I had been so busy observing London, it hadn't occurred to me that London might be observing me. On the contrary, I had assumed I would be overlooked, an ordinary woman in modest dress, and in the better part of town I am sure that is how my fellow citizens appraised me. But walking alone in this rough neighborhood, my five days' journey leaving me and my clothes less than fresh . . . I glanced along the alleys, recalling that furtive pinch, and took the carpenter's jibe as a warning. Daylight would not last forever; finding Will quickly was paramount.

"Excuse me. Which is the tavern where the players most often spend their time?" I asked a woman on the next corner.

"You're new in town then, are you?" she replied with a smirking smile.

"Yes, I—"

"Well, get out! This is my trade here, and I don't intend to share it with the likes of you!"

She spat at me—missing, fortunately—and I scurried away. Perhaps there was no need to have inquired, for the taverns came one after another, along with dicing houses and the ill-favored dwellings of who knew what inhabitants. I tried a half dozen establishments. The customers were hardly upstanding—yes, that is a pun—and the drunken crowd included sailors and rabble and lowlifes swept in from the street. It didn't seem likely Will would patronize such places—he was too fine, too fastidious—but I plugged on.

"Excuse me. I am looking for Mr. William Shakespeare, the actor."

"Never heard of him."

Finally, entering the Anchor, I caught a name that lifted my head.

"Ah, that Will's a rascal," said a dour man over his cup. "Quick to touch you for a loan, slow as a virgin to hoist her skirt when it's time to pay."

"He'll be good for it soon enough," his three companions consoled him. "He's to play before the royalty a week hence, and he'll come away with a coin or two in his purse."

"And spend it on drink before I ever see the sight of it," complained the first man. "Did you see the costume I'm to wear for our next performance? Green, all green, and baggy front and back. Makes me look like a wilted spinach."

"Hey, it's Old Sal!" another man shouted, pointing my way.

"Sal, Sal! Where's that pretty daughter of yours?"

"Right at home where she should be, earning her keep."

A woman had swayed in the doorway beside me, and her reply brought forth a roar of approval from the men. Wrinkled of face and missing half her teeth, Old Sal's appearance was as battered as if she had spent a life trodden underfoot. Her clothes looked like castoffs she had tricked up with shabby ribbons, and dirty brown hair hung in a snarl down her back. Atop this rat's nest, she wore a feathered bonnet, and I knew with immediate certainty she had stolen it, snatched it off a passing head and vanished into a crowd. Already in drink when she wandered in, Old Sal began cajoling the actors to share their mugs, lifting each tankard and slurping up. The dour fellow who had mentioned Will drew her onto his lap with a lewd remark, and there in sight of all the patrons he put his hand into her bodice. This brought forth another roar from the men, but though disgust rose in my throat I couldn't leave until I learned from these unsavory characters where Will was lodged.

"It's a shame a man should leave his wife in such a state," Old Sal was saying, in what appeared to be a familiar lament. "A shame and a scoundrel, and that's why I say never marry a sailor. Give us some money, luv"—she tickled her fingers under another man's chin—"and I'll do for you as well as my daughter."

"You old whore." The man belched. "You're riddled with the pox. A man would be a fool to touch you."

"And I have no money to give you," said the dour man, recalling his misfortunes, "not until Will pays up."

"Take us to your daughter!" another lout demanded, while one of the tavern women, a horse-faced redhead, countered, "What about us? Come sample a bit of us!"

In an instant, I decided. I needed to get out of this tavern, I needed information on Will, and unless I wanted to end up on someone's lap, it would not be safe to approach any of these men, least of all one to whom my husband apparently owed money. I grabbed Sal's sleeve.

"Sal, your daughter is asking for you. She sent me to fetch you. Come away!" I dragged her toward the door, and the men let her go with a mixture of guffaws and snorts.

"Is she ready for another?" Sal asked as we reached the outside.

"Almost," I said. "Let's walk toward your house."

"Yes, to my house." She stumbled off, too tipsy to notice that she didn't know me, and I quickly followed.

"Tell me where to find Will," I said. "Where is it he lodges?"

"Why, by the river, of course. By the devil, my head hurts."

"And so it should." Her clothes were so greasy, I could feel the oil on my fingers where I had touched her sleeve. "Look, take me to Will's address and he will pay you when we get there."

Old Sal's bleary blue eyes opened wider. "Why, I'll take you to Will Bates this very minute."

"Bates?" I stopped, then exhaled a frustrated breath. How stupid of me! How could I have assumed that even among the actors, let alone in all of London, there would be but one Will? "Never mind. Go away." I tried to shove her off, but now it was her hand that clung to my sleeve.

"No, no, I'll find you a Will, if it's not Bates you want. Is it Will Andrews, Will Cooper . . . ? No, no, you want an actor. . . . Is it Will Kempe?" She patted at me as if to find my purse.

"It's William Shakespeare," I said, near tears. "Shakespeare."

"Let me think, let me think," pleaded Sal.

"You don't know him." The tears began to fall; I had not imagined this. In Stratford, our latest news of Will was more than six months old. What if he had left London and gone on tour again with the Queen's Men? What if he had died in an accident or of illness? But surely someone would have sent word to his family? Not if he had been bludgeoned to death in some foul alley—I looked around me—like this.

"Will, Will," Sal was repeating. "Don't go. I'll ask my daughter. See? We're at my house."

She dragged me through a door, and I found myself in a hovel with a table, two chairs and a tawdry yellow curtain rigged from the ceiling to partition off one corner. Old Sal raised her forefinger and hissed at me a loud, "Shh!" There was no need for the admonition. Anyone could recognize instantly what was signified by the thumps and moans coming from behind the cloth. I sank onto one of the chairs in numb disbelief, while Sal took the seat opposite. In a minute her head was snoring on the table. It was perhaps another five minutes before the curtain parted and two figures were revealed. One was a fat man with a glistening face; beaming, he stuffed his shirt into his breeches. The other, still sitting half in shadow on the bed, was a girl. She quickly drew a shawl around her naked shoulders.

"Tomorrow, Margery?" the man said, tipping his hat to me as if his presence there were the most natural thing in the world.

The girl nodded, and he left. She turned her back and fumbled into her clothes before coming forward.

"Who are you? What do you want? I don't consort with women." Her frown went from suspicion to disgust as her gaze traveled from me to her mother. She could not have been more than fifteen, and her face was an oval of pale skin and large eyes, marred by a fading bruise below one cheekbone; she would not be pretty much longer. Nonetheless, her stiff posture eased as I explained. "Oh, you came to the wrong play-house. The Queen's Men are at the Theatre north of the city."

"Take me there," I said, straightening my bearing in imitation of the lady at the bookseller's, "and my husband will pay you."

Margery poked her head out-of-doors and pursed her lips at the lack of customers. "All right, but I want sixpence. It's a long walk."

And so it was, back through Southwark and across London Bridge, then north through the city. Margery grew talkative—it was a change, she confided, to have an afternoon out and earn a bit of money and no men to lie atop her—and she began pointing out the attractions as if I were a visiting dignitary and she my able guide. The prostitutes lodged at the Clink, she said, were called Winchester Geese because the bishop of Winchester, whose London residence was nearby, collected a fee from the surrounding brothels. The rotting heads on pikes above the bridge were a source of pride to some people; having traitorous relatives they could point out to their friends implied a link to nobility. It took some of the ache out of my feet to listen to her. We passed out of the city through Bishopsgate in the north wall and covered a half mile more.

"There," said Margery, nodding ahead to a pair of buildings that in size and shape resembled the Rose. "That's the Curtain and the The-atre. They build them outside the city walls so the law can't touch them. They're some of my best customers, the law."

"Margery," I said, "wouldn't you like to have a respectable posi-tion? Maybe one of the actors could use a maidservant."

"Huh, they'd give me a position, all right. Oh, I'll get a man to marry me, and meanwhile I take only the best customers, so I shan't catch the pox or get beaten too often. I'm lucky, you know. My mother might have smothered me at birth, as some of the women do, to save themselves the bother of a child."

"Will you tell your husband of your past?" I asked, curiosity getting the better of my manners.

She laughed. "What for? It's easy enough to become a virgin again."

I was about to ask how—who wouldn't?—when my eyes leaped ahead and something else came out of my mouth.

"Will!"

I squeezed Margery's hand, and we hurried forward. It was almost suppertime, and the afternoon performance was letting out. Will stood by the entrance to the Theatre, holding the reins of a fine-looking horse. How well he had done in just one short year! And suddenly I longed for him, for his voice and his arms, for the love we could still share. With the press of people around him, he hadn't seen me or heard my cry, and I must reach him before he mounted and rode away. But now a gentleman in a furred cape appeared, and with a bow Will handed over the reins. As the man swung into the saddle, another horse bucked into the first, the two animals neighed and reared, and Will's arms flew into the air.

"Get that clumsy clod of a groom out of the way!" one of the gentlemen yelled, spurring off, and I pushed through just in time to see Will land on his rump in a heap of fresh manure.

"Groom?" Margery's jaw dropped as the playgoers gathered around, hooting with laughter. "You said your husband was a fine actor! You said he'd pay me."

"He will, he will," I said, slip-sliding through the muck and frantically hauling up Will, only to find him besplattered but unhurt and wearing an expression of horror.

"Anne?"

"You promised me sixpence!"

"Will, this is Margery. She helped me find you. Please pay her."

"Pay her what? What are you doing here?"

"I have come to find you."

"You owe me sixpence! I could have earned twice that on my back by now!" Margery's hands clawed for my satchel.

"I'm sorry, Margery." I held her off with one arm. "Give us a minute—"

"Phew!" People laughed, holding their noses and pointing at Will's rear.

"What are you doing here, Anne?"

"You owe me!" shrieked Margery, and quicker than I saw it happen, her hand yanked at my neck. I choked, the chain broke, and she darted away among the cheering crowd, my amber necklace dangling from her fist.

Will stared at me in disbelief. "What are you doing here?" he asked.

I stared at his shit-soiled clothes and said, "What are you?"

Chapter 8

*L*iar, liar, liar.

He was not a famous actor; he was a groom-for-hire to tend the horses of wealthy patrons at the theater door.

The half dozen roles he had played were not star turns but Herald, Third Soldier, Watchman, Shepherd, Courtier. Some of them weren't even speaking parts.

He lived in one tiny rented room near Bishopsgate where the stuffing in the mattress consisted mostly of fleas.

He owed money for his meals at the tavern around the corner.

"I never claimed I was a lead actor!"

"You implied it! You had us all believing you were a big success!"

"That's your fault, your interpretation! I never said that in my letters!"

"You wrote only one, and it convinced your whole family you were the toast of London town!"

I slumped on the bed and sobbed. All that way I had come—if nothing else, a decent roof and a modicum of comfort should have awaited me. Will scoffed and feinted, trying to dodge around the truth while keeping to his untarnished view of himself. We were the ones with unrealistic expectations. He had only been trying to reassure us he was well. But whether we had misunderstood and Will was half right no longer mattered. What were we supposed to do now?

"You're a stable boy!" I wept. "You abandoned a perfectly good trade in Stratford, a chance to rebuild the family business, to stand like a lackey in the lane and be dumped ass-first in manure!"

"Gloving is *not* a good trade, not for me! I have talent! I have desires! I want something more!"

"So do I, Will. I want a lot more!"

"Then you should have waited until I sent for you. What kind of woman walks halfway across England alone?"

"A woman who's tired of waiting for her husband to grow up. If you want to act, start acting like an adult!"

"I am! I have roles! I have prospects!"

"You have shit on your breeches! Exactly when were you going to send for me anyway?"

"Soon, soon, I promise. Think what could have happened to you on the road!"

"Don't you wish! It would be your lucky day!"

"It would leave our children motherless! Why aren't you in Stratford with them, where you belong?"

I glared him down. "Why aren't you?"

Bitter words, all of them, and the most passion that had arisen between us in several years. At one point our shouting drew the landlady, and in she barged, a small, screeching woman who looked as if she had been chewed up and spat out by a dog.

"I told you before, no doxies in your room!" she yelled, and swung at Will.

Comedy, tragedy. He ducked and placated, backed against the wall. I sat on the bed and bawled. Doxies! I had known it, of course; men are always merriest when far from home. But still the truth stung. Then a hot anger flared through me, and by the time Will had hustled out the little termagant I was ready to strike back and strike hard. A stinking stable boy who couldn't keep his pants buttoned? Oh, no, I had not married Will Shakespeare for this.

"You are twenty-four years old, a husband and father. You have responsibilities to fulfill."

"I'm trying! I have two roles in the next play, you'll see. I'll take you to the theater before you go home."

"I don't care if you have two parts or ten, I am not going home unless you come too. If you refuse to take up your father's business, we'll find some other work to support us."

"But I can do that with acting. It just takes time. Do you imagine a career like Edward Alleyn's is built overnight?" A hard glint came into his eye; he was prepared to fight back.

"And you would let your children go hungry while you pursue it?" A low blow from me. Susanna, Hamnet and Judith were hardly starving back in Henley Street, and we both knew it.

"I have two roles starting soon," he repeated, his jaw jutting stubbornly.

"And what do we live on until then?"

"We can eat at the tavern."

"How, when you owe them money? Shall we scavenge leftover food from others' plates?"

His face burst into redness.

"Oh, good heavens, Will!" I dropped my head into my hands.

"It's only temporary. I have two new parts—"

The look I sliced him was sharp enough to cut off his tongue. The sun was setting, and I rose from the bed, yanked off the top blanket and shoved it into his arms.

"There is your mattress." I pointed at the floor. "Unless you want to sleep with me?"

I did not mean to say that. I had come to London to find my husband and restore our family. Now we both began to fling words that should never have been uttered.

"A bed of rocks would be preferable."

"Or perhaps the rack?" I suggested.

"I would rather lie naked on an ice floe."

"You wouldn't feel it. It is the same temperature as your heart."

"Then why have you followed me to London? Turn around and go home. I never asked you to come."

"Of course not, when you have your whores and your penniless fellow actors for company. You don't care about your parents or the children, about Gilbert and me."

Too late, I tried to gasp back the coupling of my name with Gilbert's, but Will missed the significance.

"Of course I care! Why do you think I am here but to make a name for us?"

"Then I'll stay and help you do it."

"No, you'll go home!"

"No! I am staying!"

Enough!—though in truth our argument continued until sunup, like a battle fought back and forth over the same unprofitable terrain.

"If you hadn't been so eager to lift your skirt—"

"If you hadn't been so quick to shake your spear—"

All right, all right! Enough.

~

The next day Will was attentive and solicitous. From somewhere he procured sticky buns for our breakfast. He brought a basin of water for me to wash my face and hands. He fussed over a smear of grease or tar or some black substance on the sole of my shoe and endeavored to scrape it off with a penknife.

"You stay here and rest while I go see about your journey home," he said confidently.

I let him try, guessing it would be a futile exercise. What could he do? Send me off in the cart of some country tradesman bound for the shires? Even if I walked with the pack service as far back as Oxford, we had no money to pay for my food and lodging along the road. I would be at the mercy of strangers' charity and intentions, and say what I may about Will Shakespeare, he would not put his wife in danger, nor had he the temperament to put me physically out-of-doors. Sure enough, he returned midday with no luck. But he did have better fortune minding the patrons' horses at the Theatre that afternoon.

"An extra tip," he said, flashing a coin and grinning. "We can eat a proper meal tonight. And I have secured work copying roles for the new play. Look."

He took a stack of paper from his satchel, and I studied the pages with interest as he explained. The public, Will said, was insatiable for plays. It was pure entertainment and cheap, only a penny to stand in the yard, tuppence for a bench seat in the galleries. Anyone could enjoy the spectacle, whether or not they understood every line. So day after day, people packed the theaters to gasp at swordfights and grisly murders and hear star-crossed lovers proclaim. And the theaters, to keep their audiences returning, needed a constant stream of new plays. The playwrights jobbed together, two, three or four, to churn out scripts fast enough to meet the demand.

"They outline a plot and take it to a theater company," Will said. "If the company likes it, they pay an advance, and each playwright takes away an act or two to compose. Then the acts are reassembled, and rehearsals begin. If the pieces of script are neatly penned, they can use it as is, but sometimes it is much crossed out and written over, and they require a clean text."

"And a copy for every actor," I said, catching on.

Will shook his head. "No, they cut up the script and paste each part on a separate roll of paper, so the actors get only their own lines. It saves paper and keeps the whole script from falling into a rival company's hands."

"Oh." I puzzled a moment. "But how do the actors know when to recite their lines if they never see the whole story?"

"The cues that precede their speeches are penned in, and after they have rehearsed a few times, they know how it goes."

"But they must memorize all this and a dozen other plays at the same time. . . ." In growing wonder, I turned the pages.

"We actors are renowned for our memories," said Will.

The next few days were actually pleasant, and I found a way to make myself useful. Will's room contained, besides the bed, one small table and a chair. We drew the table up to the bed to use it as a second seat, and I sat thereon, mixing the ink, reading and sorting the papers, and tending to the quill each time Will paused to flex his fingers.

"Perhaps you could do other copying as well," I said, recalling the scribe I had seen at St. Paul's Cathedral.

"Official and legal documents, no. They must be done on parchment and require special training and a skilled hand. But this"—he paused to rub his stiff knuckles—"has only to be legible."

"Then let me try." I nodded toward the half-finished role on the table.

"You can't. You've never done it."

"Of course I can. You taught me to write, remember? Give me the smallest role and let me practice on it. We could earn twice as much if I did a share."

Will considered—more money would send me back to Stratford sooner—and handed me a clean sheet. Then he badgered me like a fussy schoolmaster. "Write smaller—it saves paper. Mark the cues thus. Pay attention to the insertions. You must not skip a word, even if the actors later change the lines." I took the instruction meekly and gladly. I have always felt a thrill at accomplishing something new, and as the inked lines appeared on the paper before me, I could almost hear them soaring aloud onstage. Our room had one west-facing window, and I copied slowly but diligently until the sun set. Will looked across the table and grudgingly conceded the results were presentable.

The next day he returned from the Theatre with a bundle containing a gaudy yellow dress, scissors, a needle and a packet of thread.

"One of the actors was playing a courtesan, and he tripped on the hem and tore the skirt. I told Mr. Phipps, the wardrobe master, that you could sew it. I bragged to him what an excellent seamstress you are. If he approves of the stitching, he will send you other work."

I examined the tear. The rent was large but capable of being hidden with a clever tucking of the fabric.

"I can fix it," I confirmed.

"Then we'll be rich in no time," Will declared.

And at that we smiled together.

⸺

As long as he believed there was a chance I might leave, Will kept up his kindness, and for a month we were almost happy. I sewed in our room; he went to the theater, rehearsing in the morning, performing or tending horses in the afternoon. In between, we worked at our copying. We did not resume marital relations; a mutual wariness kept us apart. Nor did we make any great savings toward my return journey. There was his tavern bill to reconcile first, and I needed clothes. I had taken none with me from Stratford, not even a clean shift, and the first time it needed washing, I went without until it dried. I also found and repaid my debt to the surprised pie seller in Cheapside market. I never again saw Margery or my amber necklace. If it in any way helped her to a husband and an escape from her life, then I am glad.

Occasionally, Will slipped into our conversations some seemingly selfless observation. "What a shame that bed is so narrow and uncomfortable," he sympathized, gallantly not objecting to his own hard berth on the floor. I rejoined that having slept on the open road for five nights to reach London, one of those nights in the pouring rain—all right, I exaggerated—I found the bed quite luxurious. He worried at any hint of plague erupting in the city. I reminded him he had rejected that same ploy when his mother tried it in Stratford. "But disease spreads faster here," he insisted. "Better a quick death than a slow one," I said with a shrug. A week after my arrival he reported, aghast, that a woman had been murdered only a few streets away from our lodging. "Then from now on you should escort me when I go out," I countered. To curtail any argument I had only to raise my voice. He had an inordinate fear of the landlady's return.

"There is no hurry," I said when his comments verged on the idea of my leaving. "At least let me stay long enough to see the sights. Then I will be able to tell everyone back in Stratford about your bright prospects."

The hint that I might be leaning his way and would furthermore not betray him brought a grateful glow to his face.

"You can take me to the theater and introduce me to your fellow players," I continued.

"Um, no . . ."

I raised one eyebrow.

"I mean, you can't go in the theater when we are rehearsing, Anne. We'll be busy."

"Another time then. But you did promise to take me to a play."

"I will, soon. I just can't go asking for free admission and other favors when I am still new there."

I let him off, not wanting to jeopardize his standing with his colleagues. You might say that by playing along with his desire to be rid of me, I was now deceiving him. Well, I never said *when* I would go home, did I? And there were days I did waver, worrying about the children. Were they sick? Were they lonely for their mother or had they forgotten me already? Were Hamnet's sock lumps still upsetting him? About Gilbert I tried not to think or feel anything and was mostly successful. I prayed he had similarly banished me.

So there were Will and I, getting along, and I hoped the arrangement would grow on him. We had been wed almost six years, and never in that time, it seemed to me, had we become friends. Other couples achieved it. They knew each other's mind, valued each other's company. Whatever their spats or discontents they patched them up and carried forward. But Will and I had gone from lovers to strangers, from bachelor and maid to parents of three children, in such a short time that the seeds of friendship lay ungerminated in the ground. Perhaps that was what we were meant to accomplish now. I still found qualities about him to admire. He was intelligent and treasured words. If he was a trifle smug about showing off his knowledge, I loved soaking in all he could teach me. And though I was dubious that acting could provide a lucrative career, I could not fault his determination. Even the indignity of working as a groom would not deter him from his goal. If he made an equal effort to appreciate my abilities, we might recover and improve upon what a marriage should be. Whether we remained in London indefinitely or returned to Stratford tomorrow, my one resolve was that we must do it together.

Then one morning as I sat sewing, running steps and a fast knock came to our door. Opening it, I found an angelic blond boy of twelve or so years. His cheeks were flushed, and his blue eyes were bright with the importance of his mission.

"Is this Mr. Shakespeare's lodging?" he said, panting. "I'm Christopher from the theater."

"Is Will all right?" I asked, taking alarm.

"Oh, yes, he is rehearsing. But Mr. Phipps is in a terrible panic!" He took off a large bag slung over his shoulder and began to remove a lavender gown.

"Here, come in," I said, clearing my present project from the table. Thus far the sewing assignments the wardrobe master had sent home via Will had been routine repairs. One look told me this dress was of far finer quality, but as I laid it out, I sighed a sad "Ohh!" The lovely silk was riddled with moth holes.

"It was packed away in a trunk, and some of the costumes have holes this big!" Christopher held up his hand in a half curl to indicate the size of the disaster. "We need them by next week for the new play, and Mr. Phipps has me running to every seamstress we know. He's sent thread, lace and ribbons. He asks if there is some way you can save it with embroidery or trim."

I studied the damage. Since most plays were performed with a minimum of scenery and props, lavish costumes were essential to create an eye-catching show. Audiences expected them, and actors vied over them. They were often a theater company's major asset, second only to the building itself, and I could well understand the wardrobe master's despair at losing such a garment.

"I will do my best," I said, and Christopher let out a loud, "Whew!" "Are you in the new play with Will?" I asked as he prepared to go.

"I am. I act Princess Faviana."

"An excellent role," I agreed, it being one I had copied.

"I wear a wig and a pink satin gown with a beaded train. It's lucky mine was in another chest and not damaged, isn't it?"

"Yes, indeed, though if you ever do need a special costume of any sort, please tell Mr. Phipps that I can create as well as repair them."

"I will. He said when he sent me off that Mr. Shakespeare's sister is talented with her needle."

The boy swooped a bow and grinned, then scurried off before I could correct him. Oh, well, he had probably misheard, and I must set to work immediately. I fingered the lavender silk, warmed by the wardrobe master's praise and anxious to repay his trust in me. The dress was already abundantly trimmed in ivory lace, and to add more or to disguise the holes with ribbons would make it look a hodgepodge. But if I cut small patches from the lining, out of sight, and appliquéd them with delicate embroidery . . . I picked up my scissors.

Sister?

Throughout that day it came back to me, and each time I butted it from my mind. This is an important assignment, Anne. If it brings you the chance to do a complete costume, you could be earning more than Will. The idea gave me pause. Yes, I wouldn't mind that at all. Besides, the boy must have misunderstood, although he was clearly an intelligent youth to be playing the princess Faviana, whose heartrending speech when ravished by the evil duke was pivotal to the course of the play.

"At last!" said Will, when he returned that evening. "I have found a traveling party for you. They are bound for Coventry, trustworthy people, and you will have two other wives for company." He swept off his cloak, much pleased for his good care of me.

"Except that I am not going."

The cloak lost its swirl.

"Yes, you are. You leave tomorrow morning. It is arranged."

"Then unarrange it. I am not going."

For a few seconds, Will recomposed his face, curbing his irritation as if he were a parent dealing with a recalcitrant child.

"Yes, you are. You know it is the only way."

"Why did you tell the people at the theater that I am your sister?"

Caught. Caught, caught, caught. I saw it in his eyes, that instant, startled flash of guilt followed by a fluster of righteous indignation. But he couldn't pull it off, not Will. He still had a conscience. So he wriggled, squirmed and flipped excuses off his tongue, only to have them flop helplessly like fish on the floor. It was to protect me, actors were a rowdy lot, it was only a joke. . . .

"And your whores wouldn't understand?"

Ah, once more unto the breach, dear friends, though Will's whoring was actually a minor thrust—pun intended—in our reopened battle. Will was not by nature lustful. Though he had certainly indulged since his arrival in London, he was far too fastidious, too frightened of death and disease, to hop regularly between the sheets with a street-corner trollop. If he had strayed from his wedding vows, I already knew my best course was to overlook it. Thus, we both ignored my charge and proceeded straight to war.

"How can you stay, Anne? How do you imagine we are to continue living together like this?" He swept his hand from my bed to his blanket on the floor.

I swept mine back. "It is not my choice, but what matter? I don't care if you sleep on the ground forever. I don't care if we eat every meal for the rest of our lives in silence and you bed every strumpet in Southwark. But in public, in the streets, before your friends, you will treat me as your lawful and esteemed wife."

"I can't. It is impossible."

"Why? Why?"

"Because it complicates things. It spoils my chances as an actor."

"How? Other players have wives."

"Who make trouble, who get in the way, who come complaining to the theater when they can't find their husbands."

"But the Queen's Men knew you were married when they signed you on in Stratford."

"No."

"What? You lied even then?"

"Not exactly. I just let them think I was . . . unencumbered."

"What about our children? Do you deny them?"

"Of course not. Besides, you made me believe you were going home!"

He leveled an accusing finger, but I was too lost in amazement to rebut his challenge.

All this time, Will had never acknowledged me or our three children? He was that glad to be rid of us that the instant he left Stratford, he had shed his past with the relief of a snake shrugging off its old skin? With blinding clarity I grasped the situation. This last year Will had experienced a freedom not known since childhood. He had left both his personal mistakes—that would be me and the children—and his father's debts and disgrace behind him. He had shut his Stratford life away in a chest in the attic and meant never to unpack it again. Out of sight, out of mind, out of heart.

He waited a moment for my devastation to sink in. "I'm sorry, Anne. I never intended it to happen this way, but when the chance came to leave Stratford, you know I had to take it. I was young and should never have made vows I could not fulfill. Now I have years of toil ahead to earn a decent place in the theater. It's a hard life, and I can't ask you to share it."

"Why not? Let me be your wife and helpmate, as before."

And now we both waited to see how cruel he would be. I do not believe he spoke the next words gladly.

"I don't think it can be."

"Not ever?"

He exhaled a deep breath. "There is nothing here for you. Go home, Anne."

My glance went around the small room and landed on the unfinished gown, though all I saw was a lavender blur. Until that moment we had been as cardplayers with bets on the table, smiling, bluffing, each calculating what the other might hold while keeping our cards close to our chest. Now Will had laid down his hand, confident he held the trump. It was time for me to do likewise.

"I can't go back to Stratford," I said, and I told him about Gilbert.

Chapter 9

*I*f Ben Jonson is correct and the Shakespeare plays are to endure not for an age but for all time, then future readers should neither gape nor marvel at their emotional range and complexity, the deeply wrought characterizations, the powerful and cleverly constructed plots. It was all there in a powder keg between Will and me in that tight little room. Small wonder the roof did not blow off, so explosive was the air.

My revelation about Gilbert left Will dumbstruck—typical. Men don't look beyond themselves. As long as they are satisfied, they assume all is right with the world. He had consigned me to blissful oblivion back in Stratford, minding the children, cooking, sewing, cleaning, dutifully waiting upon my in-laws and refusing all thanks for my toil. A nameless, faceless saint with a beatific smile. It had never occurred to him that his discarded wife might eye another man with longing, might let her heart roam. Surprise, Will! I nearly bedded your brother! I did enjoy seeing him reel.

As for myself, the knowledge that Will had passed me off as his sister was a needful wound that opened my eyes to my singular failing. I was eight years older and twice as mature, yet in one respect I was the one who had not grown up. I still clung to a delusive hope of a loving husband and an amiable home. Wake up, Anne! His sister! It is you who are living in fairy tales. Will does not love you, he will not give up this life and you have nowhere else to go.

By dawn, bloodied and battle stained, we reached a weary truce. As the sun rose over the rooftops, I became Will Shakespeare's sister, pledged to aid him in his conquest of the stage. In return, he granted me a permanent place in London at his side.

⁓

What? I let him get away with it? I surrendered my very identity?

What identity?

Even without the problem of Gilbert, returning alone to Stratford would have compelled me to live a lie. I would have to cast myself as a happily married woman whose player husband was in such demand he could not spare a visit home to see her and his beloved children. The honest alternative was to be branded forever as a shunned wife. "Can you imagine? She journeyed all the way to London, only to have Will send her packing. How humiliating!" To divulge the additional truth about Will's impecunious situation would further degrade me, the children and the entire Shakespeare clan in the town's eyes. No, thank you. Like old John Shakespeare, I had my false pride.

Or I could stay in London and live a different lie, the role Will had already begun to write for me. His dear sister had come to the big city to look after her brother, who joyfully welcomed and earnestly praised her to everyone he knew. I added that last part. "That's *your* role," I told him. "Memorize it." This lie might actually be the easier to accomplish. Since Will was not, contrary to his claims, well-known yet to anyone here, we could start fresh with whatever story we chose to make of ourselves. Meanwhile, we sent word to Stratford that Will was delighted to see me and begged me to stay. Instead of being an outcast, I was suddenly prized in two places. Isn't it nice to be wanted?

But what about my rights as a wife? How could I concede them?

What rights? A woman and all she owns become her husband's possessions on the day she marries. A wife may be beaten, upbraided, ordered to obey. She must be silent, submissive and may be turned out-of-doors in her shift for any failure to please. But a sister, ah, a sister is a different matter entirely, and as I sat alone that next day, embroidering the lavender gown and reflecting, the advantages began to dawn on me.

I could go anywhere, anytime, without Will's permission. I could meet and speak with whomever I chose. I no longer had to abide by his standards or expectations. When shopping, I could buy the foods I liked, and if he did not care for the menu, let him sulk in the tavern and pinch off others' plates. If I could not have his affection, why worry if his socks were well darned? Of course, I would still darn them expertly and take into account his favorite foods. It is my nature to be diligent at any task I undertake, and I am not mean. But now I would do these things not to earn any kind word or look from Will or his family but only for the merit of the task itself—astounding! And if Will had forfeited his claim on my body, did that not also include my skull-encased mind? This idea was so blinding I nearly fell backward off my chair. Will Shakespeare could no longer tell me what to think or feel.

I was still cogitating three days later when I delivered the lavender gown to Mr. Phipps at the theater and another benefit announced itself. A wife must turn over to her husband any money she earns, but a brother has no right to a sister's independent income. As Will, in a forester's costume, frowned from the stage, the coins the wardrobe master counted into my hand were mine, all mine.

"Just look at this embroidery!" Mr. Phipps gasped, holding up the dress in ecstasy for the rehearsing actors to see. I had imagined him a minor tyrant and had bucked up my courage to meet him. Instead he was short, bouncy and curly mopped, and his voice squeaked when he was excited, which was often. "Lavender-on-lavender, it's perfect, and not a moth hole to be seen!"

"Wear it yourself!" one of the actors teased, and the others guffawed.

"Pay no attention to them," he huffed, putting an arm around my shoulder to guide me away. "Philistines! My dear lady, can you cut and fashion fine fabrics?"

"I can learn, Mr. Phipps," I said, forsaking modesty for an all-out sales plea. "Let me sew whole costumes for you, please!"

"I will start you immediately. You've met Christopher, our gorgeous Princess Faviana? In two weeks he must be transformed into a fairy queen for another play. I have a divine silver gauze. Wait till you see!"

An hour later, as I was leaving the theater with the materials and my instructions, another remarkable benefit burst upon me. I had stopped before the stage, adamant that Will should introduce me to his friends as befitted my new double status as both his sister and a seamstress for the company. Ever jealous for the best costume, the actors were happy to make my acquaintance, and from their compliments I was startled to learn I had suddenly gotten nearly ten years younger. Will, you see, had always told the players he was the firstborn and heir of his illustrious family. Since he was then twenty-four, his charming sister couldn't possibly be more than twenty-three. And to think those deluded Spaniards were still traipsing the alligator-infested swamps of the heathen New World to find a so-called fountain of youth!

At home that night, Will was miffed. "You needn't have been so forward with everyone today."

I shrugged. "If you don't like the way your 'sister' behaves, tell them the truth."

"I can't. It would make me look stupid."

"Hmm, I suppose it would."

And here, in a deliciously ironic nutshell, was the sweetest advantage to the lie he had perpetrated upon me: namely that I might use it to blackmail him whenever I chose. I did not flex my power lightly. I did not desire trivial things. But over the next few weeks as we grew into our roles, I learned when to lay my ace on the table.

"I would like you to tell your colleagues at the theater that I have been copying the actors' parts alongside you," I informed Will the next time he brought an assignment home.

"I can't do that. They think I do it all."

"Then they can begin to think differently. You will tell them I have ever been adept with a quill and you let me try out a few small roles for practice. You may say I begged for the opportunity, and you could not bear to refuse your devoted sister. You can assure them it is all done under your strict supervision. With the one exception, it is perfectly true, and the closer we stick to the truth, the more believable our charade will be."

"But they don't like women meddling in the theater."

"They allow women to be money gatherers and value us to sew their costumes. They exhort us to come in droves and pay to see the very same plays thought to be too indecent for us to perform."

"But copying plays is not a woman's work."

"It is now. Tell them, Will."

The company was happy to indulge the literary whim of Mr. Shakespeare's sister.

A few days later—it is best not to rush these things—I advised my dear brother I was ready to attend my first London play.

"It is only fitting that I come to applaud you," I said. "Besides, the more plays I see, and the more I understand of the theater's operation, the better costumer and copier I shall be. If you ask nicely, I am sure the company will let me watch in the yard for free."

"You'll get tired of standing there day after day."

"Then if I choose to skip a performance, I will. Arrange it, please."

Poor Will. He had liked his solo life, and it was hard on him, at first, to share his London world with me. But gradually he too came to appreciate the benefits of our newly invented sibling relationship. With our quarrels and our past buried, we could concentrate our efforts on his pursuit of an acting career. In a short while our pooled earnings allowed us to move to a better lodging, where we each got our own bed, table and chair. Also, once again he had a housekeeper, though to keep one room neat and clean is hardly a great chore. In exchange, I forbore to scold or nag—not that I ever had, but such is the view of a wife men cherish over their tankards. And, as I said, I turned a blind eye to his comings and goings, though his unlustful nature made the victory rather *lust*erless.

What Will gained most of all was a clearer conscience. No man who wants to think well of himself abandons his wife and children without some self-reproach, and with me beside him, Will could shed half that guilt. Nor did we kill off his wife entirely. I simply joined him in perceiving her as that faceless figure back in Stratford, as if I too had wriggled free of an old, constricting skin. That way, on the rare occasion when Will did become involved with some lady too insistent on his affections, he could regrettably let it slip that he had a distant wife and three children—hadn't he mentioned them? A shoe might hit his head as the betrayed female shouted him out the door, but it never failed to end the affair.

As for me, I did not—no one does—become a different person overnight. My thoughts turned often to Stratford. Were the children all right? I missed Duck and Bartholomew and sometimes even the Shakespeare clan. To gain your independence in one rush can be overwhelming, and it took me years to learn to use my freedom wisely. How much more we might all achieve if life were a straight path and we could know our destiny in advance, instead of walking into roadblocks, detours and dead ends! Yet I did feel something lying ahead for us, and the more Will and I accustomed ourselves to our revised roles, the better they fit. I credit him for the inspiration. In his clumsy disowning of a wife, he had somehow hit upon what should have been our true relationship were there any justice in the world.

Oh, one last thing, one sisterly advantage neither Will nor I had foreseen. A wife must not be unfaithful, but a pretty young sister may have admirers and even a lover or two if she is discreet. Though I saw no intriguing candidates on the immediate horizon, it did widen my gaze. In the meantime, what heat I lost by way of our separate beds was more than repaid by the fact that Will could no longer steal the sheets.

For my first play at the Theatre, I arrived in good time and prepared to be impressed. Just think—our Theatre in Shoreditch was the first public playhouse in the modern world, conceived and constructed in 1576 by James Burbage for the specific purpose of viewing plays. Before that, players had to travel to find an audience, performing at private houses and royal palaces, in inn yards, guild halls and town squares. Now they had a fixed place of their own where people could flock to see them almost every day. And though the priggish city authorities resented and tried to restrict the acting companies, we had Elizabeth's blessing. Allowing the actors to perform publicly kept them in practice to play for the queen, the argument went, and the lord mayor wouldn't want to interfere with Her Majesty's pleasure, would he?

As I shifted for a space among the rapidly growing crowd, a voice hailed me, and Mr. Phipps wedged himself over to my side.

"I don't know why they crush people in so," he fretted, guiding me by my elbow. "Well, of course I do, it's the money. Here is a good spot. I want to see the duke's sleeves in action. He claims they are too bulky and hinder his sword fighting."

"How many does the Theatre hold?" I asked, looking around the yard and along the galleries where the bettermost people were taking their seats. Six hundred? Eight hundred? A thousand?

"Up to three thousand," said Mr. Phipps. "Mr. Burbage was a joiner and carpenter before he turned actor with the Earl of Leicester's Men, and he modeled his building on the Roman theaters of antiquity. It was a success the minute it opened. Mr. Laneman built the Curtain next door the following year, and Mr. Henslowe's Rose in Southwark came third. But James Burbage was first, and we who love theater owe him an eternal debt for his vision, though he is personally a disagreeable man and I advise you to avoid him. Look, here comes the chorus to start the show."

Mr. Phipps nodded toward the stage, but for a moment my eyes and my brain failed to follow. Three thousand people? That was double the entire population of Stratford! Here, in one place, to see just one play. Though I was gradually getting accustomed to the grand scale of London, the number still amazed me. And now it all came together, building, actors, script, costumes and the most important element of all, the audience, that ring of eager faces, bodies straining forward, that press of riveted humanity . . .

Oh, brave new world! From the start I was swept away.

I hissed like the florid fishwife beside me when the villainous duke murdered the rightful ruler. I bawled—and hardened men sobbed alongside me—when the noble king sacrificed himself to save his daughter's virtue. I gaped when Will appeared. "Lo, my lord," proclaimed the rustically garbed forester, "what does Your worthy Highness in this lowly glade?" That's him! That's my hus— that's my brother! I applauded until my hands were red and stinging, and when the last line was spoken, I cried, not because it was sad but because it was over. No wonder Will loved this. Share, Will, share!

From then on I devoured plays. Each time the money collector waved me in, I floated as if Saint Peter had admitted me to heaven. Looking back, I can tell you that many of those plays were dreadfully mediocre, cobbled together and rushed onto the stage. Since the writers usually worked on several scripts simultaneously, it is not surprising the plots and characters were frequently interchangeable. As for the actors, they might portray a dozen different roles in a fortnight, and all but the best occasionally blundered. Sometimes I heard whole speeches migrate from one play to another like a flock of geese landing with a great thump in a field. Yet at the time, none of that mattered. In my inexperience, I thrilled to my soles. If there happened to be an empty seat in the lower gallery, Mr. Phipps and I sat and exclaimed over our costumes together. Best of all, the imagination I had stifled for so many years burst out again like a glittering fireworks display.

⌒

So there I was, exhilarating in my new element and coming to know the other members of Will's circle. Not James Burbage—he paid me, a lowly seamstress, scant attention, and since Mr. Phipps was right about his notorious temper, that was just as well. Burbage's elder son, Cuthbert, was also standoffish toward me. Like his father, he took up the administrative aspects of the business. But the younger son, Richard—called Dick—was jolly, gregarious and fond of hoisting a tankard. He was both an actor and a talented painter. Will Kempe, the clown who had replaced Richard Tarlton, was another merry man with a fondness for off-color jokes. A little too crude for my taste.

"You are a pustule on the arse of the universe," Kempe would shout, slapping some comrade on the back and nearly knocking him over.

Most of the company, however, were sober actors devoted to their craft, and they helped elevate the perception of their profession a step above its lowly status of vagabond and rogue. Then there were the boys like Christopher, who might or might not have the skill to carry adult roles after the first down silked their chins and their distressed voices tumbled from soprano to bass. Other troupes such as the Admiral's Men and Lord Strange's Men also played at the Theatre, and actors might jump ship from one company to another when an opportunity beckoned or they fell out with their fellows or their noble patron tightened the strings of his purse. Playwrights likewise hired out to whichever company had the means to commission their quill, and Will and I grabbed every chance to copy their scripts. We often spent more time reading than inking them, and I especially loved Christopher Marlowe's. Everything he wrote blazed. He penned not words but sparks, not speeches but conflagrations. Sometimes my fingers burned from the mere touching of his papers.

Yet despite these promising circumstances, I began to perceive a pothole on our road to success: Will's acting. Oh, dear.

At first I thought it splendid. There, there, did you see him? In the soldier's uniform, that's my brother, and in the next scene he is a shepherd. For each of his roles Will entered on cue, spoke his lines clearly and exited with precision. Bravo! In fact, I was simply too enamored of all things theatrical to apply any real judgment to his performances. If I were stupid, I might have gone on blindly applauding forever. But with every script I copied, every comedy or tragedy I viewed, discernment crept in. Like a tide, it rose slowly but inexorably, though I did my best to keep retreating from the water.

All right, he was not a standout, but what could anyone expect, given the size of his roles? It is hard to make an impression when your only lines consist of "The king is coming, my lord!" and "Madam, my master bids me give you this letter." If the whole play was badly written, that rubbed off on the actors too, and as the months passed, the Queen's Men began to reveal their shortcomings. They had been founded as a touring company specializing in patriotic plays that relied on horseplay, pantomime and improvisation to inspire provincial crowds. With the Spanish Armada defeated, that mission was over. Now they had to compete with polished troupes like the Admiral's Men, who were used to playing to sophisticated Londoners. The decline had already begun; the Queen's Men would be defunct in a few more years.

Which was why I worried for Will—in the theater, you either got better fast or you got left behind. But whether or not Will loved me or I him, I was loyal, and as the water inched from my ankles to my knees, I bailed excuses by the bucketful. I didn't want him to fail. London and the Theatre were fast becoming my home. Besides, Will was no dolt, and he was bound to improve as he gained experience. In the senior players he had many apt tutors. He never missed a rehearsal and could often recite half the other roles in addition to his own. But as one play followed another, my sinking feeling grew.

Will was average. Not good or bad, not great or awful, just adequate, mundane, ordinary. He simply did not have it in him to be a famous actor. He lacked the voice, the visage, the verve. His entrances did not flutter the ladies' fans. In a scene of six, he was as memorable as a fence post. When he spoke, his utterances carried sufficiently to the upper gallery, but the tone was flat and flinty, as if his teeth were chipping on a stone. Once, I watched him enact a part as third murderer, and as he and his fellow assassins fell on the doomed king, he affected a most savage scowl. Yet he could not bring himself to endanger anyone by stabbing his dagger too closely, and so he hung on the fringes, feinting and harmless as a puppy. In a way, I loved him for it, but the other two actors stole the scene meanwhile. Will had no *presence*—there, I have said it, an actor's death knell.

I could see the other troupers didn't know what to do with him.

They liked him—who would not? He was eager to learn and do their bidding. He hurried through his own costume changes to help them with theirs. Even Kempe, unsubtle as a thunderclap, shied away from a direct hit on Will's prospects as an actor. "Good job," he would bellow at him after a performance. "Now fetch me an ale, you pest of a player!" They strove to keep Will busy with minor roles and copy assignments or as a prompter at rehearsals. It was as if they sensed some value in him and therefore kept him around. They just couldn't put their finger on what his particular talent was or how to exploit it.

The only one who didn't know he was average was Will.

"I have three roles in the next play!" he announced, bounding up the stairs. "I am an old man in the first scene, a jailer in the middle and a friar at the end. The friar has a whole speech, twenty lines."

"That is excellent! Perhaps you could soon ask for a larger role?"

"Anne, I am still an apprentice, and they have been more than generous to me thus far. Mr. Kempe says if I keep coming along, I will be their star player before I turn forty."

He colored with pleasure at the joke, and I could only hope that no trace of a cringe showed in my smile. How would we ever support our children? Between my sewing, our copying, his acting and odd jobs, we kept food on our table, but the letters we sent home to Stratford were empty of coins. Even those few players who grew prosperous did not do so on an actor's income. They bought shares in the company or invested in property or other ventures. Edward Alleyn, perhaps the richest of all, amassed his wealth through his dealings in bear pits and brothels. To rely on acting alone meant scrabbling a living from day to day, and what of the weeks and months when the playhouses might be closed due to politics or plague? Better to be a country cleric or village schoolmaster whose salaries, if modest, were at least regular.

But Will couldn't see this either. He believed he was on a path paved with adulation and gold. He loved pomp and wearing costumes and informing people he was an actor. When he left for the theater each morning, the look on his face and the bounce in his step seemed to say, "My audience, my fellows await. The day cannot begin until I arrive." He was the center of his own attention, and there were young men like him on every street in London, the printer's apprentice striding to the shop to set type, the novice lawyer heading to advise his client. Perhaps it is a universal trait of young men, and I should not diminish it; soon enough they will be humbled and ground down. But when I looked around our neat little room—the ink bottle on Will's table, a pincushion and shears on mine, Mr. Phipps's latest commission, a saffron gown trimmed in green velvet, awaiting my needle—I thought, God, what if we are still here when we are forty? In the pit of my stomach came a gnawing sensation that mere food could not satisfy.

When the next play premiered and Will came out with the other players to take his bows, I applauded loudly. He stood at the far side of the stage, as befitted his rank, while the primary actors accepted accolades, cheers and tossed flowers. He was still dressed as the friar from the final scene, and his hooded costume of coarse brown wool must have been hot. Face shiny with perspiration, he grinned and bowed.

The stage was all his world, and I would make it mine too.

Above all, we must find a way to make it pay.

Chapter 10

$\mathcal{T}$hose first months and years in London, Will and I often felt like travelers in search of a permanent home. The acting companies remained in flux, and Will moved from the Queen's Men to Lord Strange's Men to the Earl of Pembroke's Men as fortune dictated. We also made a few trips back to Stratford. In the excitement of feting Will, the ignominy of my flight was forgotten, and though Gilbert and I had a few awkward moments, to our relief time and distance had done their work. Love had faded to liking; henceforth we would be ordinary friends.

"The children have grown so," said Will, as we blew out the candle and drew up the covers on our first night back in his parents' house. In Stratford, we had to revert to being husband and wife, sleeping in the same room with our children, sharing our old bed. I had hoped it might lead to something, but Will treated it as a simple accommodation and nothing more, the way polite travelers double up at a crowded inn. I shrugged. Wife, sister. It seemed my fate to be a woman of no fixed identity.

"They barely remember us, though," I said, gazing at Susanna, Hamnet and Judith asleep in their truckle bed. "The twins especially. They are too young."

"I know. We arrive as strangers, and as soon as we leave, they forget us again." His face furrowed in determination. "They have a good home here, but I want to do better for them, Anne. I want to make the name of Shakespeare one we can be proud to pass on."

"We will," I said. Absent though we were from our children's lives, to do well for them was one thing we could always agree on.

Gradually, we were able to send bits of income to our family, and this made us feel united and vindicated. Having money also caused me a strange anxiety. During my youth at Hewlands Farm, we had grown, made or bartered with our neighbors to obtain most of our needs. Even at the market in Stratford, we usually swapped eggs and honey for a piece of cloth; a chicken or goose brought home a new knife or a pair of shoes. Nor had I handled many coins during my six years in my in-laws' house, though I saw how the flow of them, or lack thereof, affected our living and our status.

But in London the whole world moved on money, shopkeepers required cash, and purses jangled at people's belts. To think that the very roof over our heads depended on little pieces of metal that could slip through a hole in my pocket was to me a source of constant worry. I sewed myself a drawstring pouch with double-stitched seams, and, following the practice of savvy Londoners, I wore it inside my skirt. I well remembered how boldly Margery had yanked the amber necklace from my throat, and the city cutpurses were even more adept in slicing an exposed wallet from a belt and vanishing into the crowd. Each time Mr. Phipps paid me, I pushed the coins to the very bottom of the pouch and insisted Will escort me home. Having managed his father's accounts, he was far more at ease dealing with currency.

"If you don't stop patting your hip, Anne," he scolded as we walked, "you will alert every thief for a mile what you have beneath your skirt."

I shot him an indignant look; no one likes to be mocked for her foibles. Even so, it took a mighty effort to restrain my hand, and a few times I cheated by letting my wrist brush against the spot. At home I secreted the money in a sturdy sock, which I knotted and stuffed into my pillow. Will gestured around our unadorned domicile, shook his head and laughed.

"As if anyone would consider this a worthwhile place to plunder!"

Indeed, the coins were usually spent by the next day on food, candles or rent; no fortune accumulated under my sleeping head. All the same, I kept my shoe handy by the bedside. A whap between the eyes and a broken nose would greet any thief who entered in the night.

Meanwhile, I happily sewed costumes for the Theatre. It is right to take pleasure and pride in that which you do well, and as Mr. Phipps had promised, he kept me busy. This week a crimson suit for a Turkish potentate, next week a princess's golden gown. And the fabrics! Silks and satins and brocades I had never touched in my life. When my fingers stroked over them, they almost purred. Not all our costumes were stitched brand-new. When playing common folk, the actors simply wore their own clothes. With an eye to economy and saving time, Mr. Phipps and I also bought garments secondhand and retailored them from play to play. He introduced me to his favorite vendors and taught me where to find bargains in London's nooks and crannies.

Best of all, theater costumes were exempt from the sumptuary laws, and that gave our creativity free rein. For everyone else, the edicts strictly controlled what men and women of every rank and class could and could not wear.

For example, only the queen and her immediate family could wear the color purple, and since our queen had no such living relative—how convenient!—that meant only Elizabeth could be royally empurpled. You must be at least an earl or a countess to flaunt sable; a baron and his wife had to settle for leopard fur. Tinseled satin was approved for viscounts; for knights, velvet would have to do. A knight's wife might show off in tufted taffeta, but his envious daughter wore her taffeta untufted, if she knew what was good for her. In fairness, the lower classes were allowed their finery. They might trim their wools and linens with a snippet of silk or ribbon, or—lucky peasants!—they could add a touch of homemade embroidery. And mind you heed your colors: gold, silver, indigo and crimson for the royal ilk; brown, orange, russet, green, gray and woad blue for commoners. Though the laws were nearly impossible to enforce and often ignored, to violate them could result in confiscation of the offending garment, a hefty fine and, if Her Majesty was particularly displeased, forfeiture of your property, your title and even your life. So let no one overstep his sartorial bounds!

"The laws were created to maintain the rightful order of society," Mr. Phipps explained. "Imagine the confusion if the greengrocer took to wearing ermine or a laundry maid masqueraded as a baroness. If you cannot judge a person's rank at first glance, then an honest man might be deceived by a crook in a courtier's clothes. Although that is really unfair to the crooks, since nothing stops the courtiers from corruption no matter what they wear."

Mr. Phipps knew the sumptuary laws by heart, and he also pointed out to me their benefit to our English economy. "The laws keep us from spending money on imported foreign goods when we ought to buy English instead. Think of the edict that all men and boys from the age of six must wear wool caps on Sundays. What a boon that has been to our wool industry! Besides, we cannot have poor folk overspending themselves to look like their betters. They must save their money so that it may be taken away from them in taxes to pay for useful things like wars."

"Yet actors onstage may wear clothes fit for a king," I mused. "I suppose because it is make-believe it does not count?"

"Precisely, my dear, and there are exceptions for royal servants as well. A duke may clothe his retainers in a livery befitting his station so long as his servants never outshine the queen's."

"What about that lavender dress I embroidered? Is that purple? Does it count?"

"It might, if the lady who once owned it was unwise enough to wear it in the queen's presence. But the laws work to our advantage in the theater, Anne. When ladies and gentlemen die they sometimes bequeath their clothing to their household staff, and since the servants are forbidden to wear the garments, they sell them to us and gladly take the money instead. That is how we acquired the lavender gown. And here, look what just came in." He opened a chest and brought out a deep blue damask dress.

"Oh! Mr. Phipps!"

He held the gown up to my shoulders, inviting me to take it. While

I held it in place, he straightened and tweaked the skirt. Then he picked up a glass so I could admire my reflection. The dress was trimmed in black velvet ribbon with tinseled gold edging, and the celestial blue startled awake the blue of my eyes. I sighed at the luxurious texture of the damask and how pretty I looked, how very rich. Then a man arrived, and Mr. Phipps went to speak with him, leaving me with the dress. As I swayed the skirt before me, I glanced over my shoulder. The man was Mr. Phipps's "friend," or so the actors joked, and though I understood what they meant, I chose to ignore it. Later I learned that some of those who made the rudest show of rolling their eyes had a "friend" themselves. Mr. Phipps's companion was dark, slender and shy. Their muted conversation seemed to be about their plans for the evening, when and where to meet, should they dine at the tavern or buy bread and pickled eggs to take home?

They sounded like Will and me, I thought, holding the sleeve of the dress out along my arm. From the corner of my eye I saw the two men lean toward each other and exchange a quick parting kiss on the lips. They must have thought, from the angle, they were out of my sight. I blinked—I ought to have been repulsed. Instead the scene impressed me with a sense of fleeting tenderness.

"Isn't it beautiful?" said Mr. Phipps, returning and relieving me of the dress. He touched the fabric lovingly before hanging it away.

"Yes, thank you for showing it to me," I answered. "Thank you, Mr. Phipps."

⁓

When we were not working, Will and I often strolled about the city. What a feast! I soaked London into me as a piece of bread dipped in broth draws up the seasoned juice. Even without a penny in your pocket, you could be entertained on any street corner by myriad sights and sounds. For news, we stopped at St. Paul's Cross, the outdoor pulpit where official proclamations were read aloud. On November 17, Accession Day, we might behold the queen in procession as the people cheered another anniversary on the throne. I always seized the opportunity to view the latest fashions and get a jump on my needle. A ramble to Westminster and the Strand brought us to the vicinity of many noble houses and gardens, where we gaped shamelessly. Will had an eye for architecture and would point out friezes or stonework that caught his fancy. But when I laughed at the idea of our ever setting foot inside such a place, he shook his head.

"Don't be so sure," he said stubbornly.

For both business and pleasure, we forayed to the Rose in Southwark to rate our rival actors, though as the composition of the companies shifted, yesterday's rivals might become today's friends. At the Curtain we watched wrestling and fencing matches, which took up the slack in business when playgoing was slow. Once Will took me to a bearbaiting at the Paris Garden. In addition to being crushed on all sides by the dubious inhabitants of the district, I found it not good sport. The bear was an old one, hardly fit to fight, and the short chain around its neck gave little scope to twist away from the attacking dogs. The shaggy creature raged and howled in feeble despair, and the bettors loudly protested the lack of decent odds. Some cried for Sackerson, a venerable beast whose ferocious claws had ended the life of many dogs. A small man behind us yelped at being trodden upon and complained that if the crowd kept pushing forward, the stands might collapse and people be killed, as had happened once before.

"Enough." I hooked Will's arm and dragged him out. "It is a dangerous place and a waste of our money."

"We could walk by Tyburn and see if there is a hanging," he offered. "They are free and usually afford a good view."

For fresh air, we hiked north of the city through Finsbury Fields, where windmills turned, cows grazed and young men practiced archery. On a long day we went farther, to the wooded hills of Hampstead, where you could gaze back and see a distant vista of London. It was a popular place for hunting and hawking, and I felt most fortunate that in leaving Stratford we had lost none of the pleasures of the countryside. Even within the city walls were gardens stocked with fruit trees and flower beds, and when the cherry, pear and apple blossoms opened, you would have thought we had been visited by a blizzard of pink and white snow.

Inevitably, our roamings ended at the booksellers clustered around St. Paul's. Here was a banquet of literature, high and low. Translations of Latin texts into English did a brisk business, especially Pliny's *Natural History*. While romances appealed to the female readers, Richard Hakluyt's *Divers Voyages Touching the Discoverie of America* stirred the hearts of adventurous young males. Cheap pamphlets gave illustrated accounts of murders, executions and horrific floods and fires. Bibles in English were well stocked—wouldn't my father be pleased!—and John Foxe's *Book of Martyrs* sold faster than hotcakes on a cold winter's day. For wit, Robert Greene was most in demand, and when the first three books of Edmund Spenser's *The Faerie Queene* were published, the crowds nearly broke down the stalls for a copy. The book Will and I especially craved was Raphael Holinshed's *Chronicles*, in which was recorded the whole true history of our English nation. Beautiful, but it cost £1.

"Are you looking or buying?" the booksellers would demand at our extended browsing, and we guiltily surrendered whatever volume had engrossed us and backed away. Other days they shot us a forbidding eye even as we approached.

"We have gained a reputation," Will rued. "Next time we come, it will have to be in disguise."

For dinner we might stop at one or another of the taverns favored by the actors and playwrights. The first few times, to my amusement, Will put his finger to his lips and issued me a warning, "Shh!" before we entered. Did he think I did not know how to behave in company? That I would grow tipsy and garrulous, flirt like a strumpet or snort beer through my nose?

"Now, I don't know who will be here tonight, Anne," he would begin, anxiously studying the building as we approached. "If we are lucky, it might be Edward Alleyn or even Christopher Marlowe, and we can find a seat that is close but not too close."

Poor Will, he was so painfully worshipful. He longed to be noticed and yearned for an invitation to join in their talk. If only someone would spot him as the next great player! Except there were twenty other would-be actors in the tavern intent on the same goal, and unlike my meek Will, they did not blend into the crowd. They had no fear of barging into a conversation or cajoling a playwright to pen them a breakout role. If the illustrious one swatted them away, they simply betook themselves to the next cluster of notables. The most Will would venture was a gushy compliment.

"Mr. Alleyn, I just want to tell you that I saw you in *Doctor Faustus* and could scarcely speak for the power of your performance."

"Thank you," Alleyn would reply, his mellifluous voice coating even the most mundane words like syrup-dipped cherries. Then he would raise his glass in friendly dismissal and turn back to his comrades, and Will would hem and haw a moment before slinking away. Though we could now afford to pay for the food on our plates, he was still seeking crumbs that fell from others' tables.

"They are younger than me," he said one night as we walked home.

"Who?"

"Edward Alleyn, Dick Burbage. Alleyn is twenty-four. I am twenty-six to Dick's twenty-two, and he always gets a lead role. Don't you think if I were meant to be a great actor, it would have happened by now?"

He turned to me, his face forlorn. His voice had the lonely sound of a stone dropping into a pond and sinking out of sight.

"But they started earlier, and you will catch up. Besides, Dick is the boss's son, so naturally he has first pick." I took his hand. Funny, here I was the one complaining he couldn't see the obvious, yet now that discouragement was setting in, I wanted to soften his fall. "You were excellent as the lovesick goatherd in last week's play. You had a whole sonnet to recite."

"It was a bad sonnet."

True. With two agile brains between us, Will and I were rapidly coming to grips with the structure, mechanics and poetry of the plays. We could tell, for example, which playwrights had also been actors.

They understood the possibilities and limitations of the physical space and factored in the talents of the individual players. They did not create unnecessary characters, and they paced the scenes so that those actors who doubled had sufficient time in the tiring room for costume changes. New writers often failed to grasp this, and then some long-winded and superfluous speech must be inserted to cover up the shortfall. Such had been the origin of the goatherd's sonnet that disheartened Will.

"I could write better than that," he continued.

"Why don't you?" I said. "You could write a play. You could write sonnets. Remember that one you wrote to me?"

He paused. "It was good, wasn't it?" he said wistfully.

"It was brilliant. You could write sonnets, and we could sell them at the bookshops at St. Paul's. They might not make a lot of money to start, but if your poetry were to circulate, you might gain a reputation. You could become our next Edmund Spenser."

"More likely I'll become Stratford's next unsung glover."

A long silence dropped on us, and I sensed Will wrestling with himself. He had worked hard at acting, to little avail. To switch to writing would mean starting over, competing with Spenser, Lyly, Marlowe, Greene and other established stars. What if he failed? What if he gave it his all and still we went on the same? How could we bear a future of disappointed dreams as the years slipped away and London ceased to bedazzle and our families back in Stratford dismissed all but random thoughts of us? Yet if we quit and went home, and the very next week some golden opportunity came knocking . . .

Will struggled and I waited. I banished every argument from my mind, every flicker of emotion from my face. I had spoken my support; the decision must be his. But I knew what I wanted, and I prayed, prayed.

"All right, I'll try it," he vowed. "I must have success, Anne. I must make my name."

Sonnet—a pretty word, isn't it? It means "little song," and at fourteen lines it is just the right length for a lilting love poem. The form had long been practiced in Italy, where it was made famous by Petrarch. More lately it had reached a vogue in France. Now, with the publication of Sir Philip Sidney's *Astrophel and Stella* in 1591, sonnets were the absolute rage in England. What better time for Will to try his hand? Our plan was to persuade the booksellers to stock his handwritten verses for sale as billets-doux and inspirations for the lovelorn. We would also try to persuade a printer to take on their publishing.

Best of all, the project brought Will's love of language to the fore. As an actor, he had voiced others' elegant words. Here was his chance to write them. Yet talent alone does not a poet make—it takes *practice*—and for every good sonnet that flowed from his pen, there were a dozen bad ones. I know; I helped compose them night after night, as Will scribbled and I hung over his shoulder in our room.

"I need something to rhyme with 'morn,'" he would say, scratching on his paper.

"Born, torn, shorn, forlorn, thorn."

"Thorn! I haven't used that yet. But then I'll need to insert a rose somewhere."

"Rose, toes, nose, grows, flows."

"'Grows' is good. Da-dum, da-dum, da-dum, da-dum, da-rose. Da-dum, da-dum, da-dum, thorn. Da-dum, da-dum, my love for you grows—"

"—radiant and blithe as an April morn." I tapped my finger to the paper. "All right, back to the beginning."

We also began to scheme how our poetry might lure us a patron, a highly desirable goal. Why, Edmund Spenser had so stroked Elizabeth's vanity with *The Faerie Queene* that she had awarded him an annual life pension of fifty pounds! "Think what we could do with that kind of money!" became Will's refrain, and I was only too happy to dream along. We would buy silver candlesticks for our table, a dandy's gold earring for him, a pot of French perfume for me. We would shower gifts on Stratford—let the whole town see what toffs we down-and-out Shakespeares had become! We must have spent that same fifty pounds a hundred times over and still did not tire of the game. On a paper tacked to our wall we kept a list of potential benefactors, starting with the queen herself. Why not? Aim high! We were temporarily daunted, however, when the canny bookseller who agreed to set out our first batch of sonnets for sale stipulated that we leave off Will's name.

"What we want, you see, is something your young man can snap up on an impulse and present to his lady as his own, so it won't do to have another fellow's signature on it." He touched his forefinger to his temple to indicate the genius of the notion.

"But that won't build my reputation," said Will.

"Do you want a reputation or do you want to be paid?"

Back to our ink, then. We would have to amass a body of work anyway, a sonnet sequence, to attract a patron of means. We might as well earn a few pence anonymously in the interim. And with practice we grew quick and saved ourselves much time. We mixed and matched quatrains in praise of various female virtues. Often the same sonnet would suffice for a number of suitors simply by changing the color of the lady's hair or eyes.

Most important, those sonnets moved our quills forward; we had advanced from mere copying to composing original work. That alone uplifted us, and we began to see the next level. While the candle burned low, we passed verses back and forth, wrestling with rhyme and meter and our own unformed talent. We argued, debated and growled. Suddenly a recalcitrant line would pop into place. . . . Who said that? Who thought it? From brain to fingers to paper, words had bolted of their own accord. Now we began to sense the magic, and it filled us with awe.

"This is it, what I was meant to do, Anne," said Will, and his face had the wondering look of a person to whom a long-shrouded mystery has finally become clear.

I nodded, for the same feeling had been growing in me. "Yes, I think we have found it."

"Then I should also try a play. I know the stage, I know the actors, I have been studying it for four years."

"A play would be a fine endeavor. You could put Dick Burbage in the leading role."

"I was probably never meant to be an actor at all. If only I had seen it sooner."

"Never mind, it got you to London, and you are still young enough to change course."

"I am a writer, Anne!" He held up his ink-stained palms, and with a laugh I took the cloth from beside the washbasin and wiped them dry.

"Yes, and I am proud of you."

He got up from the table, stretched his arms with real pleasure and began to undress for bed. I stoppered the ink bottle and pushed back my chair. I watched him pull on his nightshirt and slip under his blanket, then lie with hands clasped contentedly behind his head. He was better-looking than when I first met him. His face had grown lean, his beard filled in, his chest broadened. He had learned much of the world, and though he was sometimes discouraged, he refused to succumb. Whatever he took on, he worked hard to master. And we made a good team, as writers, roommates and companions. Was there any chance . . . ? He spoke before I could answer myself.

"I do write excellently, don't I?" He sighed.

"Most excellently," I replied, abandoning my notion and indulging him with a smile. I reached to stack our papers and a scratched-out line caught my eye. "Will? You should not delete this." I read it aloud.

"It clunks, Anne. Don't worry; I'll think of something fresh in the morning." He yawned and closed his lids.

My thoughts strayed to my own bed, lingered, crawled half in. Then they traveled back to the paper in my hand. Will was right, the line jerked, but the image was apt, and with a bit of rewording . . . I pulled my chair back to the table.

"What are you doing?" He squinted one eye open at the sound.

"Nothing. I won't be long. Go to sleep. I'll be quiet."

"All right then. Good night."

"Good night." I unstopped the ink, dipped my quill and bent my head.

Chapter 11

*W*riting a play is not as easy as it looks.

First, what were we to write about? I proposed a pastoral romance—exiled nobility masquerading as shepherds, lovers' trysts in an idyllic countryside, mistaken identities and comic confusion, all ending in a wedding and a merry dance. Treacle! But a writer must start somewhere, and recent offerings in that genre at the Theatre and the Rose had played to full houses. I also reckoned our boy actor Christopher should be good for one more wide-eyed heroine before his voice broke. Will preferred a revenge play, citing the continuing popularity of *The Spanish Tragedy* by Thomas Kyd.

"It has been five years since Tom penned it," he said, "yet audiences still come in droves. More to the point, it brought him fame and the patronage of Lord Strange."

"Is that still our chief goal then? To secure a patron?"

"I think so. A writer gets paid but once when he sells his play to a theater company or his poems to a publisher, but the patronage of a rich lord can fill your pocket for years. Then you can write whatever you want, aside from the odd rhyme to please him."

Who could argue? Though excellent practice, our anonymous sonnets were getting us nowhere. A hit play like Kyd's would put Will's name in everyone's mouth and boost our chances of attracting a benefactor. It would also deposit an immediate £4 to £5, the going rate for a script, into our purse.

"Let's go see *The Spanish Tragedy* again," I suggested. "It may inspire us where to start."

So off we went. You will notice, by the way, that it was now "Tom" and not "Mr. Kyd" that tripped off Will's tongue. Likewise "Kit," "Robert," "George" for Messrs. Marlowe, Greene and Peele. Getting a little cocky already, weren't you, Will? But I did not discourage his private posturing. If he was to be a writer, he must think and act like one. He must imagine himself clapping his fellow authors on the back over drinks. Look at my own snap judgment of young Christopher's availability to enact girlish parts. It was not coldhearted but realistic to match your players' talents and longevity to a role. It was how a professional playwright must think, and I was not a little proud to have such ideas blossoming in my brain. But after viewing *The Spanish Tragedy*, we emerged from the theater much dejected.

"How can I ever write anything that good?" Will despaired, and I searched in vain for a tidbit to comfort him. Kyd had modeled his bloodbath on Seneca, and besides being the first revenge play in English, it overflows with everything the genre requires: brutal murders, treachery and deceit, suicides, a ghost, a play within a play, several raving-mad scenes and a brilliant, dastardly revenge. Moreover, where Seneca did his violence offstage, Kyd littered the boards with corpses—to the horrified delight of the audience. Topping it off was Edward Alleyn's earthshaking performance as the ancient, sorrowing father Hieronimo mourning his murdered son.

> *O eyes, no eyes, but fountains fraught with tears;*
> *O life, no life, but lively form of death;*
> *O world, no world, but mass of public wrongs,*
> *Confused and filled with murder and misdeeds!*
> *O sacred heavens!*

We recited it to each other in envy and admiration. Kyd even had self-mutilation: At the end of the play, Hieronimo bites off his own tongue before fatally stabbing himself. How could we possibly top all that?

"I could poison someone," Will offered without much enthusiasm. "They could die frothing at the mouth."

"What about a slow death on the rack or being entombed in a charnel house?" I suggested.

"A strangulation? A beheading?"

"We could bash out someone's brains, hang, draw and quarter them, then set them on fire."

Will sighed. "It's been done, Anne, that's the problem. Thanks to Kyd and Seneca, every dramatist in London is writing revenge. Look at *The Jew of Malta*. Kit poisons a whole nunnery and scalds his villain to death in a boiling cauldron. All the good stuff is taken."

"Could we invent a new type of play? Perhaps it would be better to break away from the crowd rather than to repeat what has already been done."

"Except the public wants the same thing over and over."

"Then we must give it to them."

So Will began his revenge tragedy, *Titus Andronicus*. He wrote five pages. Then he rewrote them. Then he rewrote them again. Then he rewrote the rewrite of the rewrite. He refused my help. What did a seamstress know about plays? Oh, really? I held my tongue and waited as crumpled papers flew into the corners.

"I am getting nowhere!" he shouted. "Why can't I make it come out right?"

"Maybe you should set the first scene aside and go on to the second one."

"No! I won't quit until it is perfect!"

"There is no need to shout at me. It's not my fault."

We were several weeks into this testy state of affairs and the December snow was falling when Will brought home a half-written history play from Mr. Henslowe at the Rose. It was titled *King Henry VI*, and the story had been jobbed out first to George Peele and Thomas

Nashe, bosom friends and two of the University Wits, that smart set of Cambridge and Oxford graduates. Peele, when he wasn't drunk or gambling or catching the pox in Southwark, wrote charming poetry and plays. Nashe, as a hired pen for the Church of England in the Martin Marprelate controversy, had written satirical pamphlets abusing Puritans. He had also become embroiled in a bitter literary feud with the poet Gabriel Harvey, and their war of words grew as sharp as if their pens were daggers plunged into each other's breasts.

Between Peele's drunken input and Nashe's distraction with Harvey, *King Henry VI* was a mishmash. At which point Kit Marlowe had swept in and flourished a scene or two before mysteriously disappearing from London in the dark of night. Whispers in the tavern had him off to the Continent on a secret mission for the queen. While still in college he had been recruited by Elizabeth's late spymaster, Sir Francis Walsingham, for this dangerous service. Or was he merely idling in some seaside town, amused to let rumors swirl in his absence? You never knew with Kit. Meanwhile, *King Henry VI* was passed to Robert Greene, another University Wit, and worse, a whining, contentious, arrogant, spiteful, envious, ill-tempered, untalented, fornicating, underhanded—

"Greene proved so unruly," Will reported, "that Mr. Henslowe dismissed him. I heard about it from some actors and hurried to the Rose to offer my services. If I can patch it up a bit and you render a clean copy . . ."

He spread the papers on my table, and I set aside the olive peasecod doublet I was tailoring for Mr. Phipps. And isn't it interesting how Will now took my copying skills for granted, he who had once disdained the idea of my plying a pen? But it was all right when it put money in our pockets or helped him look good. Never mind. I was intrigued, though the script was a mess. A challenge—you would think a pigeon had tipped over an inkwell and traipsed across it.

"The main problem," Will said, pointing from one page to another, "is that the story is badly disjointed. The scenes skip from England to France and back again in twenty lines. The characterizations are uneven as well. How can the king be a valiant warrior one moment and a saintly simpleton the next? The dauphin and Joan of Arc are defeated and vanish near the middle of the play, and a whole new set of characters is introduced. Audiences don't like that. They want to see a coherent story line throughout. And it is way too long, the war in France and the War of the Roses crammed together. The plot must be simplified and refocused to achieve dramatic tension."

Listen to him, talking like a writer. I smiled. "What are we waiting for then?"

We spent that evening dissecting the script and gloating over our good luck to have it fall into our hands. Except it was not luck; Will went out and got it. He took the initiative, and he deserved the credit. Good work! Now all we had to do was stun the world with our new version of *Henry VI*, and he would be hailed and welcomed into the fraternity of London playwrights. And a history play was almost guaranteed to do well—why hadn't we thought of it? Since the defeat of the armada, we English had continued to ride on a wave of patriotism, and there was ample drama and treachery, murder, mayhem and rebellion in Henry VI's reign to satisfy a bloodthirsty audience. Best of all, the story was fully recorded in the chronicles of both Raphael Holinshed and his predecessor Edward Halle. We had only to straighten out the scenes and recast the tale in Will's own words. To launch this first effort, I made a tremulous decision. I wormed my hand inside my pillow and drew out the knotted sock.

"Look." I spilled money onto the table, twenty shillings, one whole pound. I had squirreled the coins away without Will's knowledge, payments from Mr. Phipps, stitched wealth. My own alchemist's gold, now to be transmuted to a higher cause. "I thought we would send it home for the children for Christmas, but if we are to write a history, we must have at least one version of the chronicles. With luck, we may find secondhand copies of both Holinshed and Halle."

For a minute, Will blinked at the pile. Then he grabbed my shoulders and planted a smack on my surprised mouth. "Come," he said, catching my hand and running me with him out the door. "To the booksellers!"

But I repeat, writing a play is not as easy as it looks, even when the plot, characters and a rough draft lie before you silver plattered.

For a start, Will and I were not experienced collaborators. We had been composing sonnets at our side-by-side tables for less than a twelvemonth. And *Henry VI* required far more than a few altered lines. We must cut, reassemble, create, then subject our work to our own scrutiny. Moreover, Will didn't think we were collaborating. He was the writer; I was supposed only to copy and assist with the research. Impossible. Ideas flurried in my head and out of my mouth like moths escaping from a trunk. Almost immediately, we fought.

"You should not interrupt the Talbot battle scenes to show the French forces onstage," I said. "Put them all together: Talbot's son arrives to join the fighting, the old man rescues the boy when he's hemmed in, then the wounded father discovers his son slain on the field, takes him in his arms and dies beside him. After that you can bring in the French."

"No, that is not the way I want it. We need a battle scene with the dauphin."

"But the father-son scenes are too powerful to break up."

"A break will increase the tension by keeping the audience waiting."

"But no one cares about the French."

"Yes, they do. They love to hiss them."

"Then let them do it after the Talbots die. Here, you could use this part where the bastard of Orléans wants to hack the bodies to pieces."

"All right, all right. I'll think about it." An hour later, grumbling and muttering, Will would thrust at me the revised draft. "I hope this satisfies you, Mistress Know-it-all."

Gradually, I learned to spoon honey over my suggestions.

"Your soliloquy for Gloucester is excellent," I might say. "You have admirably conveyed his devious nature and his lust for the crown. I wonder . . . would it enhance the speech to include some measure of his self-loathing? Perhaps the key to his character is that he despises himself."

"Does he?"

"Oh, yes. You already suggest it here when he laments that no lady will ever love him because of his physical deformities: ' . . . love forswore me in my mother's womb . . .' You have only to expand upon it." I would lean back deferentially to let him ponder.

"Well, I guess that would work."

But sometimes I lapsed and became overinsistent. Why must he always be pampered first? Why could he not simply admit when he was wrong and I was right? Just do it my way! Sometimes during *Henry VI* we went to bed not speaking, though as our beds were on opposite sides of the small room, it hardly mattered. Other times, when the changes I desired were minor, I simply slipped them in as I copied. The next day I would hold my breath as Will read them over, his eyes and brain pausing over an edited line. Then he would nod and keep on. If it was good, he must have written it, right?

Meanwhile, Mr. Henslowe was breathing on us for the script. He was as devoted to profit as James Burbage, and if we landed on his bad side, Will's playwriting career would be over before it began.

"I guess we won't be going to see the children for Christmas." I sighed as once again we slumped over our play. Susanna was eight, the twins would turn seven in January. The few letters we had received assured us they were healthy, happy and oblivious of our absence. We were glad and sad. We knew we did not deserve them, but they deserved good parents, and that should have been us. Now, Will observed, we hadn't even the means to send them New Year's presents, having spent our money on Halle and Holinshed.

"Let's buckle down and write," I said. "The sooner we finish, the sooner we can go for a visit. After all, it is for them we are doing this."

As it happened, we could not have traveled anyway, for two days later a blizzard struck, stranding everyone in London for a week. Huddled in our cold room, we solved the final problem with the script. Will was right: It was way too long. Instead of compressing two wars into one play, we boldly tossed out the War of the Roses and concentrated on Henry's battles in France.

"Like Kit did with *Tamburlaine*," said Will with a crafty nod. "You write part one, and when it is a success, you are guaranteed a commission to write a sequel. I bet we could even get a trilogy out of it."

⁓

"Should I show it to them?"

We hemmed and debated. We had finished *I Henry VI* with a few days to spare, and what Will wanted more than anything else was to walk into the tavern and share his creation with his fellow writers.

"I think so," I urged. "Some of them had a hand in it, and we don't want them to be taken aback when it suddenly appears at the Rose with your name on the playbill. It will have your name on it, won't it?"

"I hope so, though I doubt 'A New Play by Mr. William Shakespeare' posted on the door will have quite the draw of a new play by Tom or Kit."

"Nonetheless, you should make it known you have started playwriting. You are going to be one of them."

"What should I wear?"

"Hmm, let's see. You want to look confident but not presumptuous, up-and-coming but not cock-of-the-walk."

I sorted through his wardrobe and picked out a modest but well-tailored—by me—wine-colored doublet, breeches and hose. I kissed his cheek for luck and sent him out the door.

Two hours later he returned almost in tears.

"What is it? What happened?" I hurried to his side.

"They hated it, well, not hated it. But they found everything wrong with it, Anne. They tore it apart. I shall have to begin over, cut half the scenes, rewrite the battles. . . . Maybe I should give up."

I took the sheaf of papers before he could cast them aside. "Sit down and tell me," I said. "It may not be that bad."

Well, it was and it wasn't. Since he'd gone to the tavern hoping for compliments, anything to the contrary had stung Will as condemnation. I could see the damage was not fatal; most of the criticisms made good sense. But Will was too bruised to accept it, and was there any reason they had to be so rough? They could have commented nicely. They could have served up some praise along with their snide, snippy, superior remarks. The nerve of those insufferable twits! We were novices—couldn't they see that?—working under a tight deadline on their mangled script. We would show them. We would write a play to put the lot of them to shame, and in the meantime they should have a piece of my mind about treating a fellow human being and aspiring writer with a modicum of decency, kindness and respect.

I grabbed my cloak, and ten minutes later I burst into the tavern like a sputtering volcano about to blow. I marched straight to Kit Marlowe—the others had left—and opened my mouth.

"Sit down," Kit invited, patting the bench beside him before I could erupt. "How is he taking it?"

"I . . . We . . ." I stood, too furious to get words out.

"Brokenhearted? Suicidal? Swears he will never write again?"

"He . . . I—"

"So said we all and more than once. But a writer must get used to criticism, unless, like me, you are perfect."

"Why . . . you—"

Kit waited, smiling, and in sudden confusion I stopped. Good God, he was handsome. And that smile—a thousand possible readings lay behind it. Was he mocking us, himself?

"He is devastated," I confessed, and I plopped down on the bench like a sack of flour with all the air puffing out of it.

Kit gave me a moment, then he motioned to the tapster. When the mug arrived, he pushed it toward me.

"If he is really a writer, he will get over it. It's not a bad play, you know. It just needs more work."

"That is what I told him, but we haven't much time left. About the scene where Joan of Arc first meets the dauphin . . . one of you said it falls flat. Do you think it would be more convincing if, instead of simply speaking with him, she challenged him to fight? I know it is not in Holinshed but—"

"Oh, you read Holinshed, do you?"

"Yes, of course."

"And you would like to have Joan cross swords with the dauphin."

"I know it sounds silly but—"

"Not at all. Have her trounce him. If she is to win his consent to lead the French army, she must prove her skill at arms. I wouldn't let a demented peasant girl lead me into battle just because she daydreamed she heard voices from God, would you?"

"Well, no—" My tongue stumbled over itself. Among other scandalous vices attributed to Kit Marlowe, it was whispered he was an atheist, and from old habit, I glanced around, hoping no one had overheard us. One of the benefits of living in London was that your religion could get lost in the crowd; as long as Will and I attended church regularly in our Bishopsgate parish, nobody took an overt interest in our particular beliefs. Smile, pray, and you may think what you like. But for God's sake, don't speak out loud.

"Don't worry. I'll lower my voice," said Kit, dropping his tone and shading his hand to his mouth. Then he laughed, releasing me from my discomfort. "You are a good sister. If I had someone like you to look after me, as Will does, I might not be hanging out in taverns with these swillpots." He raised his ale to the actors imbibing at their tables, and they responded with hoots and offensive bodily noises. "But come, Anne, let's you and I discuss this matter of the Maid of Orléans."

Ah, me. It was never my intent to glance twice at Kit Marlowe. He preferred men, after all. But as Kit himself wrote, "Who ever loved that loved not at first sight?" And with Kit it was so easy to become smitten. He had the dark, liquid eyes of a poet, the brooding face. He had the body of a cat, languid and lithe; the simple motion of raising his mug was an act of sinuous grace. His mind was a pantheon of classical learning; from Socrates to Sophocles, they held concourse in his head. Sometimes he would pause, forgetting all else around him, and purse his lips as if some fascinating inner dialogue had called him away. "Kit? Are you with us?" His friends would poke him and jest, and he would return with a laugh. He was delighted with himself and often with life, but he dared not take anything too seriously lest it be lost or snatched away. For all his popularity, he bluffed at friendships. For all his wit, he could be hurt.

What woman could resist?

"Remember," he said, "Joan of Arc must have a comeuppance. The English will naturally vilify her throughout the play as a witch and a whore, but she herself must ultimately reveal that her courage and prowess at arms come not from God but the devil. Then the French can abandon her in good conscience—poor, deceived dauphin!—and make a coward's truce with the English after she is burned at the stake."

"Yet in the beginning of the play, the French praise her and call her fair. The dauphin prostrates himself before her." I shook my head. The ending Kit urged accorded with the story in Holinshed, but until now I had not questioned it.

"Of course. He has nothing to lose and will take a win by any means. You can write a scene where Joan calls upon the fiends to aid her in the final battle. Picture it: a shadowy, hideous gathering that silently denies her pleas and abandons her to her fate. Have the actors lurk in gauze. Besides, there has to be some unholy power on Joan's side or how else could seasoned warriors have been overcome by a mere girl? Surely you can see the devil in this story, Anne."

He arched an eyebrow at me, but I could find no reply. Was he dangerous or merely elusive? Restless against his will or reckless by design?

"Teach me everything," I blurted, and for an hour more I opened my ear to his spell. When we ended and I thanked him, he shrugged.

"I have given you a few suggestions. Now it is up to Will to write. It would not do for me to assist a rival too much."

"But you have, and tomorrow he will come thank you."

"He shouldn't. I only did it for the pleasure of your company."

I parted my lips to tease back—*You are too kind, sir*—but the flicker in his eye warned me against a flippant reply. "It was good of you to help him," I repeated, my words slowing. "I—we both—thank you."

"As I said, my pleasure." He drained his mug. "Well, Anne, I am off to the Continent soon, so tell your brother to take care of the playwriting business in my absence."

"I shall. We'll do our best."

I rose and backed out of the firelit tavern and into the winter dusk. I felt as if he had read me, and I resented it. It trapped me into trying to read him. Not until much later, not until it was too late, did I understand what he was silently asking. It was the same question he posed to all the world: *Tell me who I seem to be to you. Tell me who I am.*

But I didn't grasp it then, and all the way home I kicked myself for falling for a shallow gallantry. His pleasure, indeed. Even if he did consort with women on occasion, even if he had more than a toying interest in me, the attachment was unwise. He was a dashing boy the same age as Will, and having done without a lover thus far, why should I bother now? Men are deceivers ever. If he was a cat, I was the mouse. Ignore the quiver in your body, Anne. Do not make the same mistake twice.

The play that Will delivered to Mr. Henslowe in January 1592 is perhaps the most multiauthored play in the history of our English stage. Counting the parts we retained of the original, *I Henry VI* was written by no less than George Peele, Thomas Nashe, Christopher Marlowe, Robert Greene, Will, me, Raphael Holinshed and Edward Halle. Plus it was written by Will and me both wittingly and unwittingly imitating Peele, Nashe, Marlowe and Greene. Sometimes a speech would commence like Marlowe and end like Peele. Some nights we slashed whole scenes written by one or the other of our predecessors, only to suffer pangs of recrimination and restore them the next morning—surely they knew better than we did? Even with Kit's blessing, we hadn't the confidence to grab that play by its heart, shake it and say, "I will make you mine!"

We also botched the history, taking episodes in the original script for granted and failing to check Holinshed and Halle. Other inaccuracies jumped in by sheer mistake. We announced the loss of England's French territories, the crowning of the dauphin and the capture of Talbot in quick sequence at the funeral of Henry V, a wonderfully dramatic opening scene—except that Henry V actually died seven years before those events. Next time, we swore, we would be more accurate.

Yet for a first effort and a rush job, *I Henry VI* was not bad. And though Will's name did not appear on the playbill—no author's did— we glowed to see the notice posted on the door of the Rose. On the afternoon of the first performance in early March we were as jittery as new parents hovering over a whimpering babe.

"Is everyone here? Where is the duke's sword? Don't we have a better wig for Princess Margaret? No, no, don't let that cat run across the stage!"

"Calm down, Will, calm down," Dick Burbage soothed, as several of the actors, roles in hand, attempted to memorize the latest changes to their lines.

I was on the stage also. An hour before the play was to begin, Dick, who was playing Talbot, had caught the sleeve of his costume on a protruding nail and ripped it full-length, and I was effecting an emergency repair. It calmed my stomach to have something practical to do. Poor Will, queasy-green, was reduced to wringing his hands. As the audience poured in, I took him to stand in the yard. His eyes flitted toward the exit, and we exchanged a look.

"Do you see anyone with a sack of rotten tomatoes?" he asked in sickly jest.

I Henry VI was a sensation!

Well, maybe not quite. But the audience cheered and booed in all the right places, and it felt like a sensation—what an aphrodisiac is applause to an author's ears!

"I can't believe it, I can't believe it!" Will kept repeating as the crowd exited in a happy babble, and Mr. Henslowe and the actors pounded congratulations on his back. "Hurrah for our new scribbler!" they yelled. I had to drag him to safety, and after many celebratory drinks in the tavern, we wound homeward blissful and exhausted. We did it! We wrote a play! We were still grinning when we sat down on our respective beds, then Will's face grew quiet.

"Thank you for your help, Anne," he said, and in that moment the small room got smaller and the space between us seemed to shrink. I searched his eyes. Was he going to . . . ? Yes. His hand reached for mine, and then it was a narrow bed, chilly sheets and two long-parted bodies finding their way back. Afterward, I laid my head on his shoulder in contentment. Appreciation is not love, but it might be the first paving stone on the return path.

Chapter 12

*B*etween March and June, *I Henry VI* was acted at the Rose more than a dozen times, and for each performance, a beaming Mr. Henslowe told us, the takings were well above average. After five years of false starts, we had turned the lock and the door to the theater had finally swung wide. Thus, the applause for opening night had hardly died when we began to plot parts two and three. But though Will was diligent about his new profession, he was not impassioned about it, not completely, not yet. Once the initial euphoria passed, the astute businessman in his character emerged and weighed his prospects. So long as the muse plumped his purse, he would gladly enlist his brain in her service. But he would not entrust his heart until he was convinced she loved him back.

Our own relations were similarly warm yet wary. To renounce the brother-sister roles we had perfected was impossible. Scandal and incredulity aside, they still served us well. And though our physical relations had resumed, we did not feel like husband and wife. I suppose you could say that for the time being we were intimate friends, waiting to see where else it led. Here was the Will Shakespeare I knew that spring, as he stood tiptoe on the threshold of success.

He was twenty-eight, reasonably good-looking and terrified his hair was already thinning.

Messy with his inkwell, fastidious about all else.

Jaunty, forgivably proud. On occasion I caught him strutting in public, and though it turned a few curious heads, I covered my mouth and stifled both mirth and rebuke. He couldn't help it, and there were days I felt like strutting myself.

Happy—who would not be when your efforts have at last come to fruition and the weight of failure is off your chest?

Gracious toward his fellow actors and playwrights. Still eager to be liked.

Above all, confident.

Do you remember when I first fell in love with him, when he was eighteen and we courted and kissed and tumbled by Shottery Brook? He had been confident then, amusingly, endearingly so. It was one of the things that made him attractive to me. Then our marriage bashed it out of him, and whatever optimism he had recovered on arriving in London had been slowly dimmed by the reality of hard work for little reward. In well-behaved envy he had watched from a cold outer orbit as others cometed across the sky. Now his star had emerged in the heavens. With *I Henry VI*, Will saw who he could be. He had gained— how apt!—*authority*, and he did it without a university education, without connections, without a rich noble patting him on the back. Once he knew that about himself, he was ready to aim at the sun.

So long as I kept faithfully behind him, I had leave to follow in the streak he meant to spread across the sky.

⌒

Parts *II* and *III Henry VI* were two of the easiest and quickest plays Will ever wrote. We had the hang of it now—child's play!—and there were large chunks of the original script left over that we tidied up and put to use. The chronology was more accurate, the level of writing higher. The characters were more fully developed, although there wasn't much that we or the actors could do with poor dethroned Henry, a man so pitiful and spineless you want to shake him till his head lolls. Next time, a worthier subject, please! Nonetheless, we were still practicing, and it showed. Battles stopped for speeches. We took thirty lines to say what might have been better told in three. And the War of the Roses—It's my crown! No, mine! Whack! Give it back! Alarums! They stab each other. They die. What an empty thing to fight for, a metal clamp around your head. What is worth fighting for? Your child, your own life.

But whatever the literary verdict on our trilogy, it was soon a moot point anyway, for *II* and *III Henry VI* had barely premiered when the plague erupted, and by summer the theaters were closed.

"Damn it!" Will slammed the door as he entered with the news. "Just when I am making my mark!"

"How bad is it? Should we leave the city?"

I pushed aside my sewing and rose. A great city is never free of disease, and there had been scattered deaths from plague throughout that spring. But there had been no major outbreak in London since 1563, and, closeted in writing, we had ignored the few fatalities and adopted the general hope that this episode would be fleeting. An official closing of the theaters signaled otherwise, and a lump of panic suddenly lodged in my chest.

"No, I don't think it is that serious yet." For a moment Will paced, his old fear of the plague resurrecting. At any other time, abandoning London might be a wise move. But now?

"Let's wait a bit," he counseled. "The queen remains in town, and no one at the Theatre or the Rose has fallen ill. There is still call for entertainment at court and in private houses. If we leave and next week the closure is revoked, we will have troubled ourselves and lost momentum for naught. As long as we avoid crowds and those districts where houses are contaminated, we should be safe from the infected air. Think how much writing I can accomplish while we are hunkered down here."

"What shall we do next?" I asked.

"I think I'll revisit *Titus Andronicus*. I ought to be able to master him now."

But as July turned into August, the plague persisted and the theaters remained closed. Fairs and markets were shut down as a further precaution; even the hangings at Tyburn failed to draw many spectators. The rich deserted the city for their country estates, and the queen decided it was not too late to make a summer progress and avail herself of their hospitality. The acting companies had already departed on their summer tours, though as usual, to trim expenses, only half the troupe went along. Since they did not require new plays while on the road, there had been no need for Will to accompany them. The remaining actors dispersed to whatever employment they could find, cheering one another with predictions that the plague would wind down when the cooler weather of autumn arrived. Once, I encountered Kit Marlowe as I was passing the tavern. Nothing had come of our previous, slightly amorous exchange, and given Will's and my renewed intimacy, I felt proof against further flirtations.

"What is our golden boy working on now?" Kit teased.

"A revenge play that he started before *Henry VI*."

"Not *Richard III*?"

"No."

"Oh, come, Anne, he must. It is the logical sequel. At the end of the trilogy Will left him gnashing his teeth over Henry's corpse and plotting a bloody path to the throne. Come to think of it, didn't I write that bit?"

"I believe you did," I confessed.

"I thought so. It sounded a little too good for Master Shakespeare yet. But Richard is yours—I bequeath him to you—and what a delicious villain he will make. Crookback, black-hearted, give him fangs and claws." Kit hunched, curled his fingers and twisted his face in a sinister sneer.

"Oh, Kit!" I burst out laughing, and he joined me, resting his hand upon my shoulder. By chance his thumb touched my bare collarbone, and instantly my brain buzzed as if bee-swarmed, my tongue stuck like thick honey and every ounce of blood in my body rushed toward that delirious sting. Ohh!

"Furthermore, I bid Will to follow my excellent lead and refer him specifically to my masterful portrayals of heroic evil in *Tamburlaine* and *The Jew of Malta*. Read, reverence, then best me if you can." Kit swept a bow, and with it went his hand, his touch and my pleasure. At least it released my tongue.

"I'll tell him. *Richard III*. Thank you, Kit," I babbled.

Then he and his smile were gone.

More weak-kneed than I cared to admit, I walked home.

"Richard III?" said Will. "Well, of course I had thought of it."

The next day, we saw freshly marked plague houses near the bookseller's where we went to buy paper. Their doors were sealed—only corpses would emerge—and we reweighed the merits of returning to Stratford. To visit the children was reason enough, but what if we somehow carried the disease to them? And perhaps this episode of plague had already peaked. The weekly death count was holding steady, and most shops and taverns remained open. Having fattened our sock with the three payments for *Henry VI*, we could live awhile on our savings. We comforted ourselves with the odds. Though no one was exempt, the plague struck most ferociously at the poor, the dissolute and the elderly. With a population of two hundred thousand in London from which to pluck victims, Death was unlikely to rap his bony knuckles on our inconspicuous door.

Then in early September, Robert Greene died.

"But not by plague," Will reported. "It was pox and dropsy, sad but not surprising, given his manner of living."

I nodded. Though we hardly knew Greene, his reputation for excess was as famous as his writings. He had squandered his wife's marriage portion on ill living, then deserted the poor woman and their son. He drank, whored and kept criminal company. He wrote about his exploits and his irresponsibility, bragging brazenly, then pretending to repent. But within an hour of collecting on his latest bestseller, he would return to his debauched life. The immediate cause of his death was said to be a dinner in which he overindulged in wine and pickled herring. Deep in poverty, he would have expired in the street had not a kind cobbler and his wife taken him in.

"It is too bad," I said, and Will murmured assent, and we thought no more about it. He had set aside *Titus* for *Richard III*, and I was researching in Holinshed.

⁓

Three weeks later Robert Greene rose from the dead.

"Read this, read it!" Will banged through the door and thrust a pamphlet toward me. "How dare he? I'll show him!"

Startled, I took the tract from his hand. The title page read:

"Greene's Groats-Worth of Wit, bought with a million of Repentance, Describing the follie of youth, the falshoode of make-shift flatterers, the miserie of the negligent, and mischiefes of deceiuing Courtezans. Written before his death and published at his dyeing request."

"Farther, read farther! Toward the end!" Will commanded.

I scanned quickly to reach the part he indicated. The majority of the work appeared to be a long fable or parable of the woes of one Roberto—no doubt another of Greene's insincere self-confessions. There followed ten pious rules by which he exhorted others to live their lives, rules he himself had naturally ignored. But then, in a letter addressed to his fellow playwrights—

"There," Will jabbed, "there."

. . . for there is an upstart Crow, beautified with our feathers, that with his Tygers hart wrapt in a Players hyde, supposes he is as well able to bombast out a blanke verse as the best of you: and beeing an absolute Johannes fac totum, is in his owne conceit the onely Shake-scene in a countrey.

"I don't understand. . . ." My voice trailed, though already my stomach was cramping with dread. *O tiger's heart wrapped in a woman's hide* was how we had described rapacious Queen Margaret in *III Henry VI*. Why was Greene attacking us with our own words, accusing us . . . of what? Conceit? Bombast? Stealing his income, his thunder, his lines? Not true! Like Kit, Nashe and Peele, he had been fairly paid for his part in writing *Henry VI* before it came our way. That was how playwriting worked, jobbed scripts were the norm, and the others had taken no offense at our participation. Kit encouraged us; Nashe saluted the play. Greene hadn't complained at the time. I shook my head in bewilderment. *Shake-scene?* What had we done to deserve this posthumous bile?

"His last printed words," Will raged, "his last chance to win renown, and he uses it to heap disrepute on me! Why?"

"I don't know." Not a helpful answer, but my brain was still grappling. Though we were singled out for condemnation, Greene urged the playwrights never to trust any actors, claiming they were to blame for his misfortunes. They had profited by spouting his words. Now in his misery they had forsaken him. But even when he had appeared in Greene's plays, Will had never been more than a walk-on player. Why pick on us? Over and over the words I went, trying to fathom how we had offended this man so badly that he spent his dying breath to berate us.

"I'll show him!" Will swore. "I can write as well as anyone in London. An upstart crow! Beautified with *his* feathers? I took his dross and turned it into gold! The audience loved my play!"

"You can't show him anything," I said. "The man is dead."

"May he burn in hell!"

He stalked to his desk and grabbed his quill, vowing to pen a reply that would scorch London. I headed to the tavern to see what more I could learn. There I found Greene's pamphlet under hot discussion by the thinned contingent of actors and writers still in town. I confided Will's distress; a good sister always looks after her distraught brother. His colleagues were equally indignant.

"What did we profit from Greene's words?" said one of the actors, turning out his empty pockets. "It is we who made his writing seem good!"

Others said "Groats-Worth" was not Greene's work at all but cleverly penned by his publisher, Henry Chettle, to make one last coin on a dying man's name. This I did not believe; the pamphlet reeked of Greene. In addition to insulting Will, he had, in the guise of friendship, exhorted three unnamed but coyly identified fellow writers to learn from his mistakes and repent of their loose morals and atheism.

"Has Kit seen this?" someone asked.

"If he hasn't, Nashe and Peele will show him," said another.

That did it. I would have liked to have witnessed the scene a few days later when a delegation of prominent playwrights and actors paid a visit to Henry Chettle. The worm squirmed and promised to issue an apology, and the matter appeared to be over.

"Though I still don't understand Greene's anger toward us," I said to Mr. Phipps as I sat sewing beside him in the cozy room he shared with his shy friend, Mr. Edwards. With the theaters closed, the wardrobe master had taken on tailoring for private clients and sometimes had extra work for me.

"It wasn't anger," said Mr. Phipps. "It was fear. Robert Greene thought himself the brightest of literary lights; now here came Will to eclipse him. What Greene saw, as he lay dying, was both death and the shadow of a lesser reputation overtaking him. Poor, petty man. Whatever your fate, do not go to your grave in despair, Anne."

"I won't," I promised. And do you know how some places lift the burden from your shoulders the instant you enter the door? Mr. Phipps's lodging did just that, not only for the congenial company but because he had decorated it with the same love of color and texture he lavished on his costumes: carved chairs with tufted red pillows, gold-tasseled curtains at the window, embroidered velvet footstools to rest your feet before the hearth. Mr. Edwards, a wine merchant, sometimes came home with a bottle of sack, and we three would savor a glass together.

"But it is not the same as sewing costumes, is it, Anne?" Mr. Phipps sighed, holding up the cape he was trimming. "The theater is my life. How much longer, I wonder, until we reopen?"

"I don't know," I replied. Though the crispness of autumn was in the air, the plague had yet to abate, and a few days earlier Will and I had passed a plague physician in the street, an ominous sign. Only the very wealthy would be visited by a physician, and the doctor's long dark robe, hat, gloves and beaked mask stuffed with herbs and cloves made him resemble some huge freakish bird. Will worried that Robert Greene might get his wish after all; if the theaters stayed closed, the fame Will had gained might fade by the time they reopened. A more pressing concern was that the money in our sock would run low.

"Don't you worry." Mr. Phipps patted my hand. "So long as I have orders coming in, I will keep some for you. We artists must stick together. Ah, here comes my heart."

Mr. Edwards poked his head around the door, smiling and waggling a bottle in invitation, but for once I had to decline.

"Will needs me to copy *Richard III* for him. You know his handwriting." I rolled my eyes.

Mr. Phipps laughed and walked me to the door. "Come again soon, and meanwhile, courage. All shall yet go well, Anne."

Chapter 13

"*I*'ll show him."

For the next few weeks that mutter came repeatedly as Will labored on *Richard III*. It should have gone smoothly; hadn't we cracked the hard nut of playwriting? Moreover, Henry Chettle's apology for his part in "Groats-Worth" would soon be published, Greene's attack denounced, Will vindicated. But an apology means little if you are not at peace with yourself, and with Will's fame still new and tender, it is not surprising how hurtful and lingering one negative voice could be. So now that Will had discovered what he was meant to do, he suddenly couldn't do it. Greene's "Groats-Worth" had put a maddening hex on his writing.

First he tried to write in Greene's style, but better.

Then he forsook Greene and attempted to combine the best of the other University Wits.

Then he vowed to ignore everyone and write something splendidly new and unheard-of.

Every page was a disaster.

"I give up," said Will, and I confess to relief at the surrender. He had bristled at my suggestions, and the changes I slipped in while copying were too slight to matter. It is no fun wrestling with a script that brings you no joy and, with the theaters closed, no income either. Will went to the list of potential patrons still tacked to our wall and read off the names. "Taken, left town, taken, miserly, out of favor at court. There aren't many left, and I need a patron fast. Poems of flattery, poems of praise—step up, ladies and gentlemen, get them while they're hot."

He blew out a dispirited breath, and I inhaled it. This was not what we had envisioned a mere eight months ago, when *I Henry VI* debuted to that most glorious of sounds, the applause of a full house. With the gloom of plague and the cold rains of autumn bogging down the town, it felt as if we were floundering in a lumpy gray sea.

And how do you acquire a patron? Ah, that has ever been the quest of poets. How do I find someone who will pay me to do what I love doing but no one will open his purse for? An honest farmer need not ask that question. He has cabbage and carrots and turnips to vend. The haberdasher and saddle maker require no lordly sponsor. They put out their wares and customers flock to buy. But to sell words, ay, there's the rub. Who will pay for a puff of air? It was a subject we had often discussed with the other writers and actors, and everyone had an opinion.

"You must cultivate them like tender seedlings in the ground," said Will Kempe. "Heap verses upon them—think of it as manure."

"But beware of entanglements," warned Dick Burbage. "If you are adopted into an earl's household and his wife takes a fancy to you, you will be in her clutches."

"I hooked Lord Strange by dedicating a poem in his honor," bragged Tom Nashe.

"Some poem!" hooted the others. "It was a lewd account of a fellow's visit to a brothel and his mistress's encounter with a dildo."

Nashe shrugged. "It rhymed, didn't it?"

"I once wrote a sonnet for a lisping earl," mourned Tom Lodge, "and he had the gall to alter my lines. One of these days I am going to give it up and study medicine."

"I know the type, lads," avowed Kempe. "They cannot rest until they have left their mark on everything." He lifted his leg like a pissing dog.

Sometimes the tavern whores chimed in suggestions. "Try Sir So-and-so," they might say. Or, "I heard Lord Thus-and-such paid ten pounds for a single sonnet. Try him." Well, who knows more than a whore about securing a patron and keeping him happy? As to what that says about the status of poets, you may decide.

The upshot was that Will settled on a long poem as the likeliest route to a patron's heart and chose Venus and Adonis from Ovid's *Metamorphoses* for his subject. Leaving him to work, I set out to visit Mr. Phipps, carrying yesterday's nosegay. Its scent was almost gone, but only the foolhardy ventured into the streets without some charm against the plague air, and as I walked I inhaled strenuously the last sweet whispers of rosemary and rue. The wealthier citizens availed themselves of silver pomanders stuffed with aromatic herbs and worn on a necklace or tied to their belt, and everyone skirted those neighborhoods known to contain sealed houses. Once the disease had been identified, the sick and the well would be imprisoned together until the last corpse emerged. Still, as each day turned colder, the death toll dropped, and it appeared the worst was over.

"I have more sewing for you," said Mr. Phipps, welcoming me inside. He poured two mugs of spiced cider, and when we were comfortably settled before the hearth, he spread out a gentleman's black velvet cape lined with scarlet silk. "The client would like the hem embroidered with gold scrollwork. Here is the pattern."

"Chain stitched?" I studied the paper. "Perhaps some braid stitch for contrast and texture?"

"You may embellish at will. Let me bundle it for you to carry home."

"Thank you. Will and I are grateful for the income. But are you sure I do not take work away from you?"

"In this case, sadly, we are both taking work from the dead. A tailor of my acquaintance has died—yes, plague—and several of his customers have come to me." Mr. Phipps sighed. "Isn't it odd how in life we are fashion's devotees, yet a plain shroud suffices when we go to our grave?"

"I am sorry about the tailor," I said. "I promise my stitching will honor his memory. Where is Mr. Edwards today? At his shop?"

"Visiting his cousin by Cripplegate. He will be sorry to have missed you. Look, I have been sketching some costumes we might do when the theaters reopen. Naturally, I am no artist."

He laid before me a paper covered with a half dozen intricate drawings.

"Oh, Mr. Phipps, you should be at court sewing designs like this! The queen herself has nothing so beautiful."

"Tush, you exaggerate." His round face blushed with pleasure. "Besides, court is not where I belong. It is a realm of vicious artifice, and I much prefer our friendly little island of make-believe on the stage. Come, give me your opinion on some colors. Here I thought a yellow silk, and for this cloak, a fox-fur trim."

We spent a delightful hour talking over costumes, and my nosegay smelled the sweeter on the way home.

"So now you have a lover." The voice caught me from the side, and, turning, I saw Kit Marlowe as our paths converged by the tavern. He nodded at my dried-out bouquet.

"No." I gave a small laugh of acknowledgment. "Just a very dear friend."

"A dear friend? I didn't know there was such a thing in London." He beckoned me to the tavern doorway and invited me to look inside. "The same old boring company. You do know they are all bores, don't you? I am the only one worth listening to, and even I have been known to bore myself. Please, Anne, come in and keep me company awhile. Please? The look on your face as you sniffed your flowers . . . I don't know anyone who walks along smiling like that while thinking of me."

We went to a quiet spot, and over ales I showed him the packaged cape and told him about my visit to Mr. Phipps. Funny, I would have bet that dozens of young women would wander the streets blissfully besotted while sniffing a nosegay from Christopher Marlowe. Why had no marriage ever been arranged for him? His proclivity for men made no difference. He was twenty-eight, the same as Will, and had fame and connections. He would be expected to take a wife and beget children. Yet his name was never linked with any lady's, nor had he a particular friend like Mr. Phipps. I supposed he availed himself of prostitutes when he had the urge. Or did he? I knew more rumor than truth about him; perhaps rumor was all there was to know.

"Is your brother still in the dumps?" he asked, as our talk turned to writing. "The last time we spoke, he hinted at some difficulty with *Richard III*."

"Yes. He has set it aside and gone back to poetry in hopes of securing a patron."

"Too bad. They say the theaters will reopen any day, and I was anticipating marvelous things of *Richard*. What is the problem?"

"Well . . ." I hesitated, loath to mention my notion that Robert Greene had cursed us.

"Anne? I can't help you if you won't confide in me."

He tilted his head, teasing, and it struck me that he was lonely and craved conversation. I felt flattered that he thought I could give it to him.

"The problem is that King Richard is such a monster." I reviewed aloud Holinshed's characterization: envious, malicious, wrathful. A man deformed both in body and mind. Proud, deceitful and prone to nervous habits. When he stood musing, wrote Holinshed, he would bite and chew his lower lip and pluck his dagger up and down, up and down in its sheath, never fully drawing it. Too clever and sinister to show his blade until he was ready to stab, and that usually in the back. A man who left bodies in his wake, not least his own brother and the two young princes suffocated to death in the Tower.

"A perfect villain," Kit agreed. "The audience will love it."

"But he is so evil, how could anyone bear his company?"

"They can't, unless they are like-minded, and a gentle writer who takes a villain for his subject is bound to feel poisoned day by day. But in a small dose, in the span of a two-hour play, an audience will swallow an evildoer with righteous glee. There is nothing so satisfying as following the rampages of a monster and soaking vicariously in the blood he has spilled, then abhorring him from a safe distance as he meets a grue-some fate. We all have a vicious streak, Anne, and this is how we in-dulge it, if we are sane."

I paused, conceding the sense of his words. "But should we por-tray evil at all? Why not write only of admirable characters and thereby set an example for our audiences to follow?"

"Because then all your plays would be one-sided, abysmally dull and cheery, and as profitable as sawdust. The trick is to make your twisted king not a cringing villain but a heroic one."

"Like your Jew of Malta, who revels in his evil and brags of it in his opening soliloquy. We've tried that, but it's not working."

"Hmm," said Kit. "Why not? I assume the part will go to Dick Burbage?"

"Yes."

"Well, Dick is an excellent actor, and if you give him the right words, you can trust him to bring the role to life. Darken his features to resem-ble his black thoughts. Use that gesture from Holinshed, the dagger twitching, itching, to leave its sheath. Have Dick unloose that powerful voice of his to make Richard both malignant and fearsome. Anne?"

I stared at him. "You have solved it!"

"Well, of course. I am brilliant." He straightened, pretending to flick dust off his shoulders.

"No, no, I mean . . ." I waved my hands. "I know why we have been stuck."

"Are you going to tell me?"

"No, I have to rush home and tell Will."

"Well, I like that."

I stopped, confounded at my rudeness, my face reddening.

Kit laughed and shooed me toward the door. "Go on, tell him. I know what it is to be in the throes of creative passion."

"Thank you, Kit. You are . . . magnificent!"

"Also exceedingly witty, devilishly handsome and enlightened be-yond my time. But you know, fair Anne, one day I shall expect some-thing in return."

And there he was again, one eyebrow raised, catching me off balance and putting butterflies in my mouth. I smiled and *tsk*ed at him as if he were toying, bade him farewell and hurried home. Will wasn't there, and after several minutes of staring out the window accompanied by impatient foot tapping, I could contain myself no longer. I reached for blank paper.

Winter comes, all is discontent, yet here in our court we bask in glorious summer, thanks to my brother, the son—the sun?—of York. But whilst he capers in a lady's chamber, I am cheated of what is fair, cheated by nature who has made me so lame and unfinished that children scorn me, that dogs bark at me in the street. . . . I am a villain. I shall enact the villain. I am determined to prove a villain. . . .

Do you hear it? Can you feel it coming? I hewed at Richard III like a sculptor on a marble block, carving out the first rough chunks. But this time I concentrated on Dick Burbage speaking the part. Because that was our previous affliction: Still stewing over "Groats-Worth," we had unwittingly blotted Dick from the role and installed the only villain in our blindered vision, Robert Greene. We had tried to make Greene into Richard III and Richard III into Greene in an effort to expel and punish the dead man who had castigated us. We had forgotten one of the cardinal rules of playwriting: Always write with your actors in mind. Kit's comment had jarred Greene out of the role and allowed Dick Burbage, the rightful owner, to step in.

"Will, Will, I have solved it! Kit helped me!" I jumped up as he entered and poured out the explanation before he could get his cloak off. But he had news to top mine.

"Do you remember the bookseller who sold our anonymous sonnets? He may have a patron for me—the Countess of Southampton, no less! She wants to commission a poet to write a series of sonnets that will persuade her son the earl to wed. He is nineteen, devoted to dalliance, and his mother is anxious for him to carry on the family line. I have an appointment to call on her next Wednesday."

"That is wonderful," I replied, assimilating our good fortune. Henry Wriothesley, the young Earl of Southampton, was the darling of London society and had been on our list of prospective benefactors.

But he was already a generous supporter of several prominent writers, and, not wishing to appear as poachers, we had crossed him off as taken. To be picked up by his mother . . . We grabbed each other's shoulders and whooped around the room.

"What about *Richard III*?" I asked, happy and breathless, when we came to a halt. I glanced to my scribblings. "Can we work on that at the same time?"

Will laughed. "Leave it, Anne. Even if the theaters reopen tomorrow, poetry is the higher art. Besides, I can't be beholden to Kit Marlowe for everything."

When Will came home from his interview with the countess, he was practically kicking his heels in the air.

"Hired! I am hired!" he shouted. "I have a commission!"

He began to write immediately, reading his drafts aloud to me as I stitched my assignments from Mr. Phipps. I chimed in when he required assistance, glad to see his muse and his delight in writing both returned. But it dawned on me there was a certain irony—or should that be hypocrisy?—in what he was doing. When Will at age eighteen was forced to marry me, it was a travesty. Now here he was gleefully accepting money and summoning his poetic powers to convince another young man to do the same.

> *From fairest creatures we desire increase,*
> *That thereby beauty's rose might never die . . .*

Not bad poetry, though. A writer's ear is his whetstone, and if your lines ring dull to you, it is quite sure your reader was yawning three couplets ago. Each improvement we made affirmed we were gaining a sharper ear. We did not pause even when, in December, the theaters reopened, though we rejoiced for our actor and playwright friends. The past two years had seen many shifts in the companies. The Queen's Men were barely intact. Lord Strange's Men and the Admiral's Men sometimes quarreled, sometimes collaborated. Other troupes, such as Pembroke's Men and Sussex's Men, played at court, the theaters or in the provinces, as opportunity allowed. What better way to end the year than by having them all performing in London again? It also put Mr. Phipps and me back in the costume business, and one afternoon shortly before Christmas, I set out to visit him.

"I'll bring home sticky buns," I said to Will, who was busy sonneting.

Outside I sidestepped the icy slush in the streets. What I really wanted, I thought, as a cold trickle reached my toes, was a new pair of shoes. We had been so quick to send Will's first payment from the countess to our family in Stratford that we had kept hardly any for ourselves. The next installment, I vowed, should be put to selfish use. And forget the dainty slippers that shod royal toes and never met hard ground. Give me good stout shoes, sturdy brown leather to spurn the mud, rain and snow. Shoes for resolute walking, well laced, thick soled, able to kick off hungry dogs. Honest footwear for honest errands, tromping through the town. On I walked, head bent against the inclement weather, my frost-breathed ode to shoes stirring my blood against the cold. So when I suddenly arrived at the house where Mr. Phipps lodged and brought up my head, I did not at first comprehend.

Sealed . . . ?

God, no!

In the instant it took my raised knuckles to recoil from the door, my heart broke into a thousand pieces.

"Mr. Phipps! Mr. Phipps!" I flung myself forward, fists pounding. "Mr. Phipps! Can you hear me? It's Anne!"

A sobbing woman's voice came muffled from within. "Go away, save yourself!" Then an arm linked mine, and I was hauled back by a passing churchman.

"Do you have a friend or relative inside?" he asked kindly, restraining me as tears wet my shocked eyes. "I'm sorry. The best you can do for them is pray."

He went on, and the few passersby cast me sympathetic glances. For a moment longer I wallowed in disbelief; then I found my voice.

"Mr. Phipps, can you hear me? I am in the street! Shout if you can!" His room was on the second story, and I scanned the shuttered windows for any sign. On the front door of the house was a freshly painted red cross, and beneath it someone had nailed a paper that read, *God have mercy*. I cupped my hands to my mouth and shouted again, "Mr. Phipps!"

"I hear you, Anne! Don't come near!" His voice came through a crack in the shutters. It sounded strong, and for a moment I was reassured.

"Are you sick? Who is inside? What can I do?"

"There are seven of us, two ill. Mr. Edwards is one of them, and I am tending him."

"I will find a doctor for you." I shot a glance right and left, as if a plague physician in his outlandish costume might appear any moment and I could apprehend him.

"No, Anne," cried the boarded window, a strange sound, as if the house were speaking. "Go away from here and pray!"

I shook my head in short, vigorous jerks. I was carrying a package— a quilted doublet, a leftover project from the dead tailor—and the feel of it in my hands gave me direction. Mr. Phipps had said the client was an Italian glassmaker on Hart Street, and hurrying there I found the place with only a few inquiries. I was Mr. Phipps's assistant, I explained, opening the package, and he had asked me to make the delivery and request payment. Pleased with my work, the glassmaker complied. At a nearby apothecary shop, I obtained the address of a plague physician, and arriving out of breath, I was shown into a study filled with books and bottles. On a wall hook hung a long, gawky object that resembled a dead stork—the mask and robe of the plague physician. The man, tall and liver marked on his hands, looked down his long nose at my sum.

"It is not nearly enough." He sniffed, poking at the coins with an offended finger. "Do you imagine I would endanger my life for such small recompense?"

"You must! Besides, it is others in the house who are ill, not my friend."

"If he is not ill, he does not need me."

"But his friend is ill! And he is taking care of him!"

"The sum is insufficient, and your friends, however many of them there may be, are people of no worth. My services are reserved for those deserving the talents of a physician."

"But they are dying!"

"Then I cannot help them. No one can."

"Tell me what to do," I said, hating him and his stupid costume and my inarticulateness. "Tell me and I will go in."

"That is forbidden, as I am sure you know. If you have any sense, you will go pray and stop wasting my time."

I stumbled home and into Will's arms, crying my story. He gave a helpless shrug.

"I am sorry, Anne, but there is nothing you can do. And look at you—you are chapped red in the face, and your fingers are icicles. I bet your feet are soaking." He knelt and took off my shoes and wet woolen socks. At times he could be infinitely kind. "Get to bed or you will be sick too, and how will that help anyone?"

I cried to myself most of the night, and at daylight I went to Mr. Phipps again. Once a house was sealed, an investigator would come daily to tally the dead for the Bills of Mortality and send for the corpse wagon. Often the investigator was an old, indigent woman—if she caught plague and died in her duty, who would miss her? Such a one soon arrived at Mr. Phipps's house, and I hailed her before she could enter. She was bent and whiskered, and thin strands of white hair escaped the shawl over her head. She recited a list of curative herbs I could procure for her to take in. Bay for headache, balm and wormwood for stomach pains, licorice and comfrey for the lungs. If I brought food, that too she would deliver. But no one could come out alive except by the grace of God.

I purchased the medicines, meat, good white bread. I prayed at St. Paul's, at our parish church in Bishopsgate, kneeling by my bed. Do you hear me, God? Save him! If you can spare only one person in all England, let it be my dear friend. I will embroider an altar cloth in pure gold thread, I promise. I will come once a week and polish the candlesticks until they gleam. A tenth of all I earn forever shall go into the alms box. Please!

The next day, a girl in the house died, a pretty thing, as I saw when they brought out her covered corpse, or at least she had been. For a frightful moment the cloth slipped, revealing long blond hair sweaty and disheveled from delirium and a face ravaged by black boils and contorted in pain.

"Mr. Phipps!" I shouted at the window. "Are you there? How is Mr. Edwards?"

"He is worse, Anne! The swellings in his body are horrible to bear, and he vomits everything I feed him." So the shuttered house called back, like a man with no eyes.

I paced till the old woman came out.

"Two more sick." She sighed. "Pray God they die quickly and are spared great suffering."

The next day, three bodies emerged, though not yet Mr. Edwards.

"He fights, Anne!" cried the window. "Pray God he survives the night and perhaps the corner will be turned."

But the old woman shook her head. "Two to four days is the most anyone lasts. Go home, dearie."

"Yet you survive. And you have tended other plague houses before this?"

"Yes." She looked heavenward, her pouched eyes seeking explanation. "I was a sinner in my youth. Why spare me?"

On the fourth day, Mr. Edwards's body came out, clumsily wrapped in a sheet, one unshod foot protruding. The house sobbed, an incoherent bawling, and below the window I wept in tune for a dirge.

"You cannot keep going there," Will said that night, and now his voice grew peeved and his kindness was gone. "You risk bringing the disease home."

"How? How? I'm fine. I am strong."

"You are thin to the bone. You don't eat and you stand in the cold keeping vigil till your teeth chatter and cramp grips your legs."

"I have no stomach for food. Could you pray too, Will? Please? There are only two left, Mr. Phipps and a boy."

"Of course I will." He patted my shoulder; then we both bent our heads and he added his voice to mine.

The next morning the house did not answer my calls. "Both have the swellings," said the old woman. "It won't be long. I'll let the sexton know the bodies are coming."

I huddled in an opposite doorway. My eyes were prickly from crying, and no more tears would come. My toes had grown so numb in my leaking shoes they felt like cold peas rattling loose in my socks. All that day the house held itself as if groaning, and among the usual odors of dung and garbage in the street crawled a smell like a breath from a tomb. It was almost dusk and I was half-frozen when Will appeared and quietly fetched me home.

The next morning, the wooden cart was at the door.

I followed the two sheeted bodies to the churchyard. Each time the wheels bounced, the boy's small shape bumped and resettled, bumped and resettled, as if struggling to come alive. Mr. Phipps lay stiffly still. In the churchyard, part of the snowy ground had been reserved for plague victims, and the recent toll had kept the gnarled gravedigger busy and the earth upturned. He kicked a few stray bones out of the way.

"Get out! You've had your turn!" he yelled at the splintered remains. "Make room for the next one!"

He chortled, clearly gone in the head, and the priest, arriving, chided him sternly. In my own brain there arose a weird scene as I wondered how long it took a body to become a skeleton, a bone to become a curiosity, a life to be forgotten. Then the wrapped forms were lowered, Mr. Phipps and the boy together, and the priest beseeched God's mercy. To his credit, he did not turn away as the gravedigger lifted his shovel and flung the first heap of earth into the pit, and as it thumped and splattered on the corpses, he was thus able to catch me when I fell.

⁓

"Money, Anne! Money." Will danced into our room and plunked a purse on my table. "The countess and her son love my sonnets!"

He did another jig, and I smiled. A month had passed since Mr. Phipps's death, and I was trying to smile more often, for I knew it did no good to continue in melancholy. Once or twice I even thought I heard Mr. Phipps's voice in my ear. *Come, Anne. Don't sorrow. Sew something beautiful to remember me by.*

"That's fine," I said, and then I did gasp as Will spilled gold coins onto my table. I put down my sewing and picked one up, and it gleamed in the pale winter light.

"There is more where that came from. Guess what? I am invited to join the earl at Southampton House in the Strand. I have arrived!"

He danced again, one hand on his hip, the other snapping his fingers above his head.

"You are joining the Earl of Southampton's household?"

"Yes. I am under his wing now, and I may write what I like when I like." Will flopped onto the bed, folded his hands behind his head and crossed his legs in delight.

"You mean . . . you're leaving?"

Instantly, he sat up again, making reassuring motions. Always quick to catch on, our Will.

"No, no, not exactly. We'll still keep this place, and I will visit when I can. Look at all the room you will have." He gestured from my table to his and spread out my thread, scissors and cloth in helpful demonstration. Since Mr. Phipps's death, I had taken on his clients, and the work kept my fingers busy even when it failed to engage my mournful mind. "Or you can return to Stratford," Will continued. "No more separation, no more worrying about the children."

I watched him with a kind of dumb understanding.

"The children, you can go see the children," he repeated when I did not reply. He beamed as if he were granting my dearest wish.

"You're leaving."

"Yes," he said. "I am."

The first time he abandoned me, when he ran off to London with the Queen's Men, Will had contended it was for the good of the whole family. It would make our fortune, he said, and I had defended him to his parents despite my own heartache and misgivings. He needed no such argument now. He had been offered a glittering opportunity, and none but a fool would turn it down. He had snagged one of the richest, most influential patrons in England. But to be deserted a second time, to be discarded after all I had done for him, to be tossed aside when we were back in bed together, when I had hoped . . .

I would have stayed poor forever rather than walk away from him.

"What about us?" I said, but Will was already hunting under his bed for a satchel in which to pack his clothes.

"This won't do, it's gone threadbare. This color is out of fashion." He set one pile of garments to the left, the other to the right, folding, stacking, arranging.

What about us?

"I seem to have misplaced a sock. Where can it have gone?"

What about me, Will? Your sister, wife, damn it, I don't care which one.

"I can get a ruff now. I mean a really good, starched ruff, not this inferior thing." He pulled it off and tossed it aside. "Can you believe I ever wore this?" He laughed at the wine-colored doublet he had donned that day he took *I Henry VI* to the tavern to show his hoped-for colleagues, the doublet I had sewn for him.

"Will?" I kept the tremble from my voice. I made it an ordinary question. "What about me?"

He scooped up the coins and pressed them into my hand.

"You take it," he said happily. "There will be more where that came from."

Then he was gone, trailing socks from his satchel, and I sat in the room alone.

Chapter 14

You lie, Anne. No one could be that unfeeling. Did he really walk out, grin faced and spilling socks from his satchel, blithe to your wound? Be truthful—didn't he utter at least one salving line?

Of course I'll miss you.

No, damn him, he didn't, or if he did, what difference would it have made? He had to go—it was the chance of a lifetime—and there was no place in the Earl of Southampton's household for a sister or a wife. It was a constant bachelor party, all the rich, happy-go-lucky boys of the kingdom hanging out in the country and amusing themselves with books and archery, gambling and sports, going to plays and chasing the girls. The young earl was a pretty creature of nineteen, long dark ringlets caressing his blushing cheeks. He inclined to lipstick, earrings and other feminine accessories, but when you have a deep and titled pocketbook no one scruples about these things. Back in Stratford, we would have laughed ourselves silly at a countryman in makeup; before a rouged earl, people bow and waggle sugarcoated tongues. Exquisite, my lord! You will make carrying a lady's fan all the rage!

What hurt most is that the time Will and I had spent together lately, writing sonnets and our first plays, had reawakened for me those early months of our marriage when we passed our evenings in cozy study by his parents' fireside. We had been still in love then, a most perishable fruit, yet I thought a hardier orchard had grown from its dropped seeds: trust, companionship, respect. Didn't we have that, Will? Weren't we friends? Given your mediocrity as an actor, I can hardly believe you were dissembling. Yet there I sat alone, the countess's coins in my palm, as his footsteps skipped down the stairs.

I am afraid I reacted badly. I did what many a scorned woman—or man—has done. I said to myself, I'll show him.

⁓

"Here comes Anne!" Kit cried when I entered the tavern. "Now heaven walks on earth!" He rose and bowed, signaling the tavern keeper for an extra mug. "Where have you been? How goes *Richard III*?"

"Languishing on the shelf . . . and me too." I took the seat beside him and told him of Mr. Phipps's death and Will's new patron.

"My condolences about your friend," he said, tipping his head in acknowledgment. "As for the earl, I'd heard. Congratulations. I am formidably jealous."

"You are?"

"Why not? Shouldn't I have the best of everything?"

"Only if you deserve it." Not a particularly witty repartee, but I stuck with it. "What are you writing now?"

"I am diddling with a translation of Ovid and feeling deserted by my muse. You realize that if Will trots off on Southampton's leash and drops my favorite crookback like yesterday's bone, I will have no choice but to sink my teeth into him."

"No, he'll do *Richard III*," I protested, though I was not at all sure of Will's future literary intentions. Nonetheless, I felt a proprietary interest in continuing our War of the Roses saga and writing Richard onto and off of his ill-gotten throne. Thus is a writer a kingmaker, like Warwick! My face must have gleamed, for Kit gave a knowing chuckle. And at that, I let down my last defenses. I was lonely, and I wanted comfort and talk. I wanted him.

"Tell me about Ovid," I said.

So we conversed and drank an ale, and then we went to my room. It was as if the appointment had been made long ago, and we were simply showing up at the agreed time. From that frosty January afternoon we first made love to its cruel ending in May was a mere five months' affair. Five of the happiest months of my life. Ah, Kit, Kit, my beautiful cat. Let me tell you about making love with Christopher Marlowe.

He kissed, he always kissed first, behind my ear and down my throat, into the hollow of my collarbone, like a key searching for its lock. Then he would look up, eyes twinkling, as if to say, Do you like it? Shall I continue? Yes, yes! and I stood in an agony of anticipation as he teased loose the laces of my dress. "Hurry, I am cold!" I would bleat as the winter air brought goose shivers to my skin and one by one my garments dropped to the floor, though I would have stood naked in the frozen wastes of Iceland for the pleasure of that disrobing. Sometimes I did not wait. I pounced on him and he pounced back, and with a tiger's passion we stripped each other, our mouths so hot and deep it seemed we would suck out our souls. Then into bed! Pile on the covers! One frigid night we fornicated under a mound of blankets and wrapped in his fur-lined cloak. We steamed the room to the rafters. Those who say Kit loved not women tell but half the story, for how else but with practice could he have gained such skill? He melted my bones, and God, what delight that man could inflict with his tongue!

"Want me to do it again?" he would ask, eyes aglow. "Please, Anne, let me."

"I'll die!" I would groan. "I will die of ecstasy, Kit. Let me catch my breath . . . no, no . . ." But already he had begun, fluttering kisses down my face, between my breasts, a detour to the soft skin inside my elbow—he was going to spare me—but no, back to my rib cage, into my navel, lower . . .

"Kit, Kit, mercy!"

He claimed he learned it from a whore on the Continent, and he taught me how to return the favor. "It was the Crusaders who brought it home from the brothels of the Holy Land," he said. "Just think. Two hundred years of trying to recapture Jerusalem and the best thing to come out of it is a devilish new enticement to sin."

"Well," I said, "I am sure I never read about this in Holinshed."

When we were spent, he would lie atop me gasping, and I loved that crushed weight of his body on mine, that last furnace of heat between our skin. Then he would roll to one side, I would shift up to his chest, and we would talk lovers' talk, lazy and meandering. I felt not a single qualm of conscience. Were you there, Will? No? Then it is none of your business. Yet I had no illusions. Whatever his passion for me, Kit came and went of his own accord, keeping separate lodgings, slipping off in the company of dubious characters. But I was the last person to love him, and I can tell you things about Kit Marlowe that no other woman will ever record.

His second toes were longer than the big toes next to them. If you tickled him on the pad of his foot right under those toes he would nearly weep for giggling.

He had a small scar on his right buttock. When he was a student at Cambridge, he and his friends had once stayed up half the night drinking and daring to debate atheism. They all passed out or fell asleep, with Kit on the floor close to the fireplace. Sometime during the night he rolled onto a cinder. It smoked a hole through his best breeches and singed his flesh before he came awake yelping. His friends twitted him about "ashes to asses" for weeks thereafter.

He had nightmares, which he assured me were nothing.

In spring, when the days lengthened and warmed, he changed our lovemaking by dipping my quill in the ink bottle and writing on my body: *Kiss me here* or *Anne is mine*. But the way he would do it was this: He would mark an A on my left shoulder, an N inside my right thigh, a second N on my nipple, the E behind my knee. I must close my eyes and lie naked while he hid the letters, and to increase the mischief, he might write them out of order. Then I must lie still while he kissed out the message, knowing which places he had marked, not knowing in what order the kisses would come, dying of anticipation, here, here, kiss me!

"Write a great poem upon me!" I begged, as he straddled my hips on his knees. "Write something as wonderful as 'The Passionate Shepherd to His Love.'"

His smile curved. "Anne, Anne," he said, stroking down his nakedness and up my belly to my breasts. "Don't you understand? This *is* poetry." Then he locked his mouth and body into mine, and we rocked and surged and gave up our souls, a glistening couplet, a panting rhyme.

It was never that good with you, Will. Never.

In between lovemaking, Kit and I wrote *Richard III*.

"Not bad for a first draft," he said when I showed him the beginnings of my script.

"Do you think so? Really?"

"I never lie, except when it will get me something I want, and as I already have what I want"—he touched my cheek—"you may rest assured I am truthful. Here, though, the character is uneven, and Richard sounds merely cantankerous. May I suggest . . . ?"

I handed him the quill and leaned over his shoulder.

"Now in this scene, his speech runs long. I would cut the last ten lines. They only repeat what has been said above without improving on it."

I nodded.

"This bit is excellent, here, when he jokes to himself even as he plots his brother's murder. 'Simple, plain Clarence! I do love thee so that I will shortly send thy soul to heaven. . . .' What a dry sense of humor has our villain. Good work, Will!"

"I wrote that. I wrote all of it."

"Oh, did you?" Kit winked. "Then you have a budding talent, and it is my duty to make you flower."

So for the second time in my life I found myself a most lucky student. Will had done his part by teaching me to read and write and had stretched my mind with his love of classical learning. He had introduced me to the theater and countenanced my collaboration as we launched his playwriting career. Kit intensified my education. He could talk for hours on how a play must be shaped, a story arced, characters animated, tension created. He schooled me in blank verse, at which he was the acknowledged master. From Kit I learned to stoke a roaring fire, thrust our iron English into the burning coals, and hammer a blade so straight and true it would balance on a finger and pierce the most obdurate heart. Armed with such a weapon, a worthy character will make it sing.

"Take Richard's opening speech," he might say. " 'It is winter and into our discontent shines the bright sun of York.' Yes, that's the idea, but the sentence is flat, ordinary. You can do better, Anne."

"Shines the 'glorious' sun of York?"

"Keep going."

" 'Winter discontents us and we long to see the glorious sun of York.' "

"Keep going."

" 'Our discontented winter turns to summer when we see the magnificent sun of York.' "

"Stick with 'glorious.' Almost there."

"Agghhh! Kit!"

"You can do it."

"Can you? Are you sitting on the answer like a hen on an egg? Hatch it!"

"It is your egg. I am merely keeping it warm for you."

"You are exasperating!"

"Keep going."

Sometimes I would jump up from the table and attack him with frustrated kisses, and he would be dissuaded from tutoring as we tumbled into bed. Then out of nowhere it would burst upon me.

" 'Now is the winter of our discontent made glorious summer by this sun of York.' That's it, Kit! Let me up! I have to write it down."

"Now? God's blood, I have created a writer, a monster! Anne, look at me! Is this any time to leave a man *standing*?"

Another time we disputed over the minor but troublesome character of Lady Anne. She was the widow of Prince Edward and daughter-in-law to Henry VI, both dead by Richard's hand. Then she turned around and married him.

"How could she? It is not believable, Kit. There is no way we can make it sound convincing."

"Yet she did marry him." He drummed his fingers on my desk, as if he could rap out a solution. "We could write her off as just a pawn. Or try this: Have Richard fix the blame on her. She is so beautiful and virtuous that he murdered her menfolk so he could claim her for himself. She is the one who should feel guilty for inspiring him to these black deeds. Now her love will redeem him, and he will repent and become an honorable man."

"That's preposterous."

"Is it? Or is it the ultimate flattery? And women are forgiving by nature."

"I would never forgive a man who so wronged me."

"All the more reason you should attempt to write it. If you can persuade yourself to believe her capitulation, your audience will go along."

I did my best but still had to overload the scene with puns and cleverness to conceal its weak premise. Short of rewriting history, it was the best we could concoct for gullible Lady Anne. And as our play lengthened, Kit and I likewise fell under Richard's spell. Though the theaters had reclosed in February—the toll of plague deaths once more rising—we were engrossed by our fascinating, loathsome creature. I had not felt that way about any character in *Henry VI*, and I took it as another valuable lesson. When a strong character emerges, give him his head and half your work is done.

But time was running out for Kit and me, though I did not know it. I remember only that he began to seem jumpy, and once or twice his nightmares shot him awake in terror. He would gasp and press his chest, then spin a nonchalant tale to divert my concern.

"It's nothing," he would say. "Did I ever tell you about my first duel?"

"What duel?"

"With William Bradley."

"Who is he?"

"No one important."

"Then why would you duel with him?"

"Actually, I didn't. It never got that far. But I almost did." Then he related a story of how four years ago an argument with this fellow Bradley in Hog Lane had ended when Kit's friend Thomas Watson intervened and killed the man. Kit and Watson were held in Newgate Prison until they got off on self-defense.

"That is horrible!" I said. "Why do you relish such things?"

"I don't relish them, Anne. They just happen to me somehow." His tone was curiously pleased, as if he had reassured himself that some number of his nine lives still remained. His other narrow escapes had included two more arrests for street fighting and being deported from the Netherlands the previous year for counterfeiting gold coins. When I reminded him of his record, he shrugged uncomfortably.

"I have not always chosen the best company," he conceded, wistfully stroking my arm. "Not until now."

"Well, don't do any of it again," I scolded, and he pushed up a contrite lip.

"Kiss me, and I promise I will never, ever cause trouble."

Ah, if only it were that simple. But how do you rechart a reckless life, evade your own reputation? Or are you so bedazzled by your exploits that you are blind to the dangers? Is it like staring into the sun? Kit was brilliant, dashing and possessed of the supreme confidence that early success brings. Since whatever he undertook was bound to end in triumph, he rarely hesitated to charge in. Even the spying he had done for queen and country was a laugh, a lark, a game. He thought he could walk away, saying, "I do not wish to do this anymore," and those grim masters would reply, "Why, that's fine, Kit. Godspeed, we wish you well." You cannot expect, once you have diced with such company, to leave the table debt-free. The next roll will bring you back in, and remember, the cubes have been shaved.

Maybe he thought I could save him. Maybe he thought I could

make him be good. Why else pick me as his companion? Later, I asked myself that often, for I do believe Kit sensed trouble coming. Why turn to a woman, if he preferred men? A different kind of company? As evidence to the contrary should the sin of sodomy become too affixed to his name? Above all, why me? To ingratiate himself with Will and join in Southampton's patronage? Kit didn't need Will Shakespeare or his sister for that; he still had the greater entrée and fame. Perhaps because I was mature, comforting? He didn't know I was older, but he may have been drawn to some quality he could not name. Or was it because he truly loved me and found me superior to every other woman? I long to believe it, but even when we lay together in sated repose, I understood he was never quite mine.

One evening in early May we were working on Richard's final scenes, the fateful battle of Bosworth Field. Back and forth, back and forth, we simply could not pin down the lines. According to Holinshed, on the eve of the battle, images of terrible devils haunted Richard's dreams. Kit urged that we turn it into a parade of phantasms of his victims.

"It will give the audience a satisfying summary of the bodies our villain has strewn behind him," he said. "They'll jolt him awake with a taste of well-deserved terror and foreboding. But as for Richard's last words, I am stumped. Shall we quit for the night? It's late and maybe it will dawn on us in the morning." He went to the bed and took off his boots.

"No, not until I get this." I stood and paced, working out my stiff knuckles, spreading ink up my fingers and muttering. Richard is desperate, his foes are closing, a lifetime of evil is overtaking him. Does he cringe and whine? Does he confess the error of his ways and seek salvation? Does he flee to fight another day? Not him. Though his mount has been slain beneath him and he fights on foot, they will never take him alive.

" 'Advance our forces and I will strike to the last drop of my blood! Horse me, and kinglike I die fighting! Vouchsafe me a steed to end this bloody day! All my wealth for a stallion! A horse! A horse! My kingdom for a horse!' "

I whirled, sword thrust high, and jumped to see Kit reclined on the bed, his dark eyes brooding on me.

"That's it," he said softly. "You have it, Anne." Then he lay down on the pillow, and to the ceiling he said, "I can see that between you and Will, the theater will be in good hands."

⁓

For what came next, I blame Francis Walsingham, though Elizabeth's late spymaster was by then three years in his sanctimonious Puritan grave. In life, his mission had been twofold: to advance the Protestant faith and to protect our queen from papist plotters. It was his tenacity in unraveling plots, torturing suspects and utilizing his network of spies throughout the Continent that kept Elizabeth safe all those years while so many aimed at her demise. He had unveiled the Babington Conspiracy that brought Mary, Queen of Scots, to her beheading. You could say that Francis Walsingham, more than anyone else, determined the future course of English history, for without him, Elizabeth might have fallen to an assassin, and who knows what the fate of our nascent empire would have been then? If only Kit had withstood his enticements to join the queen's secret service. But no. Like Faustus, Kit had sold his soul to the devil, and payment was coming due.

On an afternoon in late May, he barged into my room.

"I may be an atheist, Anne."

"You silly boy." I wiped my quill, having just completed a neat copy of *Richard III*. "Don't trouble God and He won't—"

"No, Anne, listen." His face had the pallor of a man who once joked but is no longer laughing. "It's Tom Kyd. He and a half dozen other writers were rounded up by the authorities for questioning about some religious libels that have been circulating. Tom declared that a paper found in his room, a paper that denies the divinity of Christ, is really mine and got mixed in his belongings. Well, we did once share a room, but that was two years ago. I haven't seen him in ages. I have been with you, or away on business."

"But, but . . ." I didn't know which question to ask first. What paper? Who found it? Kit spoke again before I could.

"They tortured him," he said, ashen.

I jumped up and shook him. "Why? What do you mean?"

"Well, you see, they snatched old Kyd and . . ." The story was disjointed, missing facts and motives, tangled with evasions. Afterward, I spent heartbroken weeks trying to reconstruct those murky events. But all I got from Kit was that Thomas Kyd had been arrested, his room searched, an incriminating document found, Kit implicated. "A warrant for my arrest has been issued. If I am taken . . ." He shuddered.

"You must flee, now, tonight!" I grabbed his arm. "Go to your friends in the country or go abroad. You have connections. Go wherever you will be safe until it blows over." For a moment, my outlook cleared. None of these allegations were new. Kit was always being accused of atheism, blasphemy, sodomy, usually because of silly statements he had tossed off among friends, supposed friends, while all were in their cups. No matter how dire the charge, he always landed on his feet, purring. But torture—

"Go, go." I shoved him out the door, and, suddenly coming to life, he grabbed me and kissed me hard on the mouth.

Then he was gone.

I sat down, ordering myself to keep calm. Surely it was another false alarm. Despite his blood-drenched plays, Tom Kyd was a harmless sort. Why would anyone want to hurt him? And Kit had promised me he would stay out of trouble. I could vouch for his good behavior, at least for the time we had spent together. A gasp jumped from my throat. Oh, my God. They would come here to question me and I would be arrested! They would take me to the Tower and—

Tears of terror sprang to my eyes. Should I run away? Try to hide somewhere outside London? Rush to Will and implore him to shelter me with the Earl of Southampton? Who knew of the link between Kit and me? Everyone. Well, no one. With the plague now claiming a thousand bodies a week, the city was again emptying. A few writers and actors from the tavern probably suspected Kit and I were more than friendly, but who cared? I was unimportant, just Will Shakespeare's sister who used to sew their costumes. So I was safe—unless Kit was captured and tortured and gave them my name to stand as witness for him. I would do it—God give me courage!—though who would not quail at the prospect? Hot irons, mutilations. For the next week I lived in agony, diverting my mind with pointless sewing and keeping to my room. Once I skirted the tavern and risked a quick glance inside. He wasn't there, and I dared not ask, "Has anyone heard from Kit Marlowe? Is he still in town?"

No one came for me. No sinister agents in the dark of night. No cloaked men. I began to believe the whole episode was indeed a silly mistake and my sleek cat would return, licking his whiskers as if he had been off lapping cream. Then Will showed up from the earl's house in the Strand and spilled the news.

"Kit Marlowe is dead! Stabbed in a tavern fight in Deptford."

His face was puckered like a child's in disbelief, and I crumpled onto the bed, sobbing.

What happened? No one ever knew for sure. After leaving me, Kit had apparently appeared before the Privy Council and given a satisfactory explanation, for they released him pending further investigation. But instead of returning to me—oh, why not, Kit?—he went to the house of one Eleanor Bull in Deptford, five miles from London, where he was fatally stabbed above the right eye by a man named Ingram Frizer. Two other men were present, Nicholas Skeres and Robert Poley, all three said to be unsavory characters, though I had never heard Kit mention them or the Bull woman. Some said her house was also a tavern, and the incident began as an argument over who should pay the bill. The dagger was Frizer's, but he, Skeres and Poley swore it was Kit who had wrenched it out of Frizer's sheath and tried to stab Frizer in the head. Then Frizer wrested back the blade and . . . Oh, what does it matter? Kit was dead, dead.

Grappling with his own grief, Will never questioned mine. His hero, gone. A few days later, we caught a whisper that it was no simple tavern brawl but a planned murder linked to Kit's involvement with Walsingham. Had he been recruited to some fresh espionage or was it a leftover grudge from an intrigue long past? Ingram Frizer pleaded self-defense, and after a coroner's inquest, the queen herself pardoned him. That should tell you everything you need to know. Two days after the murder, Kit was hastily buried in Deptford in an unmarked grave. Oh, I cannot bear to think of it, that beautiful body sucked into the clammy spring mud.

"Maybe you should return to Stratford, Anne," Will counseled. Several more days had passed, and while he was back to normal, I only grew more morose. "Kit was rash and imprudent, but when London is not safe even for a poet, for you to continue here alone . . ." He glanced around the room, shaking his head. "I don't understand why, with the plague raging, you have lingered this long."

"I was writing *Richard III*. I saw Kit once or twice, and he gave me some suggestions on it." I paused, struggling to gather my thoughts. "Are you going back to the earl?"

"Yes. I finished the sonnets his mother commissioned encouraging him to wed. He laughed them off." Will chuckled at the private joke. "Now I have dedicated my long poem *Venus and Adonis* to him and await the public acclaim. It has already brought me more income." Grinning, he jingled his purse.

"Will, don't you care that Kit is dead?"

"Of course I do." He looked affronted, then softened, as if giving his conscience a moment to center its needle. "Kit's death is a tremendous loss, but so long as his poetry is read and his plays performed, we will have his reputation to admire. That's what he would want. We won't forget him, Anne."

I said no more. No doubt the sentiment was genuine, and it was only my grief that tinged it with self-serving. Will was ever generous in praise of Kit's writing. But did you think, Will, even for an instant did it flash across your mind that with Kit's untimely exit, the stage was clear for the understudy to emerge from the wings? A pathetic metaphor if ever there was one, but I had lost my zest for fancy phrasing. And had Kit somehow foreseen this very outcome? Suspecting his days were numbered and seeing Will ensconced with Southampton, is that why he picked me and tutored me and shielded me from his clandestine undertakings? To pass on as much as he could before he was gone?

I can see that between you and Will, the theater will be in good hands.

In the end, it is one of literature's great unanswered questions: Had Kit lived, had he survived to the same age as Will, who would have worn the crown? Kit got to his fame faster. He blazed the way, and it was his successful use of blank verse that made everyone else rush to follow. Where Will was as much businessman as poet, Kit loved writing above all else. It brought together his huge talents in one concentrated form, his energy, education, passion, brooding and introspection. Kit hadn't mastered it all yet, though it seemed to me at the time as if he had. But like us, he was still learning, and it cleaves my heart to think what he might have accomplished, the plays and poetry unborn. . . .

Kit or Will? I don't know. But my writing career was over.

"All right," I said to Will. "I'll go back to Stratford."

Chapter 15

June 1593 was a beautiful month, and I felt dead as a stone. As I prepared for my journey to Stratford, I half looked for Kit's ghost. If his death was no accident but murder, wouldn't his unquiet spirit beseech someone living to avenge him? But I saw no Kit, not in a misty apparition or in my nighttime dreams. He was scarcely missed by anyone else, it seemed, and the world went on.

Will helped me pack my belongings, catching me up on the news in higher circles. "You won't believe what the earl did," he said, laughing. "Made all his friends take a vow never to wed! I am writing a comedy about it for our private performances."

Really, Will? Well, jolly good. A comedy—how could he have a comedy in his heart when Kit was dead? Did nothing touch him, ever? Would anything ever touch me again?

"Also, I have teamed up with George Peele to revive *Titus Andronicus*, and we have sworn to make it the revenge play to top anything ever written. The subtitle should probably read, *Gore Galore!* You will probably be just as glad not to do the copying for this one."

I shrugged.

"Of course, I am still tossing off sonnets for the earl, to keep my hand in. But what I really want to do is follow up the success of *Venus and Adonis* with another long poem. That is my forte, you know, poetry."

No, Will, your forte is looking out for yourself. Your forte is justifying and rationalizing why everything you do is right and true. Go bugger yourself, Will. I've had enough of you.

Ah, but once again, I was not being fair. Within six months I had lost both Kit and dear Mr. Phipps, and in my suffering, the joy of others seemed cruelly exaggerated. Yet why shouldn't Will be happy? Resident poet for the Earl of Southampton. *Venus and Adonis* a smash at the bookstalls. He had followed Tom Nashe's advice to make it erotic. Listen:

> *I'll be a park, and thou shalt be my deer.*
> *Feed where thou wilt, on mountain or in dale*
> *Graze on my lips, and if those hills be dry,*
> *Stray lower, where the pleasant fountains lie.*

Oh! It is enough to make a nun flush to the cheekbones! You might think it odd that the man who penned such verse never guessed about Kit and me, but throughout his life the poet of love rarely heeded any romances but his own. He assumed my prolonged grief for Kit was the softheartedness of any woman, and not wishing to undeceive him, I concealed the greater part of my emotion and tried to regain some semblance of cheer. In that spirit, I invited Will to accompany me to Stratford.

"You could see the children too," I suggested.

But he couldn't tear himself away from the earl. "He cannot live without me," Will said, spreading his hands, the smiling prisoner of his own good fortune. I had to agree that when your goose is laying golden eggs, it is unwise to stroll away and risk other hands scooping from the nest.

On the day of my departure, Will walked me to St. Paul's to meet the pack service for Oxford. We had not discussed how long I would be away or whether I would return. I myself was too benumbed to know. As he helped me into a wagon, Will leaned in and gave me a peck on the cheek.

"Safe journey," he said kindly, then he shifted his eyes. "It's better this way, Anne."

⁓

In addition to the Oxford carters, our company starting out included several merchants, a young cleric headed to a living in Banbury and a widowed Jew with two children. The weather was pleasant, high summer, and as we left the city, the noise and commotion died away. The stench of garbage and piss in my nostrils was replaced by a sweet-smelling breeze, and I listened to the wrens and robins chirruping in the trees. I began to step with a lighter foot, and though tears came to my eyes at the thought of Kit and Mr. Phipps, if heaven bears any resemblance to our English countryside then they were in a better place indeed.

As we walked, I observed my fellow travelers. The Jew was a pawnbroker—or so someone whispered—and at first I did not know what to make of him. There had been almost no Jews in England for three hundred years, King Edward I having expelled them in 1290 by royal decree. Holinshed included the story of a sea captain who, hired to ferry a boatload of these Jews to France, instead drowned them in the Thames and stole their possessions. With the Spanish Inquisition, the Jews crept back in small numbers—better to brave an unfriendly shore than remain on a deadly one. Henry VIII imported another batch, talented musicians from Italy. Why let religious differences stand in the way of a merry song and dance? Now a Portuguese Jew, Roderigo Lopez, was Elizabeth's personal physician. If a few turned to the dirty business of usury, well, it helped grease the growing economy, and who better to practice it than this inferior and already scorned race? As long as they converted outwardly to Christianity, lived unobtrusively and turned the other cheek to insults and abuse, they were as welcome as anyone.

By the widower's demeanor, it appeared he accepted these terms.

He spoke in a low voice, never intruded and led his cart horse patiently over the rutted road. I wondered if he might be from Houndsditch, an area near our own Bishopsgate where a cluster of Jews made a living as clothiers and pawnbrokers. Mr. Phipps and I had visited there once or twice in search of secondhand garments for costumes. I had frowned on the inhabitants then, but this family, viewed alone, elicited different feelings. I was most impressed by the children, a boy and a girl of twelve and ten. What a contrast to the filthy, begging urchins in London; I would be happy to find my own offspring so well mannered. Both had the olive coloring, beaked nose and dark eyes of their race, though it did not stop them, the boy in particular, from being handsome. With their mother dead, they were bound to Oxford, where a small Jewish colony and close relatives awaited.

The rest of the company, especially the cleric, shunned the family, but I found myself dropping back to walk beside them. Perhaps it was my own alien state that made me sympathetic to their outcast condition. And how could Kit, in his *Jew of Malta*, have gotten these people so wrong? I wish I had spoken more with them, but it was enough to share a companionable silence while at the head of the line the cleric puffed righteousness as if God hung on every word. When they left our party at Oxford, the cleric took it upon himself to lecture me on my indiscriminate associations. He did not react kindly when I replied that I also counted actors, poets and other immoral characters among my close friends. I was glad to be rid of him at Banbury and proceed on the final stage with only a few good-natured traders and country folk.

When we reached Stratford, I walked over Clopton Bridge toward Henley Street, drew several deep breaths and knocked on the door. It had been a while since Will's and my last visit, and we had not sent word I was coming.

"Yes? Who is it?" Mary Shakespeare squinted. Then, "Anne!"

"Yes, it's me." A young man and a boy had come in talking from another room, but beyond a cursory glance, they paid me no mind. "Richard? Edmund?" I called. "It's Anne. I've come from London."

For an instant, all three stood staring. Then Richard's face cleared. "Anne! Where is Will? Come in, come in!"

"I'm sorry. Will couldn't—"

Mary pushed past me and stepped outdoors, and I took stock of Will's two youngest brothers. Richard was nineteen, taller than Will, and heavens, he had bushed a beard since I had last seen him. Edmund, once the baby, was thirteen and growing handsome.

"Where is Will?" Mary demanded, coming back inside and peering around me as if she might somehow have missed her son. "How did you get here? Did you ride? Is he putting up the horses?"

"I'm sorry, Mary. Will couldn't come. He must attend to his patron, but he sends everyone his love. Look, I have brought presents."

I slipped a bag off my shoulder. Will had accompanied me to the shops to make the purchases, the earl's continued largesse underwriting our splurge. I drew out an engraved silver tankard for John Shakespeare and for Gilbert a set of silver bells. The two men had gone to Snitterfield on a wool deal and would return for supper, I was told; though Gilbert had built up his own trade as a haberdasher, he still assisted his father in his enterprises. For Richard, we had selected an embossed Spanish leather belt. A carved wood ball and cup for Edmund, though I realized at once the toy was outgrown. For Magpie Joan, a packet of French ribbons.

"Where is she?" I asked. "Where are Susanna, Hamnet, Judith?"

"Gone berry picking by the churchyard," said Richard. "Shall I run and get them?"

"Yes, would you, Richard? Don't tell them I am here. I would like it to be a surprise."

"I will have them back in no time," he promised. "Then you can tell us the news from London. Come on, Edmund."

They left, and I handed Mary the ring Will and I had bought for her. She blinked and bit her lower lip. It was a pretty silver band set with pink coral, but small recompense for an absent son. Very slowly, she slid it onto her little finger, over knuckles that had become badly gnarled, and I held my breath in a sudden fear it would not go on. It did, and Mary contemplated it, composing herself.

"Well," she said, summoning a smile, "you must have a seat, Anne. I'll fetch you a drink while we are waiting."

She went to fill a cup, leaving me to sit alone.

When the children burst through the door, they cried, "Mother! Mother!" Then they paused, taking me in. I smiled, and while Hamnet and Judith turned to each other for confirmation, Susanna ventured a polite step forward.

"Well, well, here is your mother from the great city of London!" cried Joan, coming in behind them and ushering the twins up beside Susanna, so the three of them stood facing me in a row.

"Mother! Mother!" the twins started again.

Susanna curtseyed, her slender form making a graceful bob. "Mother, we are so pleased to see you." I saw her quick mind calculating, almost imperceptibly, the points of resemblance to herself, eyes, hair, chin. Did she like what she saw? I had no time to reflect, for now Joan crushed them all up to me in a mass of awkward embraces.

"Anne, how are you? What brings you home? Did you know we had a boy nearly drown in the Avon this spring when he was trying to catch a duck? And Cecilia Hart is to marry Benjamin Bayner in two weeks' time. Her mother swears that Farmer Grayton's new baby has the blacksmith's nose—poor homely mite! Oh, Mother, did Will send you that pretty ring? Where are our presents? Edmund said you brought presents for everyone."

Magpie Joan. Thank heaven, nothing had tamed her tongue. Mine had turned to wood in my mouth. Well, what right had I to expect instant recognition, natural affection? Give them a little time. I smiled and handed over the French ribbons, the golden trinkets for Susanna and Judith. For Hamnet, a cap with a plume. Edmund hung to the rear, guilty faced, and I sent him a forgiving glance for having spoiled the surprise of my arrival. Perhaps it was better that he had. A real surprise might have been much worse than this clumsy reception.

"Is there anything else?" Judith's eyes glinted at the new bracelet on her wrist, and she craned toward my bag in hopes of another bangle.

"No, nothing else. Your father does well in London," I teased, "but not well enough yet to shower jewels on greedy children."

She crimsoned, but at last we all laughed.

"Tell us," said Mary, beckoning everyone to take a seat. "Tell us about Will."

For two hours I obliged them, while Joan brought cold meat, bread and a bowl of pears to sustain us, all notion of a proper meal forgotten. We fed on news of our prodigal instead. Will and I had sent occasional letters. Now I filled in the gaps, especially Will's lucrative relationship with the earl, and a sense of accomplishment grew with the telling. We had done well, hadn't we? We were making good.

"Will still plays a few parts and I sew costumes, but he feels that writing, especially poetry, is the way to make his reputation," I explained.

"Tell us about the London fashions," said Joan. "Which is more popular, slashed sleeves or tied? Is the queen still wearing French farthingales and pointed stomachers? What about ruffs—the bigger the better? Last month a vendor at the market swore that changeable taffeta was the favorite of every lady and no one would be caught dead in peau de soie. Of course, it was taffeta he was selling."

At every opportunity, I smiled at the children. Susanna, ten, continued to examine me, as if matching up scraps of memory about her mother with the person before her. Occasionally, her chin tilted; presumably she had made some connection. The twins, eight, seemed content to regard me as a visiting storyteller, a traveler from a foreign country bearing exotic tales. They were as much a pair as ever. Their expressions even shifted to the same degree when they sat side by side, neither consulting the other's face. I discerned more of Will now in Hamnet, but still not much of us in either child. Both they and Susanna were blessedly healthy and happy, and I longed for a true embrace from any of them.

It was growing dusk when John and Gilbert returned. I had no chance to greet either, for the instant they entered, the rest of the family began badgering them with news of Will. John took off his hat and lowered his bags. My God, his hair had turned white since our last visit. Gilbert caught sight of the silver bells and, lifting one, he tinkled it beside his ear, smiling.

"You once said you imagined all the church bells of London ringing on a Sunday morning," I reminded him.

At supper, I sat at the end of one bench and listened as the babble about Will was passed around with the food. John proclaimed he had always known his son would do them proud. Mary quickly seconded his opinion, twisting her new ring more happily, it seemed. Every so often there would come a pause, everyone stopping to catch their breath, and then Joan or Richard or even Susanna would look to my end of the table to ask if Will had met the queen or had we seen any beheadings? A few words in reply set them off again. Except for Joan's interest in the London fashions, no one inquired any further as to what I had been doing, and as the evening shadows claimed the room, I receded into them.

Although John Shakespeare's financial position had improved, he was still far short of his former civic glory, so a visit by his daughter-in-law did not merit official attention. But over the next few days various longtime friends stopped by for reports of Will, even an alderman or two, and my in-laws derived a sense of state from these visits and never missed the chance to drop the earl's name. I played my part, smiling brightly.

"How proud you must be of your husband!" the callers said, turning to acknowledge me when their admiration of Will had been exhausted.

"Oh, yes," I replied. "My 'husband' does very well, thank you."

I was less entertained when they complimented "the children."

Not mine, not even Will's. It was almost as if our three offspring were Stratford's favorite orphans, "pretty Susanna" and "the twins," adopted by a benevolent town. Well, they had obviously thrived without benefit of any parents thus far, so why should they need either of us now? Only Joan kept entreating them to "give your mother a kiss" or "go sit on your mother's knee," which they were all too big for anyway.

Within a week, the wonder had gone out of my arrival, and I made myself useful in the household. I darned socks and trimmed a dress for Mary, made jam with Susanna, Judith and Joan. I brushed my daughters' hair. I still remember the cool silk of Susanna's blond locks running through my fingers, the sandy whorls at Judith's temples. I listened to Hamnet read from his grammar school lessons—smart boy!—and when John scoffed at my inclusion of the girls, I answered firmly that Will expected our daughters to be as lettered as our son. That brought a wink from Gilbert in memory of old times. He had not yet married and had no sweetheart.

"Much too busy," was his laughing reply.

I often walked to Hewlands Farm at Shottery to see Duck, Bartholomew and his wife, Isabella. What a batch of children they had!—though some of the little ones tumbling in and out were nieces and nephews or broods from neighboring farms. Hewlands still seemed to me a happier place than Henley Street, and I frequently dallied there until dark. Bartholomew had made more improvements to the house and outbuildings, and Duck, though slowed by rheumatism, puffed about the garden, made candies for the children and tended a wounded dove she had found. The dove would perch on her shoulder, and it was a comical sight to see Duck tending the plants, her skirts hitched up and her round bottom in the air, the dove constantly shifting its feet to counter her movements and maintain its balance. At Hewlands, they cared to hear more of me, and my tales of costumes, the theater and the sights of London brought forth "oohs" and "aahs." I told them almost everything about Mr. Phipps, and at last it felt good to remember him. I even spoke a little of Kit, and then I let him go, not that I ever had him. Perhaps my beautiful cat let go of me.

Only Duck probed into my happiness.

"What about more children for you and Will?" she asked, as we sat shelling peas by the garden wall. "Now that you prosper and have connections."

"Who knows?" I laughed. "Of course, between Will's duties to the earl and mine at the theater, we hardly have time to greet in passing. You would be amazed how quickly life fills up in a place like London!"

She didn't press, but of all those I encountered in Stratford, Duck was the one person I felt I had not quite fooled. She might not know exactly, but she guessed at something. And I could not enlighten her, for I was in even greater darkness than she. I, least of all, knew where my future lay.

⁓

So summer passed and autumn arrived. For a while Mary continued to hope Will would show up also.

"How long does it take to write a poem?" she would ask. "Maybe he will come when the next one is done."

Yes, why don't you come, Will? Is the earl's company so captivating? Don't you miss our children? Hamnet and Judith had quickly adapted to calling me Mother, though they used the word more from obedience than from filial affection. Susanna, perhaps drawing on stronger memories, warmed to me a little more. I taught her fancy stitchwork and sewed her a dress of cornflower blue with coppery trim. She practiced diligently, already looking ahead to her responsibilities. When Magpie Joan married, Susanna would assume her place as Mary's next in command. I continued to impose learning on my daughters, but whether it was a natural disinclination or the result of my in-laws' dim view of female education, I was forced to admit that neither girl showed much penchant for scholarship. I consoled myself with Hamnet's progress and compiled for him a list of his father's favorite classical works. The best days were when I took the children to Hewlands, and along with Duck, we baked bread, pressed flowers, tended the beehives or walked among the farm animals, feeding carrots to the horses and cuddling the newest litter of mewling kittens.

But I missed London.

What? Why? What is the matter with you, Anne? God's blood, look around! This is idyllic: fresh air, ripening fields, mugs of nutty ale by the fireside, the laughter of family, scampering children.

But my mind, my mind.

I would sit by the hearth with Will's family at night—Mary and Magpie gossiping, John and Gilbert hashing over the accounts and the gloves to be cut the next day—and wonder what the actors were talking about at the tavern and who was writing what play. I had left the final version of *Richard III* on my table, and as soon as the plague ended and the theaters reopened, rehearsals could begin. I would ask Will to put Kit's name on the handbill alongside his. I longed to design costumes and watch the players make splendid entrances in them. I missed the booksellers at St. Paul's, the parade of people over London Bridge, the pageants and festivals and sightings of the queen. I missed the quiet of my London abode, the privacy of my own bed. Here Magpie and I shared the mattress in Will's and my old room with Susanna and the twins in the truckle bed—you can imagine the chattering! Having lived blithely in London as Will's free-spirited sister, I missed my independence and being ten years younger. Why did these people mistake me for a sedate matron?

And why had no one here any ambition, or rather, why were their ambitions so safe and small? Stratford was a fine place, bustling, but can you really be content to plod in the provinces for the rest of your lives when in London you might achieve things you never dreamed? At such moments, I nearly tossed in my chair, wrestling with consternation at their shortsightedness. I even missed Will and forgave our differences. He *understood*.

Yet I could not simply pack up and go. Having regained a modest place in Will's family, I was reluctant to throw it away by another precipitous departure. Nor was it fair to abruptly abandon the children— "the children," you see how already I was leaving them in my mind? So I stayed through October while we gathered apples and dried herbs, and into November when we dipped candles and wove wool into shawls. Each day I absented myself a little more, talked less, dropped hints the time was coming. Winter weather would soon make the roads difficult to travel, I murmured, and who would see to it that Will wore his scarf when he went out in the cold? Each time Mary would coax me to stay a few more days. If I left, so too went the dwindling chance of Will appearing.

Finally, I found them a story; we all need our self-deceptions. Why, just look at the good time we've had hearing about Will, I chided, when half the reason he sent me is because he is dying for news of you. How goes the gloving business? How does Hamnet at school? Where are his kisses from the children? If I don't bring word soon, he will think no one loves him! And suddenly it was all right. Mary made me promise to thank him for her ring and tell him how she wore it every day. Magpie wanted her brother to know she had her eye on several young men as matrimonial prospects, unless, of course, he had someone richer in mind for her in London. Gilbert and Richard hoped to visit him themselves before too long. The family put together a basket of gifts, which they presented on my return from bidding farewell to Bartholomew and Duck at Hewlands.

"I bet you can't get kid gloves like this in London," boasted John.

"Safe journey," said Gilbert as he hugged me good-bye. "Every time I ring my bells I will think of you."

The twins waved and clamored, "Tell Father we love him!" though it was quite clear they could not have picked out their father in a group of a dozen men. "Tell my father I am learning my duties, and I pray daily for his health," said Susanna. Then she gave me the same grave curtsey she had at our original meeting. For an instant I considered sweeping them up and taking them with me, but it would have been a selfish gesture to ease my own mind. Stratford was their home.

"He will be very proud of you all," I said, embracing them.

⁓

I arrived back in early December to a joyous greeting from Will.

"Anne, what a good thing you are here! The theaters have reopened, the Burbages are in a fever of auditioning actors and launching new plays, and they still have not found a decent wardrobe master. Cuthbert swears it takes three seamstresses to replace one of you. And the copying is backing up, and *Titus Andronicus* is to premiere at the Rose in January. How soon can you do a clean script for me?" He paused and laughed apologetically. "Never mind. That can wait. Come sit by the fire and give me the news from Stratford. Here, I have some leftover rabbit pie."

"Thank you," I said, munching, for I was famished. I glanced around the room, noting his clothes hanging on the pegs. "Are you staying here awhile, rather than at the earl's? Are you still in his favor?"

"Of course," Will said. Then he flinched, the merest movement, as if a sensitive tooth had twinged. "I just find it convenient to have a place of my own to retire to on occasion. You know what they say about absence."

"That it moves the heart to fondness." I paused. Did the adage apply to us as well? After six months away, I was glad to see him, but had he actually missed me or only my housekeeping and copying skills? "So, then, what have you been up to, besides flattering your pretty earl?"

I spoke to tease, but another twinge crossed Will's face. I folded my hands and sat patiently, waiting for him to fill me in.

Chapter 16

*G*uess what. Will had written two—make that three—hit plays in my absence.

One was the comedy for the earl he had begun just as I left for Stratford, when that coy young man in lovelocks and lip paint made his bachelor buddies swear never to wed. Let's all be boys forever and ever! So Will had penned for their coterie a lighthearted romp of four noble friends pledged to forgo female company for three years while devoting themselves to study. Were you Berowne, Will, the slightly older, slightly wiser member of the quartet, the one who signs on under good-natured protest, knowing abstinence hasn't a chance? When four fair damsels led by the Princess of France arrive on the scene, the boys naturally fall to Cupid's arrow. But even Cupid is thwarted; the fun and games end when a messenger announces the King of France has died. The ladies must return to their kingdom, leaving the four gallants' rising amours to fall like a sighing soufflé.

Love's Labor's Lost, Will called it, and it is a charmer. Fancying themselves poets, the earl and company contributed to the gaudy language, and as an amateur production among the Southampton set, it was wildly popular. The earl and his friends rotated parts, and with each rendition, Will reported, they got sillier and sillier, especially as they took turns doing the female roles.

"He makes us dress in women's garments," Will grumbled, "though I told him we could hire boy actors."

"Think of it as a chance to expand your acting repertoire."

"I'd rather not."

I chuckled, but Will's mouth tightened, and my mirthful image of him gowned like a French girl was succeeded by a vague sense that something was amiss.

"Will? If you don't like it, why don't you object?"

Shrugging, he hefted his purse, and the weighty thump served as ample reminder of where our bread got its butter. "I suppose it is all in a day's work. He'll grow bored with it soon enough. I have started another long poem for him, *The Rape of Lucrece*, and meanwhile I keep him entertained with sonnets."

Will's second play was *Titus Andronicus*, coauthored with George Peele and scheduled to premiere at the Rose with the Earl of Sussex's Men in January. I lay absolutely no claim to that atrocity—take it, Will, take *Titus*; he's all yours—though I expect Peele, who adored gore, would be devastated to know his name has been omitted to posterity. My God, *Titus* was and is terrible: one severed tongue, two heads, three hands, a double rape and a dozen bodies. Who would not gasp at the sight of tongueless, handless Lavinia carrying Titus's bloody, dismembered hand in her bared teeth? And that most gruesome scene of all, when Tamora unknowingly eats the flesh of her two sons in a nicely baked pie. Will didn't invent that last bit; Seneca, the Roman revenge master, serves three boys to their father for dinner in *Thyestes*. And of course Will and Peele were still trying to outdo Tom Kyd's *The Spanish Tragedy*, though even Kyd had the sense to keep the cannibalism offstage. But not Will, oh, no. There it was, right up front, for the audience to see. Sick to my stomach, I begged Will to rewrite this, to rewrite all of it.

"If there is to be such horror," I implored, "at least give it some higher meaning. Let it shake heaven and earth. Let it move the audience to forswear violence and seek wisdom and justice. It cannot simply be blood all over the stage."

"But that is the beauty of it," Will insisted. "There is no higher meaning. The audience doesn't want to think, they want to enjoy. Besides"—he shot me a reproving look—"who is the playwright here, Anne?"

Not me. I repeat, I had no hand—pun intended—in that monstrosity. The players actually bought guts and offal from a butcher to add realism to the performances, though one afternoon it nearly turned the show into a comedy when two of the actors slipped in the slime and had to catch each other from falling. I was almost relieved when the theaters closed in February for a final, waning outbreak of plague. But when they reopened a few months later, *Titus* proved a smash. Cannibalism and all, the audience ate it up—second pun intended.

And Will's third hit play? Guess, go on, guess.

Richard III.

Wait a minute—didn't I write that in partnership with Kit?

I thought so. But on my return to London I found the whole town exclaiming over the fabulous new play about the crookback king, brilliantly acted by Dick Burbage and penned by none other than William Shakespeare. I even heard people quoting in the streets, "A horse! A horse! My kingdom for a horse!"

"I think it is one of the best lines I have ever written," said Will modestly.

Because of course he had written it. *Richard III* was the logical sequel to his acclaimed trilogy *Henry VI*. He had been struggling with the characterization of Richard since the previous spring, then it suddenly snapped into place when he pictured Dick Burbage in the title role. His sister Anne, well-known as his faithful copyist, had prepared a clean manuscript and thoughtfully left it on her desk for him before she went to visit Stratford. All he had to do was tweak the final lines and deliver it to the theater.

Will believed this so completely that I began to doubt myself. To recall the sequence of composition, I had to think back more than a year. Yes, Will had taken a stab at *Richard III*, but then he abandoned it and me to traipse off with the earl. Kit and I rescued the script, and we had used none of Will's original. Or had we? Had we banished his portion only to have it stroll nonchalantly back in when our backs were turned? But I wrote some of that original! If only I could compare those early drafts to the final product, but who saves crossed-out papers? Day after day, watching the performance, I wrestled with confused memories. Was that my line, Kit's, Will's? Surely that was my speech—I remember Kit rewarding me with kisses when I read it to him. Yet how could it be? How could I have written anything that sounded so good? Damn you, Will, damn you.

Richard III by Christopher Marlowe—that is how the posters should have read. I would gladly have gone anonymous to give him this final tribute. But I couldn't speak up for Kit without revealing our affair, and even less could I lay public claim to authorship. My word against Will's would have tipped no more weight than a feather against a stack of bricks. A woman write a play? She's lost her wits! Clap the addled, squawking creature in the stocks and pelt her with rotten fruit until she regains her senses.

I told myself it didn't matter. I did not need the money. My wants were few, and Will was happy to supply me from his bulging purse. I never really expected to see my name on the playbill, though I would have enjoyed a little private recognition from our theater friends. I told myself it was the artistry, not the artist, the play and not the playwright, that deserved the acclaim. I bit my tongue and stifled the cry of injustice in my throat. It would not be the last time, and of all the crimes I lay at Will Shakespeare's feet, this is the worst: that he taught me how to lie to myself.

The final outbreak of plague in the early spring of 1594 was less menacing, though in all more than ten thousand had died since the disease erupted nearly two years before. In anticipation of the theaters reopening, Cuthbert Burbage put me to work sewing new costumes. I rejoiced to be back, but as usual I found Cuthbert a difficult character, hard to please and lacking in personal warmth. He fired off orders when a polite request would have brought a willing response. He hired lawyers rather than settle for an obvious compromise. Perhaps that is what it takes to be successful in business; like his impresario father James, Cuthbert did not suffer others to stand in his way. Yet had he smiled more at the people around him and less at the misfortunes of our competitors, I would have called him attractive, for he was a well-featured man. It was his shrewd management that put the Theatre and later the Globe on strong financial ground and gradually made Will and me rich, so to complain overmuch of his personality would make me a hypocrite. Fortunately, except to issue my assignments, he and I had little contact.

In the evenings, I began *The Comedy of Errors*. I know—hard on Kit's death, I had said my writing career was done. But I wanted something to love again, I wanted to laugh, and with Will still frolicking with the earl, there I sat alone save for my imagination, pen and ink on my table, paper close by. Is this a quill I see before me? Let me grasp it in my hand! At the same time, browsing the bookstalls at St. Paul's, a translation of Plautus's comedy *The Menaechmi* caught my eye. Will had introduced me to the story during our lessons back in Stratford. The tale of twin brothers and mistaken identities had been among his Latin texts at the grammar school. I took *The Menaechmi* home to play with, and it began to play with me.

"What are you doing?" asked Will, observing the growing pile of paper on my table when he stopped for a visit.

"I'm not sure. When I find out, I will let you know."

Now, an author who is inspired by a classical text is expected to improve upon it. How can you make it fresher, more enlightening or entertaining? Since tales hinging on mistaken identities were extremely popular, I decided to add to Plautus's version a pair of twin servants to double the confusion of twin masters. I tangled the script into more than one knot—help!—before resolving everyone's whereabouts. Pleased with the result, I showed the rough draft to Will.

"Hmm," he said. "I might be able to make something of this."

I let him take it. For me, the fun had been in the exercise. It was the first time I had devised a cast of characters and plotted an entire play by myself—bravo! And despite the uneven pacing—my fault—and its excessive rhymes—Will's editorial contribution—*Errors* can be hilarious theater. It all depends on the actors, and this is often the hardest lump for a playwright to swallow: that your brilliant script may be mangled by an inept or miscast troupe. Comedy is especially vulnerable. When joke after joke falls flat through poor delivery, you want to bang your head on the nearest post. But when acted with rambunctious zest, *Errors* will make audiences double in belly laughs and their faces stream tears of mirth.

Will, meanwhile, had a new play of his own, which he brought me to copy: *The Two Gentlemen of Verona*—it is a bad play. A young man, Valentine, is betrayed by his best friend, Proteus, who falls in love with Valentine's betrothed, Silvia. Not only does Proteus reveal the couple's planned elopement to the authorities, resulting in Valentine's banishment, he attempts to rape Silvia when she refuses his advances. Valentine comes to her rescue, first cursing Proteus, then immediately forgiving him when Proteus says, "I'm sorry." "That's all right," says Valentine, and he offers to relinquish Silvia to his dishonest, immoral, backstabbing, would-be rapist friend. Neither of them bothers to ask Silvia's opinion of this transaction, which is prevented when Julia, Proteus's sworn love whom he had abandoned, reveals her presence. The rightful couples are reunited and live happily ever after.

"This is preposterous," I said to Will. "Did everyone suddenly turn stupid? Why would Valentine forgive Proteus? How could Silvia and Julia possibly love these despicable men?"

"It's just a play. Don't take it so seriously, Anne."

"But it is incomprehensible that Valentine would welcome Proteus back after the vile things he has done."

"It's literary convention. Besides"—Will shifted defensively—"it is natural for men to prize their friendships."

I shot him a hard look. Yes, I knew the literary tradition of noble male love, the bond between sworn brothers. Classic and contemporary tales on the theme were readily available at any bookseller's. That men stuck together in real life was no secret either. Just look at the boys' club surrounding the Earl of Southampton, the acting companies, the writers at the tavern. Since anything involving a woman was inferior, male friendships were obviously superior. But Proteus was not a good friend, and that Valentine should be so manipulated by him disturbed me. What was going on with Will that he would pen such a play?

"Is this what you really think?" I probed. "That the way to make it up with a friend who has abused you is to say, 'Here, take my mistress'?"

"Of course not," Will snapped. "But it is between men, and you wouldn't understand. Don't nag me about it, just copy."

Copy I did, and though I could not change the plot, I did improve the language on the sly. *What light is light, if Silvia be not seen? What joy is joy, if Silvia be not by?* I wrote that. I also decided that Will's charge that I took the play too seriously was incorrect; I was not taking our plays seriously enough. Why do Valentine and Proteus behave in such a manner? How would a woman react differently? Why does anyone behave as they do? Sometimes, taking a break from both sewing and writing, I would sit with my chin in my hands and my nose out the window, staring at some person below. That woman, for example. She looks careworn; see how her shoes, ill fitting, slip-slap at her heels? What if she is a widow with mouths to feed? Is she worried, praying, Please, God, let me find a coin on the way home, to buy bread? That young man—why is he running? To flee his creditors or meet his lawyer? Is he in deep debt or in expectation of a great inheritance? Would he desert a mistress for a friend? My mind chased after the disappearing figures. Stories—people are stories on two legs—and I suppose it was another effect of having lost my own identity that made me avid to know theirs.

From then on, I began to treat the characters in my plays differently. What if they were not simply villains or heroes, virgins or whores? What if they were not characters at all, but real people? It sounds elementary, but we were only a few years removed from the Queen's Men, when the main purpose of a play was pageantry and show. My notion grew slowly but steadily as I copied *Two Gentlemen*, its unlikable cast no match for what I imagined outside my window. If our future plays were to come alive, I must listen more closely to what my characters were trying to tell me. They had hopes to whisper, dreams and secrets to reveal.

As the theaters got back to business, the acting companies sorted themselves out as well. Some, like Pembroke's Men, had folded. Sussex's Men and the Queen's Men merged and became a touring company. The Lord Admiral's Men, with Edward Alleyn as their star actor, were already established at the Rose. Will, the Burbages and Will Kempe ended up with a new troupe, the Lord Chamberlain's Men, based at the Theatre. On a June afternoon came a pounding at our door, and Will, on hiatus from the earl, opened it.

"Mistress Anne!" Christopher, our once boy actor, now a handsome eighteen, flew into the room. "Mr. Cuthbert says you must come immediately!"

"What about?" I *tsk*ed at the inconvenience. With two costumes already undergoing repairs on my table, I had more than enough stitching to do. Let Cuthbert call another seamstress if he was in a hurry.

"I don't know," Christopher said, panting, "but I daren't return without you."

"What have you done, Anne?" Will teased. So like him to assume I was being summoned for some infraction. But suddenly, I worried it myself.

"I don't know, but I'm going, I'm going." I punched my needle into the pincushion. A fine state of affairs. I had worked wonders on our new costumes, sewing by candlelight late into the night to create garments that would have made Mr. Phipps clasp his hands in joy. Now here I was summoned like a miscreant for who knew what crime.

"Have you any idea what the problem is?" I asked Christopher again, as we walked through the streets. What a fine young man he had become! Though he had outgrown the girls' roles, he had found a steady berth playing parts like prince and squire while he hoped to mature into a great actor.

"No. He said only that if I do not bring you posthaste, he will dock my pay for the next three performances."

"Let's hurry then." I picked up my speed. "I would not have you get in trouble on my account."

A history play, not one of ours, was in progress when we reached the Theatre, and Christopher wished me luck and sped away. Cuthbert met me just inside the door.

"Mr. Burbage," I began irritably, prepared to defend myself even before a charge was laid. But Cuthbert interrupted.

"Come this way." He hurried me to the front row of the lower gallery and nodded upward. "Do you see the lady in the box with her attendants? Do you know who she is?"

I peered. The boxes in the gallery above the stage were considered the best seats in the house, not because they gave the best view of the stage—in fact, you mostly saw the actors' backs—but because they gave the audience the best view of you. The woman in question was elderly, regal, red haired, sharp-eyed, sumptuously dressed and jewel bedecked. And no, it was not the queen.

"It's Elizabeth, Countess of Shrewsbury," said Cuthbert in a low voice, dabbing perspiration from his forehead.

Of course I knew the name. Elizabeth of Shrewsbury, or Bess as she was called, was second only to the queen in wealth and power. She had achieved her position by marrying and outliving four husbands, bettering herself by leaps and bounds each time. She was reputed to be proud, tyrannical, a woman of formidable energy and exacting demands. A woman determined to make a grand mark—with the lands and funds she had accumulated in her marital career, she was rebuilding her ancestral home of Hardwick Hall in Derbyshire, said to be one of the most original and spectacular houses in England.

"And . . . ?" I turned my gaze back to Cuthbert.

"Twenty minutes into the play she sent word backstage that the

story was a muddle, the swordfights a disgrace, and if half the characters were not beheaded by the midpoint, she would demand a refund.
Then she said the costumes were intriguing, and I should have the
seamstress here before the final speech or she would have me arrested
and flogged."

I swallowed hard. Could she really do that? Cuthbert was quaking,
and the countess's remark on the costumes did not necessarily inspire
me with confidence.

"Are you sure she said 'intriguing'?" I beseeched him. "Do you
think she meant it favorably?"

"How should I know? She has killed four husbands!"

Good for her, I thought. I certainly admired a woman who could
strike fear into a man. Then my worry returned.

"Does she mean to speak to me? What should I do? Should I curtsey?" I remembered Susanna's curtsey to me on my arrival in Stratford
and wondered if I could be half as graceful when my knees were wob-
bling. "I must sit down."

I slid to an empty seat, furtively studying the countess and hoping
she would not spot me. If I watched, I might pick up clues from her
attendants how to behave. Instead, I became so intimidated I began to
fear I would faint rather than curtsey at her feet. And look what I was
wearing! Oh, no, I had left our room in such a hurry that here I was in
my plainest dress and cap. If only I had a piece of lace to tuck into my
bodice, a bead necklace, a pretty brooch. Oh, what could she want?
What did "intriguing" signify? Did she mean to pay me a compliment?
A ray of hope spread over me. What an honor that would be! A prominent patron of the arts might single out a great actor or playwright for
personal praise, but for a countess to speak to a mere costumer . . . !

I thought that play would never end. Bess was right: It was a muddle, and even more so in my agitated mind. The instant the players
bowed, Cuthbert grabbed my elbow and grappled me to the center of
the yard while the groundlings exited in a noisy herd around us. Elizabeth of Shrewsbury sat fanning herself until the rabble departed. Then,
after a piercing glance down at us, she and her train descended. At her

approach, I curtseyed so badly I nearly toppled over, and I reddened with embarrassment as I rose.

"Terrible play!" the countess snapped at Cuthbert, ignoring me. "I cannot understand what my son sees in them. Don't you have anything better to offer the citizens of London?"

"We have another play tomorrow, your ladyship," Cuthbert babbled. "It is a comedy called *The Comedy of Errors*, very amusing, written in fact by this woman's brother here."

"I don't see any brother here," said Bess.

"No, your ladyship, forgive me. I meant this woman has a brother who is a playwright who has written a comedy called *The Comedy of Errors* that tomorrow we will play and—"

Bess's look cut him short. But I caught the wry crook at the corner of her mouth, and suddenly my terror was gone.

"You are the seamstress," she said to me.

"Yes, your ladyship." I made another curtsey, better this time.

"You created the costume for the princess in the play."

"Yes, your ladyship."

She directed an eyebrow at Cuthbert and waited.

"Yes, yes, I will fetch it at once!" He hurried away.

"Which merchants do you patronize for your fabrics?" Bess asked me. "Who gives you the best price for black velvet?"

"I compare amongst them, my lady," I said, naming several, "and also frequent the secondhand stalls for clothes I can recut and reuse. The weight of the fabric is of special importance. Too heavy and it will weigh down the actors. Too light and it will not endure the strenuous wear it gets onstage. That is why for the princess's dress, I used a medium silk." I handed over the garment, Cuthbert having arrived with it on his arm. "You see, it looks elegant and will also prove most economical for the run of the play."

Bess snorted. "Which, for that particular play, will not be long. But economy is always to be praised. And these knot stitches, quite elaborate." She fingered the silver embroidery on the bodice. "You do not find them tedious?"

"They are tedious, your ladyship, but necessary for the image the playwright intends to convey. When the knight refers to the princess, he speaks of her cold heart, her 'chain-mailed' affection, and I wanted the dress to suggest that combination of hardness and beauty."

"So you study the plays for meaning."

"Yes, your ladyship."

"And your brother is a playwright."

"His name is William Shakespeare."

Bess shrugged. "Never heard of him." She let the fabric fall from her fingers, and I curtseyed again, assuming the interview to be over and her version of a compliment complete. Indeed, she flicked her hand and sent an attendant to fetch her carriage. "Well, then"—she turned back to me—"be at St. Paul's Cross tomorrow morning at ten and we will make a space for you."

My mind blanked. "A space for me?"

"I am in need of expert seamstresses and embroiderers for Hardwick Hall, and I know talent when I see it. I do needlework myself, you know. I find it quite satisfying. You will have meat and board and a recompense of one pound per quarter."

"But . . . but I cannot leave my brother."

"Of course you can. Since I am less inclined to travel these days, I also need someone who can come to London to buy fabrics and such. As you know the shops and can make boys look good in dresses, I have no doubt you will do. You may visit your brother then. Ah, my carriage." She swept out, and it was as if a gale had blown through and we stood leafless at its passage.

"Me? Go to Hardwick Hall?" I wondered aloud. "Isn't that a long way?"

"Yes, damn it," Cuthbert swore, "and I'll be without a seamstress again!"

Will was not happy for me either.

"Who is to tend to me, Anne? Do you know what trouble I had keeping the place tidy while you were in Stratford?"

"Hire a servant. Or get a mistress who knows how to wield a broom."

Guilt flushed his face, and I sighed. Oh, Will, if you have bedded some lady of late, do you think I care? I should have assumed it, you and your friends and the earl. Having recovered from my shock at Bess's invitation—order—I now felt almost glib. Me, go to one of the greatest houses in the kingdom, sew for a countess, live in the company of royals. I stuffed clothes in my satchel—how deliciously the tables were turned!

"But I depend upon you," Will argued. "With *The Rape of Lucrece* at the printer, I plan to start a new play, maybe two. Ideas are coming so fast I can hardly capture them. I need you to do the copying. I have always said you have the better hand."

I laughed. God help me, I sat down on the bed and laughed. It was the first time in ages Will had given me cause for genuine merriment, and I enjoyed it to the full.

"Hire a laundress, eat your meals at the tavern, learn to use a dustpan. Pick any of the aspiring young writers in town and assign them the copying. I am sure you will survive without me, as shall I without you."

I paused, sorry to have spoken the heartless words. But in wiping away Will's objections, I erased my own final doubts. Strike out, Anne! Like brave Drake sailing the seven seas, you are about to discover Derbyshire! At Hardwick Hall, I would sew beautiful designs for all to admire, and no more dealing with Cuthbert Burbage either. Of course, the countess might prove even more demanding, but as only one of many seamstresses, I did not expect her to notice me in particular. And think what she must know about life and love and the great secrets of the world! Just to travel in her wake would be an adventure.

I looked a last time around the room for anything I had missed in my packing. Will sat grumpily on his bed. On my desk lay my writing tools, and I picked up my favorite quill and tucked it in amongst my dresses. At Hardwick Hall, I would probably be too busy for any writing, but then again, you never knew.

Chapter 17

"*H*ardwick Hall, more glass than wall."

So went the saying even before the building was complete. But I must explain there were actually two houses at Hardwick, the estate where Bess's family had lived as minor gentry since the thirteenth century. Old Hall was built by her father, and there Bess was born in 1527. She rescued it, and the surrounding four-hundred-acre estate, in 1583 after her feckless brother, James, died bankrupt. Bit by bit, she transformed the existing house into a grand four-story structure, and though the result was an architectural hodgepodge, it did boast two great chambers on the upper story for dining and dancing, a spacious central hall, giant plasterwork friezes and a magnificent hilltop view over the rolling countryside.

Nonetheless, Bess deemed Old Hall too small for her household and her ambitions, and on the death of her fourth husband in 1590, she started to erect the stupendous New Hall right next door. She commissioned Robert Smythson, a master mason and surveyor, as her architect, a new profession in those days. Together they conceived New Hall to be one of the great "prodigy houses" being built by the foremost families of the realm as testament to their power and wealth. Bess was sixty-three at the time, and that she would begin such a mammoth project at such an advanced age amazed me. I took it as the statement of a woman who meant never to die.

My own first view of New Hall, as we came up the winding road, left me speechless. It crowned the hill, its six tall towers each topped with the huge initials *ES* carved in bold silhouette—just in case a befuddled traveler happened to knock at the door and inquire, "Who lives here, pray tell?" Unlike Old Hall, New Hall was beautifully symmetrical, and the rooms grew ever larger and more prestigious as you ascended the stairs. The top floor housed the staterooms, an enormous great chamber hung with tapestries and the largest long gallery in all of England. Most impressive were the size and sheer number of glass windows, hundreds and hundreds of sparkling panes. Glass was a luxury only the wealthiest could afford, and New Hall, virtually sheathed in it, outglittered the stars. Since New Hall was still under construction, we lived in Old Hall meanwhile. But at the earliest chance I wandered round and round the splendid new building, marveling at the shimmers of sunlight and the dazzling reflections in the glass.

"It cost a small fortune," Bess was fond of saying. "But then, I have a large one."

And let me tell you how she rose to such a height, for her bloodline was hardly auspicious. Her father died when she was a year old, and her brother, James, being not much older, the estate fell into wardship, its income diverted to the Crown. Though her mother remarried, the family's financial situation remained tenuous. It was a fine opportunity for Bess when, at age twelve, she went into service at Codnor Castle, the great Derbyshire estate of Sir John and Lady Zouche. Bess then married, in order:

Robert Barlow, her cousin, who was also in the Zouches' service and whose family was slightly more prosperous than hers. Robert was thirteen and Bess fifteen when they wed in a match more of friendship than love. A sickly youth, he died eighteen months after the wedding.

"Never consummated"—Bess sighed—"but then, we were only children. However, as Robert's widow I was entitled to a third of his income. About eight pounds a year—not much, but it was a start."

Bess next went into service with the Marchioness of Dorset. There, at age twenty, she married forty-two-year-old Sir William Cavendish, a royal commissioner for Henry VIII during the king's break with the Church of Rome. At Henry's behest, Cavendish had gone about dissolving monasteries and turning the monks out into the cold, and he did it so expeditiously that he was granted huge swaths of church land in return. From him, Bess acquired an excellent education in land acquisition and estate management. She could issue orders with authority to an anthill of workmen and bookkeep in her head the cost of mortar, marble and stone. The couple also ruthlessly enclosed land and drove off the local peasants, who rioted. But mostly they lived in style in London on the bribes that Cavendish, like all government officials, extracted from those seeking favor at court. Cavendish had three daughters from two previous marriages, and he and Bess produced eight children of their own, six of whom survived to adulthood.

"He was my one true love." Bess sighed. "Never a day did we quarrel—well, never did we quarrel but that he quickly admitted I was in the right, and we kissed and made up. Did you never have a true love, Anne?"

"No." I shook my head with a resigned smile. Pleased with my initial efforts at Hardwick, Bess often called for me to join her ladies as they sat sewing, and I had become her confidante. Bess's own fingers were nimble and her embroidery as fine as any I have ever seen, and as her ladies tired of stitching, she would wave them off, and she and I would continue till suppertime. I was tempted to divulge to her the facts concerning me and Will. I suspect she would have had valuable insights for me. But Bess was really talking about herself, so it was best to move on. Besides, I had answered truthfully. I had known love—Will, Gilbert and Kit had each loved me for a time. But a true love? What is that? What does it mean? It was a question I was soon to dwell much on.

As for Bess's true love, after ten years of wedded bliss, Sir William Cavendish fell ill, and despite Bess's devoted nursing, he died in her arms. Perhaps just as well, I thought to myself. Eight children in ten years? Another decade of marriage might have killed her! Or not—Bess was a bantam rooster with the constitution of a war horse and a snort to match. On Cavendish's demise, she inherited not only his sizable properties but also his sizable debts. To resolve this difficulty, she got herself appointed lady-in-waiting to the queen and went to court to find husband number three.

"Sir William St. Loe"—Bess sighed—"a most generous man."

You will notice Bess always sighed when referring to her first three husbands. It implied a lost fondness and a great distance in time, and in fact this part of her personal history was nearly thirty years old. St. Loe, wealthy, elderly and twice widowed, was a close friend of the queen, who had made him both captain of the guard and butler of the royal household. He brought Bess two more stepdaughters and willingly assumed her debts from Cavendish. On his death five years later, he left all his lands to his "own sweet Bess," much to his family's indignation.

"If not for me, St. Loe's brother Edward would have been his heir," Bess conceded. "But they had a terrible falling-out, and Edward even tried to poison us."

"Poison you?" I gasped.

"Oh, yes. Luckily, he was a most incompetent man."

For her fourth match, Bess returned to court, and at the age of forty she snagged one of the richest men in England. George Talbot, sixth Earl of Shrewsbury, was a widower with seven children. To further cement their union, two of Bess's children by Cavendish were then married to two of Talbot's offspring in a double ceremony. The little brides were aged eight and twelve.

"What is the point of marrying money if you don't keep it in the family?" said Bess.

But Bess did not sigh when recalling her final husband. Though the marriage began smoothly enough, it gradually grew rancorous. The main cause was disagreements over her money and lands, which led to increasingly bitter accusations and harassments. "No curse or plague in the world could be more grievous," wrote the furious earl, describing Bess. But the most important player in the Talbots' domestic drama was a third party. In early 1569, barely a year into their marriage, Queen

Elizabeth sent them a royal visitor. It was Mary, Queen of Scots, and Talbot had been appointed her custodian, or rather, her jailer.

"At first we were thrilled," said Bess. "It was a great mark of the queen's favor. But every time there arose a hint of intrigue involving Mary, we had to pack up and move. Tutbury Castle, Sheffield Castle, Wingfield Manor, Worksop Manor, Buxton Lodge, Chatsworth—we shifted her forty-six times in sixteen years. The queen provided an allowance for Mary's maintenance, but it was never enough, and we were forced to supply the difference. Her private household sometimes numbered up to sixty people, so you can imagine the constant strain on our budget and our nerves. Yet I determined to make Mary my friend."

"Your friend?" I interrupted, too fascinated to check my curiosity. "Why?"

Bess shrugged. "Keep your friends close and your enemies closer. If Elizabeth died childless, Mary might become queen of England. The trick was to keep each of them thinking I was on her side."

"Whose side were you on?"

"Mine."

I breathed admiration. "How did you accomplish it?" I asked. "Make Mary your friend, I mean."

"Simple," said Bess. "By sewing."

Of course. All those long hours and days and years of Mary's confinement, almost half her life spent under English house arrest, what would keep a deposed queen occupied? Sewing and talking with her female companions, just as Bess and I were doing. Still, her befriending of Mary ultimately proved unsuccessful, especially after the birth of Bess's granddaughter, Arbella Stuart, in 1575. Orphaned by age six, Arbella was second in line to the English throne after her cousin King James VI of Scotland, Mary's son, and Bess's dynastic scheming on the little girl's behalf aroused Mary's fury. The caged and spiteful Scots queen retaliated by playing Bess and her husband against each other and caused such aggravation that the Talbots were soon separated more often than not.

"It got messy," said Bess.

Indeed. In 1584 the couple broke completely, and Bess fled to Hardwick amidst allegations of mutual abuse and rumors that Talbot had fathered a child by Mary. Summoned to court by Elizabeth, Bess denied on her knees that she had initiated or spread the vicious slander. At the end of the year Mary was finally taken off the Talbots' hands and eventually transferred to Sir Amias Paulet at Fotheringay, where she got into the conspiracies that cost her her head. But although Bess asked the earl to take her back and the queen herself tried to reconcile the warring couple, it was to no avail. Instead, Bess caught Talbot with a serving wench and accused him of infidelity, and he called Bess a bitter shrew and ran off with the wench.

"Then what happened?" I demanded.

"He died," said Bess, "and I inherited my widow's third. Lands and castles, forests and timber, coal pits and mineral rights, ironworks, glassworks, smithies. Mine, all mine."

"But did you kill any of them?" I begged to know. "Did you actually kill any of your husbands?"

"Oh, good heavens, no." She paused. "Well, I did weigh the benefits of eliminating Talbot."

"And . . . ?"

Bess harrumphed. "If I had tried, I would have succeeded. I am *not* incompetent."

I let out a long, satisfied breath. Bess appreciated a rapt audience, and I was happy to oblige. Thanks to my playwriting, I could craft our conversations with an ear for pacing and punch, giving her double pleasure in the telling. Bess had also quickly divined that I was educated, if not in the usual fashion, and she sometimes bade me set aside my needle and read to the ladies as they sewed.

"Your brother has tutored you well," she observed, raising an eyebrow at me in mild suspicion. "I have no time for books myself, but Arbella sends for them from London, so you may choose from her library. And I should like you to be her dressmaker. My granddaughter is headstrong and romantic, and it may soothe her to have someone of your calm, steady nature close by."

"I will do my best," I promised, grateful to be so favored. And skills aside, I believe the final reason Bess trusted me was because she saw I desired nothing from her. Unlike almost everyone else fawning and bowing at Hardwick, I had no secret ambitions or relatives to advance. Nor did I ever steal from her, not the least crumb, unlike some of the servants, who were promptly caught and dismissed. I would have done my work without any pay at all, simply for the roof over my head, as long as I could sit beside her, listening and learning.

"Men boast endlessly to women of what they know," Bess once said as we stitched panels for a wall hanging. "Then they claim women know nothing. Nonsense! Not only do we reap the ample knowledge they let fall, we store up our own wisdom besides. But since they disdain to glean anything from us, they are deficient by half. I bow to no man, Anne. I will have my name in the histories yet to be written, and so long as Hardwick stands with my initials on its roof, there I am."

Though heavy rains drenched England that summer and autumn of 1594, I continued to enjoy my new life at Hardwick. The household varied in size depending on which of Bess's offspring joined her in residence. In addition to the family, there were never less than thirty servants. The upper servants were more like courtiers, the sons and daughters of gentlefolk who had gone into service, as Bess had done at the start of her career. The lower servants included the cooks, scullions, ladies' maids, laundry maids and other manual workers. Officially, I was a lower servant and ate and slept with them in the hall, but Bess's friendship and my position as Arbella's seamstress elevated me slightly. The atmosphere was always busy: sewing, baking, washing, brewing, meals, music, dancing, entertainments, and of course, the construction on New Hall. When the downpours slowed the work, Bess rotated the men to indoor projects. Ever one to turn a situation to her advantage, she decided the deluge would be a good opportunity to build fish ponds, which she had stocked with pike, bream and carp.

"It's England," she said with a snort. "If you wait for the rain to stop, you will never accomplish anything."

To pass the wet evenings, I composed a few sonnets to an imaginary lost love. I suppose I was mimicking Will—or missing him. Either way, the exercise loosed the literary rust from my brain, and my fingertips tingled to have a quill back in my hand.

"What is it you scribble by candlelight in the servants' hall?" Bess demanded. Nothing happened at Hardwick that she did not find out.

"Sonnets," I confessed. "I hope I have not disturbed anyone by my late hours. I pay for my paper and ink out of my wages and use only the candle stubs."

"Sonnets. Tut, tut, and I thought you had such a clear head. Bring them to me."

I obeyed.

Bess read and arched an eyebrow. "For someone who denies any knowledge of love, you write remarkably well about it."

"It is not the topic but the writing that intrigues me."

"Ah, that is the influence of your brother, the playwright. No doubt it runs in your family. Too bad." Bess handed back my verses. "Well, I see no harm in it, so long as you dash any romantic fantasies that may occur to Arbella."

I readily agreed to her command. At nineteen, Bess's granddaughter and her young ladies did enough sighing over love to waft a fleet of ships to the Indies, and as I fitted Arbella's dresses I was sometimes privy to her confidences. But while I tactfully discouraged her dreams of romance, I began to indulge a few of my own. Hardwick was swarming with men: masons, carpenters, artisans, gardeners, gamekeepers, plus all the household servants. Half a dozen tried to catch my eye, and one or two stirred my desire. With Will far away and our future uncertain, had I not as much license to commit adultery as he? After the bed pleasures Kit had shown me, why should I forgo them? But to go beyond fantasies could cost me my position, and besides, most of those at

Hardwick were honest men; what they sought was not a lover but a wife. I must have seemed the ideal catch—Bess of Hardwick's personal seamstress, healthy, attractive, hardworking, intelligent and good-natured. With such attributes, no wonder my single state caused puzzlement. Bess herself offered to find me a husband.

"I suspect you are as finicky about men as you are about your stitches," she chided, a little ungently, as we embroidered a bed hanging one twilight after the other women had gone. "Surely on all my estates we could find someone who pleases you."

"My freedom pleases me. I am happy where I am. Is this not a pretty velvet?" I held out a sample for her approval, but she was not diverted.

"Tut, tut. You could rise in the world, as I did, by the right match. My bailiff at Chatsworth is recently widowed, and Simpson, who manages my glassworks, is quite a decent man."

I bowed my head, pretending to frown over a stitch.

"And children," Bess continued, "surely you want children."

My head fell lower, and for an instant I longed to tell her the truth. Here was a woman, a great woman, who had befriended me, and I was deceiving her. Bess's finger lifted my chin, and she gazed into my shame-flushed face. For a long moment she held my eye.

"There *is* a child," she said quietly.

Her finger let go, and with a slight nod, I lowered my head. Her guess was close enough.

"Well," she said, more kindly, "most men would overlook it. They may have got one or two outside the sheets themselves."

"I know." I drew a breath and stroked my embroidery while she awaited a further reply. "It's only . . . have you ever felt . . ."

My mind skipped back to that first afternoon Will had come upon me at Shottery Brook. I had been thinking it too bad the religious orders had been destroyed, for I would have fared well in a nunnery. In a way, a nunnery was what I had here at Hardwick, a part to play in a great house, to pursue sewing and reading and writing amongst gentle company. Nowhere would my name or initials appear on my work, as did Bess's proud ES on her six towers. But did that matter? I was a member of a community with a purpose, creating beautiful needlework that would please and inspire those who saw it in years to come. It might even please God. Perhaps celibacy was a fitting price to pay.

"It is only that I am happy here," I concluded lamely. "I don't want anything to change."

Bess patted my shoulder. "Then I shan't pry. Besides, between Arbella and my other grandchildren, I have enough matchmaking on my hands."

Good to her word, Bess tossed away the idea of my marrying, and the men of the estate gradually shrugged their shoulders and left me alone. I tore up the sonnets to my imaginary love and lay awake in the dark nights, listening to the rain drumming down.

Chapter 18

They say the sun-kissed climate of Italy makes the people there naturally amorous and carefree. If that is true, I suppose the abundant rain in England dampens our national character to the opposite degree. You never hear of a passionate English lover, do you? Yet inured as we are to our drizzly skies, it was rapidly becoming obvious that autumn of 1594 that we were experiencing far more precipitation than usual. Rivers overflowed, people and animals drowned. Corn did not ripen; fields of wheat and barley were reduced to sodden stalks. Carrots and turnips had to be dug up at half their size or risk rotting in the soggy ground.

Nonetheless, Bess did not allow the mud and mire on the roads to stop her from making a December journey to London, where she bought chests, chairs, candlesticks, carpets, pitchers, plate, tapestries, mirrors, sconces and every other thing you could imagine. Shopkeepers went into a flurry at her approach and sank moaning afterward at the hard bargains she could drive. She took me along, sending me to scout fabrics, threads and trims and granting me an afternoon to check on Will. It is always strange to come home after an interval away. I looked around the room to see what had changed—not much, yet it felt different somehow. Smaller, outgrown—I had become used to the grandeur of Hardwick. Lonesome—if Will had a current mistress, he did not bring her here. I sensed no woman's touch.

"How goes it?" I asked, sitting on my old bed. "How does everyone at the theater?"

"All right," said Will. He had smiled on seeing me, but his face grew shadowed as we began to talk. The bad news was that the playhouses had closed again for the summer soon after I went to Hardwick. The crop failures and higher food prices caused by the rain had led to serious riots in London, and the authorities feared any place a mob might gather. Worse, poor Tom Kyd had recently died; he had never fully recovered from his torture. On the brighter side, the Lord Chamberlain's Men, led by the Burbages at the Theatre, and the Lord Admiral's Men, starring Edward Alleyn and based at Philip Henslowe's Rose, were now established as the two principal acting companies, and a sense of stability was returning. And Will had had an offer.

"I have been invited to become a partner in the Lord Chamberlain's Men," he said. "I have only to raise the funds."

"But that is excellent! And as for the money"—I laughed—"just ask your rich friend the earl."

He shrugged uncomfortably. "I'd rather not."

"You are still on good terms, aren't you?"

"Yes."

"And you finished *The Rape of Lucrece* and dedicated it to him as planned?"

"Yes."

He handed me a copy, and opening the handsome volume, I felt an unexpected thrill. Never mind what Will and I had been through, whether we quarreled, whether we loved, whether we had chosen the right path. "Will, this is wonderful!" I said. "You have created a beautiful poem that no one else could have written. Could you ever have imagined back in Stratford that you would do this?" I read over the effusive dedication. "The earl must have been enchanted."

"He liked it enormously."

"And the public response?"

"It is as popular as *Venus and Adonis* last year."

"Then what is troubling you?"

For a moment Will did not reply. "You remember how I thought having a patron would solve everything? It's more as if . . . I feel like a pet dog." He turned to the window, watching the rain as he spoke. "At first you are so excited to be taken in, you gladly perform any trick your new master requires. You sit at attention, twirl on your hind legs, wag your tail, all for whatever scraps he cares to toss your way." Will mimicked the pose of a begging pooch, followed by a face of disgust. "I am thirty years old, Anne. Enough, damn it!"

He struck his fist on the wall, and I started at his vehemence. From those first commissioned sonnets exhorting the teenaged earl to wed, Will had understood his pen was in paid service. He had been tickled to do it, and poetry was indeed his forte; he set words into poems like a meticulous jeweler arranging gems in a crown. As for the monetary rewards, Southampton's "scraps" had been extremely generous. Had some tiff arisen, a falling-out? I recalled Will's discomfiture over the French dress, the female roles he had been forced to play in *Love's Labor's Lost*, and once again a vague unease crept over me.

"What is it, Will?"

He never quite told me, not that day or any day thereafter. He muttered and mumbled and brushed it away. He was thirty, he said, and though his name was steadily becoming known, he was still neither a great actor nor a great writer nor a great anything else. Every path he tried seemed promising, yet he ended up at the same crossroads, unsure which way to go. Should he seek another patron? Forgo poetry and concentrate on the Burbages' offer? And meanwhile he had to subject himself to . . .

"To what?" I coaxed.

His eyes slanted to the sheaf of sonnets on his table, and I picked them up and skimmed through them. The first short batch was the original commission from the earl's mother, the pleas to marry that Will and Southampton had chuckled over. Still more ladled praise on the earl himself. A few were sublime:

Shall I compare thee to a summer's day?
When in disgrace with fortune and men's eyes . . .
Let me not to the marriage of true minds admit impediments.

But even in Will's capable hands, they often gushed the same ostenta-
tious flattery: You are young, beautiful, wondrous. You outshine the sun.
I adore you, I am at your mercy. When we quarrel, it is surely I who am in
the wrong. How divine you are to forgive me and take me back. Oh, do
not let a rival poet steal your affections! No one else loves you like I do.

How much did you love him, Will? Was your body in paid service
along with your pen? Did you shake him with your spear, or did he shake
you? There were places in the writing I could not help but think something
had occurred. *The master-mistress of my passion . . .* Thus he termed that
alluring boy, lamenting that nature had not given him a woman's parts. If
Will did truly love him, I would not censure. The deep affection I had witnessed between Mr. Phipps and Mr. Edwards had given me to understand
that love takes myriad forms. But theirs had been a relationship of equals,
whereas an impossible gap lay between Will and the earl. The sonnets were
tinged with disparity and discomfort; after the first flush of being taken up
by a noble patron comes the reality of subservience. You laugh at the bad
jokes. You don the French dress. You trot at their heel. When someone has
the wealth and power to advance you, it is hard to say no.

But the murkiness did not end there. The final poems were addressed to a third party, a mysterious Dark Lady. Will seemed to have
disliked her as much as he was enthralled by her, and this sly creature
apparently captured the earl's eye as well. Then he and Will shared her,
amicably, jealously, in an ever-shifting triangle. Who was she? I don't
know and I don't care. I do not blame her either. She only did what a
woman must to survive, and she did me no personal harm. But the
wrangling over her between Will and the earl—think of *The Two Gentlemen of Verona*, the inexplicable friendship between Valentine and
Proteus, their distasteful trading over Silvia. Was that too a disguised
record of Will's relationship with Southampton, true love forced to endure and forgive the indignities of a fickle friend?

"Leave him," I said, looking up.

"I can't. Not yet." After a moment's silence, he changed the subject. "I have a new play on the boards. I call it *The Taming of the Shrew*."

Well, it is an age-old tale, and every man in the audience is bound to cheer Petruchio as he bends and bullies the bad-tempered Kate to his will. Smug wives probably approve her capitulation and acknowledgment of him as her master. I myself think Petruchio did Kate a favor; she was intolerable. But even when they both reform, I did not like either character, and after I bade Will good-bye and headed back to rejoin Bess, it occurred to me that this play too was just a bit coincidental. After all, here I was employed by the Countess of *Shrews*bury, a woman who refused to bow to any male. Perhaps I was the shrew as well for flouncing off and deserting him in favor of Hardwick. And was there yet another shrew, the Earl of Southampton, and another, the Dark Lady, all of us troubling Will? He should have called this play *The Taming of the Shrews*, for I sensed between its lines the chafing discontent of a man who longs to browbeat an unruly force into submission just as he feels himself to have been browbeaten by others. I could only hope he would find a way out of his unhappy entanglements.

Never let anyone tell you that a piece of fiction is not personal.

⁓

The contact with London must have stirred me, for on our return to Hardwick I knew what I wanted to do: write a play entirely by myself. I had come close with *The Comedy of Errors*, producing a reasonable first draft before I turned it over to Will. Consider also that I had left Stratford in the summer of 1588 and we were now embarking on the year 1595. I had thus spent almost seven years, the term of a typical apprenticeship, learning and practicing the craft of writing among the best teachers, actors and theater companies England had to offer. It was high time to see what I could do.

Very well. What should I write about?

"A love story," I whispered, it being late and I the only one left awake in the servants' hall. The night was freezing as I huddled at the long table, my blanket pulled around my shoulders, but the feeling of embarking on something special helped me ignore my shivers. And the choice of a love story was sound. Tragical romances like Kit's *Dido, Queen of Carthage* were by far the favorite literature when I read to Bess's ladies, and as usual I had only to take an existing tale and transform it for the stage. To appeal to the male audience, my romance should also encompass brave speeches, heroic swordfights and plenty of slaughter. I mused over King Arthur and Guinevere, Tristan and Isolde, before settling on my subject. *The Most Tragical Drama of Helen of Troy*—how you would have laughed to read the first scribbles. Aeolus with his huge puffed cheeks could not have blown a bigger bag of wind. Wisely, I did not wear myself out long on that endeavor.

"A history then." Another cold night; my whisper turned to an icy mist before my face. Once again, the choice made sense. We had done Henry VI, followed by Richard III. What about going back to Richard II? It was his overthrow by Henry Bolingbroke that led to the War of the Roses, where our modern English history began, and I could refresh my memory from Arbella's copy of Holinshed's *Chronicles*. It was one book Bess insisted her granddaughter study deeply; it would never do for a potential future queen of England to be ignorant of her country's history.

"Help yourself," said Arbella. "Holinshed is boring."

Oh, no, he is fascinating, and on those frosty winter nights as I wrote *Richard II* I strove to understand the clash of arms between the king and Bolingbroke. Some would say Richard deserved his downfall. He was greedy and made serious political blunders. How could he fail to see that his illegal seizure of Bolingbroke's inheritance would alarm the other nobles and turn them against him? The banished Bolingbroke had only to choose his moment to return and rally his followers to rebellion. But when the first draft was complete, I found my strict adherence to historical facts had produced a very dry play.

"Richard"—I blew on my cold hands—"the stage is yours. Come forth and claim it!"

He did. In my second draft, Richard became self-absorbed and altogether taken with his own posturing. I pictured him surrounded by and openly admiring himself in imaginary mirrors. In short, he overacted being king—wouldn't Dick Burbage have fun with him?—and when I brought Richard up against the calculating and emotionless Bolingbroke, I saw the real story was not the clash of their arms but the conflict of their personalities. Frightening to think how often the fate of a kingdom and the wars and suffering that overtake ordinary people hinge on the character of a single man. If our kings are indeed God's anointed, why did he anoint so many flawed ones? But there was still a problem with my play. Why did Richard seem vaguely familiar? Because as a deposed monarch he naturally called to mind Edward II, another fallen king, and of course Kit had written a play about him which, I now realized, I had unwittingly imitated.

"Damn!" I pulled my hair in exasperation. After several fruitless attempts to reposition Richard, I bundled up the play and sent it to Will via Bess's steward Timothy Pusey, who made frequent trips to London to settle her legal matters. Though I asked only for Will's opinion, he took *Richard II* and blatantly edited. He improved it, and while grateful, I was also angry—with him for meddling and with myself for once again falling back on someone else's judgment.

"Courage, third try," I whispered, dipping my quill.

I revived the idea of a love story and found a promising source, brought from London by Mr. Pusey in Arbella's latest batch of books: *The Tragical History of Romeus and Juliet* by Arthur Brooke. The story was well-known in several languages; Brooke's version was a rhymed poem of over three thousand lines. I would turn it into a play in blank verse. My one doubt was Romeus, a silly boy. Well, what about those lovesick swains pining at court and buying sonnets at the bookstores? Men could be as silly as women about love. Besides, the lovers' families are feuding, and Romeus does kill Juliet's cousin, Tybalt. One body down, an excellent way to hook the male audience. As for the Hardwick ladies, when I read them Brooke's poem, they gave it their highest approval: They bawled.

Very good then. Begin . . .

I began with Romeus bemoaning his bad luck in love. His bad luck in love? At such a tender age, boy, you don't know what bad luck in love is.

I rebegan with Juliet, pining for fear she will never be wed. Oh, stop weeping, girl! To be married is no rosy enterprise. Do you think you will still possess that shining hair and slender waist when you have birthed a half dozen squalling imps?

I made another false start with Juliet's parents arranging her marriage to Paris, a man so lifeless she might as well marry a stick.

Another opening scene landed in the fire when Juliet's prattling nurse butted in.

Some nights I could not face that blank paper and made excuses to stay away.

"God's blood," I groaned, "why can't I get this? Where is my muse?" Kit had always seemed so inspired, so animated. Will was spurred by his desire for wealth and fame. Well, I wanted a play of my own, and stubbornly, I slogged on. Somewhere was a path to the top of this mountain, and I was determined to get there alone.

～

On an evening in early April when the day's sewing was done, I was strolling the grounds when I came upon Arbella. It was the second day in a row of soft blue skies, a welcome break in the endless rain. Warm air had crept in from the south, and the scent of spring flowers lingered in the gardens and along the paths. You could feel the change in everyone's demeanor, as if the door of a dank underground prison had swung open and the inhabitants of Hardwick had been let out to breathe sunshine once again. Arbella was facing westward as the sun set over the valley in a wash of pink and dusky blue. She seemed to be yearning toward it, her wave of light brown hair flowing loose down her back. So lovely was the sight that when I first glimpsed her from the side, I thought the glistening tears on her cheeks were the happy tears of heart's ease. Then she turned at my footsteps, and I gasped.

"My lady, what is it?" I hurried to her.

She closed her eyes and let the tears drip, shaking her head.

"Come, come." I led her to a stone bench and drew her down beside me. She was still a beautiful girl then, slim and twenty, pale complexion and wide blue eyes. Yet her ragged face that night presaged the tormented woman she was to become.

"I am rebuked," she said, her voice dazed and hopeless. "The queen has cast me lower than the least peasant in the kingdom."

I put my arm around her. "Shh, shh, come now, don't talk so," I implored, though my brain immediately took fright. Any instance of royal displeasure was cause for alarm. "Tell me your trouble. Surely it can be mended."

All my life people have confided in me, told me their woes. An unfair burden—when have I ever been allowed to tell anyone mine? But I asked, and Arbella poured out her griefs, which as always were entangled with her proximity to the throne. How much happier she might have been as a country milkmaid; instead, from the moment of her birth, she was everyone's pawn. The question of whom she would marry was paramount, though even to discuss a potential match could bring charges of treason. A decade before, Elizabeth had been furious when Bess connived to betroth Arbella, at age nine, to Lord Denbigh, the two-year-old son of the queen's favorite, Robert Dudley, Earl of Leicester. It all came to naught when little Lord Denbigh died. Subsequent candidates had included Arbella's cousin King James, the son of the Duke of Parma and a host of other ambitious princes, depending on which way politics and religion swung.

The latest development in these dynastic scramblings should have relieved the pressure on Arbella. In 1589 King James had married Anne of Denmark, and the couple had lately produced their first child, a boy, pushing Arbella a step away from the throne. Instead, the Catholic factions that opposed Protestant James grew more united in favor of Arbella, though she herself was raised Protestant. They must have thought her malleable, an easily controlled marionette.

"I don't want their stupid crown." Arbella wept. "Catholic or Protestant, I don't care. Can't they see that?"

No, they couldn't, Queen Elizabeth least of all. How dared anyone meddle with the succession? How dared they treat Gloriana as an ordinary mortal who might one day expire? She would outfox them and live forever. The queen had commanded Bess to desist from marriage schemes for Arbella, but although Bess outwardly complied, I do not believe she discouraged others from intriguing on Arbella's behalf. Some said that was the real reason she was building New Hall, as a "palace of the north" for her granddaughter's future court. Ah, so alike, Bess of Hardwick and Elizabeth Tudor, in name, in appearance, and above all, in strength of will. Perhaps that is why they quarreled as often as they got along.

Meanwhile, where as a docile child Arbella had once been petted at court, as a restless and attractive young woman she was kept at Hardwick under strict guard. Desperate, she had smuggled a letter to the queen and begged to be readmitted to her presence. A mistake. The just-received royal reply scorched like a coal too hot to handle.

"I am never to leave here but as a virgin in a coffin," said Arbella, weeping on my shoulder.

"Poor lady, poor darling." I patted her and stroked her hair. Pointless to tell her that love was often an illusion and she would be better off without. Like all her young friends, male and female, she believed true love existed and that to be denied it was the worst fate that could befall. She clung to it, despite ample evidence of marital failures all around her. *Mine will be the exception. Ours will be the love that burns bright as a flame unto death.* Blame it on the poets—those scoundrels!— but what if they are right? If true love exists, it should be our holy grail. We should desire it more than life itself. Unlike Arbella, at least I had had my chance. If I could fly this minute to London, rush into Will's arms . . . I blinked at the impossible turn my thoughts were taking. It must have been the spell of the April evening, the colors of the dying light.

"There, there." I hugged and comforted, rocking Arbella in the darkness until her sobbing and pain were exhausted. She thanked me and wiped her eyes, then slipped away, begging me to say no word to anyone of her folly. I sat quietly, my body chilling as the warmth where she had huddled against me evaporated in the night. Then in my mind's eye I saw another woman, kind and elderly, consoling a distraught girl.

More than consoling—plotting, conspiring to give the young creature she had nursed her heart's desire.

I jumped to my feet and ran to the house, hitching up my skirts.

"Stay with me," I breathed. "I'm coming!"

I careened into the servants' hall and snatched up my quill.

In my youth, there had been in Stratford a crazy old woman who talked aloud as if conversing with a realm of unseen inhabitants. The children pelted her with stones, and people said the devil had gotten into her head. I do not know what became of her, but when Juliet's nurse emerged in my brain that night, I suspected I had entered that lunatic land. I have since found that in starting any play, the story cannot begin until one of the characters speaks up. You answer back, they seize your ear and soon other characters are clamoring to be heard. Like the figures in a tapestry they step off the wall, turn to one another and begin enacting their tale. Who needs a writer? They have substance, flesh, a pulse, and they know their own story better than anyone else. Give them scope and the whole play unfolds before you; you have only to scribble down the words. If this is the devil's work, I contend he is divine.

Two households, both alike in dignity, In fair Verona, where we lay our scene . . .

But firmly rooted in England. The houses of Tudor and Stuart in uneasy balance. The fractious elders, Montague and Capulet, Elizabeth and Bess. The skirmishes marital, political, religious. Juliet—Arbella—at first a demure daughter, willing to accept her parents' choice of Paris for her husband. Romeo, the ardent suitor of whom every woman dreams, moping over Rosalind until he invades the Capulets' ball, where he is stunned by Juliet. Then nothing else matters, in heaven and earth, nothing else. They are as much in love with love as with each other, and they have to die—we know it, we who are older and wiser— yet to the last we yearn to believe it can end differently, if only Juliet awakens a moment sooner, if only the vial is empty when Romeo raises it to his lips. We curse the feuding parents, the interfering friends, the complicit nurse and bumbling friar. Damn you and your stupid quarrels! Look what you've done! Oh, my God, they're dead!

I wept over my papers. Some sheets were so tear soaked, they puckered into soft spots that I had to write around. I let the language fly. *What light through yonder window breaks? It is the east, and Juliet is the sun!* In Brooke's poem, the story of the lovers' courtship, marriage and death took nine months to unfold. I condensed it to a mere five days, a whirlwind of passion and grief. I put traces of Gilbert, Will's brother, into good-natured Benvolio, and if you cannot see Kit in mocking, troubled, reckless Mercutio, stabbed by mischance in a duel, then you have no eyes. There are bits and pieces of my life crushed everywhere into that play, and this is another great thing about being a writer: that nothing you do in your life ever goes to waste. You cut it out in little stars and scatter it into the heaven of everything you write.

I showed *Romeo and Juliet* to Will on my next visit to London. Bess had not come, sending me with Timothy Pusey to buy fabrics and trims. Will paused over the play an anxiously long time.

"Well?" I asked, twisting my hands.

"Well . . . it's good."

He tried to keep his tone light, but I saw the struggle that worked the muscles of his face: admiration, confusion, trepidation, jealousy. Then I knew too. It was very good, wasn't it, Will? But you didn't write it, so how could that be? And suddenly I was as frightened as if an earthquake had rumbled beneath my feet. I hadn't meant to challenge or equal him, to drive another wedge between us. I just wanted to write something very fine that would make an audience gasp with astonishment and my chest swell with pride. For a long moment, Will and I stared at each other, the color drained from our cheeks. Then Will swallowed and cleared his throat.

"It's excellent," he said. Then his voice shriveled. "Now what?"

Chapter 19

Romeo and Juliet by Anne Shakespeare.

Why didn't I do it? Oh, God, God, God, why not?

I think Will would have let me, though as he stood there, ashen, every instinct in his body fought to disbelieve what he held in his hands. To admit I could do this shook him to the core. It would have confounded every man and most women throughout Christendom. Women are inferior beings. They are incapable of writing plays, let alone an excellent one. And if an ordinary woman could do this, what did it say about him? He had worked, studied and sweated to rise to the top of his profession. Now here came a piece that made him think he might as well pack up his quill and go home. From another man, he could have borne it more easily, slapping congratulations on a comrade's back while enviously gritting his teeth. But to comprehend it from a woman? Above all, from me?

For a long time we looked, the scales rebalancing themselves.

Will drew a breath. "What now, Anne?" he repeated.

"I don't know."

And that is the truth. I didn't know. I had no example to guide me. There were few other women authors during Elizabeth's reign. The only one of whom I had any inkling was Mary Sidney, Countess of Pembroke, sister of the great poet Sir Philip Sidney. She was a patron of the poet Samuel Daniel and several other writers, and her name had been high on

Will's and my list of potential benefactors. She did translations from French and wrote poetry for her own amusement, mainly turning psalms into verse—ho-hum. She also maintained a literary salon, but only for her court friends, not a nobody like me. And wait, there was one other, for I am forgetting that Queen Elizabeth likewise composed poetry. You can be sure whatever she wrote, it was "Brilliant, Your Majesty!"

Now here was my chance to step forward. Take it, Anne!

But when I tried to envision emerging from my shell, I felt immediately unnerved. I had not been raised to be forward or bold. I was a writer, not a pioneer or a revolutionary. Whenever in my life I had acted courageously—like running after Will to London or skipping off to Hardwick with Bess—it was usually because circumstances forced it upon me. And even for me the notion of a professional female playwright was almost beyond imagining. A man might as well give birth, a fish sprout wings. Finally, standing there facing Will, I cared far less about making history and far more about what this would mean between him and me.

"What should we do?" I asked.

Confused, he shook his head. He seemed to understand I had not done it to sabotage or betray him. If the pupil had bested the master, he had only himself to blame. And in his way, he too cared what became of us. A marriage is till death, no matter what form it takes, no matter how mismatched and wavering the affections, and for the most part we had made our odd arrangement work and enjoyed mutual benefits thereby.

"Even if I tell the company, I doubt they will believe me," he said. "Kempe will hoot me out of the Theatre. And if I do persuade them . . ."

He grimaced, and I caught his meaning. To put my name on *Romeo and Juliet* would inevitably cast suspicion on the authorship of the previous plays. While that might elevate me, the far greater effect would be to diminish the reputation of William Shakespeare that we had labored so hard to build. Will would be a laughingstock, a subject for farce, a poet in skirts. No one would ever take a play by William Shakespeare seriously again; literary reputation aside, it would almost certainly destroy our livelihood. Could we put both our names on *Romeo and Juliet*? Then if I did write another good play, the second one would be more easily received as a solo effort while allowing Will to brag of his protégé. Will must have thought of this also, but having swallowed his pride and acknowledged my feat, he would not now suggest anything that implied he was claiming half the credit. Besides, how could we have authored jointly when he was in London, I leagues away in Derbyshire?

"On the other hand," Will offered, "your play might be seen as a phenomenon, a reason to draw a crowd."

For a moment I brightened. That people would come just for the novelty of a play by a woman might make it worth the company's support. Then my stomach gave a twist.

"Or it might bring down the authorities."

I sagged onto the bed. Until now, I had always had Will to hide behind when one of our plays drew criticism or fell flat. He also handled the tricky business of placating the Master of the Revels. This functionary, Edmund Tilney, scrutinized every script for the least deviation from political expediency or religious orthodoxy. No play made it to the stage without his approval, and the changes he dictated could eviscerate both the script and the writer's soul. Thus, while I had had the pleasure of writing, Will took the brunt. Even if *Romeo and Juliet* passed censorship and proved popular with audiences, the shock of a female author was guaranteed to provoke attacks. Just recall the malicious pamphlets our fellow writers like Thomas Nashe and Gabriel Harvey were forever hurling at one another; none of them would be as gracious as Will in admitting me to their club. My stomach wrenched tighter. Was I up to the controversy, humiliation, scorn?

Will said nothing, regarding me sympathetically. He must have known how it would end. Perhaps if he had thrown off neutrality—"You can do it!"—but he held back. For reasons good and bad, practical and selfish, he gave me the choice. Had I grasped it, had I borne the abuse and demanded the acclaim, I might have been the first acknowledged female playwright in the English language. I might have made it easier, sooner, for those women who followed. I like to believe Will would have championed my cause. Would you have, Will? Or was your response all a clever manipulation, and I am once again deluding myself? We both knew something had changed between us. But at the crucial moment I was weak. It was my own character that failed me, and I lost my chance.

"No," I said. "You take it."

Romeo and Juliet and every subsequent play went out the door with Will's name. Ambition should be made of sterner stuff.

~

During the two weeks I was in London, Will and I spent almost every day together. *Richard II* had just opened, but even with Will's edits some scenes were still giving trouble, and we made further adjustments. *Romeo and Juliet* was snapped up by the Lord Chamberlain's Men and—Will wrote me later—made it through production with only minimal changes. I could wish there had been more of them. Gawky rhymes, excessive punning—well, it was the style of the day, and if Will and I were too caught up in the story to notice the occasionally overwrought wording, the same must have been true for the audience. Their roar of applause confirmed *Romeo and Juliet* a great success. Dick Burbage excelled as Romeo, and the sweet-voiced boy who played Juliet gave her the courage to brave the tomb in search of true love. Yet whichever actor played Juliet over the years, it was always Arbella's face I saw in the role and myself as her nurse.

"I miss London," I said with a sigh to Will as we strolled the streets, munching sticky buns and licking our fingers. Though the rain had returned in force that summer, I remember it as a beautiful afternoon. And wasn't it funny how naturally we had fallen into our old routine? At one point, Will even slipped his arm through mine and let it rest there awhile. It helped that his situation with the Earl of Southampton had finally begun to resolve itself. The beautiful boy had found a new playmate, Elizabeth Vernon, a cousin of the Earl of Essex, and whether Will and the dark mistress had lost favor by comparison or whether it was a mutual cooling of the triangular passion, both Will and the dark one were drifting to the periphery of Southampton's circle. Though he felt the pangs of departure and regret, Will was ready to move on. Having a patron had served our purpose, sustaining us while we mastered our craft and enabling Will to purchase a share in the Chamberlain's Men. As for the earl, when you are rich, you can always buy new friends.

"Being a shareholder means I get a slice of the profits from every performance, not just a onetime payment for a script," Will said as we walked. "I have a say in the running of things, how the company is managed, what plays we perform. I won't act anymore, unless I am needed for a small part. I can see I was never very good at it to begin."

I smiled to myself, and Will caught it and elbowed my ribs.

"What about competition from the Admiral's Men?" I asked.

"Ned Alleyn and Philip Henslowe are a formidable team, and they have signed on a new young writer, Thomas Dekker. But we can cooperate. We have a common interest in keeping the theaters open and audiences streaming in."

"Then we must keep writing."

"Yes. If you are willing, together we can turn out twice as much."

"We can send manuscripts back and forth by Mr. Pusey," I suggested, "until I come again."

"As we reap profits from the company, we should think of investing," said Will.

"In what?"

"Land, a house in Stratford. I plan to make a great deal of money from the theater and retire as a gentleman."

"And as the greatest playwright in England?" I teased.

"Of course!"

We laughed, then paused. It was as if we looked at each other in pleased surprise and said, "Wait a minute . . . I know you. We used to be friends." Now a new stage lay before us—pun not quite intended, but I'll take it—and with the theaters thriving, Will's business sense and our combined literary talent put us in a position to make William Shakespeare the foremost writer and a rich and respected man. For once in our lives we had arrived at the same place at the same time.

By the day of my departure, we had plans for three plays. The first, a comedy, sprang upon us as we supped one night at the tavern. The Chamberlain's Men had given a performance at court that afternoon, and Will was reporting to me on the appearance of the queen.

"She wears so much paste and powder to conceal her wrinkles that it dries and cracks like plaster," he said, shuddering. "She flirts with men young enough to be her grandson, fluttering her eyelashes and simpering. Kempe claims he saw her fondle the Earl of Essex when she thought no one was looking. It is grotesque, Anne."

"To think it has been twenty years since she visited Kenilworth," I said. "What a glorious occasion that was. Do you remember how you pushed me out of the way to see her?"

"What? What are you talking about?"

"You pushed me out of the way after I got you to the front."

"I don't remember that. We never met there."

"Yes, we did, and you were a spoiled imp."

"Well, if I did, please forgive me. I was only a boy." He offered a share of his baked apple in apology. "Do you remember the giant trumpeters and the fireworks on the lake?"

"It was like stars exploding. Do you remember the story of how Harry Goldingham played Arion on the dolphin, and he mixed up his lines?"

"His nose was red from drinking, and he blurted to the queen, 'I am none of Arion but honest Harry Goldingham!'"

"Poor silly man," I said, both of us chuckling. "What an ass he must have felt, yet the queen laughed and everyone joined in."

"It was a fantasy, a dream. We should write it, a tale of lovers and fairies in an enchanted wood."

"Let me have first crack," I begged.

Our second choice was a history, King John. A play on the subject already existed—the Queen's Men had performed it in Stratford that fateful summer of 1587—but Will was eager to redo it and burnish our reputation in that genre.

"People should think: history—William Shakespeare," he said, snapping his fingers.

Our third idea arose from a visit to London Bridge. I had gone into a shop to buy a special gold lace requested by Arbella, and when I emerged, Will was staring toward the south end where the traitors' heads bristled on pikes.

"Do you recall the trial of Roderigo Lopez?" he said.

I cast my mind back a year and nodded. Lopez, a Portuguese Jew turned Christian, was a learned doctor and had been Elizabeth's personal physician. You might have thought that would keep him safe from harm. But somehow he ran afoul of the Earl of Essex, who accused him of being a foreign agent and attempting to poison the queen. Damning testimony was wrung from Lopez's servants by torture. Elizabeth did not intervene. Lopez protested his innocence all the way to the scaffold, where he was hanged, drawn and quartered. Many felt it was the least any Jew deserved, yet in a few minds there arose qualms that an injustice had been done.

"Why do you want me to remember that?" I asked, taking Will's arm to turn him homeward. The execution had taken place about the time I left for Hardwick, and I shied from the grisly evocation.

"Because it revived Kit's *Jew of Malta*. Ned Alleyn has been playing it all year to huge crowds at the Rose, and as long as the subject is popular I think we should mine it."

"But we cannot keep traveling in Kit's shadow. We should do something different."

"There is nothing different," said Will, squeezing us both past a cart as we exited the bridge. "Sometimes I think there are only twenty stories in the whole world. Lovers part and reunite. Kings and usurpers vie for crowns. Murdered spirits cry for revenge. The task of the writer"—he paused, ready to hear himself being clever—"is to infuse the language with such beauty and truth that the audience gasps in astonishment to think they have never heard it before."

"And who more qualified to do that than William Shakespeare?" I said, and we grinned.

On my last day, walking toward St. Paul's Cross, where I was to meet Mr. Pusey, we both dragged our feet. Ask me, Will. *Ask me to stay.* I might have said yes, though my conscience reproved that I owed

Bess too much to desert her without warning. And perhaps we needed more time to absorb the changing relationship between us; by the look on Will's face, his thoughts mirrored the caution in mine. Wiser but sadder—the heady days when we could rush into anything were gone. Besides, there was Mr. Pusey waiting, and with a few awkward phrases, Will kissed me on the cheek and helped me up to the wagon.

"Good-bye!" he called suddenly, as the wagon creaked away, and the crowd merged between us. He flung out his arms in imitation of a heartbroken lover. "Parting is such sweet sorrow!"

I doubled in laughter. Then, mimicking his gesture, I rose to my role. "Good-bye, good-bye, until it be morrow!"

This time, all the way to Hardwick, I looked backward.

~

Rain, rain, rain. It drips, it splats, it pours. You cannot know in advance how long a spell of bad weather will last, but by the summer of 1595 we had endured more than a twelvemonth of wet gray skies, and along with the damp, a dread pervaded the kingdom. If the harvest failed again that autumn . . .

It did and for another year after that. In the end, the calamitous weather lingered from 1594 to 1597 and brought famine and poverty to many unfortunate people. Hardwick was not immune, and though she persevered in her building, Bess's income dropped by a quarter. Everywhere you looked, life was less jolly, and our leaders did little to provide relief. The government's affairs were in a muddle, the treasury drained by mismanagement and corruption. The never-ending war with Spain continued to simmer on the Continent, rebellions erupted in Ireland, and the cost of maintaining garrisons on foreign soil pushed the country further into debt. Plots and persecutions became more blatant. Was Elizabeth losing her grip on power? Was this the twilight of a once dominant queen? The political maneuverings invariably involved Arbella, at least by name, and included rumors of kidnap schemes. It is no exaggeration to say our nerves were often under siege.

Rain, rain, rain. Do you know what I think? I think it is because of the rain that England has produced so many great writers. What else is there to do on a soggy day in a cold northern land? You sit by the fire and read and write, shivering. You chastise your runny nose with a handkerchief and concentrate on the lines. It is the only reprieve from our dour climate: to escape with a cast of imaginary characters to some more exciting realm of mind. If you were in Italy, you would be out picking grapes, flirting by the fountain, dew-grass dancing with upflung arms. But in England, you huddle by a stone hearth and strive to warm the world with your pen. Laugh if you like, but I maintain it is true. Where Italy sows lovers, authors sprout from our sodden English soil. As half of that hot commodity William Shakespeare, I was one of them.

"What are you scribbling at night now?" Bess demanded. "I thought you had given up those silly sonnets."

"Only some ideas for my brother, for his plays."

"Can't he do his own work?"

"Yes, of course, but I . . . I like helping."

Well"—Bess harrumphed—"so long as you do not ruin your eyes for sewing."

Meanwhile, the muse was murmuring sweetly in Will's and my ears. Over the next year, sending our manuscripts via Mr. Pusey, we completed three plays. *King John* is my least favorite. Once again we tossed historical accuracy out the window; it would have made a tedious and unwieldy play. On the other hand, we whipped so much together that events galloped across the stage at breakneck speed. The main problem, however, was that the Bastard stole the show. Rough and irreverent at the beginning, rising to heroism at the end, he took all the best speeches and left the politicians in a sniveling heap.

Let's kill them off and crown the Bastard king, Will wrote, frustrated, after we had both tried and failed to rein him in. Ah, well, still learning, always learning.

I give higher marks to *The Merchant of Venice*. Where the typical story of the evil Jew piles one act of violence and revenge atop another, Will based our play on an Italian tale in which the threat revolves around a single pound of flesh; sometimes brutality is more chilling in small doses. Nonetheless, in his first draft the character of Shylock was an undisguised copy of Kit's Barabas.

"It's what the audience wants," he said when I expressed misgivings at our next meeting. "This is what they come to see."

"But it is wrong. That time I traveled back to Stratford alone, there was a Jewish merchant in our company, a widower with two young children. He was kind. He was polite. He did not scowl or snarl or curse us. The children were educated and respectful. None of them had horns."

"I know." Will gnawed his lip. His parents' religion had long worn off, and privately we both wished that common sense would prevail over ignorance and intolerance. "When I pass the Jews' quarter, they keep to their business and molest no one. But Shylock must be greedy and cruel enough to set the stakes for his loan at a pound of flesh. Otherwise, what will he say? 'Here, Antonio, help yourself to my money. If your ships sink and you cannot repay me, I will just forgive the debt and go bankrupt.' "

I gnawed in return. Will was right. Even a comedy must have a conflict. No conflict, no play.

In the end, I think we achieved the right balance on our Jew, though when *Merchant* was first performed, most in the audience booed that Shylock, stripped of half his earthly goods and forced to convert to Christianity, got off so lightly. Now I would say the play is best viewed as an unintended milestone, for our English theater was once again maturing. As we playwrights outgrew our childish dependence on stock characters and plots, our infatuation with puns and verbiage, the actors took up the challenge. Given clean poetry to speak and complex characters to play, they stopped spouting words and striking poses. Their portrayals became varied, subtle, elegant, deft. In the Chamberlain's Men, we had a stellar group of players—Dick Burbage, Will Kempe, John Heminge—and they inhabited and enlarged our characters even beyond what we had imagined.

Our audience was also growing more sophisticated. Presented with Shylock, they were initially puzzled. Where was the evil Jew they loved to revile? Who was this man who, despite the huge fake nose, did not fit the familiar beaked profile? I watched their faces scrunch as they tried to comprehend. They were being asked to work harder, to use their brains, and, struggling, they complied. One day, unobserved by the doorway as the crowd exited from a performance, I overheard two laborers rating the play.

"Ha, that'll teach the filthy Jew," crowed one.

"Maybe," muttered the other, a crude fellow with a bushy beard and pockmarked face. He scratched his head and frowned. "But that pound of flesh and no blood trick . . . I wouldn't be happy if it were played on me."

So we were all working harder, and we loved it. Funny, then, that the best play of the three came with the greatest ease. *A Midsummer Night's Dream*—who would want to wake up from such a delightful reverie? In Bottom the weaver, bewitched with an ass's head, we even immortalized a bit of honest Harry Goldingham.

"Wonderful!" Will wrote when I sent the script via Mr. Pusey. Then he eliminated one character, cut two scenes and added three. This time, I thanked him. We had matured enough to accept each other's critiques with good humor, valuing the corrections. And how can you not like and admire someone who shares your talent and your passion? I think Will and I were closer then in thought and affection than at any previous time. In the spring of 1596 he wrote that Cuthbert had fired their latest wardrobe master, and that "the actors still ask after my sister, the seamstress. They beg that you come back to sew for them."

Almost, but not quite. *Ask me, Will. Ask me.*

Fool that I was, I was falling back in love with Will Shakespeare, and I hoped and believed he felt the same.

⁓

By now we were making quite a bit of money, and after sending a generous sum to Stratford, Will determined to get his father the one thing sure to gladden the old man's heart: a coat of arms.

Ah, me, a coat of arms. What a vain and trifling accoutrement when you are rapping on death's door. Does God care if you are a gentleman? On the contrary, it is to your detriment; you are the camel squeezing through the needle's eye. But in this earthly life, you must strive to obtain wealth and position and bring glory to your family name. To possess a coat of arms would certify John Shakespeare a gentleman, a recognition he had once sought and been denied, and this time Will's reputation should procure a different outcome. Above all, it is a son's duty to avenge a father who has been wronged.

With childish pleasure, Will set about sketching a design. A good coat of arms, he wrote me, should be bold and distinctive to ensure it stood out and was not mistaken for any other. John's original petition had featured a bird and a spear, and in his application he asserted that his grandfather was a hero in the War of the Roses who had been granted land by King Henry VII. This was pure invention, yet despite the lack of warrior forebears, a spear was inevitable; might as well leave it in. Will's preference was for a gold spear on a diagonal black band on a gold shield. The crest featured a spread-winged falcon atop a helmet clutching another spear in its talons. But Will was stuck for a motto and requested my assistance.

Honor is ours?

Valor and glory?

Honor and valor?

Triumph and wisdom?

The two greatest writers in the English language, and this was the best we could devise? I left it to Will in London, and in between sewing Arbella's dresses and embroidering a set of cushion covers for Bess, I perused Holinshed. We had decided upon Henry IV for our next project, but the crafty Bolingbroke was eluding us, and I was annoyed. Our collaboration had become so fruitful that I expected more plays to drop into our lap like ripe plums. I have since come to accept that even with two of us writing diligently, there is often a needful lull after finishing a script. You cannot begin to savor a new play until the taste of the old one has left your tongue.

Thus my sojourn with Holinshed, while Will stewed over the motto. Once he submitted the application, the College of Arms would investigate our claim. To be successful, an applicant must have a worthy profession, own property, be free of debt and be adjudged pious and of good moral character. I found the latter qualification particularly amusing. Since the single most important criterion in obtaining a coat of arms was the ability to slip the college officials the payment to get one, the first place to look for a scoundrel was the college itself. Nonetheless, the process would soon be complete, and we arranged to meet in Stratford to present his father with the long-awaited honor. In early August I asked Bess for leave.

"A coat of arms? You are moving up, Anne," said Bess. "By all means, you may visit your family. Mr. Pusey is traveling to London in two days and can escort you. Arbella has more than enough dresses to last her until Christmas."

I thanked her and packed a satchel with my clothing. Too late to buy presents for the children. Besides, with the money Will regularly sent the family, I pictured them already prettily dressed and amply supplied with toys, Susanna and Judith rocking new dolls, Hamnet showing off his skill with juggling sticks. Though Will had made a trip to Stratford while I was at Hardwick, it was going on three years since I had walked up Henley Street. John and Mary would embrace me—yes, I could imagine that—and I warmed to think of John's reaction when Will unveiled the coat of arms. I pinched myself as a severe reminder, in the event I beat him to Stratford, to say nothing that would spoil the surprise. When our wagon reached Clopton Bridge, Mr. Pusey helped me down and promised to hail Will if he passed him on the road. I headed up Henley Street, picturing the fine curtsey Susanna would make and hopeful the twins would recognize me this time.

"Hello!" I called, opening the door and seeing only a figure bent over the table.

"Mother?" Susanna lifted her tear-streaked face from her crossed arms. "You're too late. Hamnet died this morning."

Chapter 20

*N*o. *No, no, no. NO!*

I grabbed Susanna by the shoulders. "What are you saying? What do you mean?" I shook her hard, and her throat disgorged a piteous sob.

"Hamnet is dead!"

She fell into my arms, weeping, and as if in answer, a spasm of grief broke out in the bedroom overhead. I clutched my daughter and rocked her with a fierce fright. No, this was not true. My son was fine. All my children were fine, pretty, red cheeked. I had walked into the wrong house. I had walked into a dream. I must stop this bedlam and take control. I pushed Susanna from me and ran up the stairs. In the bedroom doorway, Mary stood sideways, clutching the frame. Eyes closed, muttering some prayer, she knocked her forehead to the wood. At the bedside knelt John. All those years he had bellowed, too angry, too hearty, too bluff. Now he roared like a bear in the baiting pit, his arms thrown across the bed, covering the blanketed body thereon. From nowhere Judith appeared, flying at me out of a corner, screaming.

"We sent Gilbert! Why didn't you come? Why didn't you come?" Her fists pummeled me, her unkempt hair and tormented face the living image of a harpy child. In her eyes welled the utter misery of one who has lost half her soul.

"Let me go!" I shoved her away and dropped to my knees at the bedside. John lifted himself from the blanket, shook his puckered face at me and fell back to give me room. Hamnet lay as if asleep, the blush still upon his cheek—please, God, let him be sleeping! I brushed back his fair hair. "Hamnet, Hamnet," I pleaded softly, as if to wake him too abruptly would cause undue alarm. "It's Mother. I've come."

I reached beneath the cover to find his hand. It was warm to the touch, and my heart lightened. All this commotion for nothing! Beside me, Judith had sunk to the floor, panting, her glance darting like an animal that feels the hunter stalking. John encircled her waist with his arm and dragged her away.

"Hamnet," I said reasonably, though my voice had begun to quake. "Hamnet, wake up." His lips were parted, and his girlish face looked sweet on his pillow. But when I lifted him to my breast, his head fell back like a broken doll and his jaw sagged open, and where a beating pulse should have shown in his throat, there was only a cold blue vein. "Hamnet!" I shrieked.

Susanna had arrived in the doorway, and she and Mary clung together, moaning. John still held Judith at bay.

"Get the doctor, get a doctor!" I screamed at all of them.

"The doctor has come and gone," said John. "He's dead, Anne."

They stared at me, helpless spectators, while the words sank in.

"No! But what happened? What sickness?" The tears started in my eyes. I could see no marks on my son, no rash, no sores. And slight, he had always been slight, but there was no wasting away of his flesh.

"Two weeks ago." John tried and failed to wipe his face dry. "A simple ague, it seemed. Then a fever that broke. Then chills."

"We kept him warm," Mary insisted, as if she had already repeated the plaintive words many times. "We gave him beef broth for nourishment, honey to soothe his throat. We chafed his feet and cooled his brow. We brought the doctor and the priest. Oh, God! Why have you taken him?" She buried her head on Susanna's shoulder.

I sat on the floor beside my son's deathbed and watched the room fall apart before my eyes.

⌒

They had sent Gilbert riding to London three days before. But the night of my arrival a rain began, and by the next morning it was a torrent, delaying Will's and Gilbert's return. While Mary kept Susanna and Judith downstairs, Magpie Joan sat beside me as I kept vigil by Hamnet's bed. For once even Magpie had ceased to chatter, and we cried together, she hugging my shoulder by the flickering candlelight as twilight came down. Richard and Edmund hung around the fringes, sixteen-year-old Edmund trying to be manful in the face of his nephew's death. John disappeared, and Richard brought quiet reports to the bedroom. A grave would be dug as soon as the rain let up. The priest was preparing for the funeral.

"You must know his sweet soul is in heaven," Magpie said, holding my hand. "He was a blameless child, the joy of all who knew him. I promise you he did not suffer much, Anne."

"I hate God." I clenched my fist.

"You don't mean that. It is your grief speaking."

She paused and glanced apprehensively around the room. A stirring of air had given us both a sudden chill, and I pulled up the blanket to keep my son warm. What did it matter if I hated God? What difference if this was his will or some cruel trick of fate? My son was dead, and his body would be laid in cold, damp ground, and his flesh would rot away—

I covered my face in my hands as fresh anguish burst forth.

"There, there," said Magpie. "There, there."

⌒

I wondered if Hamnet's ghost might come that night, and at every creak of a floorboard or skittering of mice in the roof, I searched the room. I longed to see him. If he could only tell me that he was in paradise. If only

I could say good-bye. Ghosts come most often, they say, to be avenged for a wrongful death, and what is more wrongful than the death of a child? But no misty figure appeared; no piping voice comforted my ear.

"Did he ask for me before he died? Did he ask for me or his father?" I implored John, who came to the bedroom sometime after midnight and took the chair beside me. He looked a corpse himself, gray skinned and unshaven.

"No. He didn't know he was dying, and neither did we. The day after Gilbert left, he seemed to be getting better. He sat up and ate some fruit pudding, and I joked with him what a scare he had given us, sending his uncle to London for nothing."

"Maybe he is not really dead but just sleeping," I said, as if it could still be true, and I shook Hamnet's shoulder as I might to wake him for school in the morning.

"Don't." John clamped my hand and held it tightly until I stopped shaking.

"Do Susanna and Judith sleep?" I asked, trying to sound reasonable again.

"Yes. They are worn out with crying."

"And Mary?"

"Fitfully. I expect it will be so for many nights."

He reached out and patted the coverlet, and I remembered that he and Mary had done this three times before, kept vigil over the two infant daughters who had preceded Will and then over Will's little sister Anne. In this same bed? I fingered the coverlet, a pretty piece of my own work embroidered with purple gillyflowers. Over the hours Hamnet's face had grown waxen and his body stiff. My son was a corpse. My shoulders shook, and John opened his arms and I sobbed inside them.

⁓

Will and Gilbert arrived midday. Will, who was no rider, had clung to the saddle, enduring jolt after jolt and cramps in his thighs, and he nearly fell off the horse into the street, his legs bent in agony. One look at my face and Gilbert cried, "I am too late!" Afterward, he berated himself—if only he had ridden faster, if they had plunged on through the mired roads, though their horses were spent from the pace.

Red eyed, I watched Will endure the same shock and disbelief that had engulfed me. All that day he mourned by our son's body, and each time our eyes met, the pain was so terrible we could not speak for sobbing. He begged God to take his life instead—I had urged the same bargain many times during my night's vigil—but both our pleas fell on ears that were not deaf but unimpressed, perhaps, with the littleness of the offering.

Waves, that is how grief comes, waves that overwhelm and tumble you without mercy, like a shipwrecked body rolled in the surf, cast up on the beach near drowned. Will and I held each other, and I did my best to comfort him. He gathered Susanna and Judith and hugged and rocked them. Mary tried to feed him. She tried to feed everyone, more to keep her own mind from despair, I think, than to fill our bellies, for no one was hungry. I had neither eaten nor slept since my arrival, and by that second evening a charitable numbness claimed me. I remember sinking almost in slow motion there in the parlor, my hand slipping from the mantel where I had just set a candle, and nothing more until I came awake in bed the next morning.

As we carried the shrouded body to the churchyard, friends and neighbors turned out of their doors and joined the procession. Nothing of what the priest said has stayed with me. I know that Will held my arm, and we tossed sprigs of evergreen into the grave. Susanna bowed her head and dutifully recited the prayers for her brother, but as the first clump of earth hit the shroud, Judith covered her ears and ran away shrieking.

The rain had ceased, and it was a beautiful day.

～

That evening my brain wandered in search of memories. Once, when Hamnet was little, he accidentally poked his finger into Judith's eye, and when she set up wailing, he crumpled the offending finger into a fist and hit himself in the face. It happened in a blink, yet in that split second his small visage showed horror and remorse for the misdeed, then surprise at the self-punishment. Another time, perhaps he was three, he had eaten a cake left on the table and stoutly denied it despite the icing stuck to his chin. He was quick to laugh and to sing, and Gilbert said he was becoming accomplished on the flute—might he have become a musician? His ears were a little low-set, and I had worried about that. Did it signify anything? No, just one of those oddities that gives a mother pause. I remembered how the lumps in his socks would drive him to distraction, and that time I brought him the hat with a plume. He had worn it throughout my stay, doffing it with courtly pomp to his grandmother, sisters and me when he entered a room.

Were these all the memories I had of my child? I hung my head in shame.

Will must have been doing the same.

"That such a sweet child could be taken," he said numbly, as the family sat by the fire.

How do you know he was sweet?

"I remember how he loved playing at swords, and extra jam on his bread."

No, you don't remember that. You remember your mother telling us he did.

"I have lost the joy of his laughter, the light of his eyes."

When did you ever have them, Will? How often did either of us hold him in our arms?

"I remember—"

I shrieked and leaped to my feet.

"This is your fault, yours! If you had not run away with the Queen's Men, we would have stayed in Stratford where we belonged! We would have been here taking care of our children, not playing at make-believe in London. Damn your vanity and your aspirations! Was it worth it, Will? Was it worth losing our son?"

I knew the charges were unjust even as I uttered them. Hamnet might have died wherever we lived, whatever our occupation. And neither of us could have given up London or turned our back on our talent as it flowered there. Will loved our child and had as much right to mourn as I. But I could not stop the hateful accusations that spewed from my mouth.

"You abandoned him! You only loved the idea of him! We never missed him as much as we ought!"

The others gaped, too shocked to reply, but Will took it like a dumb beast endures a lashing. When I was spent we stared at each other, then I fell to my knees before him.

"I'm sorry, Will, I'm sorry," I cried. "I didn't mean it."

He shook his head and wordlessly bent his forehead to mine.

Over the next few weeks, the household returned to life around us. Richard and Edmund were first. I heard them laughing over some jest in another room, and I wanted to rush in and slap them for the sacrilege. But why should they continue to hurt over what could not be remedied? Why should anyone hurt, if they don't have to? So the next morning, when I heard Susanna chuckle at a bird that had pulled a squiggling grub from the garden, I held the sound to me as if it were something I might someday imitate. John and Gilbert got back to business. They had trading to do, gloves and leather goods to sell. I followed their industrious example and sat in the garden, embroidering pillow covers. Mary and Susanna kept me company, and I instructed them in the elaborate stitches. Susanna at thirteen had grown still lovelier and was now taller than her grandmother. They were eager to hear about Hardwick Hall, and my recitations passed the time.

Only two did not recover, though outwardly it appeared they were coming around. Judith resumed playing. She stayed at some distance from us, within sight but out of the conversation, putting her doll through the motions of some story in her head. She would become quite absorbed, her head tipping or her mouth pouting as the doll whirled or jumped or sat on a stone. Her lips moved, and once, straining, I caught snatches of her monologue. She seemed to be talking not to the doll but to someone beside her, the way she and Hamnet had played of old. I let her be. If it gave her solace to think her brother still kept her company, where was the harm? I would have spoken to him myself if I believed he could have heard.

And Will. He walked to the churchyard every day and stood by the grave. I did not join him. In the grave was a body, and if my son's soul were anywhere, it was back in this house, this garden. Otherwise, Will was eating, sleeping and had a new purpose. Forgoing the surprise, he informed his father of his endeavor to secure the long-coveted coat of arms. It raised John's spirits—it raised everyone's—and Will and John spent hours reworking the petition and design. The gold spear acquired a silver head; the motto was still undecided. I listened as the Shakespeare lineage became ever more illustrious and did not contradict the two men.

By the end of August Will was ready to return to London.

"What do you want to do, Anne?" he asked as we walked back across the fields from Shottery. It had been a painful visit with Duck, Bartholomew and Isabella, the sight of nieces and nephews running over the farmyard, children being happy.

"I want to come back to London." For a while after Hamnet's death I had considered staying in Stratford for our daughters' sakes. More belated guilt—what good does that do anyone? Susanna was already perfectly competent at life without any assistance from Will or me, while Judith shunned us both and lurked like a stranger amidst the rest of the family. My other choice, Hardwick, might have restored my spirits in time. But it wasn't a *place* I wanted to return to, it was Will, and when I said, "London," he nodded. During the past weeks, sharing our old room with our daughters, we had listened each night for the rise and fall of their breath to confirm sleep so that we might release in silent streams the day's dammed-up tears. Even if we never touched like husband and wife again, neither of us wanted to go on alone.

So we departed Stratford in early September, Will to London, me to Hardwick to give notice to Bess. I suppose I could have sent a letter. The few clothes and belongings I had left there would have been no great loss. But I am not that sort of person; I require endings, no trailing threads but stitches neatly tied off. As I walked up the winding road, the bright sunlight glinting off the windows of New Hall made it sparkle like a lantern on a hill. The building was finally nearing completion, and before heading to the servants' quarters in Old Hall, I paused for a view. Here and there a crew of laborers hauled away plaster buckets or a stone carver chipped the final details into the Hardwick coat of arms glorifying the roof. I wondered where these men would disappear to next and if they had jobs to move on to, or whether, as Bess sometimes claimed, they were deliberately slowing their pace to make the work and their pay stretch a few months more. On that day, in my state of mind, Hardwick looked sharp and empty, flinty and angled like Bess herself, and I was less enamored of her than I once had been. How could she value wealth and possessions over her fellow human beings? But of course it was I who felt detached from everyone around me. I was like Hardwick Hall, more glass than wall, a brittle surface sheathing a hollow within.

It was several days before I had an opportunity to speak privately with Bess. She had just seen off a horde of family and guests, and the activity had aggravated her rheumatism. She rubbed her knee beneath her dress, and I asked after her health.

"It will greatly improve when I have some peace and quiet," she said with her usual snort. "However, at my age I do not complain. It is a miracle to me that I have lived through conspiracies, plague, four husbands and eight children, yet I can still chew my food and bedevil my servants and offspring." She stopped, an adept reader of faces.

"My child is dead."

"Ahh."

I lowered my head, and for a moment Bess said nothing, granting me a sympathetic silence. Then her hand touched my sleeve. "I am very sorry, Anne. When? What was the cause?"

"He fell sick. He died the morning of the day I arrived."

"And you had but the one."

I did not answer, and after a minute she spoke again.

"All children are dear, Anne. I lost two, and I mourned them as any mother would. God cuts many lives short, and we cannot know why. In time, the heartache eases, and we can keep you as busy as you desire meanwhile."

"Thank you, but . . ." I faltered. Hardwick had been my home for two years; quitting it would be harder than I had imagined. "I must leave your service. My brother needs me in London."

"Your brother the famous playwright, William Shakespeare."

I started. Bess, who disdained the theater, finally recognized Will's name?

"Yes," she said. "My son saw a recent play of his in London. Some nonsense called *Romeo and Juliet*. Was that not the story you used to read to my ladies?" She eyed me, lips pursing. "For what exactly does your brother need you?"

"To keep his lodgings and look after him. To encourage him. Writing is an all-consuming endeavor."

"Tut, tut, it is a job like any other. Tell him to get on with it."

"He has also become a partner in the Lord Chamberlain's Men and has many responsibilities therein."

"Then he can afford to hire his own servants, not steal mine. I will increase your wages."

"No, please!" I pressed my fists to my chest, trying to hold the truth in. To explain myself at this point, to spill out my tangled history of dissembling, was more than I could bear. "You have already been more generous than I deserve. But my brother is the hope of our family. He has gained an auspicious place in the theater, and I must be there to assist him. And the child who died was dear to him too. We are so far from Stratford, and we want to be together."

Tears burned my eyes, though when I raised my face halfway to Bess, I saw there was no need for further protestations.

"I shall be sorry to lose my best seamstress," she said, "especially when you also happen to be of superior intelligence to most silly women. The next time Mr. Pusey goes to London, you may leave with him. And do not carry away any sadness or rebuke yourself that you have deserted me. Women do far too much of that. Men don't look back." She reached toward me, and with her finger she lifted my chin. "You are not who you seem, are you? Tut, tut, get on with it."

⌒

It was early December before Mr. Pusey's next journey, and I spent the time sewing one last gown for Arbella. Rose satin, her favorite color. Each stitch was bittersweet, drawing me forward, tugging me back, but when the gown was finished, I was pleased at the happiness it gave her.

"One day my wedding dress shall be this color," she said, twirling. The morning of my departure, she presented me with £1 as a parting gift, half of which I later disbursed in pennies to beggars along the road. Bess wished me an unsentimental farewell and sent me off with a pearl ring to remember her by, as if anyone could ever forget Bess of Hardwick.

When I arrived in London, Will greeted me with momentous news. The Shakespeare coat of arms had been granted, and John and all his male descendants henceforth were entitled to call themselves gentlemen. Will had commissioned an artist to render a colored drawing, and it was handsome indeed: the spear-holding falcon suitably warlike, bold red accentuating the mantles that flourished on either side of the helmet and gold shield. But the motto, chosen by Will, struck me wrong.

Non Sanz Droict, Not without Right. How could Will have missed the irony? Because to say you claim something *not without right* implies there are those who say you have no right to claim it. Perhaps it was a preemptive "So there!" as if Will and his father were snicking their thumb at those who had shunned John twenty years ago. Now that petulant phrase would forever stick to our name. Were it up to me, I would replace the spear on the shield with a quill in an inkwell and a motto thus: *Scribendo Surgimus*, We Rise by Writing. Yet I pretended joy for Will's sake, and Will pretended it for his own. Afterward, he put the drawing away and did not look at it again for a long time.

The real irony, of course, is that having obtained a coat of arms, we no longer had a son to whom we could pass it on.

Chapter 21

*B*efore our journey to Stratford, before Hamnet's death, we had chosen *Henry IV* as our next play. It was the logical sequel to *Richard II* and would continue our streak of English histories. Few, I think, have done them better. For God's sake, let us sit upon the ground and tell sad stories of the death of kings! Even the most unfit, inept monarch soared to a moment's nobility—or pathos—on our wingèd lines. I looked forward to the project. Neither of us being in much cheer to celebrate Christmas, we could spend the holiday quietly writing.

First, however, we had to move to new lodgings Will had arranged across the Thames in Southwark. To live cheek by jowl amongst the brothels, bear pits and gaming houses gave me pause, but a new theater, the Swan, had opened there that year, and the Chamberlain's Men had recently begun playing at that venue. Their usual home, the Theatre in Shoreditch, had developed complications. When James Burbage built the Theatre in 1576 he had taken a twenty-one-year lease on the land. That agreement would soon expire, and with the landowner, Giles Allen, threatening a steep rise in the rent, the players had regrouped at the Swan until the negotiations were resolved. Though the rooms Will had taken were spacious and could be made comfortable, in the December dark our new abode had a disheveled feel. I unpacked, straightened and tidied. Will was often out until suppertime or later, and I made sure to have venison pies or currant buns and a pot of ale waiting by the fire.

"It is good to have you back," he said, coming in one night and making gratefully for the hearth, where he let out a shivering, "Brrr!"

"I am glad to be back, even if only to tend to you," I said wryly. "But good heavens, Will, no hat or gloves in this weather?" I took his hands, which were freezing. Men—how do they ever survive without us? "Were you at the theater? I would have thought it too wet for a performance. Here, I have kept our meal warm." I lifted the plate from the hearth.

"No, thank you. I ate at the tavern, but I could do with some ale. And I am glad you're here, Anne. I didn't mean that the way it sounded."

He gave a sheepish smile; then a tired look reclaimed his features as he sat down in his chair. In addition to our own recent sorrow, his friend George Peele had lately died of the pox. I poured him a mug and joined him, helping myself to the food.

"A difficult day?" I asked, noting the dark moons beneath his eyes.

Will sighed. "The Master of the Revels has been riding us hard of late, and the city authorities are once again calling for the closure of the playhouses. As for the dispute with Giles Allen, we are making no progress. The better news is that the Burbages have taken a lease on the dining hall of the old Blackfriars monastery near St. Paul's and plan to open a small indoor playhouse for an upper-class audience. The performances can go on day or night, rain or shine, and the rich will gladly pay a higher price to sit comfortably among their friends and avoid the rabble."

"But that is unfair. Why should the rich have their private theaters and the common people none? Where would we be if not for all the plays we stood and watched as penny groundlings?"

"I know, but as a shareholder . . ."

Will shrugged, and I finished reluctantly for him.

". . . you must do what is most profitable."

"And despite all, we have had good earnings this season," he concluded. "I should be happy." He picked up the poker and nudged a burning log, and for a moment we fell silent.

"Shall we talk about him?" I asked.

"No."

We watched the fire, thinking of our son.

"Maybe we should begin *Henry IV*," I said, rousing myself, "now that we are settled. I thought you might have started it while you waited for me to finish at Hardwick."

Will grimaced. "My mood was wrong. Anne, we must try to regain our spirits, not spend the holiday festering here. Let's be merry, shall we? We'll go to plays and the winter fairs and clap for jugglers and musicians. The Chamberlain's Men will probably be called to perform for the queen. Would you like to come along?"

Would I!

From then on, I was in a flurry of anticipation, though Will cautioned against any wild imaginings. Even as principal playwright of the Lord Chamberlain's Men, he had yet to be singled out by our gracious monarch. The most he could promise was that I might see her from the rear of the hall. Nonetheless, my brain shot up a thousand fireworks. There I was, bowing before Gloriana, kissing her bejeweled hand.

"So you are the sister I have heard so much about," she would say, and give me a Bess-like look of far deeper meaning than the polite phrase implied.

"Your Majesty!" I would exclaim, and here my sparkling rockets fizzled as my tongue failed to launch a reply. What on earth did one say to a queen? I would stutter and be mortified. I would trip on my hem and fall on my face. But Elizabeth smiled! I was forgiven! She expected her subjects to be humbled and awed. Then *bang!*, my brain would explode a hundred delightful new pinwheels starring me and the queen. Go ahead, laugh—I knew they were mere flights of fancy. But I enjoyed every last one until they burst and sprinkled in glittering colors to the ground.

On the appointed night, we arrived at Whitehall Palace. I wore a new dress. "Have one made, Anne," Will urged. "We can afford it." What, trust another seamstress to do it as well? I paid strict attention to the sumptuary laws, and Mr. Phipps would have beamed to see me in a modest but becoming brown velvet edged in gold ribbon. Even if I only stood in the background, I wished to acknowledge the importance of the occasion. Me, a farmer's daughter from Shottery, in the same room as the queen! As Will, the actors and I were led through the palace, my head twisted and turned to peer down corridors and guess at closed doors. Which were Elizabeth's personal apartments? Where lodged her ladies, councilors, secretaries, messengers, guards, servants, footmen? Painted ancestors presided over the torchlit walls, and as we marched this royal gauntlet, the younger actors nervously recited their lines. Will Kempe bustled them along.

"Have no fear. Kempe is here! Bungle a verse and I will rescue you with my rapier wit. I will skewer your mishaps like doves on a spit and serve them up fit for a king. Why, the old girl won't even notice you when I am onstage." He enacted a sword flourish as he strutted along.

"Show-off," Will whispered, rolling his eyes and guiding me to a corner of the great chamber where the actors were to perform. The room was already crowded with lords and ladies, and it was the Lord Chamberlain's job, Will informed me, to make sure no one sat above his or her station on the rows of upholstered benches. As Will began naming off notables, I took in the tapestries and candle sconces, the mingled perfumes, the rustle of conversation and the sibilance of silk gowns. On a dais at the front of the room was the throne, magnificently carved and furnished with scarlet cushions embroidered in gold, *ER*. The back of the throne was surmounted by a carved lion's head wearing a crown. She must have one in every palace, I thought, perhaps in every room. Was a queen even allowed to sit in an ordinary chair? Or did a chair become a throne when she sat in it? A strange prickling crept over me. How would it feel to ripple your spine against its back, lay your arms on the armrests and grip the knobs—

In a sudden whoosh, the audience rose, and I jumped. Will gave me a bemused glance and tipped his head toward the figure seating itself in the place where my imagination had just been. I saw a glittering gold gown with an enormous ruffled collar that fanned over the shoulders like the wings of an exotic bird, a cake white face topped by an imperious red wig. Then Elizabeth commanded the play to begin. *Romeo and Juliet*—that did plump my pride!—and though Kempe proved a scoundrel, stealing as many lines as he spouted of his own, the young actors did brave work, and the queen clapped and brayed. The dashing Earl of Essex and a select company sat by her, and was it really true, as Kempe claimed, that he had once seen Elizabeth's long fingers squeeze Essex between the thighs? I alternated between shock at the impropriety and rabid curiosity. She was twice his age! He was also unabashedly ambitious; he leaned on the throne, smirking, and let everyone see. At least no one could accuse me of openly coveting—

Hard as onyx, the queen's eyes fixed on me. She knew! Oh, God, she knew I had imagined sitting on her throne. *Not to usurp it, Your Majesty, I swear! Just to see how it felt.* An empty wood chair, yet it had exerted a magnetic pull. And not like Kenilworth or the times we had watched Gloriana borne on a litter in a procession through town. Those were excusable daydreams of pomp and ceremony, an invitation to picture yourself the center of attention, feted and adored. This was a call to power, the terrible itch that infected Essex and Mary, Queen of Scots, and every other claimant before them. And if I could feel what they felt . . .

Romeo and Juliet were dying, and Elizabeth's eyes had moved on, but my brain hovered over the experience like a hawk scanning for the best place to land. I found it, marveling: Whatever a person's state, there is no emotion exclusive to highborn or commoner, rich or poor. Ambition is ambition, whether for a king's throne or a glover's coat of arms. Fear is fear, whether of a lurking assassin or fumbled lines. Grief cuts everyone with the same knife at the death of a child. Simple, obvious, yet thinking them ever above us, Will and I still portrayed our kings and queens mainly as heroes or villains, not characters of flesh and blood. I know these people now, I thought. Henceforth, I know how to write them. Thus illumination, by way of an ordinary chair.

When the play ended, the queen thanked the actors and departed on the Earl of Essex's arm. One of her gentlemen came around to weight each player's purse with a coin or two, depending on the size of their roles. Then we all left together, bound for the nearest alehouse to celebrate.

"Did you enjoy it, Anne?" Will asked as we settled amidst our noisy comrades with our mugs. "Even if you did not get to meet the queen?"

"It was excellent," I said, ducking my head as Dick Burbage tossed a shilling over the table to John Heminge to settle some wager between them. I could see I would have no chance to share my insight with Will tonight. Half the actors were singing and thumping the table, the other half replaying their best lines. When the congratulations finally died down, they turned to politics, and having spent my time at Hardwick mostly in the company of women, I listened to the men's voices with renewed pleasure. The problem, everyone agreed, was Philip of Spain, as usual. It did not bode well that he was rebuilding his navy and supporting the rebels in Ireland.

"We have nothing to fear from that bird's pizzle Philip," said Kempe, emitting a scornful belch. He raised his cup to the tavern whores. "Excuse me, fair ladies. Be thankful it did not exit by the rump."

"If you are so bold, go enlist," scoffed Dick.

"No need," said Kempe. "Far better to pray for Philip than to fight him."

"Pray for him?"

"Indeed, for the recovery of his memory."

"What ails his memory?" asked Heminge.

"Why, he has clean lost it, for if he had it, he would remember what happened to his invincible armada the last time. Besides, who gives a fig for honor in battle? What has it got that sorry lot?" Kempe motioned toward a group of grizzled men. A dark-eyed girl was seated amongst them, and at Kempe's raised voice, she rose and flounced over to him. He plopped her onto his knee and planted a sloppy kiss on her mouth. "Smart whore!" he cried. "Come toss in the sheets with me. I will prove a better jouster than those slack soldiers."

Cuthbert cast the men a disgusted look. "How we are to be defended from the Spanish by the likes of them, only God knows," he muttered. He swigged his ale, and I was reminded that I did not like him. From the way the ragged crew hoarded their mugs, I guessed they hadn't the coin for a drink often.

"England has more to fear from the Earl of Essex than from Philip of Spain," said Henry Condell, and others nodded. "He has dangerous visions, and the more the queen indulges him, the more reckless he becomes."

"Play Elizabeth and Essex!" called a customer at another table, and since actors never need coaxing, two of the troupe began to improvise a bawdy scene. Will laughed and covered his mouth to prevent spewing his ale, but I found it distasteful and returned my gaze to the soldiers. They were five in number, their eyes sunken, beards tangled, scraps for clothes. One of them bent to rub his knee, and I saw there was no leg below it and a crutch by his side. Had they once marched off to battle confident and bantering? How could anyone walk toward the point of a sword without quaking? I tried to catch snatches of their conversation, but their voices were too low.

"When are you coming back to sew for us, Anne?" Cuthbert demanded, interrupting my meditations. "Since you've left that crusty old countess, you will need something to keep you busy."

"I am busy," I said, noticing Will's eyes drooping at the late hour. "Will, it is time we were on our way."

"Oh, ho," said Kempe, shoving him. "You have drunk too much again, you slobbering sot, and your sister has to drag you home. Arrest him, Anne! Jail him and put him to work! We need a new play, and we need it soon!"

Will waved him off good-naturedly, and after a bit more teasing, I got Will out and we headed for our lodging.

"That Kempe can be most annoying," I said. "I am not dragging you home."

"Of course not. Pay him no mind. He wants a new role, that is all."

"Well, unless he behaves, he won't get it." I shook off my animosity, refusing to let an irascible loudmouth spoil my evening. "Thank you for letting me come, Will." I slipped my arm through his and squeezed, and he returned the slight pressure. He had seemed happy tonight; too often his responsibilities for the company weighed him down. And Hamnet's death still shadowed us both, though we were mending. What we needed was to resume writing—might it even bring some special light for me back into Will's eyes? Ah, you are hopeless, Anne. But meanwhile, a touch was good enough; friendship would suffice. I walked home from seeing the queen, a farmer's daughter from Shottery.

New Year 1597, and I was ready to begin *Henry IV*. But Will was embroiled in company business. The Blackfriars playhouse project was under way and the lease negotiations for the Theatre land had grown antagonistic. With Gilbert acting as his agent, he was also exploring the purchase of a house in Stratford.

"Go ahead, you start," he encouraged. "I will pitch in soon."

I cut a new quill and set to work, my fingers cramping in the January cold. From the outset, I knew *Henry IV* would be different from our previous histories. My revelation at Whitehall had given me the confidence to shape my royal characters in a more rounded, more human way. Yet I also could not forget those tattered soldiers at the tavern. England was flush with them in those days, the stray dogs of war. When there was a campaign in progress in Ireland or the Netherlands, they might find employment, rations and a blanket to wrap themselves in. But between battles they were discharged with nowhere to go, and whatever pay they brought home soon vanished into the brothels and dicing dens. Some took to being highwaymen; others were hanged for poaching to put food in their bellies. Still others died in rancid alleys, broken down from disease and wounds, drunk, if they were lucky, to ward off the cold and pain. As might be expected, Southwark was a favorite haunt, and Will and I observed them often that winter in the taverns where we took our meals. In my mind they juxtaposed with Kempe—that braggart would desert at the mere whiff of gunpowder!—and he ballooned into a fat knight leading a band of motley warriors with scarcely a sword or a uniform amongst them. This had nothing to do with King Henry IV, however. Shouldn't his play be about him?

"A history is meant to be serious," I argued to Will, who was not arguing back. I waited while he signaled the tavern keeper for a refill of his ale and waved my hand over my mug to indicate no more. "To insert a comic or low-life figure unbalances the story. Look at *King John*. We indulged the Bastard, and he got too big for the play. I can hardly remember the other characters, and we wrote them."

Will shrugged. "I wish all our characters were as memorable. If this fat knight you picture insists on having his say, give it to him."

"I may have to. It seems the only way to evict him from my head. He could be one of Prince Hal's companions." I paused. Yes, that might work. I had been debating how to include the usual stories of the prince's wild youth and the trials he caused his father, the weary king. Conflict on and off the battlefield, the father-son angle, the contrast of high and low society—the play was shape-shifting itself into being.

"A cowardly knight would suit Kempe enormously," said Will. "It doesn't have to be a large role. Whatever the length, he will ham it to twice the size you intend."

"Then we can easily divide the writing. I'll take the comic cast, you do Bolingbroke and his court. We'll splice them together and have a new play ready to premiere this spring."

"Well, perhaps not that soon." Will sighed regretfully. "I am pressed with other affairs, remember, but you go ahead."

The next weeks were almost happy ones, despite pelting winter storms and if any time can be considered happy when you still mourn a child. Little things catch you out, flashes of memory too quick to censor, the sight of a towheaded boy running up a street in the snow. Sometimes I cried. Will would hold me then, though he himself remained dry eyed. It brought us back to bed together, for comfort, for friendship, for solace in the dark.

Meanwhile, the lard-belly knight of my play continued to bellow and bluster his way forward, and the snatches I read aloud had Will and me roaring with laughter. I had named him Sir John Oldcastle after a comrade of Prince Hal's in *The Famous Victories of Henry the Fifth*, a popular farce that, along with Holinshed, afforded good source material. Later a descendant of the real Oldcastle protested the usage, and we were compelled to change the surname to Falstaff, a capitulation that left me growling. One of the secret pleasures of being an author is the privilege of bestowing names upon your characters, and to be told you must relinquish your first choice is akin to unbaptizing your children. Meanwhile, instead of whittling the role down to size, I kept embellishing it.

"You had better write your share soon," I warned Will, who had come home late after another meeting of the company. "Or there won't be any room left for Bolingbroke."

"Bolingbroke must wait, Anne. The Blackfriars project has run into trouble. The Burbages have gone to great expense to convert the building into a respectable theater, yet the residents are raising a cry against even a private playhouse in their neighborhood."

"What will happen?" Alarmed, I put down my pen. While I had been rollicking with Falstaff, Will, as usual, was dealing with real-life unpleasantries.

"We don't know. But if this keeps up, the company may be homeless."

The following week, the blow fell. In response to a petition from the well-heeled citizens of Blackfriars, the council shut down the theater only days before its opening. Will had taken me once to peek inside, and despite my misgivings that it would exclude the common folk, I could see how the intimate setting offered possibilities unimaginable in a huge, unroofed playhouse. Effects of light and shadow by torches or candle glow. The delicate music of flutes, lutes and viols instead of noisy horns and drums. More subtle writing and acting, no need to shout above a boisterous crowd. Now that enterprise was thwarted, and every penny spent by the Burbages—some £600!—was lost.

Far worse, James Burbage died soon thereafter. Though he was sixty-six, he had commenced the Blackfriars project with his usual vigor, and no one suspected his health was in jeopardy or that the stress of the venture would prove fatal. Mr. Phipps had once said every actor and playwright in London owed James Burbage a debt for building the Theatre, and I agree. It was his foresight and vision that launched our world. If any of us are to be remembered, let it be him. Now, at this critical juncture, we were without our longtime leader, and we were about to lose the Swan as well. A new acting troupe had secured a year's lease there, so while Cuthbert and Dick Burbage wrangled with Giles Allen over the Theatre land, the Chamberlain's Men moved their productions back across the Thames to the Curtain. Unable to help in any other way, I continued writing the adventures of Falstaff and Hal and prodded Will to start the king.

"Soon," he promised. "We are trying to get accustomed to the Curtain, and I may have to journey to Stratford to inspect some properties Gilbert has found."

"Stratford? But the company needs you here. I need you here for *Henry IV*."

"Don't worry. If I go, the visit will be short."

"But we must maintain your position as chief playwright. The Chamberlain's Men expect constant new scripts."

"Not so much in winter. Even Kempe can't pack them in when icicles are hanging from their noses. Besides, thanks to me"—he smiled—"and thanks to you, half the young men in London fancy themselves writers and spit out scripts like melon seeds."

"All the more reason we must spit faster to stay ahead of them. What if I block out Henry's scenes for you?"

Will agreed, and I set to work, glad to relieve him of some toil, not that writing ever is. But you must recall that of the entire company, Will was the only one who did it all. Actor, writer, director, producer, partner. Small wonder they found him indispensable; many nights he was exhausted. Then I discovered that dull headaches had begun to op-press him.

"I am not ill, just tired," he reassured me, rubbing his brow. "Let's go to the tavern and relax awhile." Then he joked, "At least in South-wark, we don't have to walk far."

True, and what more convivial way to pass a winter night than sur-rounded by friends, good food and drink, beside a dancing fire? But as sleety March gave way to balmy April, the tavern's charm began to wear thin. We should be at home writing. Will might have other employ-ments, but I had none. Having declined costume assignments to con-centrate on *Henry IV*, my pen was everything to me now. I chafed in silence while he drained one mug, then another. When he went outside to relieve himself, I counted in my head. Three mugs? Four? Though like anyone Will might grow tipsy on a festive night, he was no drunk-ard. It was overwork and those headaches; he was using drink to ease the strain. I tried to speak to him about it and got a sharp reply.

Then Gilbert wrote of a house for sale in Stratford. And not just any house: New Place, one of the largest dwellings in town. It had been built in the late 1500s by Sir Hugh Clopton, Stratford's famous son and benefactor who became lord mayor of London. The five-gabled brick-and-timber edifice comprised over a dozen rooms and property that included two barns and two gardens. Unoccupied in recent years and badly neglected, it would require extensive renovation. Still, I shook my head, amazed. After we had struggled so long, the idea of owning this grand abode required a major shift of perception.

"We have a coat of arms now," Will reminded me, though the pa-per remained tucked away. "We have an obligation to live up to it."

"But we won't even be living there, you and I. Who will look after it for us?"

"Gilbert can manage it, and eventually we will move the family in or find tenants. The point is to acquire property and investments for the future." He chuckled. "I know it is hard to break a lifetime habit of thrift, but we can afford this. And don't be afraid to buy pretty things for yourself, Anne, or for Susanna and Judith. I have to go to Stratford to complete the sale, and I could take them presents. What about braided gold rings or perfume from France?"

"What about *Henry IV*? I have nearly finished the adventures of Falstaff and Hal. We need the king."

"When I return," he promised. "Or you could come, and we could stay awhile. We could go a-Maying."

He took both my hands and swayed them as if to dance, but though I laughed, my heart recoiled. In the Stratford churchyard was a grave I could not quite face.

"You go. I will stay here and write, and you can add Henry when you get back."

Will rode off in late April, and I sat down to polish off Falstaff. Unfortunately, that corpulent rogue grew again. He became so gargantuan I began to suspect the only way to make space for Henry was to extend the play to two parts. Will would approve; twice the receipts in the collection box. But just when you think you are almost finished . . . I gnashed and growled. I should never have split the roles with Will in the first place. If he was too busy to write his share, I should have done both from the start. Trying to insert Bolingbroke now was like trying to wedge new bricks into a building after the mortar has set. I fiddled the pearl ring on my finger. Tut, tut, get on with it.

In early May Will was back, the beaming owner of New Place. He had bought me a pearl pendant to complement my ring, a touching gift. But when I pressed him on my plan for *Henry IV*, he begged off. Whatever I wanted to write was fine. The trip had put him far behind in his obligations to the Chamberlain's Men, and he must catch up. Within a week, his headaches recurred. Enough! The company demanded far too much of him, and the next time I crossed paths with Cuthbert I would tell him so. Two days later, amidst the usual gathering of actors in the tavern, I cornered my foe.

"What are you talking about?" Cuthbert bristled. "Will is the one who insists on being present at every rehearsal and performance. If the truth be told, he is making a nuisance of himself. Dick and I have urged him repeatedly to go home and finish *Henry IV*. He claims he has penned a brilliant part for Kempe, but where is the rest of it? Instead of dragging him out to drink every night, why don't you let him stay home and get it written?"

Cuthbert glared at me, and I backed away, confounded. Slowly, I rejoined Will. His eyes were glassy, though when I suggested we leave, he rose steadily and bade the company good night in unslurred tones. He slept well, while I lay awake puzzling. When he strolled in from the theater the next day, I had two plates of mutton and potatoes waiting, and a fresh quill, ink and paper on his table.

"We will stay home and write tonight," I said, a cheerful command. "I know where we must insert Bolingbroke, and here is Holinshed for reference."

"What, no supper first?" Will joked.

"Right here. We can eat while we work."

"And ale?"

"If we get a good portion edited, we can stop by the tavern later."

"Let's write at the tavern. We'll take pen and paper."

He picked up the quill and started to shuffle the papers into a stack. I moved slowly toward the door.

"There," he said. "Ready to go."

He straightened with his armload and turned toward me. His smile turned queasy at seeing my back to the door.

"Will, what is wrong?"

I had thought he would feint or make more excuses. I had feared he would blurt that a fatal disease was consuming him, a tumor in his head. I had suspected another woman—what better way to allay suspicion of an affair than by being overly attentive and agreeable to the wife, sister, you are betraying? Instead, the papers spilled from Will's arms, and he crumpled onto the bed and pulled the blanket over him. His body shuddered as if with convulsions, and I rushed to him. Oh, God, oh, God! It was a serious malady after all.

"I cannot write, Anne," he said, his voice hollow as a skull. "Not plays, not poetry, not anything."

I shook my head, uncomprehending. Cannot write? This from a

man from whom words used to flow like a rushing brook, a flooding stream, a river dashing and splashing to sea? It should have been funny. But the voice, muffled beneath the blanket, came from a place of such misery that a shiver ran over me.

"What do you mean? Of course you can write," I said, shaking him.

"No, I can't, Anne, not even when half the job is done for me. I stay at the theater all day to avoid it, the tavern by night."

"But that is the problem. You work too hard. Let the theater run itself for a few days while you clear your mind. "

"No, this is different. You don't understand. I cannot write, not a word since Hamnet's death. I tried to start *Henry IV* while you were still at Hardwick, and for days on end I stared at a blank page. And the paper just keeps getting whiter and whiter, and my head hurts all the time. . . ."

"Oh, Will."

I laid my hand upon his shoulder. My grief for Hamnet had ebbed and flowed with my tears, but Will, it seemed, had dammed his like a poisoned lake, and it was drowning him. He huddled under the blanket, curled wretchedly on his side like a gut-sick child.

"Everything is wrong," he whispered. "I lost my son, and I never knew him. I keep trying to make him up in my mind. The Blackfriars playhouse is gone, the Theatre in danger of following. I have no reason to work and cannot work to save my reason. I wake every morning praying it will be different, but the dawn brings no change. I cannot write. I have lost the grace of God."

I slipped into the bed and drew him into my arms.

Chapter 22

There began a hellish time.

At first, I thought words could fix it. Words had started it, my cruel accusations following the funeral in Stratford. *You abandoned him! You only loved the idea of him!* God, I was to blame. I thought if we talked enough, reminisced of Hamnet, Will's pain would gradually fade. So we tried—we talked of all our children—but it only revealed the truth, that we hadn't much real knowledge to go on.

Sadly, Will shook his head. "You see, Anne? You weren't wrong. Now Hamnet is gone, and the rest is falling apart anyway."

"But it will get better," I urged, though I could see how the company's recent misfortunes also weighed on him. Between the loss of the Theatre and the private playhouse at Blackfriars, the death of James Burbage and our ouster from the Swan, none of the Chamberlain's Men were cheerful that spring.

Yet Will did try to write again. He sat at his table, he dipped his quill, he stared at the blank page. He tapped a string of dots across the paper . . . *tap, tap, tap* . . . as if the release of ink would travel up his arm to his brain and trigger a return message that would spill out words.

"I know how to do this, Anne," he insisted.

"Of course you do."

"It should not be hard. *Henry IV* is just another play, another history. I have penned a half dozen already."

"And they were excellent. Perhaps if you reread the passages in Holinshed?"

"No, I know the story." *Tap, tap, tap . . .*

And another night:

"I am just too tired, Anne. We had a long day at rehearsals, and my head aches."

"Then rest awhile. You mustn't force yourself. I will cover for you."

"No, I'll do it. You are not to write my part."

"I didn't mean that, Will. Of course I won't take over your writing. I only meant I won't let on to anyone that the play is . . . is . . . going more slowly than anticipated."

"Oh, thank you for your charity."

"You needn't sneer. I am only trying to help."

"Well, you're not." *Tap, tap, tap . . .*

The next day he apologized, and I gladly forgave him. It was as if part of his brain had locked up shop, and he could not find the key. I encouraged him to write when he seemed in the mood, bit my lip when he faltered, tried to soothe his and my own growing worries over the fate of the Theatre. I made sure he ate, surprised him with sticky buns and the other sweets he adored. If he felt like walking, I was good for miles. If he wished to spend the evening at the tavern, I tagged along and held my tongue while he drank, slowly and steadily, to soften the edges of his pain; he never went beyond and into a stupor. I began to shrink from that tapping of his quill.

"Perhaps a history is the wrong choice," he said. "That new play of George Chapman's takes an entirely different direction."

I made a reluctant nod. In March, the Admiral's Men had premiered at the Rose a comedy by George Chapman entitled *A Humorous Day's Mirth*. The principal roles—an elderly, jealous husband, a young Puritan wife, a foolish gallant and a melancholic misanthrope—were immediately recognizable as various humors, and Chapman's skillful plotting kept them entangled in folly until the last laugh. Some of the other writers and actors swore this "comedy of humors" was the coming thing, causing me a flash of fear. Were we pursuing the wrong trail with *Henry IV*? Would this new type of play render ours stillborn? Did everyone else know something we did not? Ah, the insecurities of the artist; first the dread that you will never rise above the horizon, then the constant anxiety that you will be eclipsed. Robert Greene was probably chortling in his grave.

"All the same, I don't want to drop Henry," I said. "I believe Falstaff could be a hit."

"But if the audience craves more plays like Chapman's . . ."

"Well, then, you should try."

Tap, tap, tap . . .

"Never mind," he declared one night, pushing aside another paper. It looked as if a trail of pepper had been sprinkled over it. "I have already more fame than most. If it is God's will that my future role in the theater is as a manager and investor, then I will carry forward and make us rich. There is nothing wrong with that, is there, Anne?"

"Of course not," I said, and inwardly despaired. Give up writing forever? He couldn't mean it. The field before him might appear barren, but surely if we planted new ideas, new seeds, they would sprout and grow. But while I suffered for Will—and chafed for myself—I dared not usurp his share of *Henry IV*. In his troubled state, it might alienate him from both me and writing forever. Thus I hovered around him like an anxious nurse or fretting mother, afraid to make things worse, at a loss how to make them better.

In July, more discouraging affairs. Some of our actors had broken away from the Chamberlain's Men, and with a like number of deserters from the Admiral's Men they had formed a new troupe at the Swan under the patronage of the Earl of Pembroke. We lost no one of importance, and to a few, good riddance. But their first performances were a success, creating a fresh source of competition to prey on our nerves. Then Pembroke's Men pulled a stupid, no, a dangerous stunt. They staged a new play called *The Isle of Dogs* by the ever vitriolic Tom

Nashe, a satire so full of sedition and slander that the Privy Council immediately shut it down. Nashe skipped town to escape punishment, but three of the actors, including a noisy newcomer by the name of Ben Jonson, were imprisoned. To ensure we learned our lesson, the council closed all the other playhouses as well.

"What now?" I asked Will.

He shrugged, wiped his pen and capped his ink.

⁓

The theaters remained closed until October. Three months of lost revenue, of Cuthbert snarling, of grumbling actors out of work. Some went on tour, and a few privately commissioned performances kept others in practice, but as the days wore on, the mood grew bleak. Looking back at the various closures we endured in our career, I rue our lack of clairvoyance. Could we have guessed how long they were to last, we might have gone to visit the children or developed a secondary business to profit from the slack time. But no one could ever tell; the shutdowns came swiftly and without an ending date. We protested, we negotiated, we promised to behave. We waited out politics and the plague. But like spurned lovers waiting outside a hard-hearted mistress's gate, we could not tear ourselves away. What if we left today and the doors reopened tomorrow?

We did keep busy. I embroidered; we probably had the prettiest pillow covers in Southwark. Will sent a constant stream of letters to Gilbert detailing improvements to New Place. Increasingly, however, he slunk off to the tavern. "There may be news," he would say, and I let him go. Kindness had not prevailed, nor nagging nor indifference. Now I had a new tactic: I cheated.

The instant Will left our room, I shut the door, sat at my table and pulled out *Henry IV*. I am sure I sound unfeeling. Shouldn't Hamnet's death and our other anxieties have affected me as deeply as they did Will? But I had grieved, and it was writing that got me through it, and if that seems uncaring, then so I am. There is no such thing as an unselfish artist. To be an artist of any kind is the most selfish occupation of all.

I reviewed the scenes of *Henry IV* already completed and confirmed there was material enough for two plays. Better still, Hal and Falstaff rejoiced to see me. *We thought you had abandoned us*, they exulted. *Anne is back—hurrah!* I apologized for my absence, though I warned them it was the king's story I must concentrate on now. It proved more difficult than expected, for after drinking sack in the merry company of Falstaff and Prince Hal, King Henry IV was a pail of sour milk. I could not admire him; he was cynical and expedient. Nevertheless, he got the job of kingship done. I suppose most of all he reminded me of Cuthbert. And I did sympathize with his bitter disappointment at his dissolute son and was glad to lift his spirits with Hal's defeat of the glory-hungry Hotspur at the end of Part I. Yet I liked Hotspur—that tender scene with his wife—whose side was I on? Which was exactly what I wanted, characters too complex, too human, to permit simple judgments. It dawned on me that *Henry IV* was becoming quite good. Above all, that deadening *tap*, *tap*, *tap* had been replaced by a silky, beauteous, inky flow.

Will remained unsuspecting. At the slightest noise I would leap to my feet, shove the papers under my bed and snatch up my embroidery so that I might appear innocently employed when he walked in the door. From my pounding heart, you would think I was hiding an adulterous affair. I meant to tell him, when the circumstances were right; discretion is the better part of valor. I still hoped his muse would return of her own accord. But Will rarely sat at his desk anymore. He half resided in the taverns, seeking that fixed degree of numbness, as if he were creating a deliberate fog between himself and the rest of the world. Enough to blur the features without wiping out the vision. He could not quite obliterate himself, but neither could he bear to be who he was.

"What is the point in being sober when it only makes me more dull-witted?" he asked one night when I tried to reason with him. "The theaters are dark, and my muse has gone to bed with other men. Farewell, fickle whore!"

"The muse has not abandoned you, Will. Maybe she just can't find you in those crowded taverns." I had continued to sympathize with and encourage him. Now his self-pity tipped the scale, and I let my exasperation show. "I forbid you to go to the alehouse," I said, as if I had any such power. Yet for a few days he meekly obeyed. *Tap, tap, tap* . . . By the end of the week, the melancholy was so severe he crawled into bed and lay there the entire day, unmoving.

"Stop it! Get up! We cannot go on like this!" I shrieked, angry and terrified. I tore off the blanket as he lay with his face to the wall.

Will didn't flinch. "It's despicable, I know," he said blankly. "But my gift is gone." He waggled his fingers at me, as if they were evil snakes and only poisoned words could flow from them.

"Your gift has nothing to do with your hands. It is in your head, your heart."

"They are empty."

"Look." I pulled *I Henry IV* from under my bed and shoved it at him. "I wrote it while you were drinking. You can polish it, and that may get you started."

"No, I'm sure it is fine. I don't care."

I dropped the papers and huddled in next to him, pulling the blanket over us both. "But you must, Will. The playhouses won't stay closed forever. And though Hamnet is gone and we can't resurrect him, he does not want you to suffer."

"We could have another son."

My heart gave a painful beat. As his melancholy had deepened, Will had pushed me away, and I had ached at the loss. But there was no pressure or warmth from him toward me now. It was a wistful statement, not love or even bodily desire.

"We have two daughters," I said, "and we must work to provide for them. They deserve good husbands, men who are esteemed and prosperous, and for their sake we must maintain your reputation and our income."

"Then maybe we should return to Stratford and invest in more property. I shall become a country squire."

"No, Will, no. Your muse will come back. She has to." I hugged him, squeezing tight. Then I got out of bed, wrapped my shawl around my shoulders and pulled my chair up to my table.

⌒

When the other playhouses reopened after *The Isle of Dogs* scandal, the Theatre remained closed. The land lease had expired in April, and Giles Allen refused to modify his exorbitant terms. The Chamberlain's Men resumed performing at the next-door Curtain, and it was there that *I Henry IV* debuted at the end of the year. Falstaff won raves—the audience nearly carried Kempe off on their shoulders—and I proceeded directly to Part II. Determined to involve Will, I would set each finished scene before him, only to have him sweep it away as if I were trying to force-feed a clamp-mouthed child. Occasionally, he did make a scoffing suggestion, few of which were worthwhile.

But one proved critical. Given Falstaff's popularity—and our resultant profits—I felt compelled to make him even more prominent in the sequel. Hal's presence diminished in contrast; poor King Henry withered even more. Lapping up the attention, the fat knight grew spoiled. He became less funny, more immoral, his misdeeds criminal. Hal and I both wished to be rid of him. Should I kill him off? I was muttering and pacing before the fire, executing subtle dagger thrusts, when Will entered. I smelled the ale on him before he said a word.

"Go to bed." I waved impatiently. "I have to stab Falstaff."

Will snorted. "Terr'ble idea. Loud boo! Make Hal spurn 'im. Out of my way, old man."

He toppled over—onto the bed, fortunately—and in amazement I stared. Of course! Let Hal do the dirty work. He already knew that on mounting the throne, he would have to distance himself from the irresponsible companions of his youth. A public rebuff would break Falstaff's heart, at the same time proclaiming to one and all that Hal meant business. Kempe would wring the scene, the audience would approve and the stage would be set for *Henry V*. Brilliant, Will! But when he awoke the next morning he had no memory of our exchange.

"What are you talking about?" he interrupted as I started to thank him.

"Don't you remember? You came in, I said I needed to kill Falstaff, and you said . . ." I paused. Will was giving me a curdled scowl; I would not have liked to encounter that stubbled visage in a Southwark alley at night. "Never mind. You went to sleep, and I had a brilliant idea," I concluded, and it became my idea from then on. Why not? He stole plenty from me and still put his name on the playbill. Just once, between us, I took credit for something of his. So there, Will.

Yet I understood his plight. What happens when you lose your talent, when the musician goes deaf or the carpenter is paralyzed in his good hand? Who are you then? Livelihood vanished, you must either adapt yourself to a new profession or rely on the charity of others—a shame to an industrious man. But you can never forget what you lost, and while the humble acceptance of your fate may make you a saint, who wants to be one? Having to dissemble to his friends further increased Will's burden—and mine. With our literary reputation riding on my shoulders, what if inspiration deserted me as well? Some days as I walked in the street, I looked backward as if my muse might be one of the faces behind me. Please, I begged, do not get lost in the crowd!

To keep my finger on the pulse of the theater—and on Will—I resumed sewing for the company. Since Mr. Phipps, there had been several wardrobe masters, and the latest one was amiable enough and most appreciative of my work. It gave me an excuse to come and go, to view the actors in rehearsal, to pick up news, to be included in their circle when they gathered over ale. When *II Henry IV* premiered that spring, the takings merited celebration.

"Did you hear how the crowd cheered me today?" said Kempe, downing a tankard. "My Falstaff was a mountainous marvel!"

"Perhaps the playwright had something to do with that," I observed dryly.

Kempe reached over and rudely pinched my cheek, then slapped his arm around Will. "Of course he did, and you are a loyal sister to make sure he gets his due. A clever move, seeming to have Hal reject

Falstaff at the end. I lust to see my triumphant comeback in *Henry V*. Three cheers for our besotted bard! We must keep him here at the tavern, good and drunk. He has never written so well!"

Will raised his mug, grinning, as they shouted, "Hear, hear!"

I decided I might have to murder Falstaff after all.

If the mood of the country, like Will's and mine, was unsettled that spring, we had plenty of cause. Nearly four years of crop failures and starvation, the lingering fear of a second Spanish Armada, political and religious persecutions, an elderly and increasingly irritable queen who refused to name a successor. In Stratford the harvests were likewise bad, and the number of paupers grew. Yet a few bright spots surfaced when we paid a May visit. New Place was shaping up, and Gilbert had found tenants. Will's parents and our girls fared well, and Magpie Joan got married to William Hart, a kindly, soft-spoken hatter. Will tempered his drinking during our stay, only to return to his usual haunts when we arrived back in London. Then one day, I looked up from my table to see a strange golden light filtering through the window. Was the bad weather finally over? I rose and opened the pane, and my chest swelled with the first sweet breath I had taken in a long while.

Inspired, I began a comedy, *Much Ado About Nothing*, and this time I ignored Will. I did not solicit his ideas for a topic or ask his opinion on the writing. I was quite capable of conducting a merry skirmish of wit on my own. I based the story on an Italian novel and relished the perverse irony in opposing two such stubborn characters as Beatrice and Benedict and making them fall in love. Who was self-deluding now? At least Kempe, hounding Will for more Falstaff, would be pacified with the plum role of Dogberry.

Then along came Ben Jonson.

First, nothing Ben Jonson says about himself is true. His grandfather a gentleman in Scotland? Ha! Besides, his father lost their supposed estates, became a clergyman, then died a month before Ben was born. His mother remarried, to a bricklayer. If that is the lineage of a gentleman, John Shakespeare deserves his coat of arms. Ben acquired a decent education but never made it to a university, being apprenticed instead to his stepfather's trade. I am sure any building in which he laid a brick has long since fallen down.

To escape his ill-suited vocation, Ben soldiered in the Low Countries, where he killed an enemy warrior in single combat, or so he claimed. That Ben would distinguish himself by anything so noble as solo combat is laughable. More likely, as Falstaff with Hotspur, he drove his sword into some poor wretch already dead on the ground. On his return to England, he transformed himself into an actor and was soon in prison for his part in *The Isle of Dogs*. Would they had kept him jailed! But no, Ben got out and decreed himself a full-time playwright. He penned a lopsided piece or two and muscled his way into the writers' circle.

In the late summer of 1598, shortly after I completed *Much Ado*, he struck.

The piece was entitled *Every Man in His Humor*, and in addition to immediately popularizing the humors genre, it was the yardstick, Jonson declared, by which we would measure every future play. Henceforth every script, however funny, must also serve a moral purpose. In a comedy of humors, for example, the point of the eccentric characters was to reveal, ridicule and punish folly. We must also adhere to the precepts of classical literature and craft our stories with strict regard to the three unities of action, time and place. I am the expert, trumpeted Ben. Do as I say! *Every Man in His Humor* even took sideswipes at our histories—grrr! What goaded me most deeply was that the Chamberlain's Men produced it at the Curtain, and Ben insisted Will act one of the parts.

"The role of the old father," he said, slapping it down on the tavern table in front of us. "It is a perfect fit."

Smiling, Will accepted. Let them once smell your fear and the dogs will tear you to pieces. Yet not a hint of Ben's machinations was lost on us. Will as the ancient pater—you are washed up and done for already, old man. May I point out that Ben was only eight years younger? Nonetheless, I simmered in silence. Will had not played a part in ages, and though I had no illusions he would resurrect himself as an actor, it might reawaken his muse. Instead, it further crushed him, while *Every Man in His Humor* became a roaring success.

The very night the play opened, Ben showed his true colors. After the show he met Gabriel Spencer, one of the actors who had been imprisoned with him over *The Isle of Dogs*. They got into an argument, over what I never heard, and like idiot men they could not let it go but must adjourn to a field to settle it with swords. Spencer wounded Ben first, then Ben ran him through. He killed a man who a year ago had been his friend, and when he was convicted of manslaughter, he escaped hanging by reciting a Latin verse and pleading benefit of clergy. During his brief stay in prison, he converted to Roman Catholicism, as if he ever believed seriously in religion at all. He was also stripped of his possessions and branded on the left thumb, which he proceeded to brag about. I don't care if Ben Jonson is a brilliant writer, he is a duplicitous, deceitful, despicable—

Ah, me. I know I sound petty and jealous. I am sorry to sink so low. And Ben did have another side—we all do—but my own state was so despondent, I had no charity for anyone else. Two years had passed since Hamnet's death, and though Will and I had prosperity, friends, family, fame, we had lost any semblance of happiness. We took refuge in our separate occupations, me in writing and sewing, Will in drink and his doings with the company, but the strain of opposite minds living under one roof was becoming unbearable.

What happened next, I remember clearly. It was a beautiful October day, and knowing it would be one of the last before winter set in, I ordered myself out to the countryside to view the scarlet palette of autumn leaves and inhale the fresh air. When I got home late that evening, I found Will sitting at his table, the paper before him speckled with an aimless trail of black dots. His left sleeve was rolled up, and across his wrist, across the veins, was a thin stripe of ink.

"We played *Every Man in His Humor* this afternoon at the Curtain," he remarked, not looking at me. "An excellent play. Then we went to the tavern, and Ben ordered a round, though naturally he couldn't find his purse to pay for it. He made quite a few toasts, including one to me. Not every man, he said, would condescend to play a role in his rival's first theatrical triumph. 'Here's to Will Shakespeare, a good sport!' Tell me, Anne"—Will flexed his marked wrist—"is this how the ancient Romans did it? How deep does one cut?"

I hit him, Bess's pearl ring drawing blood from his cheek. Then I grabbed his face in both my hands and kissed him violently on the mouth.

"Damn you and your grief and your melancholy," I swore. "Get into bed. If this is the only way to do it, then I will give you another child."

I shoved him toward the mattress, pulling at the ties of my bodice as I followed. Whose fault was it if we had only one son? Whose fault was it we had slept apart so often over the years? In a rage, I tugged my sleeves down my shoulders and advanced on him. For an instant Will looked appalled, then his anger kindled in return. Hurling hateful words, we fought with each other's clothes, tearing at the garments as if they and not we were somehow to blame. He scratched my breastbone. I raked his chest. We struggled to hurt each other and hurt me he did. Our thrashings brought me to tears and him to animal grunts, and when he pulled out of me, I turned away, cupped my hand between my legs and bawled.

The next day Will got drunker than ever before. Nor did the episode bring us a child; I suspect the difficult birth of the twins had forever damaged my ability to conceive. But it did make me wonder if Will might have another son somewhere. He had been unfaithful to me before I joined him in London, and the Dark Lady had come between him and the earl. Prostitutes would have found him charming, and if he consorted with other women while I was at Hardwick, who could tell? Will was not promiscuous; still, all it would take was one fleeting encounter. But if there was a bastard, no mother or child ever came forward. Or maybe the mother miscarried or the child died at birth or the whore didn't know which of her customers was the father. Too bad, poor tyke. I would have taken you in and loved you, and you could have been our son. Or so I told myself in the bitter dusk of that unhappy year.

Then finally, Will's muse returned, though it was not by the intervention of any living being or even by God himself.

Chapter 23

"*T*he man is a scoundrel!"

Will slammed the door and threw himself into a chair. I knotted my thread and clipped the end. As a refuge, embroidery can be highly satisfying. You envision a design, pick your colors, sort your threads. Each stitch adds to the growing picture, and though you may alter or embellish as you go, the final work is entirely your own making; you are in control. It is creative yet methodical, and I suppose that is why, in the weeks following Will's and my tawdry brawl, I found it so soothing. It also meant I did not have to look at him as we spoke, some conversation still being necessary in the course of a day.

"He has no principles!"

I steeled myself to absorb Ben Jonson's latest shenanigans. It was almost Christmas, and *Every Man in His Humor* was continuing its popular run when the weather allowed. Will had wiggled out of playing the old father after only a few performances, taking advantage of a slight cold, and another actor had assumed the role.

"It is the wood he wants, the timber. That has been his plan all along."

Jonson wanted wood? At this I did give Will a puzzled look. He had been at a meeting of the Chamberlain's Men, and I was not so angry with him as to underrate his business skills or ignore his worries.

Whatever was amiss, it concerned me, and I must pay attention and help if I could.

"What do you mean?"

"Giles Allen has given us his final terms to renew our land lease for the Theatre."

Ah, wrong scoundrel. "How bad is it?" I asked, catching on.

"It is impossible! Nearly double the rent and only a five-year term, after which he gains ownership of the building. He has deliberately crafted an unworkable document, knowing we could not sign."

"But that does not profit him either. Why drive off a paying tenant and lose the income? Does he think another company will move in and pay more? And how can they when we own the building?"

"Not for much longer."

"What?"

Will gave me a glum look. "The original lease of land to James Burbage stipulates that if the lease is not renewed at the end of twenty-one years, the building must be removed from the property or its ownership transfers to Allen. As legal owner, he can then demolish the structure and sell the timber for a pretty price. That's what he is really after."

"Why, that . . . !" I jabbed my needle into my embroidery and set it aside. Tear down the Theatre? "That Philistine!"

"Worse, he is a Puritan. He would like to see every playhouse close."

"What can be done? Can we bring a lawsuit to stop him?"

"We are considering our options," Will said darkly.

For the next several days Will was absent from dawn to dusk. When I questioned what progress they were making, he would only hint, "We are forming a plan." Premonition coiled like a cold snake inside me. If tempers erupted, if threats were spoken . . . Though Will carried a sword, as befitted a man of his station, he had no experience using it beyond a little stage fighting. But plenty of our actors did, and if hotheads prevailed, it was not my imagination running away with me to think that Will could be impaled trying to prevent bloodshed. Then

I noticed something else. Will had stopped drinking. Even the slight glaze that was his preferred state of intoxication had left him, and he was clear-eyed and hardheaded.

"We have rented a new piece of ground not far from the Rose," he reported a few days later. "We'll build our own theater and have complete control. It will be the finest playhouse in England."

"Thank heaven!" I let out a long breath. Yes, sad though it was, let the Theatre go. We would lose money but no lives, and we could all keep our peace of mind. You see again that I am a coward, and perhaps it is true that for physical bravery, a woman can never match a man. I would not do battle for the Theatre. I would not risk my life for a pile of boards. Is that wisdom or weakness? If the latter, then cowards live the longer.

But Will gave a grim smile. "We are not done with Giles Allen yet," he said.

We passed the Christmas holiday pleasantly enough, dining at the tavern on roast goose stuffed with chestnuts, potatoes in thick gravy, stewed plums and a fine Madeira. Will contented himself with a single cup, turning it in his hand as if knowing he could set it down. They say a crisis sharpens the mind, and the consternation over the Theatre seemed to be having that effect on him. On Christmas night, I went to sleep heartened. In the morning, I awoke to find him sitting on my bed, rubbing his hands.

"Tonight, Anne."

"What?" I tensed.

"Tonight we shall have our revenge on Giles Allen."

"No, Will, whatever it is, no." I sat up, snatching the blanket around me to ward off the dark chill of dawn. Will was grinning like a schoolboy plotting some mischievous escapade. "Tell me," I demanded.

"We are going to demolish the Theatre ourselves, cart it away and rebuild it on our new land. Tonight! We'll leave not a stick of it for Allen."

"Can you do that? You will be arrested for theft, trespassing!"

"Who is to stop us? Allen is away from London, the Theatre is outside the city wall, and Cuthbert has hired a crew of sturdy men. We can have it dismantled before sunrise."

"Take down the whole building in one night? Even if it can be done, some passerby will raise the alarm."

"Not if they value their lives. We go armed."

"Will!"

Men! Why must they always aggravate matters? Why, when a civil word might suffice, must they rush to fisticuffs and bloodletting?

"Stay home, Will." I clutched his sleeve. "If it must be done, let the others manage it. You will only be in the way. Besides, someone must stay clear and run the company when they are caught and imprisoned."

"No, Anne. It is my theater, my life, my fellows and friends."

Simple words, simply spoken.

"Then I am coming too," I said.

We passed a restless day. I could not even concentrate on my embroidery, twice pricking my finger. Still, it was better than sitting idle while fear chewed my insides.

"We'll be all right," said Will, as the hour drew near. "You are imagining battle cries, cudgel blows, skulls cracking."

"Aren't you?" I hugged my arms to my chest and gazed out the window at the gray twilight settling over town. "I would this night were over and we were safe home in bed."

"I suppose that is how soldiers feel," Will conceded, "looking across at the enemy camp and wondering which of them will still be alive at day's end. You should go back and insert more of that for Falstaff in *I Henry IV*, some meditation on honor being wasted on the dead."

"What? How can you think of writing at such a time? Besides, *Henry IV* is done."

"A play is never done, even a good one."

He smiled at me, a warm and tender smile that lit his eyes as well as his lips. It awoke such long-buried feelings, memories of when we were

young. There was rue in it but also optimism, something I had not witnessed in Will for a long time, and I understood how unhappy he had
been.

"You will write again," I said.

"Yes. The new year is coming, and I'll make a fresh start." He came
to me and put his arm around my shoulder. "It will get better, Anne."

For a moment I let myself feel the warmth of him. "If we survive
this night," I said.

～〜

We left our lodging as soon as it reached full dark. Thank heaven it
was December; a long winter night stretched before us. Clouds blanketed the moon, not that the absence of light would conceal us once
the noise began. Yet we practically tiptoed as we ran through the
streets, across the bridge, hugging our cloaks close to keep out the icy
air. Oh, it was cold! The frozen ground penetrated my soles, and each
puff of breath frosted on our cheeks and noses. Everywhere the
shadow crowd was beginning to emerge, the cheap women and drunkards, the thugs and cutpurses, the beggars curled in doorways shivering in their rags. Whom would they prey on tonight, when all proper
people were home in their beds? One another, I supposed. We passed
them and hastened on.

As we neared the Theatre, other footsteps joined us, burly men in
rough clothes. I recognized no one until we saw Cuthbert directing
several wagoners to positions around the building. He beckoned to
Will, scowled at me and nodded upward.

"We have begun."

It was quieter than I had imagined, no shouting, low voices, lan-
terns lit in a ring around the open roof. Cuthbert had hired the master
carpenter Peter Street to supervise the dismantling, and the men moved
under his command like an army taking a building by stealthy storm.
Bent shapes tore off tiles, pried apart rafters and passed down boards.
The dull thumps blended into the other night sounds, the barking of a
dog, the hoot of an owl, a horse and cart clopping homeward. Though

there were no doughty inhabitants to battle the men off, the Theatre offered a resistance of sorts. Sturdy beams, once pegged into place, have a formidable integrity; they marshal their defenses, lock arms. As the men panted and yanked, the topmost gallery fought back, and curses rang out as the wood split and stabbed into bare hands. Two men lost their balance, and a long plank slid off the roof and drove into the yard, nearly hitting Dick Burbage like a battering ram. Defying Cuthbert, I made it my job to keep track of the candles, issuing fresh tapers as the old ones guttered out. Though my stomach was knotted, the task was oddly consoling—to be in the midst of destruction passing out light.

Despite our efforts to proceed quietly, a small group of onlookers gathered, and the news soon spread among the night people that a rare entertainment was at hand.

"Here, what are you doing?" demanded a crew of carousers.

"Private business. Be off with you," Cuthbert ordered.

"We can do business anywhere we please," countered a pock-marked whore.

"We'll help you tear it down!" shouted another man, though he weaved as he stepped forward.

Cuthbert made the mistake of giving them a shilling to go back to the nearest tavern. They cheered and departed, only to reappear a short while later, more drunk, with their hands out. The third time, one of the burly men Cuthbert had hired drove them off with a stout stick. That group did not reappear, but as the demolition continued, others did, along with a few respectable-looking citizens. In a festive mood from Christmas and with the merrymaking of New Year's and Twelfth Night ahead, they took the event as an unexpected bonus to the revelry. A few of the most drunken attempted to make off with the wood them-selves, only to be collared by the guards. Several sober, hollow-cheeked men approached Cuthbert and Peter Street, caps in hand.

"Could we earn a bit for a night's work?" they implored, and they were hired on to fetch and haul.

I went to and fro with candles, trying to stay out of the way, rubbing my hands to keep warm. Those scraps of wood too small or splintered to reuse had been gathered for a bonfire, and the workers took turns holding their fingers to its glow. Will had gone to the upper gallery to help demolish the lath and plaster walls. What was he thinking? If a hammer struck him in the head or he fell off and broke his neck, where would we be then? But he needed to do this, to feel he belonged in the thick of it, to say when it was over that he had taken a bold part.

"Will, get down!" Cuthbert ordered. "Do you think we want to lose our playwright?"

"I am in no more danger than you are," Will retorted, laughing.

Where are the officials? I kept wondering, swiveling my head at any hint of approaching authority. Why had no patrol descended on us with complaints or warrants? True, we were outside the city walls, but I began to feel indignant. A fine town we lived in! Where was the civic order that a bunch of brigands could pull apart a great building in the middle of the night and no one cared? Suppose we were ruffians bent on arson or enemy soldiers mounting an attack. Where was the night watchman?

I had no sooner thought it than a constable appeared. He was a little, mustachioed man, whose zealousness quickly deserted him as he saw the large and noisy horde. Another shilling from Cuthbert's purse, and in gratitude and relief the constable slunk away. With no one to challenge them, the men began to joke as they worked, and the strange spectacle took on a holiday atmosphere.

"Here, catch this, you clumsy oaf!"

"Don't drop that board on your head or it might knock some sense into you!"

"Keep working!" Cuthbert warned. "It won't be so funny if we fail to finish and Giles Allen gets word."

By midnight, the top tier was down, and as the major timbers were removed, Street marked and cataloged them for reassembly. I began to study the workers' faces, brothers to the carpenters, joiners and stonemasons I had seen at New Hall. Though they might regret they were unbuilding, when it was in their nature to build, it would surely be a good night's pay to take home to their families. As if the same thought were in his mind, Will came to ask if I would not rather go home? When I stopped to think about it, I was both weary and cold, but I could no more quit the scene than anyone else. Lantern in hand, I walked about, collecting more stray wood to add to the bonfire. By three in the morning the second gallery was gone, and carts rumbled away, carrying pieces of our Theatre to Southwark. I was trimming candle stumps when Will came toward me, face pinched, his right hand holding his left to his chest.

"What have you done? Oh, Will!" I held up a lantern and clucked over the injury, a nasty sliver driven almost straight into his palm. "Sit down and let me see. How am I ever going to get this out?" He winced as I examined the hurt. "Of all the silly . . . ! If this becomes infected . . ." Shushing his protests, I got a small knife from one of the workers. Will bore my probings bravely until the offending splinter was out.

"There, you have been wounded in battle," I said. "Are you happy?"

"I believe I am," he said, his face shining beneath the dirt.

The dark began to thin, and the work sped up. When the men started on the roof, it had taken time to rope and maneuver the heavy oak frames to the ground. The lower they got, the faster the dismantling.

"How strange it will be not to see plays here anymore," I said to Will Kempe, who strolled up, naturally, when the job was almost done.

"Ah, but wait until our new theater opens," he vowed. "I shall make it rock with laughter. Build it strong enough to withstand an earthquake of mirth!" he commanded Street, who ignored him. He went off to hail Dick Burbage, and I shook my head. Did no one share my sense of loss? Even Will did not sigh at the demolition, all the men's talk that night being of the grand new playhouse they would erect. Perhaps that is the best way to see life, to move continually forward with no regrets. But women are sentimental, attaching meaning to things our opposite sex might disdain, and as the painted heavens broke apart and the columns of the stage were lowered to the ground, I recalled the costumes I had sewn, the lines I had penned.

As dawn broke, the night onlookers drifted away, yawning, and the daytime citizens began to stir. Cuthbert stopped a man pushing a cart-load of bread and pies and bought half his store to feed the workers. The baker blinked in delight; the sun not yet up, and already he had a profit. He proceeded toward Bishopsgate, smiling a toothless grin, and the men devoured the food. They had labored more than twelve hours and were cold and bruised. Bellies sated, they shrugged off their weariness and took up their tools to finish the job.

I was growing droopy eyed, and I sat on the ground by the remains of the bonfire to wait for Will. The Theatre was down to the stage and a portion of the back wall, and there was some consultation about how much was salvageable. What an adventure! I was feeling proud myself to have been part of it, a witness, to have lent a hand. *I was there the night they dismantled the Theatre and carted it board by board to its new home*, I would tell my grandchildren, and their eyes would grow round. If it was not as impressive as saying you sailed to the New World or fought off the Spanish Armada, at least it was proof I had done something daring, and I yawned in satisfaction.

The next thing I remember was awakening amidst shouts and ruckus and being buffeted by some dark assailant. In terror I screamed and flailed, a bright light leaping before my face. Then pain and horror—

"Smother her! Roll her!"

Hands thundered me on the ground, beating at my back and head.

"Rip off her cloak!"

They did, the scrolled metal clasp gouging my throat as the garment was torn away. I choked and cried. My hair, they were ripping out my hair by the roots! Pain seared up my legs, red flames sizzled my sleeves. Blankets and cloaks were piled atop me, and heavy bodies flattened themselves on mine. I felt my ribs crack, and my lungs gasped for air.

"Anne!" Will gathered me into his arms, his face stricken. "My God, you set yourself on fire!"

"You must have rolled too close to the embers. Good God," said Cuthbert, "are you all right?"

I drew a sharp breath and began to shake. I hurt in so many places I could not tell which were burned, which broken, which bleeding and which bent the wrong way.

"Yes, I'm all right," I said too loudly, trying to overcome the ringing in my ears. Tears flooded my eyes as I smelled the smoke and stench of my cloak and the burned skin on my shins and arms.

"Get her a drink!" yelled Will Kempe, and several figures dashed off.

I pressed a hand to my stinging skin, though my head hurt more and a long chunk of hair lay caught in the cloak clasp. And my ribs— Will told me later it was several stout workers who first saw me alight and threw themselves on me to smother the flames. I could have wished they had been less precipitate; just one of their burly lot could have done the job. But I thanked them, and Will pressed on them his gratitude and his purse.

Several pots of ale were thrust at me, and Kempe took one back. "God's blood, I need a drink even if you don't," he declared, and the breaking of tension brought forth laughs.

I drank a few gulps, then handed the liquor away. My injuries were beginning to assert themselves, and if I did not get up and home to bed, I would soon be unable to move. Will helped me rise and beckoned one of the wagons about to leave with a load.

"Thank you . . . I should have taken more care. . . ." I hung my head, and although voices immediately assured me not to worry, I also heard a few belated, low-spoken growls. "What's a woman doing here anyway?"

At home, Will undressed me and tucked me into bed. He sent for a doctor, who treated my burns with a salve that took away the sting. But my body was black and blue all over, and between the scratches and cuts on my face where they had rolled me on the ground, and the chunk of hair missing from my left temple, and the gouge on my throat and my tender ribs . . . I started to cry.

"Was I all aflame?" I asked, not sure I wanted to know. "Like a martyr at the stake?"

"It seemed to me you were sheeted in fire. If you hadn't been wearing so many layers against the cold . . ." He shuddered. His eye sockets were purple from lack of sleep, his own wound, exhaustion and fright. "Shh, shh, it was a terrible accident, but thank God you were saved."

I sniffed, unable to see him clearly through my blurred eyes. I had nearly died—*died!*—and not until it was over did I know I had never been more frightened in my life.

"Just hold me," I cried.

And he did.

Chapter 24

$\mathscr{I}$ do not know why God spared me from that fire. If I had sufficient vanity I might pretend it was so that I could continue writing and enlarge the talent he himself gave me. Yet God had snipped Kit, Tom Kyd and others already in full flower when Will and I were but hard green buds. Why clip those bursting blossoms and leave us? Or did he prune them precisely to give us room to flourish? Then why not push Ben Jonson in front of a horse or trip him into a well? What a boon that would have been to civilization and great literature.

Or perhaps my slight scorching had a much more uncomplicated explanation: It was simply God giving me a foretaste of hell's eternal blaze.

Whatever the reason, I was alive, and once we got over the shock it became a week's jest between Will and me. He called me "Torch," and in retaliation I dubbed him "Splinter" for the wound in his palm. We chuckled at the vision of me being rolled on the ground by the workmen, until I had to stop laughing for my aching ribs. Will proposed enshrining the remnants of my filthy, burned cape in a frame on the wall as a reminder of how close I had come.

"Too gruesome, and besides, it will molder and attract moths," I objected.

"Then let's burn a sacrificial scrap in the hearth and raise a toast to being alive," he said, pouring us each a cup of Canary wine. So we did, and went on talking late into the night long after the wine was gone.

How did we become so merry?

Well, for one thing our adventure in stealing the Theatre proved successful. We had the wood and we had managed to snick our thumbs at Giles Allen, and you can guess which gave everyone the greater pleasure. Though Allen was furious and brought a lawsuit against the company, after the usual lawyerly wrangling it was decided in our favor—hurrah! By that time the new playhouse was rising in Southwark, and Will and I often strolled over to observe the construction and chat with the laborers. Three storied, multisided, a hundred feet across—room for up to three thousand cheering spectators. O, magic encircled! Just to stand in the yard and look up to the sky was exultation. The underside of the heavens was painted with a celestial design embellished with gold leaf, and the stage pillars were so cleverly marbled you would swear they were real stone. On the practical side, the yard was surfaced in a mixture of soap ash and hazelnut shells for drainage in wet weather, while the north-facing, roofed stage protected the valuable costumes from sunlight and rain and the swordfighting actors from sun in their eyes. After much debate and after rejecting appellations that included the Venture, the Castle and the Phoenix—the latter my suggestion—the company named our new home the Globe.

"I like it," I said. It was important-sounding and visionary. It disdained boundaries, proclaimed horizons. It smacked of adventure, fearless expedition, a brave new world. Best of all, it was a beautiful, round, weighty word, and we intoned it like giggling children, making our voices deeper and more sonorous with each rendition.

The *Gloobe,* the *Gloooobe,* the *Gloooooobe!*

Another reason we were merry was that thanks to our raid on the Theatre and my near immolation, Will had rediscovered how to write. There is nothing like a heart-pounding, death-defying episode to scare awake somnolent senses and set fresh blood coursing through your veins. It yanked Will's talent back from the grave and laid Hamnet's soft soul to rest. On second thought, was that why God had seared yet spared me? To revitalize Will? I shouldn't be surprised. Men do stick together, don't they?

But there was a reward in it for me as well, for once Will's muse was restored, so was his affection toward me. It seems unfair I had ever lost it, but when we are unhappy, our instinct is to lash out at those nearest us whether or not they are to blame. We are injured dogs that snap and snarl at the very hand that offers to bind our wounds. And with me deftly penning *Henry IV* while his quill had run excruciatingly dry, Will's pain and resentment had been doubled. I must have seemed a traitor, especially when his judgment was wallowing in drink. Now that blackness had lifted, he forgave me for his unhappiness, and I forgave him for the same. Almost without a word, we were friends again.

And soon we were more than friends.

To be loved, to be touched, is a heavenly thing.

That year of 1599 was a time of leapfrog plays.

Will sprang back into the game with *The Merry Wives of Windsor*, and that by royal command on very short notice. Falstaff had proven so popular in *Henry IV* that the queen requested a reappearance of the bellowing bed presser, horseback breaker, huge hill of flesh in time for the Garter Feast in April. Since Prince Hal and I were fed up with him, we gladly relinquished him to Will. He unearthed a dusty comedy from the company's repertoire, patched in the lard-bucket knight and his roguish accomplices, and rounded out the cast with a jealous husband and a silly young gentleman, two of the "types" Ben had popularized in *Every Man in His Humor*. The twist was that Will turned the tables on Falstaff by making the unreformed rascal the butt of the comedy. Nice work! More to the point, *Merry Wives* put Will to the test and forced him to write to a deadline, and when he passed it, he let out the relieved sigh of a student who has just passed his examinations.

Meanwhile, at our side-by-side tables I wrote *Henry V*. A pleasant change, since so far none of the monarchs Will and I had immortalized were particularly admirable men. Henry VI was a simpleton, Richard

III a villain, Richard II undone by poor judgment, King John a boring miscreant. Henry IV, though efficient, was forever tainted by his usurpation of the throne. But with Henry V, England finally had a ruler of whom it could be proud, and I had a king worthy of my pen. I saw him clearly, a man of the best qualities, strong, handsome, courageous, an able administrator and leader of men. I had particular fun writing the tennis balls scene between the king and the French ambassadors, my father's old story. Henry V was that rare thing: a monarch who viewed England not as his personal plunder but as a nation to be governed for the betterment of its citizens. If that also sounds like Elizabeth, it should. Yet he was still his father's son, crafty, ambitious, willing to risk other men's lives to achieve his ends. He understood that giddy and ungiddy minds alike are happy to embrace foreign quarrels if they sense profit in it. What people respect most is a ruler who, by whatever means, enriches them.

"I have included a touching report of Falstaff's death offstage of natural causes," I told Will, for I had indeed decided to do the fat man in.

"Kempe won't be happy."

"Too bad. What I need next is some French. Henry has to court Princess Katharine, who speaks no English."

"Easy enough," he replied. "I have picked up a few choice expressions, and between the writers and actors, there are a half dozen who can bandy words in that tongue. Tell me what you want, and we'll plug it in."

Then back to Will, who, having warmed up on *Merry Wives*, was ready to tackle weightier matter. Long ago Stratford grammar school had plowed into its pupils' heads a thorough knowledge of classical subjects and authors, and Will's fondness for them had never abated. One of his favorite volumes was Plutarch's *The Lives of the Noble Grecians and Romans*, available in either Sir Thomas North's translation or the original Latin—which Will could perfectly well read; so there, Ben! And *Lives* is no dry recitation of dates and accomplishments but probing portraits of men's characters and minds. As he skimmed its pages,

Will read passages aloud to me and spent even more time perusing to himself and frowning. A frown is always a good sign in a writer poring over a book; it means you think you can take what you are reading and make it better. Thus, Will commenced *The Tragedy of Julius Caesar*.

I finished *Henry V* and lighted upon *Rosalynde*, a popular pastoral romance by Thomas Lodge. I rewrote it for the stage with the title *As You Like It*, and it is as carefree as a butterfly on a summer day. Lodge set his tale in the Forest of Ardennes, a pleasant coincidence that allowed me to picture my setting as our own Forest of Arden. As for the twining lovers, it has all been done before. We did it quite well in *A Midsummer Night's Dream*. Yet audiences never tire of the panting pursuits of fair youths and maidens, and the subject suited my happy mood. I still chuckle to recall the lovelorn shepherd Silvius pining after the scornful shepherdess Phebe while Phebe bats her eyelashes at Ganymede, who is Rosalind in boy's garb, and Orlando makes pretend love to Ganymede, who is tutoring him to woo his lost Rosalind. . . . Well, you get the gist.

Throughout, Will and I read over each other's shoulders, buzzing to and fro like pollinating honeybees.

Once more unto the breach, dear friends—his.

Friends, Romans, countrymen, lend me your ears—mine . . . no, wait, that was his.

Cowards die many times before their deaths—mine.

True is it that we have seen better days—we blurted it together.

"How was ancient Rome today?" I would ask at sunset as we wiped our pens.

"Brutal," he would reply. "How was the Forest of Arden?"

Will also helped me with one of my best speeches ever. In the midst of the lighthearted forest company in *As You Like It*, I had inserted one down-in-the-mouth character, the melancholy Jaques. It irks me to admit it, but in creating him, I too had succumbed to Ben Jonson's nefarious influence, for Jaques was nothing more than one of Ben's "humors." His character was so unimportant, I could have booted him from the play, and no one would know he was gone. But I needed a melancholic type to fit the vogue, and that character needed something to say, and I was racking my brain one afternoon as Will and I walked to the Globe. Will pointed to the theater's motto on a banner above the door.

Totus mundus agit histrionem—the whole world plays the actor.

"Why don't you make something of that for Jaques?" he said.

"Such as?"

"I don't know. A reflection on the roles we play throughout our lives as we progress from childhood to maturity to feeble oblivion."

"The seven ages of man? It is a tired chestnut, Will."

"Not in your capable hands. Start with something like, 'We are born onto a stage,' or, 'What a stage we live upon!' "

" 'All the world's a stage?' "

"Something like that. Play with it. Have fun."

⁓

Regrettably, the mood in our English theater was not nearly so sunshiny as Will's and mine. Will Kempe's demanding and often disruptive nature had been causing increased friction among the Chamberlain's Men. Now he took the loss of his Falstaff role as a personal insult and quit the company in a huff. Though we were not unhappy to see him go, to lose our famous clown could seriously affect our receipts. A new actor, Robert Armin, took Kempe's place, and we held our breaths to see whether the audience would embrace him.

Ben Jonson also caused fresh problems. When our beauteous Globe opened in July 1599, among its premiering plays was Jonson's follow-up, *Every Man out of His Humor*. In supreme arrogance, he opened that work with three characters discussing his theory of humors; naturally, his ideas are deemed superior to everyone else's. Dictator! Where is Brutus when we need him? Jonson also granted one of his characters a coat of arms featuring a boar's head and the motto "Not Without Mustard." Sound familiar? Will shrugged it off—I am glad he could. I am also pleased to report that while our plays that season attracted full houses, *Every Man Out of His Humor* was a complete flop. In a fit of pique, Jonson vented his jealousy by publicly criticizing

Julius Caesar. He rated some of our lines to be so "ridiculous" that they forced him to laugh aloud. Well, a script can always be improved, and Will did change the lines, over my objections. But is that any way to speak of a fellow writer? If a line was ill conceived, Ben could have advised us in private.

"The ingrate!" I fumed to Will. "We bought his play for the Globe, it loses us money, yet he turns around and attacks ours."

"He is an oaf," Will agreed. "Unfortunately, he is a talented one. Let's be thankful he has stomped off to the Admiral's Men at the Rose to write drivel with Tom Dekker."

"But if he continues to slander us . . ." I growled and strangled the air with my hands.

A few weeks later, I nearly had the chance. I had gone to the tavern to meet Will for supper, but he sent a boy to tell me he was delayed at the Globe. I was sipping my ale when Jonson entered. He glanced around, spotted me, then made straight in my direction, hat in hand. Instinctively, I drew back on my seat.

"Mistress Shakespeare," said Ben, making a slight bow. "I have come . . . I am sorry . . ."

He fumbled his hat between his fingers, then set it on the table. Though he had once or twice seen me in Will's company, we had not been formally introduced, and now he pulled at his ear and shifted his feet.

"Yes?" I said, half-curious, half-wary.

"I have come to apologize. Your brother says you were very angry at me. He said you wanted to throttle me. I don't blame you. Most people do."

"You have been talking to Will?"

"Yes, about those comments of mine regarding *Julius Caesar.* And about *Every Man out of His Humor.* I don't know why it wasn't successful. Do you?"

He sat down with a thump, and though he had asked my opinion, he scarcely let me utter a word in reply. I probably could not have advised him anyway, for just as I had not thought *Every Man in His Hu-*

mor to be particularly good, I had not found the sequel particularly bad. In my mind, they were both mediocre, and if the opinion of the audience had landed at either extreme, that judgment might even out in time.

But for Ben, any criticism was an impossible lump to swallow, and he was baffled that a piece of his had gone awry. Listening to him trying to reconcile it was like watching a man wrestle an invisible opponent. Unable to grapple with the poor reviews, he ended up talking himself into the stout conviction that he was not wrong but a genius misunderstood. It reminded me how hurt Will and I had been by the University Wits' initial reaction to our *Henry VI*, and coming on the heels of his first big hit, it was even harder for Ben. Who doesn't like to think that once you have reached the top, you have earned the right to stay there awhile? But no, that's not how it is, ever. Back to work, always back to work.

"Did Will send you?" I interrupted, when he finally stopped for breath.

"No." Ben lowered his head in guilt, seeming to remember why he had come. "I was at the Globe, and we got to talking, and we made it up about *Julius Caesar*. Then he said you were the one who was most angry, and you wanted to strangle me." He loosed his collar, pulled down the edges and leaned his bare neck toward me. "Go ahead."

I pondered. "No, thank you. If Will has forgiven you, the matter is closed. But perhaps you could behave differently next time?"

He shook his head. "I try, but it doesn't work. You really should do it while you have the chance."

He stuck his neck out farther, and I gave a slight smile, tipping my head just enough to signify acknowledgment of his offer. Relieved, Ben made his farewell and departed, leaving me mulling. Though it was probably not the impression he intended to make, what struck me most about Ben Jonson from the encounter was an unconfessed fear of poverty and failure. It may have sprung from his lowly beginnings. Like Will and me, he was trying to make his mark without benefit of a degree or rich connections. Unlike us, he could not grasp how to learn from his mistakes. His preferred reaction was to deny he had made them. Then, armored in arrogance, he went on the attack. A flawed but, as Will had said, a talented man.

When Will arrived, I asked him. No, he had not sent Ben. A rare instance of remorse and humility, we agreed.

"Don't expect it to happen often," Will said.

⁓

In the autumn of 1599, two new companies appeared as rivals on our horizon. They were mere children—the sweet-voiced choirboys of St. Paul's and the Queen's Chapel Royal—yet to our chagrin they were soon in serious competition with both the Chamberlain's and the Admiral's Men. Though primarily singers, the boys had also, in the early years of Elizabeth's reign, performed playlets for Her Majesty at court, specializing in elaborate but lightweight productions. To earn extra income, the enterprising choirmasters had opened their rehearsals in the old Blackfriars Monastery to a paying audience until, caught up in the Martin Marprelate controversy, both companies and their playhouse were closed in 1589. Now the St. Paul's Boys revived, engaged John Marston as their writer and began acting at a small private house near the church. The Queen's Chapel Boys likewise resurrected and moved into the Blackfriars Theatre that James Burbage had constructed and been forced to abandon. And whom did they take for their writer? Ben Jonson.

Ah, me, two playwrights given to extremes. Marston, twenty-three and the son of an esteemed lawyer, was already a skilled dramatist who considered himself too much the gentleman to write for the public playhouses. Yet he felt no qualms about composing the most savage satires and the lewdest poems; that very year, the Archbishop of Canterbury ordered his works to be burned. What's more, his language was so extravagant and ranting that his meaning was often drowned in a gale of words. Since Ben's extreme consisted in anointing himself the arbiter of English playwriting, it is no surprise he and Marston were soon quarreling. For the next two years what came to be known as the

War of the Theaters was on, Ben and Marston vehemently attacking each other in a series of retaliatory plays. Other playwrights jumped in as well—it was a glorious mud fight all around.

Ben usually got the worst of it. Unlike Marston, he was a slow writer who often struggled for words, and it made him fume in frustration. He knew himself to be superior, yet here was this puny poet writing circles around him. He was like a bully who picks a fight, then roars in outrage when his skinny victim turns on him and bloodies his nose. Nor did this battle confine itself to the stage. Some nights Will and I would set off in search of an hour's pleasant diversion at the tavern, only to hear an ominous noise growing in volume as we neared. We would look at each other in regret. All we wanted was a quiet drink among friends, and here came vitriol—and sometimes several writers and actors as well—brawling out the door.

"It is a good thing London has so many taverns," Will would say as we turned our steps elsewhere. "Our throats would be parched else."

"I'll drink to that," I said.

The dawning of the new century in 1600 ought to have been a time of jubilation, and despite a sleeting rain that December night, some hardy revelers did take to the streets. Will and I heard the shouts and the bursting of firecrackers as we supped late by the fire. That afternoon we had received a letter from Gilbert with sad news for me. My dear stepmother, Duck, had died, passing in her sleep as easily as a leaf from a tree. How could I cry when I knew she and my father would finally be reunited? I did anyway. The rest of the family, Gilbert wrote, fared well. Susanna and Judith, seventeen and fifteen, were proficient in their household duties; I suspected the blanket comment applied more to our older than our younger girl. New Place, nicely renovated, was well looked after by its tenants. Were we interested in more property? Not at present, Will concluded. Now, the hour late, we were both yawning, and Will was fighting off a cold.

"I'll see you in a century," he joked, going to bed early, and I replied with amused tolerance, "Ha, ha." He had stolen that jest from our new clown Robert Armin, as I knew very well.

I lingered by the fire. Lest any of our London friends drop by our room, Will and I still maintained separate beds, and tonight, weighing the benefits of shared bodily warmth against the likelihood of catching his sniffles, I concluded my own mattress would be preferable. But I was reluctant to undress and expose my skin, however briefly, to the wintry air, so I sat and drew my shawl closer. A sense of time came over me, and I wondered if, on the first day of January of the year 900, for example, people everywhere said, "I am so glad the eight hundreds are over, aren't you?" No, of course not. I doubt that, huddled around campfires or freezing in their hovels, they espoused with any fervor the idea that the new century would be markedly better. But we, reviewing a much greater sweep of history, could comprehend how different our lives had become in this modern age. In a little over a hundred years we had discovered the New World and circumnavigated the globe. We had invented the printing press and typeset books and made such advances in science and medicine that we laughed at our former ignorance and the dark superstitions of ages past. Here in England, we had broken from the Church of Rome, defeated Spain's invincible armada and become a world power.

But we had a very old queen.

She came out in procession shortly after New Year's Day, and Will and I joined the throng of spectators. Overall I had seen Elizabeth perhaps a dozen times on public occasions and during that one visit to Whitehall Palace. Now I craned to see the figure in the litter, thinking this might be the last chance. She wore a white satin gown decorated with jewels and richly embroidered with pansies and roses, English spring flowers. Ropes of pearls crisscrossed her chest, sapphires and rubies flashed on her waving hand, and a small golden crown perched atop her red wig like a bright little bird clinging to a curly nest. Her posture was very erect. It was hard to see her face, for her ermine-trimmed cape was pulled close to her cheeks for warmth. Even her high white forehead, always so admired, was decorated by a garland of golden spangles that draped across her brow. All that showed of her visage was a tiny circle of dark eyes, nose and a pinched mouth. It was almost as if no living creature existed inside that consuming structure of clothes, and perhaps that was the intent, to rivet the eye and forestall the mind long enough for the litter to pass. And, of course, everyone cheered and waved, a distraction in itself. But there was one moment when the cold winter sunlight struck her just so, and I gasped at the skeleton head. The next instant she was gone, and I experienced one of those physical jolts that makes you question whether what you have seen is real.

"Huh, queen," muttered a slovenly man butting against my shoulder, "nice work if you can get it."

"Get away, you! That's our Gloriana!" several voices cried, and the offender was thumped and whacked with canes and driven off. But others in the crowd snickered like children at a naughty joke.

She had the dust of mortality on her, that was it. She had frailty, if not in her heart, then in her bones. For forty years she had skillfully portrayed herself as the Virgin Queen, an ageless Diana with a snowy bosom and dewy face. Vain Elizabeth went so far as to banish every last looking glass from her chambers, she who had once delighted in receiving ornate mirrors as gifts. Believe me, I knew the allure of charades, especially for a woman as the rude years added up. As Will's "younger" sister, I was still deluding myself. But here we had a whole country joining in the feint, the male courtiers gushing compliments, the portrait painters pinking her cheeks like a girl's.

But for how much longer? Who could revere a wrinkled hag with half her black teeth gone? After the procession, we heard bets being placed in the tavern.

"A year at most."

"I give her two. The old girl is tougher than she looks."

"James of Scotland must be her successor."

"Then she should name him and clear the way so there will be no doubt of his authority."

"She'll never name anyone. They'll have to pry her clutching corpse off the throne."

"Unless someone decides to relieve her of it sooner."

"Maybe Essex."

Voices lowered. The Earl of Essex was sulking in disgrace after a disastrous military campaign in Ireland. Sent in March to attack the Irish rebels, he had misused his army, wasted his supplies, ignored his orders, made peace with the traitors and then abandoned his command. He gave Elizabeth no choice, and when he returned to London in the autumn she had him arrested and banished from court. That there would be a next move was certain. The question was, where and when?

"I give her six months," someone said, and the bantering tone resumed.

"Let's go," Will whispered, taking my arm, and I nodded, uncomfortable with the morbid wagering. We retraced our steps along the procession route, ducking our heads against a cold wind, and I recalled Elizabeth's crown bobbing on her red wig.

You had better clutch tightly, I told the little bird. The vultures are circling.

Chapter 25

$\mathcal{I}$f 1599 was a fertile year for our writing, 1600 was almost barren. Intending to follow the success of *Julius Caesar* with another classical subject, Will commenced *The Tragedy of Troilus and Cressida* but was forced to put it aside. The War of the Theaters was blasting away, the Chamberlain's Men were often caught in the cross fire and Will would come home sighing. Marston had done this, Jonson had done that, Tom Dekker was itching to reply.

Then the Privy Council shut the theaters for Lent. We were supposed to close for Lent every year, but rarely did anyone obey. This time, the council meant business. The still out-of-favor Earl of Essex was becoming a rallying point for malcontents, and an inflammatory play—should anyone be foolish enough to produce one—could set the intrigues ablaze. Even after the Lenten season was over, the council restricted performances to twice weekly. It cost us not only lost income but also actors. With families to feed, they scattered to take whatever other work beckoned. Will Kempe, in a clever bid to earn money, issued a bet that he could Morris dance the hundred miles from London to Norwich. He covered the distance in nine days, spread over several weeks, gathering crowds along the road. On his arrival at Norwich he received a hero's welcome, which so elated him that for his next feat he proposed to dance over the Alps to Rome.

Meanwhile, the boys' troupes had become the preferred entertainment for genteel Londoners. I am sure their repertoire did not equal ours for either quantity or quality, nor could the little actors compare to the virtuosity of the veteran performers in the Chamberlain's or the Admiral's Men. But the comfort and exclusivity of their private theaters bested the rough-and-tumble of the open playhouses, so while the yard at the Globe suffered no loss of groundlings, our galleries were sometimes sparsely populated. It was most discouraging counting those empty seats and knowing our profits were parking their upper-class bums on someone else's benches. Besides the usual advertisements— posting playbills, flying a banner on the flagpole, hiring a drummer to attract attention on play days—what else could we do? The Admiral's Men at the Rose fared even worse. Unable to withstand the competition from both the boys and the Globe, they packed up and erected a new playhouse in St. Giles Cripplegate north of the city. It was called the Fortune, presumably in hopes of better times to come. Privately, we cheered at running them off, and their departure from the immediate scene did give us a slight advantage.

My own muse began the year by resting. But some literary effort was soon called for, because—and here was the year's bright note—our new clown Robert Armin was proving a pearl in an ordinary-seeming shell. "Will Kempe who?" Will and I joked between us. Where Kempe was loud, lewd and riotous—in brief, a Falstaff—Armin was small, slight, subtle and intelligent—a philosopher. He could improvise so quickly you would swear he had wizardry in him. Let someone in the audience toss him a word or a phrase and he would compose an instant poem upon it. And when he sang, what a lovely, feeling voice. The entire house would fall silent to listen. I went back to *Much Ado* and *As You Like It* and revised the roles of Dogberry and Touchstone for him, improving both plays. When, in late summer, I began *Twelfth Night*, Feste was his from the start.

"Do you think Feste and the others are too mean to Malvolio?" I asked him after several mornings' rehearsals. I had borrowed the outline of my play—the separated brother-sister twins, the lovesick duke's pursuit of the countess—from a twenty-year-old romantic tale by Barnabe Riche, who copied it from a French narrative that came from a still earlier Italian version, which was lifted from . . . well, who knows? I would swear stories have secret ways of propagating themselves, sending off shoots like insidious vines ever in search of fresh soil. Also, I should not say "my" play, for once I had blocked out the scenes and the characters, *Twelfth Night* became a joint effort, and together Will and I added the subplot of Sir Toby, Maria, Sir Andrew Aguecheek and Malvolio. But just as Falstaff had begun to rub me wrong by verging into criminality, repeatedly watching Toby and his gang abuse Malvolio was beginning to blunt the fun we had taken in writing it.

"Too mean? Perhaps," Armin replied. "But that is Will's point. Everyone in the play goes too far, Orsino in his melancholy, Olivia in her mourning and her ardor for Cesario, Toby in his cruelty and Feste in going along with whatever prank comes to hand. Of course, that is the fool's job, to reveal folly by aiding and abetting it."

"Does he enjoy his job?"

" 'Better a witty fool than a foolish wit.' "

"But he ends the play alone."

"We all end alone. Only Feste is wise enough to know it."

He went back to the stage, leaving me musing. Funny how ideas insert themselves in plays without even the author knowing.

In the dawn of the year 1601, a familiar conversation was playing in the alehouses.

"The grave'll swallow her soon. No one escapes forever."

"I'll wager three months at most. There's naught but a bony skull under that crown."

"The sooner the better. It's time we had a king again."

"Shh! Do not be so quick or so loud to bury her. There are spies and factions everywhere, and the wrong words could land a man in the Tower."

Would that the Chamberlain's Men had shown equal discretion, for to recall what happened next still makes me shudder. In October 1600 Elizabeth had finally broken irrevocably from the temperamental Earl of Essex by declining to renew a grant she had given him on the tax of sweet wines. With his private estate already deep in debt, the loss of the grant stripped the earl of his last source of income. Outraged, he began plotting revenge. On February 6, a group of his friends appeared at the Globe to commission a special performance of *Richard II* for the following afternoon. Had Will or Cuthbert been present, common sense might have prevailed. But they were elsewhere on business, and in their absence Dick Burbage and the remaining players naively accepted.

"But you don't want an old play like *Richard II*," they advised Essex's friends. "Let us give you something fresher, *As You Like It* or *Every Man in His Humor*."

"No, it must be *Richard II*," the men replied, and as the leader drew out a bulging purse, the actors' eyes grew wide.

Oh, you numbskulls! Cogitate! Why would Essex insist on *Richard II*? Do you suppose the plot—a faltering king overthrown by a vigorous champion—has anything to do with it? Could there be a parallel between Elizabeth as Richard II and Essex as Bolingbroke, who proclaimed himself Henry IV? Have you forgotten that Sir John Hayward was tortured on the rack for publishing the same story, or that when our play was issued in quarto the deposition scene was glaringly cut? Are you being duped into stirring up passions and instigating a riot that could lead to the dethroning and murder of the queen?

But all the actors and their ever-empty bellies saw was that pear-plump purse, and, salivating, they agreed. The next day the play was performed to a cheering crowd from Essex House, after which the actors scooted off to the tavern with their takings. That night the earl received a summons to court. He spurned the messenger, and when a deputation of Privy Councilors arrived in the morning to pursue the matter, they were roughly taken captive. Essex and two hundred armed followers then thronged into the city, shouting rebellion.

In hindsight, of course, it sounds laughable. How could this wild charge hope to prevail against the established order or even reach the queen's staunchly defended person? But the country was in turmoil, and the citizens were tired of decrepit leaders and bad government, of religious divisions and foreign intrigues. Elizabeth had lost her luster; she was a setting sun. A fading magician, no more tricks up her elaborate sleeve. The grumbles in the taverns had been growing louder daily. Time for a new generation to run this new seventeenth century! You are holding us back, old woman. All the rebels had to do was whip up a groundswell as they stormed through town.

Yet not one citizen rose up to join Essex. Not one. Ah, we are timorous, bleating sheep, we mortals. It is why, from birth to death, the vast number of us remain unknown. Essex at least will be enshrined in future chronicles for his audacity, for daring to aim at a crown. Perhaps in the end that was what he wanted most, to leave a name that would not be forgotten, even if it was a perverse fame. Still, I try to imagine how he felt as he charged through the city and saw those deserted streets, closed shutters, locked doors. I try to pinpoint the moment when the hollow taste of defeat came into his throat and he knew he had lost the game.

"What about us?" I cried, clutching Will as news of Essex's ignominious surrender swept through town. "What about *Richard II*? We will be implicated, tortured, put to a horrible death!" I began to shake, for although no one would ever credit me for any of the plays, I fully believed that if Will were arrested, I would and should share his fate. I would have stood by him.

For a week our stomachs churned in anxiety. While the authorities investigated, London remained in a state of rumor and alarm. One of Essex's misguided followers was Will's former patron, the Earl of Southampton, who three years ago had impregnated and married his mistress Elizabeth Vernon, a cousin of Essex. The former beautiful boy had accompanied Essex on his military expeditions, including the debacle in Ireland, where, it was said, he spent most of his time in bed cuddling with a captain. Though Will shied from the subject, I knew memories and a helpless sense of loyalty tormented him. On February

18, the Chamberlain's Men were summoned for questioning in the Essex affair. They chose Augustine Phillips, who had the steadiest nerves, to represent them.

"Stick to the facts," they coached. "Just answer the questions and don't give excess information. Tell them we only did it for the money."

On his return, they pounced on him.

"I'm not sure how it went," he said, exhaling heavily and accepting the sustaining drink they thrust into his hands. "They rendered no immediate decision."

The following day, Essex and Southampton were brought to trial for high treason, and the whole city hushed while we awaited the outcome. Will burst in with the verdict as soon as it was proclaimed.

"Guilty, both condemned to death."

"Oh, Will! And us?"

"Absolved."

He sank onto the bed, and though it was a cold day, the sweat of relief poured off him.

"Thank God! But how? Why? What happened at the trial?"

"All we know is that although the council severely criticized the playing of *Richard II*, they determined the Chamberlain's Men had no part in the conspiracy. They decided"—Will gave a wobbly smile—"that actors are far too dim-witted to organize and execute a rebellion."

Six days later, Essex's handsome head dropped into the straw. Southampton was reprieved and sentenced to prison instead. The night before Essex's execution, the Chamberlain's Men were called to court to perform. It was not a Shakespeare play, and Will and I were not present, but those actors who were reported later that they quaked in their costumes throughout the performance and the queen watched them with a particularly baleful eye. The headman's ax is not the only way to send a sharp message.

Yet Elizabeth surely had more on her mind that night than intimidating our hapless players. In the Tower, her last love was counting his final hours on earth, and you knew she was counting them too. I pictured her barking laughter at the comedy while her hands clawed onto the arms of her throne, her knuckles protruding like knobby white rocks through the desiccated flesh. No more gallant young men would come to flatter and amuse her, to whisper warm breath into her dry spinster ear. No more dashing, virile attendants would hover beside her to prop up the myth of agelessness. Oh, Elizabeth, I thought, how tired you must be. How weary of pretense. All your life you have done your duty. Now that you have entered your seventh age, don't you deserve a rest? But that was the very lesson of Essex's betrayal: that to relax for even a moment could be fatal. So while the players played and the minutes preyed on her nerves, she cackled and clapped. Ironic, isn't it, that women were still banned from the stage, when the greatest trouper in England was a red-wigged crone who for forty years had stuck doggedly to her part.

We all end alone, Elizabeth, and oh, God, how you know it.

Even after our escape in the Essex rebellion, 1601 was a lean year for the Globe and the Chamberlain's Men. The boys' theaters continued to be strong contenders. Actors drifted away, and there was little call for new plays. The War of the Theaters intensified with a comedy by Ben called *Poetaster, His Arraignment.* Belying his usual reputation for slowness, he completed it in a mere fifteen weeks. In *Poetaster*, Ben portrayed himself as the Roman poet Horace holding forth at the court of the emperor Augustus. From that lofty height, he proceeded to mock and condemn quite a number of his fellow writers, all thinly disguised as characters at Augustus's court. He also denigrated the actors, the professional players who had given him his start, proclaiming he was now too good to write for them. Let me tell you, no man made enemies with more ease than Ben Jonson.

Now here comes the fun part—childish fun, I call it. Word leaked out what Ben was writing, and the Chamberlain's Men determined to reply. At first I begged Will to desist. Throughout our career he had shielded me from the slings and arrows of our outrageous profession, the tedious negotiations and cutthroat competition, the battles over censorship, the enervating squabbles and retaliations that wasted so much time. He shouldered the business, while I, snail-like, ducked my sensitive antennae into my shell and coiled there, writing. But a sheltering snail may still be crunched underfoot when heavy boots start stomping.

"Let Jonson write what he pleases," I argued. "We should not dirty our hands and our reputation."

"Yet you are the one who wanted to strangle him when he criticized *Julius Caesar*."

"And you wisely counseled we remain above the fray. What about *Troilus and Cressida*? You hardly have time for it now, and they want you to drop everything to write a play insulting Jonson?"

"The retort will not come from me. We have commissioned Tom Dekker."

"But he was Jonson's former writing partner for the Admiral's Men."

"Exactly." Will grinned.

Well, Dekker knew his man, and he knew how to goad him. In no time he had penned *Satiromastix; or, The Untrussing of the Humorous Poet*. The title alone was a triumph. The image of a bellowing Ben with his breeches yanked to his knees and his bare bottom exposed to the world was a marvelous feather to tickle the fancy. In the play, Jonson, in his own favorite guise as Horace, is vilified, crowned with nettles and forced to reform. Dekker had incorporated many of his former friend's most irritating traits and deftly ridiculed them, and I roared with approval at the first performance. Jonson was so offended, he skulked off and stopped writing. Once again, the bully got his comeuppance. It was quite all right for him to bait and scorn others, but he could not stand it when he was twitted in return.

"Is it over now?" I asked Will. "Can we get back to writing, please?"

"With pleasure. Where is *Troilus and Cressida*?"

"Languishing on your table."

"I'll brush it off. What about you? Do you have anything in mind?"

"Not yet. I'll copy for you while I await inspiration."

"Don't take too long, Mistress Bard," Will teased.

What does a writer do when she is not writing?

Many things!

For a start, housekeeping, and when a play was finished I often looked about our lodgings with a guilty uh-oh. A thick fuzz of dust on the mantel, smoke grime on the walls. Who stops to scrub the floor when your pen is calling? I would plunge in with broom, bucket and goose-feather duster to set matters right. There were also the everyday routines of making the beds, tending the hearth, running errands to the shops, the wine merchant, the booksellers, the cobbler, the laundress. I enjoyed these rounds and found it pleasant to exchange conversation with the tradesmen, their wives and apprentices. There are many good people in the world, and their numbers and resilience are often overlooked. Of course, they were also fodder for characters in future plays.

Always, I had some sewing project to occupy me, especially costumes, beading and embroidery for the Globe. Lately, more time was spent on Will's and my own wardrobe. Will, in particular, must make an impression befitting his reputation when he walked about town or appeared at court. Many a morning when we got a good eastern light, he stood while I draped and pinned fabric about him. "Turn . . . a little more . . . hold there . . ." I never had to admonish him for fidgeting. He liked fine clothes, and the old sumptuary laws that had restricted and defined the dress of every class were, like Elizabeth, losing their grip. At least he did not go so far as some of the foppish men at court, who dyed their beards orange or purple to match their garb. My own dress was more subdued. I was content with a modest appearance and felt no need to draw attention.

In the afternoons, I took long walks. Here a nose, there a face, a voice, a hat. Stories on two legs—it was how I had gotten Malvolio's yellow stockings. Ambling to the meadows and marshes south of South-wark, I picked wildflowers or observed the migrating ducks. Will and I also partook of the seasonal diversions—All Fools' Day, May Day, St. Bartholomew's Fair in August—though even these festive events were more subdued than usual in the twilight of Elizabeth's reign. Naturally, I read the latest books and attended performances at the Globe and the Fortune, where Ned Alleyn and the Admiral's Men continued to dra-matize and declaim. A decade ago everyone had found that style of acting riveting; now, much as I respected Alleyn, it struck me as windy and overdone. But to repeat, it was not an auspicious time for the the-aters, and we all dropped anchor in the safe harbor of repetition while we waited out the storms.

It would have been nice to have some female friends, but what other woman was there like me, in my circumstances, in all London? When the cobbler's wife confided her long list of physical complaints or a neighbor detained me to brag of her children, I could hardly reply with a discussion of high poetry or the mechanics of foreshadowing. For those conversations, I relied on our cohorts in the theater, who took it for granted that Will's sister would be enlightened and talked to me as if I were one of them. Nonetheless, it had been a long time since I had had a close connection with someone like Mr. Phipps or Bess of Hardwick. Bess would be nearly seventy-five now, more wizened than ever and a miniature firecracker all the same. Whenever I felt myself falter in bargaining with a merchant, the memory of how she could leave a grown man whimpering would stiffen my spine. I imagined the fun of catching up with her.

"Anne!" Her sharp eyes would glint with instant recognition. "What is this nonsense I hear about your brother entangling himself with the Essex rebellion? A playwright has no business in politics."

"Well, he—"

"A lucky thing they let him off." Here, a knobby finger shaken at me. "I have had to make do with inferior seamstresses ever since you left, and with inferior company. Come back and I will pay you better."

"I am sorry. My brother—"

"—could very well get along without you. Or could he? That recent play of his, *Twelfth Night*. Does it not contain a brother and sister so alike that the sister substitutes herself for him?"

"Well, she . . . I thought you had no regard for plays," I would tease. "Have you seen *Twelfth Night* then?"

"Of course not. A complete waste of time. That Romeo and Juliet story you used to read to Arbella permanently softened her brain. My granddaughter will marry when and whom I say she will." Here, the finger would crook me closer and Bess's voice drop low. "The queen cannot last forever. Tell your brother to be patient and behave meanwhile. Talent in any form should be respected—not hidden."

Then, motioning to her attendants, Bess would march on her way. I hoped she would live forever; even an imaginary Bess could inspire me. And though I was sometimes lonely, I did not lack friends. On the contrary, my plays were peopled with them—men, women and children of every background, temperament and disposition. I regret that in our early plays it was too often a shallow acquaintance; we hadn't the experience to plumb our characters deeply. Now I could pursue their complexities and inhabit their souls—as they did mine.

All of which is to say I was ready that summer afternoon of 1601 when, backstage at the Globe, I opened a large costume trunk. I was digging for a snippet of brown velvet—acorn brown was the exact shade I sought—when underneath the bolts and ribbons I came across some misplaced scripts from the company's repertoire. I scanned the titles and flipped a few pages. I was short on reading material just then, there having been nothing juicy at the booksellers' of late, and I hated being bookless. Oh, well, this would do for the nonce, and, selecting a Danish play by Tom Kyd, I took it home.

⁓

I had barely turned the last page of Kyd's *Hamlet* when death paid a visit, though not the one we were all expecting. Elizabeth lived on; it was John Shakespeare who died that September. Gilbert sent word the old man was ailing, and we made the journey in time to sit by his deathbed, a grisly episode. He was in pain and exhausted, whey-faced and waxen. A twisted rag was all that remained of that once bluff man. In his last hours, he became positively frightened, begging that he be spared an eternity in hell. Why he should have thought it a possibility, I cannot say. His sins were no better or worse than anyone else's. It may be that a delirium had entered his brain, for he moaned and thrashed as if wrestling with some unseen force. Then he gave a horrified suck of air, his eyes rolled back and his body arched with a grotesque cry. God, it was awful. Mary sobbed piteously, and we all were badly shaken. I pray my own death when it comes will be much more decorous and expeditious.

With John's passing, Will became the head of the Shakespeare family. Since he had long ago paid off his father's debts, settling the small estate was uncomplicated, and as none of his brothers cared to continue John's gloving business, that also ended. Will decided to seek a tenant for the Henley Street house and move the whole family into New Place.

"I may turn the Henley Street building into an inn," he said, "and I want to look into buying more property."

"What for?"

"An investment. Farmland, perhaps, that I can let out to accrue rent."

"Why not invest in London? We could have a proper house there."

"That is hardly necessary for just the two of us, Anne. For our girls' sakes, we need to maintain our position in Stratford and see to our obligations here."

"It seems to me you have already more than fulfilled them. You got your father his coat of arms, you bought New Place, and you send money regularly to support our daughters and your mother. One has but to ask and you provide. I want to get back to London, Will. Gilbert can manage for us, as always."

"Yes, but Gilbert also has his own livelihood as a haberdasher to pursue, and I must take a more active role." Will sighed. "Things have changed, Anne. Everyone is looking to me."

"So are the Chamberlain's Men. The boys' theaters continue to outdraw us, and you haven't completed a play in a twelvemonth."

He made a noise that meant he did not like to be reminded. "I will resume work on *Troilus and Cressida* as soon as I can. I don't see you turning out anything meanwhile."

"But that's just it. I have a great play in mind, Will. I am onto something."

"Write it here then."

Very well, since I have your permission. In fact, I was soon sneaking off at every chance to scribble. Susanna was so adept at directing the move from Henley Street and commandeering New Place that no one missed me. I could disappear into one of the dozen-plus rooms, write undetected for several hours and reemerge at mealtimes as if I had been part of the activities all along. Thus, while Will and Susanna supervised the family's installation at New Place, I began *Hamlet*. I leave it to you to decide which was the better use of time.

Chapter 26

$\mathcal{I}$ suspected early on that *Hamlet* could be my greatest play. An exhilarating sensation—many writers are never granted a masterpiece at all, and here I could feel mine taking shape. Thank you, God! Thank you, muse! But also bittersweet—what if nothing else I wrote henceforth, no matter how compelling, ever matched it? Would it undercut the pleasure of every future endeavor, enervate the result? And the weight of responsibility, to live up to it, to get it right . . .

Hamlet also knew what we were about, although for him the promise of immortality was cold comfort to the grief of being sacrificed to avenge his father's death. Hamlet knew? Oh, yes. He breathed from the start, his presence so close upon my shoulder that I could feel the soft stir of animate air. It helped us both that the revenge genre was still in vogue and the formula easy to follow. It helped that the story's dark mood was in tune with the times. It helped that the tale was set in Denmark, another small, northern sea kingdom. When Will and I returned to London in midautumn, I had only to look out our window to capture the atmosphere: cold, damp, foggy, glum. But it was Hamlet who pervaded my bones and dragged me ever deeper into the mire of Elsinore. And if you are now crying, "Cart that woman off to Bedlam! Her wits are as scattered as stars spinning across the sky!" then you still understand nothing of writing, of creating, even after all my attempts to explain.

"I am doing *Hamlet*," I told Will when his focus returned to the theater.

"That Danish story?"

"Yes, I found a version by Tom Kyd in an old trunk at the Globe. As I recall, he wrote it soon after *The Spanish Tragedy*, and it was popular, remember?"

"Of course I remember. I helped him write it."

"You did not. When? Where?"

"I made suggestions."

"Do not take credit for others' work, Will," I said, a bit testily. "I make suggestions to you all the time, and I get no recognition for it." We scowled at each other a moment before I continued. "Anyway, it is a good story with meaty parts, and Dick will excel in the lead. Would you like to act the old king's ghost? It is a pivotal role."

Will paused, considering, and I knew I had him; he could be a bit of a ham. I even expanded the role to give him extra stage time. In Kyd's version, the dead king appears but once, pleads his case and disappears into the fog. In mine, his first appearance is silent, and Hamlet must await a second visitation from the specter to learn of the shocking fratricide. You see what happens as a favor to an actor? Give me a bigger part! Oh, all right. But in this case, it improved the play, heightening the suspense and sending a shiver of premonition up the spine. It set the tone of doubt—can you trust the word of a ghost? I also enhanced the role of the old councilor Polonius, transformed the harlot who tempts Hamlet into Polonius's daughter Ophelia, and inserted the play within the play to reveal Claudius's guilt. Despite these changes, I like to think Tom Kyd would approve of my keeping his work alive. And while I discerned no hints of Will in Kyd's script, I did detect a faint, sweet whiff of Kit. He and Tom had shared lodgings, after all.

The genesis of the graveyard scene was perhaps the oddest occurrence in writing the play, and here you must bear with the tentacled crawlings of my octopus brain. I was sitting in the tavern with Will one evening, listening to the conversations, when my eye fell on a man across the room. He sat in a pensive pose, chin propped against his fist, and his hand seemed extremely large in proportion to his head. I put my own head in a similar position, feeling the space my palm covered from my jawline up to my cheekbone. Then I scanned the other tables for a comparison. There—one of the whores, a chubby girl, clapped her fingers to her mouth as she giggled over a customer's joke. Her palm almost covered her face. Despite her fat body, was her head smaller than average? Then right beside me Robert Armin lifted his fingers to scratch his ear. I have said he was a slight man, and when he set his hand back on the table, it was smaller than mine. Yet in relation to his skull . . .

"Is something wrong?" he asked me.

"No, no, I was just noticing . . ."

I squirmed off my embarrassment at having been caught staring, and Armin laughed. But inwardly I was piqued. How could I, a constant observer, have missed this intriguing detail of human anatomy? I spent the rest of the evening mentally measuring hands and skulls. Then the skulls took over, and for two weeks it was all I could do to keep from openly scrutinizing people in the streets, amazed at the infinite variety of faces that could be constructed upon one barren bone. Wide, narrow, pinched, bulging, long nosed, low browed, lantern-jawed, oval, squarish, lopsided, deformed. Some carried their brains all on top, others wore them out the back like a rear balcony. The slightest deviation in structure could change the entire aspect and stamp a child forever as a beauty or a toad. I imagined turning these passing craniums in my hands; I confess it sounds macabre. One night I made Will sit by candlelight while I probed over his temples and his emerging bald spot.

"What are you doing?" he said, exasperated.

"I don't know yet. Humor me."

Three days later Hamlet and Horatio were strolling by the grave-yard—Why did they go there? I didn't send them—when Robert Armin's spade tossed up a dirty skull. The prince wandered his fingers over its contours, imagining the soft tissue that had fleshed it, the lips that once smiled.

"To be or not to be," he whispered, shivering.

Later, of course, I moved that line. But I sat reeling over those thirteen letters for the rest of the day. Does God know? I asked Hamlet. Is this why he has fixed his canon against self-slaughter, not because it is a sin, but to pretend the taking of life is his sole perquisite when the power lies in our hands? And if it does, what other power matters? Have I just dethroned God? And if the expression of this awful truth can be reduced to such blinding simplicity, have I wiped out the need to ever write anything again? What else do we need to understand? With a cry, I shut down the thought. To demote God was one thing, but to be guilty of murdering all writing forever . . . I would rather lose my faith than my soul.

But it is hard to close your eyes once you have seen the light, and Hamlet and I took another step toward it. In a typical revenge tragedy, the point is to achieve vengeance, the bloodier the better. Now Hamlet began to sense that no matter how justified the revenge he enacted on his treacherous uncle Claudius, it would be an empty victory. It would not change the fact of his father's murder or bring his pale ghost back from the dead. It would not absolve his mother, Gertrude, of her lust, her complicity, her weakness, her failure to stand up for her son. It would not absolve Hamlet of his guilt for having killed Polonius, for though he declares the meddling old man deserved his accidental death behind the arras, he lies in his throat. He knows in his heart he has spilled the lifeblood of an innocent human being, and he is repulsed by the violence he has done not only to Polonius but to himself. He has become a murderer—no, no, no, no.

Oh, my poor sweet prince. How much easier had you been a seasoned soldier, a battle-stained man. Henry V would have had no hesitation in executing a murderer and usurper. That champion of justice would have hewn Claudius with a single virtuous stroke, kicked his corpse to the dogs, and walked away with his conscience not only intact but magnified. But Hamlet is a student, a poet, and murder sickens him. He abhors the taking of any life—would that all men felt the same. And once Polonius is slain, it is too late. Now Laertes must avenge his father, and the sinister cycle of vengeance has begun. The shadow is creeping over Denmark, and dispatching his uncle will bring Hamlet no satisfaction when he sits on his ill-gotten throne. So he wavers and prevaricates, hoping some other path will open. Is there no chance for forgiveness and redemption? Why must this unwelcome duty to set things right fall upon him?

"Take this cup from me!"

He did plead that, in an early draft; then, shaking, I struck the line. Struck and double-struck it, smeared the ink and hurriedly burned the paper before God's sweeping eye could land thereon. You can see what a problem I have with God. I am not sure I entirely believe in him, but I cannot seem to cast him out either. And heaven help me if the authorities discovered my blasphemy. The last thing we needed after our blunder in the Essex affair was to reantagonize them. While I sat breathing heavily, Hamlet pressed his advantage.

Release me, he said. *Find another way. Bring Fortinbras in sooner and let him assume the throne.*

How can I? There is no drama in that, no tragedy, no great woe.

Then have him kill Claudius, vanquish me in a duel, and I will abdicate in his favor for the good of Denmark.

You can't. You are the son, the rightful heir.

I don't want the job. Besides, I could be illegitimate. You know what a whore my mother is. The funeral meats did coldly furnish forth the marriage feast, so quick was she to jump into my uncle's bed.

Don't joke! She is suffering too.

Then release her. Make Laertes her son and give him the crown. He will make the far better king.

No! That is not how the story goes. You stray too far from the script.

But I don't want to die.

You have to. You must be sacrificed. The slate must be wiped clean.

Change it. You are the writer. You can do anything.

It will ruin my masterpiece. It won't be the same.

Don't be selfish. Another masterpiece will come along.

No, this is it. I forbid you to disobey me.

"Why are you crying?" Will quizzed me with a rude look. "It is only a play."

"I know. It is nothing, silliness." I wiped my cheek with the back of my hand. "How are you getting on with *Troilus and Cressida*?"

Will grunted. "I would be a lot farther along if you did not interrupt me with blubbering."

After that, Hamlet ceased speaking to me and retreated to a corner, sad, reproachful, resigned. The final draft was devoted to the language, the words that would lift this story above any other ever written, and I trimmed and tuned, reading aloud, listening. No more poetry for poetry's sake. Every word must be necessary, beautiful, true. Every line must resonate; when you have it right, it is like plucking the string of a harp and hearing it thrum. I hardly noticed when the New Year's Eve fireworks burst over the Thames—1602 and Elizabeth still lived; fooled you again! Late that night I put down my pen.

There. I had it, I did it, and I would die fulfilled even if I never wrote again.

⁓

Will knew it too. I would come home from an errand and catch him reading my papers.

"Not bad," he would say, lightly setting the script aside. "I have marked a few changes you might want to consider."

"I will look at them," I agreed, and I did but declined to incorporate them. *Hamlet* was finished. I was only letting the script rest a few days before I let it go out in the world.

"You could do the same for *Troilus and Cressida*," he offered. "Glance it over, give me your opinion."

"All right." I edited and made a few suggestions. Though neither of us was ever quite happy with *Troilus and Cressida*—it is one of those plays that cannot seem to define itself—it did not occur to me that Will was soliciting my help in a surreptitious hope I would salvage it. Unfortunately, my creative faculties were temporarily exhausted, and when I failed to transform *Troilus and Cressida*, he grew grumpy.

"You have *Hamlet*. Take it to the Globe," I said, and naturally he did with his name on it, and he and Dick Burbage got the acclaim. That I did not mind—well, not too much anyway. Nor did I disagree when he decided our takings should go toward the purchase of more property in Stratford. What irked me was that he began to act as if *Hamlet* should have been his. He did not deny I wrote it, yet he behaved as if I had somehow stolen it from him. I can't help it, Will. I don't know why me and not you. I am sorry you are jealous, but you cannot be the best every single time.

Oh, dear. Ever since that night of dismantling the Globe, the affection between us had held steady. We continued to couple, if not with the frequency and passion of youth, at least with mutual enjoyment and tenderness. We had matured into a comfortable living arrangement that met both our needs, and we had rediscovered solid reasons to like each other. Couldn't liking grow back into a modest love? Couldn't you say, "I love you," to a friend? But I suppose where I saw Will and myself as partners in a joint enterprise, his pride still pricked at any hint I might exceed him. And if the only way he could love me was for me to forswear my talent and brick up my brain, then no. *Hamlet* didn't drop on me from the sky, Will. I earned him. Haven't you been paying attention?

I stalked to the tavern, ordered a sherry wine and took it to a corner to sulk. I was doing a good job of it when a sneering voice interrupted.

"Well, well, if it isn't the sister of our illustrious Will, the genius who wrote *Hamlet*. Drinking all alone in the tavern. Is this any place for a lady?"

Ben Jonson. He swayed on his feet and a beery fog wafted from him.

"I enjoy being alone," I replied, but the subtlety was lost on him, and he lurched onto the bench beside me.

"Ah, don't go," he said, grabbing my sleeve as I started to rise. "Don't you want to stay and hear how I have given up writing? That's one fewer playwright in London to trouble your precious brother."

He belched in my face, and I leaned back. Jonson smelled not only of beer but of garlic and sausage. Since storming off the literary scene the previous year when Tom Dekker raked him over in *Satiromastix*, he had kept out of sight, and the War of the Theaters had mercifully subsided. Now the popularity of the boy players was beginning to wane, and the professional players were coming back in demand. Philip Henslowe and Edward Alleyn at the Fortune had commissioned Dekker and several new writers to produce a fresh crop of plays for the Admiral's Men. Another troupe of players, the Earl of Worcester's Men, had also lately arisen. They were acting at the Rose, and our old clown Will Kempe had joined them. His quest to dance over the Alps to Rome had not been the popular or financial success he anticipated, and since Robert Armin had become firmly established with the Chamberlain's Men in his absence, Kempe had taken up with our competition.

Which brought me back to Ben Jonson, who, although he claimed to have renounced writing, obviously had not quit London. Hmm. In the midst of these shifting theater loyalties, perhaps he should be endured long enough for me to determine whether he possessed any inside information.

"So you have laid down your pen?" I echoed, trying not to appear overly curious.

"Sworn off it forever, as I should have long ago. It is a fickle, an ungrateful profession, fit only for hacks."

I made a consoling sound, for I was sorry to see any writer suffer such pangs. At the same time, I proceeded to study Ben's skull. We had procured a real skull for *Hamlet*, by the way, and Dick Burbage always wrung an eloquent scene from poor Yorick's pate. Ben Jonson's skull was not his friend. It was broad and blunt, flat cheeked, a peasant's noggin fleshed over with too much meat and drink and set upon a thick neck. Perhaps his habitual belligerence was partly in rebellion to that skull, a protest that he was not what his face portended. Too bad his behavior usually had the reverse effect of confirming that the brawling visage suited him after all. Still, somewhere in that lout there resided a talented brain.

For a full hour that day I listened to Ben's griefs. Naturally, he had done no wrong, oh, no, not Ben. If he had abused and satirized and slandered others, what other course had been open to him? He had to speak up; their conceptions of playwriting were patently wrong.

"Think of a crossroads," he said, diverging his palms in earnest demonstration. "Would you allow a friend to take a path that you knew would lead him astray? Never! You would set him on the proper route to the proper destination, and if he insisted on pursuing his misguided course, you would throw yourself in front of him and block the road. Just so did I endeavor to prevent my fellow writers from traveling a path to literary ruin. And they attacked me—attacked me!—in return. Was ever a man of genius so misused? I will never write again!"

Good! I thought, though of course Will and I had more than once vowed the same. And Ben had shown me he had it in him to be a better man; he would be welcome back when he unearthed him. Meanwhile, I had gleaned no news of interest from his lament, and mumbling a few more condolences, I rose to go. Jonson's meaty hand clamped my wrist.

"What is that famous brother of yours writing now, anything?"

"He is taking a break after *Hamlet*." I twisted my arm free. "You may expect something equally brilliant when he is ready."

"When he is ready? Oh, ho, aren't we the fine author, doling out plays like royal favors, making us bow and scrape at his feet to receive them. So where is it then? Where is the next great play coming from?"

"Where is yours?" I shot back. "You ought to quit while you are behind, ha!"

I gathered my skirts and swept out. It is the one advantage of being a woman. Unlike a man in breeches, you always have on you the makings of a dramatic exit.

All the same, Jonson's taunt nagged at me over the next few days. With the situation for the public theaters improving, the Chamberlain's Men and the Globe required strong plays to stay in competition. Though *Troilus and Cressida* was surely not Will's best, it was time to finish it and move on.

"I can't," he said when I prodded him. He held up a newly arrived letter. "Gilbert has found another property. Good, arable land, a hundred and seven acres at three hundred and fifty pounds, and he thinks we can bring the price down."

"Fine, have him buy it so you can get on with writing."

"He has other properties for me to consider as well. I need to see them in person."

"But that will take weeks, and the Globe and the players need you. Your place is here in London."

"I won't be away long." He waved his hand to make my protest disappear. "Besides, I have written more than two dozen plays in barely ten years. Don't I deserve a holiday?"

"You had one at your father's funeral." Angry, I did not spare him. "Will, this isn't fair to me."

"Not fair to you?"

"To leave me alone in London."

"Who is leaving you? You are welcome to come to Stratford, and if it happens that we decide to stay awhile—"

"Stay? What do you mean? You can't be ready to retire to the country?"

"Maybe."

"No! I want to write plays in London." Bewildered, I shook my head. How had we leaped from Gilbert buying us a property to Will taking a holiday to our moving back to Stratford for all time? How long had he been planning this?

"You said you wanted a proper house." He spoke as calmly as if we were discussing whether to have kippers or cutlets for our supper. "In Stratford we have New Place, the finest home in town."

"Will, I agree we should return to Stratford eventually, and I know that between your father's death and the slump in the theater, last year was a difficult one. But now that the playhouses are reviving, don't you want to see what more you can accomplish? And Ben Jonson is out of the way, at least for the time being. He confirmed it to me at the tavern. We won't have to contend with his nastiness."

"Jonson is a small fish"—Will shrugged—"but so are we all."

"No, we . . . you are a great playwright. You must continue. I need you to write!"

I grabbed his arm, my brain still reeling. I suppose I shook him roughly—I was as tall as him—and, startled, he wrenched loose.

"Let go, Anne! What possesses you? Why are you so anxious to remain in London? Do you have a secret lover of whom I know nothing?" He arched an eyebrow at the comical idea. Then he repeated with dawning seriousness, "Do you?"

"Of course not! How can you think such a thing? Do you accuse me of infidelity? I want us to stay so you can write plays."

"I can write in Stratford, if an idea strikes me. Besides, nothing is decided. I am only going to check out properties."

He turned up his palms and smiled, and I cautioned myself to have patience. Will had talked this way before and always rebounded. Perhaps if I sent him off cheerily to Stratford, he would play out this latest whim, realize what he was missing, and return.

"Very well," I said, and for the next week, until he left, we smiled at each other often.

But once he was gone, I curled onto the bed in the shape of an unborn child, whimpering disconsolate sounds.

Chapter 27

Separated again. In a bitter mood I pictured Will in Stratford, embracing his doting mother and our blooming daughters, clapping Gilbert on the back as they sat down to discuss the properties Gilbert had scouted for his consideration. I imagined him strolling about the town and countryside, beaming at the people clustering to speak with Stratford's most famous citizen, offering his wise opinion on everything from the price of wool to the general hardships of the times.

"Stratford is well situated at the market crossroads," he would say, "but the dismal state of the national economy threatens us with decline. We must encourage commerce and develop better transportation with an eye to becoming the hub of the Midlands."

Who did he think he was, the mayor? All right, I understood he would be flattered. I appreciated the allure of yet another prodigal return, his *Non Sanz Droict* claim to premier status in the town. And I granted he deserved a holiday. Will worked hard—I always said so—and was present at nearly every rehearsal and performance, coaching the actors not only in his plays but in every play in the company's repertoire. He filled in when an actor was sick or otherwise missing, which meant memorizing their parts. He read and critiqued the scripts thrust weekly upon him by aspiring authors. The Essex affair, the War of the Theaters and the competition of the boys' troupes had made the previous year especially difficult. So it was surely tempting to sit in the Stratford alehouse and contemplate a permanent life of ease as a country gentleman—the very respectability for which John Shakespeare had aimed. With the old man's death, was Will becoming his father?

In mid-May a letter from Will informed me he had purchased the hundred-plus acres of land Gilbert had identified, the price reduced to £320. *Good, now come home.* But the brothers were in pursuit of more investments, and I became annoyed with Gilbert's complicity in this business. How could I once have trusted him as my ally and friend? I muttered recriminations in his far-off direction, though of course he had no inkling that in his enthusiasm to do Will's bidding he was undermining my happiness, my position. As spring turned to summer, a queasiness began to dog me, though I suppressed it in my daily walks about London. How could anyone dream of giving up this life, this hurly-burly place, this gleaming existence? We had the intellectual pursuits of a capital city, the green array of nature just outside town. Will would come to his senses and return. But at night, looking across at his empty bed, I felt the unease creep back in. He meant to stay in Stratford. He meant to give it all up and retire. How could he, the young man who had once declared he would be the greatest poet of the age? I would have gone to him and groveled, had I believed it would do any good. And how ironic that I, who had once been left behind in Stratford while he ran off to London, now found myself deserted in the opposite direction.

"Please, Will," I begged the night. "We can't give this up. You will kill me. It's like dying."

Fortunately, as far as the Chamberlain's Men were concerned, Will's absence thus far was no longer than usual. They also had family obligations and side investments and took time off to address them. To cover up for him meanwhile, I began a new play. Given the success of *Hamlet*, I fully expected something miraculous from my pen. Instead I coughed up *All's Well That Ends Well*. The theme—that nobility resides in a person's character, not his rank—is trite and belabored. I made penniless Helena such a paragon of virtue and highborn Bertram such an unworthy snob it was inconceivable any woman would want him. I fell back on the old bed trick to have her win him—fine for the audience, who would approve her sneaking into his bed in the guise of another woman as both justified and clever. But I found it distasteful, their reconciliation far from romantic. Couldn't I come up with anything better? Apparently not. I tucked the lumpy script under my bed, never intending it to see the light of day. Just when you think you know how to write . . .

"This is your fault," I muttered at the empty bed, and the next day I avenged myself by prowling the shops. If we could afford a hundred acres of land, then I was certainly entitled to a pair of silk slippers or a garnet ring—take that! But Will was always generous to me and never complained how I spent money, and besides, he had no need to worry. I was woefully frugal by nature and must coax myself to splurge even when a full purse was at my command. And it wasn't really new slippers or a garnet ring I craved. I came home from shopping with my desires deflated and my basket empty save for a single sticky bun.

That night I pulled the pillow from Will's bed and hugged it to me, my mind arguing back and forth. Was Will calculating that after reaching the literary peak with *Hamlet*, we should quit while he was ahead? Had I unwittingly dug my own grave along with Ophelia's, thrown in my pen?

He had no right!

I got up, lit a taper and cleared a space on my desk. I divided a paper in two columns—no, three, to include collaborators like Kit, Nashe and Peele. Then I started from the beginning with *I Henry VI* right up to *Hamlet* and the moribund *Troilus and Cressida*. His, his, a quarter mine, a third Kit's. His, half mine, ours, a third his. In every instance, I gave him the benefit. Where we had so interwoven our efforts that I could no longer separate them, I assigned an equal percentage. Mine, half his, then mine, mine, mine, for that spell after Hamnet's death when the ink crusted on his pen. To the end of the tally, I expected his share to top what I had done. But as I reached the final sum, a strange sensation dawned over me, and I could swear it grew lighter in the room.

Not by much, but my column was the greater. Belatedly I realized the exercise did not include *Venus and Adonis*, *The Rape of Lucrece* and the Southampton sonnets that Will had unequivocally penned. If I could have devised a way to weight them in proportion to the plays, it would probably have brought us even. But for plays alone, I came out ahead. And when I went back and cautiously rated them for popularity and critical praise . . .

The knowledge infused me like the first swallow of a potent drug. Will might yet tire of his squire's role. He might discover Stratford's boundaries stifling and scurry back where he belonged. But the stage should not suffer meanwhile. The next morning I strolled to the Globe and informed the Chamberlain's Men that although Will was delayed indefinitely in Stratford, he planned to write a new play while he was there.

"How could you imagine you would lose the greatest playwright in the English language?" I teased Cuthbert, as he sighed his relief. "Now if you will excuse me, I must go look through our costume trunks for a bit of velvet ribbon."

Considering my boast to Cuthbert, I did not find my next play as quickly as I would have liked. Instead, I spent several weeks lugging scripts back and forth to the Globe, chewing over ideas, and to pacify Cuthbert, I gave him *Troilus and Cressida* meanwhile. Too bad, Will— you weren't here, so I copied it over and declared it done. Then I fetched another batch of scripts home, confident that inspiration would arrive soon.

But jealousy was on my mind. No one escapes it; it is too basic a human emotion. From girlhood, I remembered playmates who were prettier than me or had more dresses, a new necklace or nicer toys. In the early years of my marriage I envied loving couples, happy wives. As a writer, I resented the freedom and opportunities accorded to men.

And Will and I both gnawed over the successes of our competitors, though we strove to be magnanimous when someone else carried off the prize.

Now I suspected the green-eyed monster was preying on Will. Why? When confronted with *Romeo and Juliet*, he had manfully conceded my role in the creations of William Shakespeare and admitted me to partnership. I had thought the arrangement worked; we laughed, we collaborated, we planned. But as Will's stay in Stratford lengthened, I began to fear I had been blind. Was he a better actor than I suspected, concealing his jealousy until *Hamlet* became the deciding straw? Why hadn't he confided in me? *It's all right, Will. You too are human.* We might have devised a different manner of working or adjusted our routines to give him more writing time. Yet had I asked, I am sure he would have denied any such petty feeling, and while he was being noble, the monster's fangs were sinking in.

"Do you have any stories or plays about jealousy?" I asked the bookseller.

"Try this. It has just been translated from the Italian."

I skimmed the offered volume. The author, Cinthio, was unfamiliar, but the opening pages were intriguing. A Moor, a valiant soldier, falls in love with and marries a Venetian lady. His ensign also lusts after her, and when she ignores him, the treacherous ensign persuades the Moor his wife has been unfaithful. Promising—I read all the way home. That Cinthio's tale was only recently available in English and not yet widely known made it a change from the usual recycled material, and I congratulated myself on spotting its potential. By that evening I was blocking out scenes in my mind.

"Will writes that he has a new tragedy in the works," I told Cuthbert. "Be patient. It's coming."

The long summer days aided me in writing *Othello, The Moor of Venice*. I could break for my midday meal and a stroll and still have ample light well into the evening. Increasingly, I ran into Ben Jonson. If he had forsworn writing, why did he stay in London, hanging around the theaters and forcing himself on other writers, an injured bear with rude manners crying into his beer? I was not the only one who wished he would either buck up and take it or put himself out of his misery. The tavern regulars groaned at his entry. He developed a particular knack for finding me, whether I was en route to the Globe or browsing at the booksellers. Was he stalking me? I chided myself for nerves, though whenever possible I asked one of the spare actors at the Globe to escort me the short distance home. But Ben kept showing up and did not scruple to address me.

"Is our esteemed Will back yet from the provinces?" he would ask. "I wouldn't want him to lose the preeminent position he has achieved in the theater."

"Wouldn't you?"

"Oh, no, dear me, no. It is not as though he trod on another's back to get there."

"What are you saying, Mr. Jonson?" I had been hurrying to get away from him in the street. Now I turned and faced him.

"Why, nothing. I wish only the best to our sweet swan of Avon and am humbled to tread in his footsteps."

"Huh! If you were any kind of writer at all you would not mix your metaphors in such clumsy fashion. You might float in his regal wake or glide on the fluid crest of his aqueous passage, but I have never heard of a swan with footsteps."

Ben sneered. "Shall I tell you what is wrong with your brother's writing?"

"No. Good day to you."

I shouldered away, but I did not feel entirely triumphant. What did the man want? Why was he pestering me? Was this his bizarre idea of flirting? I consulted my mirror on my return home. I had more or less forgotten my real age. I was Will's younger sister, and I looked it, my hair still a glossy golden brown, my face showing only the faintest wrinkles about the eyes, my bosom high. Ben was another eight years younger than Will, and although I had always appealed to younger men, if this was Ben's intent, it was no blessing. I pitied his poor wife, a woman named Anne Lewis from whom he was frequently separated and whom he declared to be "a shrew, yet honest." Who would not turn shrewish, married to him? Why could he never once be fully generous and loving? And the next day . . .

"Shall I tell you what is wrong with your brother's writing?"

I did not trouble to hide my heavy sigh as Jonson sat down opposite me at the tavern.

"Mr. Jonson," I said, "my sympathy and my patience are running thin. I will give you a quarter hour, one quarter hour and no more, to hear your grievances. Then you will acknowledge I have heard you out, and you will trouble me no more. Are we agreed?"

"Ha, it would take years to elaborate where Will has gone wrong. His whole conception of theater is malformed. Now, in a comedy of humors . . ."

Blast him! I should have known that my being polite would only provoke a dissertation. And here I had before me a lovely dinner of beef, buttered parsnips and a gooseberry tart. Well, I would not let Ben Jonson spoil it. I concentrated on my meal—the beef was just right, a succulent slice with a little red juice running out of it. I remembered how I had too often overcooked the meat in those faraway days when Will and I were first married and I lived under my in-laws' roof. I probably acquired the habit from my stepmother, Duck—what a good woman!—because my father liked his meat cooked shoe-leather brown. Come to think of it, much of our country food was brown: brown eggs, brown bread, brown gravy, brown beer. I wondered what Bartholomew and Isabella were growing in the garden at Hewlands these days. Green leeks, fat red radishes, purple beets, bright orange carrots—there was color for you.

"And that is not Will's only fault," Ben expostulated. "You tell him I said . . ."

I smiled blankly at him. The parsnips were excellent too, boiled and sliced and simmered in herb butter. The cooking at the tavern had improved of late, and one of the benefits of being a middling cook like me was that you could appreciate someone else's fine work all the better. Speaking of work, I was having a slight problem with *Othello*. In

Cinthio's story the Moor dispatches Desdemona by beating her with a stocking full of sand. Doesn't that sound silly? Couldn't she jump up and run away or at least shriek for help? In their rich house, there would have been servants everywhere to rush to her defense. Then, to cover up the murder, Othello pulls down part of the ceiling and blames that for his wife's death. I supposed we could construct some sort of fake roof for Dick Burbage to demolish, but the idea of a man beating a woman to death with a sand-filled stocking . . . I chuckled.

"So you think this is funny?" snarled Ben.

"Oh, no, not at all. I beg your pardon. Do go on."

"Then, as I was saying, your brother's obsession with prying into his characters' minds and analyzing their emotions is completely unwarranted. As I demonstrated in *Every Man in His Humor* . . ."

I savored another bite of beef, took a drink from my mug and began visualizing other deaths for Desdemona. Strangle her—that was it. Simple. Efficient. Highly moving. The two of them face-to-face, Desdemona pleading but with no chance of fighting back against such a powerful man. Given Othello's jealous nature, the naive young woman was doomed from the moment the ensign, whom I had named Iago, insinuated she had been unfaithful. In Cinthio's tale the ensign was in love with Desdemona and acted against her because she felt nothing for him. Believable, but I could add another layer to this motive of slighted love. If the ensign was also secretly angry with Othello because the Moor had passed him over for promotion, much like Ben's fury at having to take second place to Will . . .

"Aha!" Ben pointed at my face. "You do see what I mean."

"Yes, yes." I waved at him in happy oblivion. It was as if the sun had leaped into the sky right over my head. The ensign, a conniving, malevolent man, feels he has been denied his destiny by a greater light. That was Ben toward Will; though Will had never personally stood in his way, after Ben's trouncing in the War of the Theaters he blamed everyone. Whether he meant to seduce me as a dubious way to get even with Will or merely to harass me in Will's stead, the comparison held. And Will, the noble captain—not only was he jealous that my writing surpassed his, he had recently voiced the completely ludicrous notion that I had taken a lover here in London. And he had tried to kill me—in my mind, I accused him of that very crime. He was strangling me by trying to take away the main thing I lived for, my writing.

I gasped aloud, and at the same instant Ben stopped talking. I had half heard his last jibes, scorning Will's work as overwrought and sentimental. Now his jaw dropped as if he too had just reached some blinding conclusion.

"The problem with your brother"—Ben's eyes narrowed—"is that he writes like a woman."

"Nonsense!" I jumped, brain racing, conscience stricken for my inattention. What was Ben up to? Had he read my face, my mind?

"Is it? All his prying and probing into dainty matters, his empathy for the outcast and downtrodden. That's womanish talk, womanish thinking."

"No, it is just . . . just . . ."

"Take Hamlet. He is half a woman himself, prancing around graveyards, draping himself in melancholy. I would have run the lecherous uncle through without a moment's pause."

"You know very well Hamlet never had a chance. He could not kill Claudius when he was at his prayers and in a state of grace, and that is the only time in the play he ever encounters him alone." There, I had him.

"So he prattles in a graveyard with a skull bone instead. A real man would have avenged his father's murder, claimed Ophelia to wife and set himself on the throne. Maybe your brother isn't a real man."

"You . . . you are abominable! You exert yourself to be offensive. You don't even believe what you are saying."

"Then why defend him so hotly? Methinks the lady doth protest too much. . . . Not going to finish your dinner?"

I stormed out, Ben laughing behind me. He hadn't even the common courtesy to be ashamed. I would show him how Will could write. I would prove my brother was a man. You want a noble, tragic hero? Just watch me! I wrote that night until my fingers cramped, Othello, a great soldier with a soldier's faults and virtues, a man used to making life-or-death decisions, unused to puzzling over subtle problems. He takes the simple road, the first answer, the physical option. The possibility of an ulterior motive in his helpful ensign is not within his ken. He never suspects as Iago dupes and convinces him with a single prop, an innocent strawberry-patterned handkerchief. Like her forthright husband, Desdemona is incapable of committing disloyalty and of detecting it in others. It is almost too easy as they both become the wily Iago's pawns. Well, I may gnash about Ben Jonson, but he fired me to write what might be my second-greatest play. And when it was finished and performed to thunderous applause, what did Ben say?

"A simpering girl, that Desdemona. It is uncanny how well our Will portrays the female mind."

I threw my ale in his face, to a roar of approval from the tavern.

"Go home, Ben!" several voices shouted.

He grinned, and with a leering tongue he licked the brew from his lips. It was I who went home, shaking, unaware that he had followed me until I was at my door.

"I apologize," he said, pulling a long face and pouting like a child, mocking me.

"Go away, you horrible man! You will never be the writer Will is. Do not block my entrance. Let me go."

He grabbed my wrist, and though I twisted, he was far stronger and cared not if he hurt me.

"Let me go! When Will finds out how you have treated me—"

"He'll do what? Thrash me? Your brother is a pansy, a powder puff—whufff!" He blew a beery breath into my face, and I kicked him in the shin. I hurt my own toes more than those stocky legs of his. "I have been thinking a lot about your brother and his plays in my copious free time," Ben continued. "You know, while I am not writing."

"Huh, you don't think at all. Your shaggy skull is as empty of fruitful thoughts as a coconut husk."

"Oh, ho, an apt image. You have a way with words, haven't you?"

"I could give you plenty more to describe your behavior, but you are not worth them."

"Then you underestimate me." He twisted my wrist tighter, and his eyes glittered slyly in spite of his drink. "I suggest you listen. As I say, in my idle time I have done a lot of thinking. I have studied your brother's plays in depth and compared them with the other tripe that passes for public entertainment."

"Let me— Ouch!"

"I said, *listen*. Your brother writes like a woman, but your brother isn't here. He hasn't been in London for some time. But you are and you have a remarkable talent with language. Even in your casual conversations with the tavern whores and street vendors—"

"You have been spying on me? How dare—"

"And when you sit among the actors, you display an intimate knowledge of every scene your brother has written. You prompt the players on their lines."

"That is hardly surprising. Everyone knows I do Will's copying for him."

"But he isn't here, yet back and forth to the Globe you trot, your arms full of scripts. Who are they for then?"

"For me, to read. Besides, when I sit sewing at the Globe I hear the players rehearse. It is bound to sink in."

"Then I have never heard of another seamstress with such acute memory."

"Then perhaps you, like every other man, undervalue a woman's mind."

"Ah, no, that's just it. I don't undervalue *your* mind at all."

He let go of my wrist—it was bruised for a week—and though I huffed my outrage, my heart was shaking. Did he really know or was it still a half intuition of his crude and brilliant mind? For a long moment, I could not think whether to brazen it out, taunt him with his own deficiencies, lambaste him for such a foolish idea or shriek for help against an assailant in the street. And in that womanish moment of indecision he caught me with his eye.

"As I said, I don't undervalue you at all," said Ben. "I think you and I are going to become very good friends, Anne."

Chapter 28

For a long time I had no idea what Ben Jonson wanted from me. I don't think he knew himself. He was like a devilish boy who, having caught a defenseless bird, cannot decide whether to cage and taunt it, pet it on his finger or crush it beneath a rock. As the mood struck him, he might do all three. Meanwhile, I scoffed at his nonsense and held it too ridiculous to deny. He had no proof, that was certain. If he began to air his drunken opinions, I had only to roll my eyes, and he would be laughed out of town. But Ben was in no hurry. Would that the man were as stupid as he looked!

"It is no matter whether I can prove it or not." He leered, catching up to me yet again as I headed toward the Globe. I had tried to avoid him by keeping to my rooms, but I could hardly stay inside forever. I cut him a scathing look and hurried on, but he persisted. "I have only to insinuate, and people will begin to wonder if it is true. Our glorious Will, an empty sack, a shadow, a straw man. What do you suppose Marston, Dekker and the others would do with that information?"

"You have no information, and unlike you, they are gentlemen," I said, breaking my silence in frustration.

"No, they're not. They are hacks who will write anything for a few pounds. They were for me, then against me. For a shilling, they'll turn their opinions inside out. They will demolish your brother for the fun of it."

"Go away."

"Wouldn't you like to have some credit, Anne? That *Hamlet* really is a fine play."

"You said it was sentimental and overwrought."

"I could change my mind."

"Then for all your high opinions of yourself and your writing, you are as easily bought as the rest of them."

"You wound me, madam! Here I am ready to sacrifice my own honor to see you get your due, and you repulse me."

"No, you repulse me. You have no honor to sacrifice. Now leave me alone!"

I shuddered away from him and into the Globe, feeling dirtied by his mere presence. But his words teased my mind. Was there some way I could use Jonson to my advantage? If he did air his suspicions, might it force Will to return? I wanted him back and us writing together. I wanted his voice in our rooms, his habits, his company. When Will had fallen into despondency over Hamnet's death and the misfortunes of our old Theatre, the adventure of the Globe had revitalized him. Whatever his misguided reasons for stalling in Stratford, the jolt of Jonson's accusations might now do the same.

"Go ahead then, tell the world," I said, the next time Ben caught me at the market. I gave a weary, indulgent laugh. "No one will believe you."

"Won't they?"

"No."

"Ah, you don't want them to. You enjoy this charade."

"I don't care what the world believes." I turned a corner, and Ben dodged several people and followed.

"Then you are far too modest. You have written some excellent plays."

"Such as?"

"*Romeo and Juliet*, for example. That has your touch upon it. Not that I like it myself, but it is a crowd pleaser."

"Then go on, tell everyone I wrote it. Why do you hesitate?" I selected a loaf of bread and handed the vendor his money.

"So you admit it was conceived by your pen."

"Oh, yes, I wrote everything, the plays, the sonnets, *Venus and Adonis*. Dashed them off in my abundant free time." I waved my basket of purchases at him. "In fact, Will doesn't exist at all. He is merely a country boy I use as my front so I have a man's name to write under."

"Do you?"

"Yes, and you have my leave to shout it from the rooftops of London."

That quieted him for all of two days, and I was not sure how I felt about it. *Othello* completed, I was once again seeking inspiration and missing Will more sorely than ever. I longed for someone with whom I could exchange ideas, talk writers' talk. What about the literary company at the tavern, we few, we happy few, we band of authors? But I would have to do so surreptitiously. "Will advises me in his latest letter from Stratford that he is mulling a new play on the subject of . . ." I sighed at the necessity of subterfuge. I never had the advantage Will did of being able to openly solicit opinions on a work in progress, and I know some of my plays suffered thereby. Even so, Will was careful to withhold crucial details until a play was firmly in his grasp. Ideas, plots and characters are all fair game, and a smart leopard does not alert his spotted friends to his quarry, lest they pounce first and haul it away up a tree.

But these reflections did not solve my problem, and I wrote to Will, craving his return and stating plainly that Jonson might expose him.

"Expose what?" Will wrote back. "Your only role in my plays was to copy them in a clear hand."

What?

I strode to the tavern and found Ben. "Why haven't you exposed me?" I demanded.

"Gladly." He crooked his finger toward my bodice, and I slapped his hand.

"You know what I mean. Why haven't you revealed your absurd claim?"

"Because now you want me to. Why is that, Anne?" He shifted

sideways on his bench and smacked down his palm for me to join him. I walked disdainfully around the table and sat opposite, and Ben raised his mug and called for the tavern keeper to bring me an ale.

"I will have cider," I corrected, lifting my voice to the tapster, who tipped his head in return. How like a man, to usurp even a woman's choice of beverage, though in truth I would have preferred the ale. "I simply wish to have this matter resolved," I said to Ben, resuming a gracious tone.

"Good, because you know what I think? I think you would like to have the credit."

"Yes, I would, and I would therefore be much obliged if you would tell the world the truth, Mr. Jonson."

"Still Mr. Jonson? Come, come, Anne. I told you we were friends." He guffawed and clamped his paw over my hand. "And that is precisely why I cannot tell the world what you have done."

"What on earth are you talking about?"

"Well, don't you see, Anne, lovely Anne, brilliant Anne, that even if I had the proof and could swear to it on the queen's own Bible, and even if the world believed me, what would that accomplish?"

I pulled loose my hand. "It would give me recognition for everything I have done, every word I have written, story conceived, play penned. It would make me the foremost writer in the land."

I hadn't meant to let out that secret knowledge, that tally I had done, but the flash of pride across my face was not lost on Ben.

"So you wrote that many of them? I wasn't sure about the histories, particularly *Henry IV* and *V*. They seemed a little too manly in dealing with politics and war. I apologize, madam. You have sufficient spirit to don a suit of armor. Why then do you creep about like a mouse in a dun-colored gown?" He fingered the sleeve of my gray-brown dress, a perfectly suitable garment for those not fond of ostentation. "Because you do not wish to draw attention to yourself, of course. Yet now you urge me to proclaim your true identity and declare you a superior writer to everyone else, including me, the colossus of the English stage. How ill you use me! Have I no friends?"

His volume had risen, and the tavern, expecting another self-pitying speech, gave a groan. Someone tossed a turkey bone at him amidst calls to pipe down.

"We can talk about being friends later," I said, leaning in and tapping my forefinger on the table to rivet his attention. "I want you to reveal what you have guessed. Tell them, Ben."

"I can't." He huddled in, glancing around as if we were the conspirators scheming to overthrow Caesar.

"After all you have been threatening? Why not?"

"Because the plays would suffer in consequence, and I am not that mean." He straightened, took a maddeningly slow draft from his mug, wiped his sleeve across his mouth and set down his ale with a satisfied belch.

I snatched the mug away from him. "What are you talking about? You are mean enough to do anything."

"No, I'm not."

"Yes, you are. Mean and cruel and hateful."

"I am mean in my pockets, which is to say, they are empty. Could you pay for my drink, Anne?"

"No!"

"Come, Anne, don't be mean. Or do you mean to be doubly mean to one who means only to be your friend?"

"Stop it!" I was near tears. "I will not play these silly games!"

"But you were so fond of them in your early plays, all that punning in *Romeo and Juliet*, the extended metaphors, the cleverly embedded sonnet at the lovers' first meeting. Don't you recall?"

"Of course I do, damn you! What a beast you are!"

I rose to leave, but as I passed him, Jonson caught me around the waist and dragged me down.

"I am the kindest beast you will ever meet," he said sadly, and I halted at the change in his tone. "Don't you understand? I would love to knock Will Shakespeare from his pedestal, and it would tickle my fancy to see a woman revealed as the playwright of our age when I myself am done for and can write no more. But what would happen instead is that your plays—and though I say it to no one else, I confess it to you: Some of them are so magnificent I could weep—your plays will never be accounted the same, but always relegated to inferior status once it is known they come from a woman's brain."

He put his head on the table and began to bawl.

"Ben, you pissing drunk, go home!" came the shouts and another hail of turkey bones.

I jumped up and ran out, cutting right and left through the people on the streets, hurrying I knew not where. Finally, out of breath, I stopped on a corner where a crowd had gathered to watch a juggler perform. He wore orange-and-purple motley and a fool's cap jingling with silver bells, and he mocked the audience as he tossed three leather balls in the air.

"Leap and laugh, you bawds and whoremongers!" he jeered. "See here my three balls, where most men have but two. I'll bed your wives and your mistresses too! Throw me your coins! Fling me your money and I'll jest with more cunning."

Huh, he couldn't even make a decent rhyme—the incongruity of my situation made tears spurt to my eyes. I will never know how much Ben plotted to hurt and confound me or if his cruelties were merely the genius of the moment. I could neither outwit him nor win. He ignored logic as it suited him and changed arguments on a whim—oh, damn the rhyme! I wiped my cheeks and hurried away before anyone could see, though they were far too busy taunting the juggler to remark an ordinary woman in a dun dress. I returned to my room and faced facts.

I was alone.

Will might or might not return to London, but I could not count on him.

Ben might or might not expose me.

If he did not, I would lose my last chance to see my name on my work. I had already forfeited my best opportunity when Will and I faced each other over *Romeo and Juliet*. Since then, the reputation of William Shakespeare had grown so large, only someone of Ben Jonson's stature and aggression could puncture the myth. Otherwise, I would die an anonymous wife, and barely that. Look at me! I am flesh and blood! I am alive! I thought of Bess of Hardwick carving her initials big and bold on the stone turrets of New Hall just to say the like.

Yet if Ben did speak up and if he were believed, what then? All the same bitter consequences that would have attended my name on *Romeo and Juliet*. Will mocked, me beset by critics, the plays relegated to secondhand status and left to molder in the dust. What will these women think they are capable of next? And where Will and I might have preserved our relationship had the revelation come from us, he would never forgive me if I made Jonson the source. I still did not understand what his latest letter meant, his assertion that I had only copied. Was he merely sticking to our story or had he reverted to believing it?

For the next week I barely left my room, sending a street boy to the market when I needed provisions and to deliver sewing to the Globe. To steady my mind, I outlined a new work about a virtuous young woman forced by a lustful deputy to choose between saving her brother's life and surrendering her own honor—I groan to think of my transparency. And since I had no solution to either my character's dilemma or mine, *Measure for Measure* quickly became a quagmire, the self-righteous and potentially tragic first half melting into a syrupy pudding with another bed trick ending. I stuffed it under my bed with *All's Well That Ends Well* and assured an impatient Cuthbert that I expected something new from Will very soon. I almost wished to see Ben. He was at least a fellow writer, and I hurt for a like mind. But how could I trust him? I was miserably lonely, but I was not stupid.

The year 1602 wore to a dull and rainy close. Will wrote that he had purchased a cottage in Stratford; what did we need with a cottage? I was afraid to join him, even for a visit. It might dislodge us from London forever. Ben came and went, sometimes remorseful, sometimes with new mischief to spread. I was alternately irritated and sorry for him. I knew how it felt to have your opportunities and your muse with-draw to a corner. Occasionally I pulled out *All's Well* and *Measure for Measure* but occupied myself mostly with sewing.

Throughout London, a similar inertia had taken hold. Rumors of Elizabeth's imminent demise were once again circulating, and this time the tone was ominous. People trudged with heads down; conversations were muted. Few plays were performed anywhere, and the government fell quiet. The air was stagnant, listless. Then a dangerous royal scandal erupted involving Bess of Hardwick's granddaughter, Arbella.

Still unwed at twenty-eight, Arbella had schemed to elope with Edward Seymour, the eldest grandson of the Earl of Hertford and ten years her junior. She had never even met him—all was done by secret messages—but Seymour's bloodline, like Arbella's, gave him a claim to the throne. Elizabeth was furious and dispatched an interrogator to Hardwick. Arbella was forced to write a confession, then the terrified girl collapsed and, to all appearances, went insane. Until early March, when she attempted to stroll casually out of Hardwick to meet up with two supporters and a troop of forty men. She made it as far as the porter's lodge, where Bess's authority prevailed and she was turned around. Considering the episode also involved Catholic sympathizers and threats on the queen's life, the whole country went into an uproar.

Stunned, I absorbed the news swirling in the market and around St. Paul's. What could Arbella have been thinking? Most of us outgrow *Romeo and Juliet*. We know that if we cannot have this one, another will come along. But it was beginning to seem Arbella would never be allowed to have anyone at all, and in her desperate, single-minded pursuit of love I found something to admire. For all my reputation as Will's seducer, perhaps I never pursued him hard enough.

As for Elizabeth, the great agitation she suffered over this betrayal proved too much to bear. It overwrought her aged body and exhausted her indomitable mind. Rumors swept through the streets.

She's dying! The queen is dying!

Really?

Yes, really this time.

Chapter 29

*W*ell, it's about time.

Those last words were not spoken aloud, but the thought rippled through the land. I have said how distressing it was to be present at John Shakespeare's passing, but there is a strange fascination in hovering around a deathbed from afar, especially the deathbed of a king. They who have loomed above us are mortal after all. Why were we so in awe? And however high their station in life, does not God promise to judge them exactly like us for the hereafter? Depending on their sins, they would now suffer or be saved like any greasy commoner with his finger up his nose. You too, Gloriana, though we loved you more than most. Yesterday you played at eternal youth, our Diana, our Cynthia, our bounding red-haired girl. Today the silent Reaper has emerged from behind your throne, fingering his sickle blade.

Yet as word of the queen's deteriorating condition leaked from Richmond Palace, a single question emerged in our narrowing minds. How may I profit by this turn of events? What's in it for me? Though Elizabeth still refused to name a successor, all odds were on Scottish James. Whiskers twitched, eyes glinted northward and the creaky hold erupted with furry bodies as the vermin fled our sinking ship of state. It was later revealed that Sir Robert Cecil, Elizabeth's principal secretary, had been in secret correspondence with James for years to ensure a smooth accession. Nothing personal, Your Majesty, and most people would agree Cecil's sly diplomacy was in England's best interests. The last thing we needed was another War of the Roses.

It was less easy to excuse the courtiers who had fed off the queen's table. Perfumed letters and costly presents streamed to Edinburgh, each bearing a request to be remembered when James plumped his rump on the throne. Those longest in power were in the greatest panic, their comfortable livings likely to be swept aside by the new regime. They would have propped Elizabeth up with sticks and put a talking parrot behind her head to make it appear she lived on. But even those who truly grieved Elizabeth could not afford to wait until she was laid in her grave. They must join the rush to James or be left at the end of the line, begging for scraps from the royal hand.

The theater companies and the players were no exception. Who is more likely to command entertainment: a sick old woman or a beaming bumpkin who has just inherited the purse strings of a kingdom? Thus, the queen's impending death accomplished what I could not. It brought Will back to London.

"How are you, Anne?" he asked warily.

"Fine," I said, and for a moment it was as if I glanced on a familiar but altered acquaintance. Still attractive, though his hairline had once again receded and he had put on weight, not too much, but noticeable. Had I passed him on the street I would have pegged him as a prosperous country squire come to town, and so he was. He studied me in the same cautious vein, offering nuggets from Stratford—tales of our family and New Place, local gossip—in an awkward attempt to bridge the gap between us. After a while we moved on to the safer topic of business.

"The queen is secluded in Richmond Palace," I said, "and they say the end is near. The authorities fear disturbances, and Cuthbert is worried they will close the playhouses."

"I'll speak with him and the other shareholders. We must be in a position to take advantage of the situation. By the way"—Will gave me a sheepish look—"have I written anything lately that I can take to show them?"

I handed him *All's Well That Ends Well* and *Measure for Measure*—I was sick of them anyway—and off he went, leaving me musing on injustice, a subject on which I was expert. Since he couldn't admit it was jealousy of me that had propelled him to Stratford, he had to resort to nonchalant behavior to deflect his sense of guilt on his return. Nonetheless, I had survived enough loveless spells with Will not to get overexcited, and no doubt we would sort ourselves out in time. And I did enjoy a sweet taste of revenge, for when *All's Well* and *Measure for Measure* were later performed, both fell short of expectations. Stuck your name on a couple of duds there, didn't you, Will?

But I was speaking of Elizabeth, and it was a dragged-out death over those last weeks and days, gruesome details leaking to the public ear. They said she was glassy-eyed and listless, sitting on a pile of cushions on the floor, the stench of death consuming her, clothes unchanged, hair unkempt, sucking her finger like a child. A few days before the end she took to her bed, breath rasping in and out, oblivion inexorably closing. Dimly, she must have marked the scurrying around her, the rush to fortify the city in case of chaos and disorder, a last-minute invasion by anyone with a claim to the throne. Did the news reach her that an even more unwelcome visitor was already within the gates, a worrisome new outbreak of plague? Was she glad to let go, to surrender at last her great burden of care?

The end arrived in the early morning hours of March 24. By then all London was in a hush, people barely whispering in the streets, tiptoeing on only the most necessary errands. When a cart wheel creaked, the offending driver received a glare. The weather was gray, damp and cloaked. Yet when the bells suddenly clanged, we jolted, and some cried aloud at the discordant peals. She's dead! Really? A few people cheered in confusion, then immediately looked shamefaced. In truth, we had no idea how to react. Only the old folk among us could recall the passing of an English king. So while some crossed themselves and prayed for Elizabeth's soul, others hung about stupidly, as if there were more news to hear.

By midday James VI of Scotland was proclaimed King James I of

England. Will and I heard the news at St. Paul's Cross, where it was received with widespread rejoicing. More bells rang, bonfires were lit, liquor and dancing filled the streets. I observed but held back from the celebration. James was expected to end our long-running quarrel with Spain and put a halt to the huge military expenditures that had bankrupted the nation. Even so, how could people think all their troubles would disappear merely by his accession? The rain and disastrous crop failures of the last decade could return at any time; I have never yet heard of a monarch who could control the weather. Nor of one who could prevent corruption; you can see what a cynic I had become. Moreover, James was completely unfamiliar with our laws and our ways. He had never set foot in England, and poor, craggy Scotland, inhabited by feuding clans, had experienced nothing like the massive changes that had transformed England during Gloriana's reign. Why were we dancing at the prospect of this unprepared man rising to the highest position in the land?

At Richmond, the queen's body was placed in a lead coffin, then sailed up the river to Whitehall Palace to lie in state. The funeral took place in late April, and Will and I watched the cortege wind its way to Westminster Abbey. The funeral carriage was drawn by four black-draped horses, and an effigy of the queen adorned the purple velvet-covered coffin. The procession included Elizabeth's riderless palfrey and over a thousand officials, peers and mourners. Sighing, groaning and weeping people lined the route. In the abbey, Elizabeth was interred beside her half sister Mary, that long-ago, unhappy Catholic queen. As Will and I trudged home, I pictured the dust motes stirred up in the sun shafts settling slowly back onto the tomb.

She's dead.

Really.

What happens now?

In the weeks following the funeral, London buzzed with news and rumors of our new king. What sort of man was he?

Pale skinned, soft bellied, barely above medium height.

Brown hair, a sparse beard, and large, almost protruding eyes.

Said to be intelligent and well educated; he had written two books asserting the divine right of kings. Also, a volume entitled *Daemonologie* alerting the world to the danger of witches. In 1590, when storms had kept him from returning to Scotland from Denmark with his bride Queen Anne, he had a group of women tortured until they confessed their witchcraft was the cause.

His tongue was too big for his mouth, an affliction that, combined with his thick Scots accent, made him sound when he spoke as if his mouth held a block of wood.

Ungainly. He jerked and shambled, and he had an embarrassing habit of fingering his codpiece.

He had male favorites and kissed them openly on the mouth. Some said we had traded King Elizabeth for Queen James.

He was terrified of assassins and wore a thick quilted doublet to ward off their knives. Who could blame him? When he was still in the womb, his mother's secretary and reputed lover, the Italian David Rizzio, had been violently murdered while the horrified Queen of Scots looked on. His father, the useless Lord Darnley, was similarly dispatched before James's first birthday. His grandfather was fatally wounded in a coup attempt when the boy was five. At sixteen, James himself was abducted and held prisoner for ten months by treasonous Scottish nobles. Finally, there was his mother's beheading to haunt his dreams. But Elizabeth had endured many similar tragedies and still ridden out on her white horse to proclaim her defiance of the whole Spanish Armada that day in 1588. A symbolic gesture, but God's blood, she inspired men with courage. No one was inspired by James.

By the way, where was he? For weeks we peered and craned, but as it turned out our new king would not arrive from Scotland anytime soon. The plague was gaining ground, and where is the fun in inheriting a crown if you must hazard death to set it on your head? Yet even from a distance, there were offices, patents and trading rights to be awarded, loyalties to reward, past injuries to avenge. Talents for flattery and backbiting were called forth; old debts were called in.

Whatever Will, the Burbages and the other shareholders were up to, they have my admiration. By May, the Chamberlain's Men had been appointed the King's Players and Grooms of the Chamber Extraordinary, an excellent turn of fortune's wheel. It meant far more than a fancy title. Under Elizabeth the various companies had been allowed to perform publicly on the glib pretext that they must keep in practice to play for her occasional pleasure. Now, by right of patent, the new King's Men were officially royal servants and recognized as the premier company in London. The usually tightfisted Cuthbert hosted a dinner to celebrate, Ben Jonson showed up, and in the general enthusiasm and inebriation, all was forgiven. Ben had even written a new tragedy, *Sejanus*, depicting the rise and fall of Tiberius's favorite.

"It was kind of you to tolerate me when I was so insufferable," he said, hanging his head before me.

"I am glad to see you recovered," I said sincerely.

He nodded and took my hand. "I am your friend, believe me, Anne."

I lay down to sleep that night almost optimistic. Perhaps the new reign would indeed set the country right. And Will and I had rebuilt a modest friendship, though we kept to separate beds. We had also taken new lodgings near St. Paul's in Cripplegate, less convenient to the Globe than our Southwark residence, but a better neighborhood. So if I had not everything I desired, I had enough to sustain me. Let us all now live happily ever after.

But as summer bloomed, so did the plague. In late July James ducked into the city for a quick coronation at Westminster Abbey in pouring rain, then scooted back out to put a good distance between himself and his diseased subjects. A wise move, for the death toll soon exceeded a thousand a week, and by the time the epidemic petered out at year's end, more than thirty thousand in London would die. Among the early victims was Ben's only child, a boy of seven whom Ben called his "best piece of poetry." More than once, he came to tears in front of Will and me, and we did our best to comfort him.

To escape the illness, the court went on progress, many residents fled the city and the playhouses were closed. Following their new monarch, the King's Men accompanied James on tour, and after escorting me to Stratford, Will joined them. I had a pleasant visit. Mary Shakespeare was in fair health, Susanna had New Place well in hand, and the household was large enough that Judith could enjoy the illusion of issuing orders without affecting her sister's overall command. Magpie Joan and her husband, William Hart, had just been blessed with their second child, Gilbert and Richard remained unwed, and the youngest Shakespeare brother, twenty-three-year-old Edmund, talked of coming to London and training as an actor. In midautumn I returned to London, counting on the cooler weather to reduce the incidence of disease. Will was still away, and I was alone.

One evening I came upon Ben in the tavern. Not drunk—he seemed to have curbed that inclination—but sad and subdued. His son's death still pained him, and he had separated from his wife again. I tried to cheer him with talk of writing, but he shook his head. Even before the plague arrived, his *Sejanus* had met with a bad reception from both the public and the censors, and he had been hauled before the Privy Council for questioning, the councilors comparing Sejanus's career to the rise and fall of Essex.

"I had no such idea in mind," said Ben, "and as for the wretched audience, I try to give them the benefits of my learning. I poured my knowledge of the classics into that play, including the utmost details of Roman life and customs. I was accurate in every instance, Anne."

"I know. You tried." Tried too hard, perhaps, for the understanding of those in the yard and even the galleries. It is lonely and dispiriting to have a brain so far in advance of the average man. "What will you do next, Ben?"

"I don't know. I am at loose ends."

"Me, too."

"Nothing in progress?"

I shook my head. On tour with James, the King's Men were stick-ing to their old plays. James had never seen their repertoire, so why bother to produce new scripts and learn new lines when you can drag out tried-and-true ones?

"What we really need," I said, "is for the public theaters to re-open."

"Then we could collaborate," said Ben.

"You and I?"

"Yes, why not?"

"You would listen to my opinions?"

"Well . . ."

"You would put my name on the plays?"

"Well, not exactly . . ."

I stood, laughing. "I'm going home."

"No, wait." He put out a hand to detain me, then drew it back, aware of past offenses. "I only meant that here we are, marooned in London, no jobs, no income. . . ."

I softened. Between Will's position with the King's Men and his investments in Stratford, we had a steady supply of funds. But Ben had bounced from company to company, alienating and reconciling but without a permanent stake in any of them. Was he finally developing a sense of remorse and responsibility?

"Ben, I can give you a loan if you are running low."

"No, I won't ask you for money, Anne. A friendly ear, that's all. Someone to listen to my projects and offer an opinion before I make a fool of myself again." He flinched.

"You don't want to write another *Sejanus*," I concluded. "You want—poor Ben!—you crave a popular reputation."

"I need a hit," he confessed. "But must I compromise everything I believe in? You do not compromise, Anne."

He was wrong, of course—I had spent my whole life compromising—but he looked up at me with such wistfulness that I sat back down. A fatal moment, for there began the affair between myself and Ben Jonson.

⁓

At first it was a meeting of the minds. Ben was ready to work and behave maturely; I needed a fresh direction. We talked long hours of the recent tastes in plays, the entertainments at court, the possibilities when James returned to London and the theaters reopened.

"Perhaps I should compose something to praise the king and show my loyalty," said Ben.

"Flattery is always in season," I agreed. "But what has James accomplished to write about? He has no heroic background like Henry V and no great vision for our country. He was handed the crown and had only to put it on his head."

"Last spring, before the plague, I did a fairy playlet for the queen that was very well received. Maybe I could write a love story that would appeal to both her and the king, a *Romeo and Juliet* with a happy ending. Think of the rewards if I managed to reconcile them."

I made a doubtful sound. Though raised a Lutheran, Queen Anne had converted to Catholicism after her marriage. James was tolerant of her beliefs, and many English Protestants and Catholics alike took it as a hopeful sign that our religious divisions were coming to an end. Until the queen publicly humiliated the king by refusing to take Anglican communion at their coronation. How are you going to govern a country, the tavern denizens hooted, when you can't even keep your wife in line?

"I would not meddle there," I said. "Besides, though James and Anne go on having children, everyone knows he would rather bed men. Are you still Catholic, by the way?"

Ben put his hands together in mock prayer. "I did convert that time I was in prison, but it is wearing off. Don't hold it against me."

I laughed. "Well, in any case, *James and Anne* lacks a romantic ring, and you could no more write a *Romeo and Juliet* than could a monkey."

"What about something Scottish?"

"Fine for him, though that might rub it in our English faces. Doesn't he have any other interests that would make safe topics?"

"Hunting," said Ben. "Food, drink and spending the treasury. There is his fascination with witches."

"Then do a play about them."

"Probably not a wise idea." Ben held out his thumb where he had been branded, and though the T for Tyburn was old and faded, it made me shiver. "I have a knack for getting into trouble, even without courting it. Let's not add a suspected alliance with Satan to my list of crimes."

The year turned, 1604, and if not for Ben's friendship it would have been a dull time. I heard little from Will until March, when our dillydallying king finally showed his face. The plague had departed; time for a procession! As royal servants, Will and the King's Men were required to walk in the parade. The event started at the Tower at eleven in the morning and took a full six hours before it ended at Westminster. Ben had received a commission to help design one of the seven triumphal arches, and he and I watched from the throng. The sights and sounds included James on a white horse under a canopy held by eight gentlemen, Queen Anne in a coach with her ladies, three hundred singing children from Christ's Hospital, a Fountain of Virtue flowing with wine, speeches and Latin orations, the Nine Muses, the lord mayor—all the usual displays of royal extravagance and wasteful spending. To my delight, Arbella Stuart rode in a carriage right behind the queen. With Elizabeth's passing, Arbella was back in favor. Also riding in the procession was the Earl of Southampton, pardoned by James for his role in the Essex affair and released from the Tower. A fresh start for one and all.

I stretched for my glimpse of the king. He read and wrote books; surely I would spot that glimmer of intellect in his eyes. Instead I saw a vain creature who reveled in pomp, and though it is wrong to make hasty judgments, you may as well know what we soon learned: Although he loved to orate on the supremacy of kings, James was far too lazy to exert himself in the job. Where Elizabeth had kept a firm finger on every pulse beat of politics, James turned most of the business over to Sir Robert Cecil, his principal minister. He could not even manage his own household, which quickly became mired in corruption. The only things he knew how to do were spend money and go stag hunting, frequently falling off his horse.

"Here they come," said Ben, as Will and the other King's Men strutted into view in their scarlet liveries. I have never thought that Will, with that ginger shade to his hair, looked good in red, but since he once again had a few less hairs and a few more pounds, why should I care? Will obviously thought he looked most excellent, and both his lips and his balding pate were beaming. "Life is his oyster, isn't it?" Ben murmured into my ear, then he added quickly and penitently, "Forgive me. I should not make fun of your brother."

"Go ahead," I replied. "I was thinking the same thing."

When the parade ended, Will went off to celebrate at court, and Ben and I repaired to the tavern with the other left-behinds. But soon Ben's fortunes, too, began to rise. He found a way into the royal presence, and that was through the masques.

⁓

Ah, the masques. In their amateur form they had been popular among the court crowd for ages. They were easy and fun to produce; the aristocrats simply donned masks and costumes to dance and entertain the king or local lord. Will and I had made brief use of the device in some of our early plays. *Love's Labor's Lost* and *Much Ado* both contain scenes of masked dances in which the love-struck characters engage in witty flirtations. It was also how I gained entry for Romeo and his friends to Capulet's ball—they slip in with the masquers.

Now, under James, the masques exploded into elaborate displays of scenery, music, costumes, song and dance—think of the spectacles at Kenilworth. They usually presented a mythological theme, such as Queen Mab, or an allegorical subject, and the massive sets might recreate a wooded bower with pools and sweet-smelling flowers or a glittering, turreted palace. Ships, moats, drawbridges, waterfalls, trapdoors, rising platforms and other ingenious machines were constructed. Rich draperies, gilded arches, painted hangings and glowing candles adorned the stage. A masque might be commissioned for almost any occasion, a marriage, birthday, holiday or simply to sing the royal family's praises. What is the point in being king if you can't order people to fawn over you?

Queen Anne was enamored of the masques, and there was a great call for pieces in which she and her ladies could perform. You see, women *can* act, I was tempted to say. If the queen is allowed to do it, why not the rest of us? But of course this was not true acting, only a chance to dress up and play. Nevertheless, the size and scope of the productions required professional writers, actors and musicians to provide scripts and support to the royal amateurs, and the Stuarts were thus good for all of us in the entertainment business. Queen Anne adopted our former rivals, the boy actors, whose piping voices were ideal for musical parts. Ten-year-old Prince Henry became the patron of the Admiral's Men. I hardly saw Will, the King's Men were in such constant demand. Ben was appointed chief writer for the masques and seemed to have found the perfect home. His only complaint—typical!— was that his poetry was better than the Stuarts deserved.

"You think it is better than anyone deserves," I said, giving him a playful nudge, and he chuckled. Busy as he was, he came often to find me, and I started sketching costumes for the masques. I couldn't help it. As soon as he began to tell me the theme, visions of gowns and fairy wings, wizards' cloaks and emperors' trains danced before my eyes. He made me a gift of paints and brushes, and though I was a poor artist, I had fun inking out my ideas and coloring them in. Besides, to tell Ben that a doublet required picadils or that a dress should have Spanish-style sleeves only furrowed his forehead. It took a sketch on paper to bring an "ahh" of comprehension. Officially, the scenery and costumes for the masques were the province of the architect Inigo Jones, but like Ben, Jones had a large opinion of himself, and no sooner were they commissioned to work together than the friction began. It delighted

Ben to slip one of my anonymous, amateur sketches to the queen and have her prefer it to Jones's designs.

"I told Jones I know a costume designer so talented she would mince him for pie," Ben boasted, as he escorted me home from the tavern.

"Ben! You should not antagonize him. You must work with him."

"Let me take you to the market and buy you something pretty." He jangled his purse. "I am a newly coined man, and you know that won't last long."

"All the more reason you should save your earnings."

"No, let's be *un*reasonable, Anne. Let's be merry. Life is short and I am a fool, and things may never be so good again!" We had reached my doorstep, and he fell at my feet and grasped my hand.

"Ben!" I laughed and pulled him up before the neighborhood could see, and he bounded with me into my room and grabbed my hands.

"Dance with me. We'll show a leg!"

"You are a bear, Ben. Don't knock over the candlesticks!"

"I am a bear in clover and honey. I am in love with you, Anne!"

I stopped short, yet for a moment he kept whirling, until my dead-weight wound him down.

"What?" he asked.

"You are in love with me?"

"How could I not be? You are kind, witty, smiling, wise and amazing. I know of no other woman like you, and of none that could put up with me so well." He came closer and his face grew serious. "I am in love with you, Anne."

He touched my forearms, and his big fingers rested there, awaiting my permission.

"What about your wife?" I whispered. "You are married, Ben."

He lowered his gaze, and I knew I had also awakened memories of his dead son.

"I am a bad husband," he said, sadly and humbly. "My wife is better off without me."

For a moment, I closed my eyes. I was still married too, if only in name, and unlike my deliberate falling into bed with Kit, this time I did not pick up caution and throw it to the wind. I held it in my mind and let it rest there like a feather, and it took no great gust of passion to send it aloft. It was the merest puff of air, a faint ruffling of the edges, and the feather lifted and vanished, and I stepped into Ben's arms. His kiss was soft, his beard fuzzy, his chest broad. When our lips parted, he looked at me in gratitude and wonder that I had not refused him. And now that rough, rude man became a shy lover, overwhelmed by good fortune. He held me so tenderly, murmured so fondly, I could scarcely have sworn it was the same man. He had grown on me, and I think truly without design. He understood me, and I understood him better than he did himself. We were nothing alike, but we had everything in common.

"Your brother will be angry," he said afterward, as we lay nestled in bed. "He will walk in any moment and challenge me to a duel to avenge your honor. I would if you were my sister."

"Fear not," I replied. "My private life is of no consequence to him. But can you, Ben, as a gentleman, keep your tongue to yourself?"

"I will keep my tongue only to you," he swore, and we broke into laughter. The lovemaking had not been without pain for me—it had been so long—but it would get better, and meanwhile what content to be held in his arms. When all else is past, when all battles have been lost or won, when glory and ignominy have fallen away, to lie in the warm darkness of a bed sated with love makes earth a better place than heaven.

"I think I love you, Ben," I said, and he buried his face in my hair and sighed.

Chapter 30

For a long year, Ben and I were happy. Will must have known, but he came and went and turned a blind eye. He was too absorbed with the King's Men, and as for needing to defend his sister's honor, Ben never gave him cause. He was endearingly, impeccably discreet.

Quite a contrast to the royal court. We had gone from a Virgin Queen to a licentious nobility where pimps flourished and prostitutes flaunted their assets and their prices. For sixpence, you could have it in a dark corner; for a courtesan of the highest rank, bring jewels. Whether James, who had recently commissioned a new translation of the Bible, was a pious hypocrite or simply powerless to control these activities, you may decide. Ben declared that the king stuck to his male favorites and did not partake of mistresses.

"Too limp," he stated. "Probably damaged himself from all that falling off his horse."

Ben had even less regard for the queen. "A mushroom has a bigger brain," he said, as I poured us each a cup of Madeira wine. I generally met him at his room in the late afternoon, and he would walk me home at twilight. "She cannot sing but insists I compose songs for her, which she then mangles to death in her Danish accent."

"Let her do a dance instead," I suggested.

"She has two left feet."

"Sneak me in to see her. Please?"

"All right," Ben grumbled, as if he were a put-upon husband, though already a smile tugged at the corners of his mouth. He liked being teased out of himself, liked thinking he could deny me nothing.

A few weeks later he found occasion to slip me into the palace as a seamstress during costume fittings for a masque. While my fingers hemmed one of the ladies' skirts, my eyes surreptitiously observed the queen. Even if her intellectual capacity fell short of a toadstool, I hoped to find a woman of independent spirit. Hadn't she stood up to the king and refused Anglican communion at the coronation? But as I stitched, I reluctantly concurred with Ben's view. It was not that she did anything particularly stupid. On the contrary, she did little but pose and frown at her costume. It was one of Inigo Jones's designs, not mine, and I thought the silvery gown and ornate headdress made the best of her long-nosed face and average charms. But although her garb already incorporated enough feathers to billow her aloft like a great snowy bird, she required additional plumage.

"I want them all about my shoulders, waist and headdress," she said. And here is the vital difference: Had Elizabeth Tudor voiced the same command, you would have rushed to pluck ostriches. When Queen Anne spoke, you merely sighed and said, "Yes, Your Majesty."

"And her ladies—twitter, twitter, twitter," said Ben, fingering the air as if canaries fluttered at his ears. We were back in his room, sharing our impressions of the afternoon.

"Featherweights," I agreed, stretching the obvious pun. "But guess who else I saw, Ben, though it was only a glimpse as she passed in a corridor, and she didn't see me? Arbella Stuart." I brightened at the memory. One of the other seamstresses, a gossipy woman, had informed me that Arbella had fine apartments in the palace, attendants befitting her station and an annual income of three thousand pounds, which she was quickly overspending. Most important, though still husbandless at thirty, Arbella had appeared fresh cheeked and happy.

"Anyway," I continued, "maybe we are being too hard on the

queen for her frivolity. What other occupation has she? Married to James at fourteen, a royal brood mare for the begetting of children. Seven so far, four living. James hasn't been limp there."

"Leaving us a passel of feebleminded Stuarts to rule England from now on. If not for my masques, there will be nothing worth remembering in their entire reign."

"Yet you lavish flattery upon them."

"I am court poet, that is my job. And how is that Scottish play of yours coming?"

We raised mocking eyebrows at each other, then laughed and kissed. You can see that whereas with Kit Marlowe I had had a breath-panting, bed-heaving affair—the kind every woman deserves at least once in her life—with Ben I had almost a marriage. You would have thought on our evenings together we were an old domestic couple, mellowed by years of companionship. And though in our writing we were antipodes, we shelved our creative differences to hear out each other's literary conundrums. Now I pulled off Ben's shoes, took his left foot in my lap and began massaging the sole.

"My doodling about witches and Scotland is at an impasse," I confessed, for I had taken up the subject Ben had rejected. "You know the legend of the Three Sisters and the glorious future they foretold for Banquo's descendants? Macbeth is to be king first, then the crown goes to Banquo's son."

"Which our royal lump James, claiming descent from Banquo, cites as evidence of his ancient right to the throne."

"Yes. Now picture these three witches on a foggy moor in Scotland, crook-nosed hags cackling over a boiling cauldron—at least, that is how the silly and superstitious choose to portray them. But Holinshed describes them only as three women in strange and wild apparel, resembling creatures of the elder world, the sight of whom causes Macbeth and Banquo to gaze in wonder. Suppose they were not hags then, but beautiful, seductive women. Why would anyone listen to a witch or her prophecies if she were too repulsive to approach?"

"To remedy which, you would make them alluring."

"Quite so. If they were comely, wouldn't you be more likely to believe them and do their bidding?"

"Most likely I would. And for the rest of your story?"

"There lies my problem. According to Holinshed, Banquo, to hasten the witches' prophecy, conspires with Macbeth to kill the reigning king. James has apparently forgotten his ancestor was a murderer, and I doubt he will take kindly to anyone reminding him. Here, give me the other one." I put down his left foot and beckoned for the right, and he heaved it into my lap with a contented sigh.

"That feels good."

"You're welcome. Back to my play. Well, between evil Banquo and beautiful witches I am temporarily stalled. Maybe they just need time to take shape, or am I growing lazy?"

"I like you lazy. You are my quiet spot in the day, when the hectic hours wind down and we drink a slow glass of wine and listen to the minutes ticking."

We paused, weighing the words.

"Nice image," I said, lowering his foot.

"Thank you." He slid his hand behind my ankle and cradled it on his knees. "Here, your turn."

So time passed, and it was pleasant. If I died the next day, I reflected, it would scarcely be noticed I was gone. And this was not a bad thing. The yoke was off my shoulders. If my muse was desultory, I could dawdle along. For once I had a soft spot in my life, ease, comfort, love and attention. I went to plays almost every afternoon. I strolled across town. Ben purloined a lute from one of the masques, and I took lessons with no real hope that I would ever learn to play. I found an old cat shivering in a doorway and sheltered it in Ben's room. The creature came and went for several weeks, and after lapping the cream I offered, it would lick my hand and meow unmelodiously. Until one day it did not return. I cried for an hour on Ben's shoulder—for a flea-bitten cat—but when in my life had I ever had the luxury to cry over a cat before?

Most of all, I treated myself to a spate of uninterrupted reading—

or tried to. When you are a writer, much of your reading is directed to your profession, perusing novels for fresh subjects, studying the competition's latest plays, researching history and famous personages. Now I purchased a half dozen juicy, sensationalist volumes, eager for scandals, tattle and titillation. Alas, years of honing my skills had paid off too well. Mushy, derivative, overwrought, misplotted, devoid of tension—one by one, I tossed them aside like a finicky buyer sorting through a basket of bruised fruit at the market. Even for recreation's sake, I simply could not abide incompetent writing.

Will continued to pass me with a friendly wave. He was now a serious man of forty-one, intent on the profitable management of the Globe and the King's Men. He had also concluded another deal in Stratford, purchasing half the parish tithes for the sum of £440. "We will reap sixty pounds a year," he informed me, and I congratulated him. Some nights, Ben, Will and I ended up in the tavern together, and I would listen in quiet amusement as my two playwrights vigorously debated their various styles of writing, Tom Dekker often joining in. Both Will and Ben seemed to forget entirely my contribution; this was a jousting match between men. The evenings always ended with an amicable toast, then my considerate brother would walk me home.

⁓

In the early autumn of 1605 there occurred two astonishing eclipses of the sun and moon. Depending on their degree of bravery, people either hid beneath their beds or flocked outside to witness the celestial omens. I was torn. Long ago, Kit had taught me to be skeptical of religion and superstition. But two eclipses so close together—what might that portend? I joined the sky gazers, and when I found myself unscathed after peering at the first obscuration, I was emboldened to enjoy the second one. But perhaps the superstitious were right to cower, for it was about that time the tide of fortune began to turn.

First came a personal scare that left me shaking. In addition to writing poetry and masques, Ben had partnered with his former rival John Marston and the playwright George Chapman to compose a new work, *Eastward Ho.* The plot was inoffensive enough: A goldsmith has two daughters; one marries the industrious apprentice, the other a spendthrift knight. Unfortunately, thinking themselves in good graces with the king, the playwrights rashly allowed one character to imitate James's Scottish accent and another to disparage the Scots themselves. Ben, where did you leave your brain? The king was incensed, Marston fled town and Ben and Chapman were imprisoned until the tantrum sputtered out. I crushed myself into his arms when he was freed and came strolling home.

"Please, Ben, please watch what you write!" I implored, breathing in his earthy scent, his solid bulk.

"Why can't the man take a simple joke?" Ben grumbled. "Come, come, no harm done. Not even a new brand to match the other." Grinning, he held up his thumbs.

But in other matters, Ben was not laughing. Though my shaggy bear continued to behave admirably toward me, at court he quarreled increasingly with Inigo Jones. It seems inevitable that anytime you put together two men of talent, they will rub each other wrong. They are each so sure of their vision, so jealous to relinquish the least jot of control. To expect Jonson and Jones to collaborate on the masques like good chums was like asking God to share his throne. Aside from the later, harmonious partnership of Francis Beaumont and John Fletcher, the only man of genius I have ever known to maintain consistently amicable relations with his creative peers was Will. But then, he was only half a genius, wasn't he?

Meanwhile, an autumn of discontent crept over the nation. It was now more than two years since Elizabeth's death, and the country's hopes for James were greatly diminished. I have noted the licentiousness at court, now add rampant corruption. Though the king had brought peace with Spain as promised, no rainbow of prosperity arced over us at home. Political divisions remained unhealed, and simmering religious tensions, that real witches' brew, began to bubble in the cauldron.

In early November, a group of Catholic conspirators made their move. Having expected more freedom of religion under James, they decided to express their disapproval at the lack thereof by renting a cellar beneath Parliament House and stocking it with thirty-six barrels of gunpowder. They planned to ignite it on November 5, the opening day of Parliament. James would have been there, the Prince of Wales, the Privy Council, nobles, judges, bishops—the entire government destroyed in one massive explosion, the country laid open to foreign invasion.

The Gunpowder Plot was discovered scarcely twelve hours before the fuse was to be lit, and we citizens learned of the horror only after it had been averted. We stood blinking at the Sunday-morning sermon at St. Paul's Cross, hearing the news and mingling shock with prayers of thanksgiving. Whatever our disappointment in James, this was not what we had in mind. Within a week, most of the conspirators were either killed or apprehended and conveyed to the Tower of London. What was done to them there, I will not think on. The trial took place in January 1606; the outcome, guilty of high treason, was a foregone conclusion. The executions were carried out at the end of the month, and the heads and disemboweled body parts of Guy Fawkes and his cohorts provided grisly decorations at vantage points throughout London. I encountered one by mistake—a lower torso, a crow pecking at the purpled, hairy area where the privates had been. For weeks afterward, I walked with my unnerved eyes on the ground.

"Some days I want to curl inside and ignore everything," I told Ben, hugging myself by the fire against the winter cold. I would rather it were Ben hugging me, but that evening he was not in the mood. He had picked another fight with Inigo Jones, then refused to concede when he lost, the usual outcome. Poor Ben. His mind was acute, but his articulation lagged. Even when his ideas were better, a rival could twirl and truss him up with clever phrases before he could expound his meaning. He brought his defeats home, and when I tried to console him, he grew belligerent.

"Why am I wasting my talent on these masques?" he swore, thrashing his arms. "Fluff for prancing nobles with dyed beards and silly ladies who can't remember three lines. They don't sing, they squeal like castrated pigs. They dance like bumping hippopotami. I should have stuck to writing plays."

"Write one. Any of the companies would be happy to have a new play by you."

"That's right, they would. I am the best."

"Then show them what you can do."

"I will, and quickly too. They have mocked in the past that I am a slow writer. Watch me confound them."

It is not always wise to encourage a man, for if he fails, he will turn the blame upon you. This time, luckily, Ben excelled. In just five weeks, he wrote *Volpone; or, The Fox*, a feat he boasted of until even I tired of hearing it. Produced by the King's Men, it was a brilliant and bitter piece of satire. Other writers that year were in a similarly contentious mood, tired of trying to please a modern audience that had become increasingly jaded and critical. What, another tragedy? We've seen dozens already. Give us something new, astound us! Very well, the authors replied, and they resorted to plays that turned on and castigated the audience for its cynical nature. A strange atmosphere, and meanwhile new playwrights had entered the scene: John Day, Francis Beaumont, Cyril Tourneur, Thomas Middleton.

Time for me to buckle down.

⁓

My next play, *King Lear*, is no doubt the most depressing in my canon. No one lives happily ever after. For that matter, hardly anyone lives at all. I killed them off right and left, die, die, die. England is going to wrack and ruin, the king is blind to everything but his own whims and pleasures, his elder daughters are cruel. And Cordelia is stupid, yes, stupid. When Lear childishly commands a declaration of love from each daughter, he is not asking for the truth but for a sop to his pitifully dwindling power. Since Cordelia does love him, it would be no lie to soothe him with sweet words. Go on, make the senile old man happy, humor him, girl! But no, saintly Cordelia cannot permit the slightest inexactitude to pass her lips and needlessly angers him with a less-than-fulsome reply. So he disinherits her. A kingdom lost for a quibble! If you pack with wolves like Goneril and Regan, you have two choices: Be torn to pieces or learn to howl.

Of course, up to that point I was only following the well-known story of King Leir in Holinshed and other sources. In the old tales, Goneril and Regan drive out their poor father, then Cordelia raises an army that defeats her wicked sisters and restores Leir to his throne. He dies peacefully, Cordelia inherits, the good live happily ever after. Until years later, when, according to some versions, the wolf pups of the two sisters grow up and exact revenge. They overthrow and imprison Cordelia, who, weary and wretched, eventually hangs herself. I must have been in an impatient mood. If Cordelia dies anyway, why drag it out?

"Pretty grim, isn't it?" said Ben, when I showed him the script.

"If you think so, you have grown too used to glittery masques. Did you notice the way I built Lear's madness from scene to scene? I am rather proud of that."

"Yes, I noted. Another great role for Dick Burbage. Does the man have any idea how much he owes you?"

"No, but I owe him as well. He is the only one who can pull off the range of emotion demanded of Lear."

"And Robert Armin for the fool?"

"His subtlety will balance Lear's rantings."

"All the same, it is a savage play. Murder, treachery, gouging out eyes. I should fear meeting you in a black alley."

"As flies to wanton boys are characters to my pen," I quipped, badly. "Tremble before me, Ben."

Though Will had no part in writing *Lear*, he took a particular interest in its staging and persuaded Cuthbert they should create special effects similar to those in the masques. The idea made good business sense. Incorporating the latest features from the court spectacles in our productions at the Globe might be just what we needed to attract a wider audience. However, I did not realize the full extent of Will's project until one morning when I visited the Globe during a rehearsal. As the actors left the stage, he turned to two carpenters waiting in the yard.

"We must have thunder, lightning, a storm on the heath," he ordered, gesticulating. "I will devise some moving scenery and provide you with sketches for the construction."

The men nodded agreeably, though I had to chuckle at the looks they exchanged as they departed.

"A storm may be hard to achieve when the play is presented in midafternoon on a sunny May day," I observed, coming forward. "What will you do? Have boys pour buckets of water down on the actors from the heavens?"

He paused—England's greatest playwright and he didn't recognize sarcasm when he heard it?

"Not a bucket, a sieve," he said, after mulling the idea for a moment.

"What?"

"A sieve, or rather, many of them. Then the water would fall in droplets, not a stream. Or if we had a single long sieve, a trough, with a handle on either end, we could have a boy hold each side and together shake it gently." He spread his hands and jiggled them in demonstration. "The water would sprinkle down."

"A sprinkle is hardly a storm."

"They would shake forcefully then."

"How would they replenish the water if it ran out too quickly?"

"Buckets. Two more boys with extra buckets could hide in the heavens and refill the sieve as necessary."

"And if the trough or the buckets are too heavy and the boys happen to drop one or the other on Lear's head?"

"Lear must keep to the front of the stage and not walk under the opening to the heavens."

"And when the stage becomes wet and the actors begin to slip?"

"Not too much water then."

For the lightning, Will envisioned jagged strips of silver metal, nailed to long poles. More boys in the heavens could stab these bolts downward just far enough not to reveal the artifice. Then of course there must be cracks and booms of thunder to accompany the lightning, easily produced by still more heavenly boys banging pots and fry pans or beating on drums. Will was quite pleased as this picture began to knit together, his face bathed in boyish optimism, his bald forehead shining with beads of perspiration. I pictured soaked actors with head injuries and terrified boys spilling from the sky.

"If only we had a windmill." Will sighed.

"A windmill?"

"Yes, onstage, with sails and a pulley. A boy could hide inside and work the ropes and that would create a wind to blow the rain to create a gale."

Thus far, I had swallowed his nonsense with a dose of dark humor. Now I drew a breath and chose my words carefully.

"Will, the gale scene is supposed to take place on a barren heath, save for a hovel in which Edgar, the good but banished son of the Duke of Gloucester, is hiding. Edgar's troubles have driven him out of his wits, and he is now known as Poor Tom. Yet even an idiot, when presented with the choice of sheltering in a filthy, leaky hovel or a nice, dry windmill, will choose the saner accommodation."

Will opened his mouth to protest, but I held up my finger and continued.

"Now Lear arrives on the stormy scene, battered, bedraggled, half-naked, raving. Picture the dramatic possibilities of this once mighty king crawling into a demeaning pile of boards versus the sight of a cozy windmill waiting. He'll just go into the windmill with Tom, who probably has a hot supper waiting."

Will responded with the petulant look of a child denied his wishes.

"We need wind, noise, commotion," he insisted. "We want to billow Lear's cape and make the fool clap his cap to his head. I can make this work. Maybe, if many boys were to stand offstage, each with a bellows, all pumping as hard as they can . . ."

I pumped a breath in exasperation, threw up my hands and walked home.

In the end, after numerous complaints from the drenched actors during rehearsals, most of Will's special effects were abandoned, except for the boys banging the pots and fry pans. At the opening performance, they banged with such lusty enthusiasm that Dick Burbage was drowned out as he tore his breast upon the heath. That did it. Dick grabbed Will by the ear, and the boys were reduced to an opening salvo followed by quiet thereafter.

⁓

About the time I finished *Lear* in the spring of 1606, I fell ill. Was it bad air, bad food, some punishment from God? For the first few weeks, my only symptom was an uneasy stomach, and I ignored it. Who had time to be sick when my Scottish play was finally asserting itself? Faced with the choice of either eliminating Banquo from the story or transforming James's thug of an ancestor into a model of nobility, I chose the latter. It made for better drama anyway, good Banquo versus evil Macbeth. From then on, the writing went smoothly, especially as I was aided by my new spectacles. What a boon to mankind is this simple device! No longer will poor eyesight at any age deprive people of the joys of reading and writing.

But early into the second draft of *The Tragedy of Macbeth*, my guts cramped and I began to vomit a greenish bile. My bowels gave way, and what I did not spew up my throat burned through my stomach and exited in a malodorous stew. Will and the King's Men were away at Hampton Court entertaining James, and it was almost a week before Ben came to find me. He had been so grumpy of late that I had taken to visiting him less often. Now he drew back at the sight of me, sweaty and shaking with fever in my bed, the piss pot near to running over.

"Why in God's name haven't you called a doctor?" he demanded, keeping his distance.

"I did. He said it was the flux and wanted to bleed me. Don't let them do that, Ben."

"Where is your brother? Why isn't he here to take care of you?"

"He's with the king—you know that. You might have stopped by. Didn't you notice I was missing?"

"Of course, but I have been busy."

"Help me, Ben."

"All right, all right. I'll get a doctor."

"No! He will bleed me!"

"Then you must be bled. Pfeuw!"

I hate men, I hate men. He could have tended me, bathed me, brought fragrant broth and a little roast meat, pressed a cold cloth to my forehead. He could have sat by and read to me, burned sweet herbs or brought flowers to freshen the air. But let there be a quick and violent solution at hand, and that is the one men will choose. Ben was back in an hour with an evil-looking man, and, ignoring my terrified cries, Ben pinioned me on the bed while the physician slashed open my arm and squeezed a river of blood into a copper bowl.

"I'll send someone to nurse you until Will returns," said Ben, gruff patience restored when the ordeal was over. "You should have sent for help immediately, Anne, not left it until you were truly ill."

"I didn't wish to inconvenience anyone." Tears of hurt wet my eyes. "I thought you would come."

But even with Will back in town looking after me, my recovery was slow, and I missed a beautiful spring. I turned fifty—good God, could that be true? For eighteen years I had been Will's younger sister, a decade miraculously shaved off my age, and until this illness, I had looked and lived the part. Now it was as if I had been stripped of a sacred belief. Fifty? Me? For a full day I recalculated. I was born in 1556, Will in 1564. He was eight years younger than me, but the whole world thought me two years younger than him. Wasn't that right? I looked in the mirror, a sideways glance. Well, my skin was pinched and pale, but that was the lingering effects of the illness. I put extra effort into my hair and dress and bought a pot of softening lotion to rub into my cheeks. Ben's time for me had shrunk since I fell sick; men have no stomach for reality, and having seen me at my worst, he had retreated because of it. But as soon as I built up my health, he would be back. We had everything in common, our writing, our companionship.

I filled my hours writing *Macbeth*. The witches could not escape being hags after all; they were probably fifty. It made for better theater—hair-raising scenes announced with thunder—and accorded with James's idea of what a witch ought to be. But the idea of a seductress would not go quietly, and one day as I was dipping my quill, she possessed Lady Macbeth. Formerly a minor character, she became a full partner in her husband's schemes, ruthless, beautiful, lusting for power, each driving the other forward when stabs of conscience threatened to turn them back. As the Macbeths' murderous plot crumbled and madness crept into the lady's midnight hours, she contemplated her downfall and uttered her heart's cry on the meaninglessness of life: a tale told by an idiot, full of sound and fury, signifying nothing. Then, center stage, she plunged her dagger into her breast, leaving Macbeth to be run through by Macduff's sword. That was my original version.

Then Will ruined it.

"Queen Anne's brother, the King of Denmark, is coming on a state visit, and I have been commissioned to write something for the occasion," he announced, rummaging in my papers. "I need it quickly, perhaps a sequel to *Hamlet*, the return of glory to the Danish throne. Where is our quarto version?"

"Don't . . . touch . . . *Hamlet*." I inserted myself between him and my table and put a menacing finger to his chest. "Don't you dare touch a word." In my still haggard state I must have looked exceedingly wrathful. He backed away, and to ensure he stayed there I handed him *Macbeth*. "Here, I have a new play with a Scottish theme. Take it."

Will's eyes brightened. "Excellent! I will get to work."

He worked on it all right. *Macbeth* was near completion when I passed it to him, and in my tired state it was not wrong of me to hope Will would polish it. But he was too much in a hurry to do a proper job, and he failed to flesh out the minor characters, as I would have done had my health and time allowed. Far more distressing, he stripped my lady of her best speech and dramatic suicide. He turned her into an ambitious, mocking wife who pushes her husband to commit regicide; then he set her aside and gave the second half of the play to Macbeth. When she reappeared briefly near the end, she was a sleepwalking, conscience-stricken wraith who dies offstage and is dismissed in two lines.

"Life's but a walking shadow," cries Macbeth. I would have liked to make a walking shadow of Will. His other contribution was to add a dumb show of eight kings to the scene in which the witches show the line of the Scots kings' descent from Banquo down to King James. James loved it.

"I hate it," I told Ben. I had not seen him in two weeks, and I had gone to his room, willing to forgive his neglect and resume our companionship. He was probably still frustrated by the inanities of court, and I had my grievances. We two writers could surely commiserate.

"Never trust a collaborator," Ben agreed. "But you ought to stay home and get some more color in your cheeks. After such a serious illness, you can't expect to recover overnight. Maybe you ought to have a holiday in Stratford. The country air would do you good."

"Perhaps, but there is no need to journey that far. What if we both took a short holiday? You like to walk, and you need the exercise." I patted his protruding tummy. "We could take a week's interval in Surrey."

"I don't think so, Anne. I am very busy at court."

He shrugged regretfully, but I saw how when I touched him he had flinched away. I gave him a long look. Why, Ben? Did you just get tired of me or did my illness reveal me to be past my best? Was there someone else or were you ready to try again with your wife? I was still weak and hadn't the stomach to mount what seemed likely to be a fruitless protest. But unlike Ben, I would not end this affair with dishonesty.

"I love you," I said, and waited.

Ben shambled a bit. "Faugh, love, what is that?" He twitched one shoulder and cocked his head as if to make me laugh.

"I love you."

"Well, we did have some good times, didn't we, Anne?"

"We had wonderful times."

"All right, yes, they were wonderful. But you knew it couldn't last."

"Couldn't it?"

"I am married."

"I know. How suddenly convenient."

"Well, then, I must get back to work. The queen has ordered another masque, and I can't let Inigo Jones get the upper hand."

"You swore you were my friend."

Ben huffed in frustration. "I have been your friend, Anne. I listened to your plays, let you sketch costumes for the masques, took care of you in illness, told you news of court. I have kept your secret and treated your brother as an equal." His voice was rising, irritation forming his face into a scowl. He grew clumsy in his movements, and in trying to back away from me without seeming to do so, he kicked over a stool with a mug on it. The empty mug clattered onto the floor, and he made exasperated and exaggerated motions to retrieve it. My bear was becoming untamed again, a muttering, growling creature who had used up his good behavior and was reverting to himself. Good-bye, Ben.

I waited, unmoving, until the stool and mug were ostentatiously restored to their place. I waited until he had no choice but to look me in the eye.

"I loved you," I said.

Chapter 31

$\mathcal{B}$en was right; I should have known we couldn't last. His was not a steadfast nature, and he never stuck to any friend, male or female, longer than it suited his mood or his ambitions. It would have surprised him to receive loyalty in return. In Ben's view, you took people for what they offered, they took you, then both moved on. So don't take it seriously. It's nothing personal, Anne.

But that refrain brought no comfort each night as I cried myself to sleep. I had asked for so little: friendship, a familiar routine, the occasional lovemaking, the security of knowing there was someone in the world who cared about me. I tried to keep my tears to my pillow, but one night Will rose in the dark to come pat me on the shoulder. I bawled then, and he held me, and in the morning we pretended it was past. But my heartache continued, and the arrival of the leaden winter months further depressed my spirits.

Will tried to coax me back to life with little kindnesses, carrying my basket home from the market, complimenting me on my sewing, offering tidbits for conversation when I seemed open to talk. Ah, Will, why were we so often apart when we could have shared so much? Why did we keep taking separate paths if they were forever destined to reintersect? Why could we never, permanently, get it right? It wasn't a question of infidelities. Without a word, he forgave me for Ben, just as

I had excused Southampton and the Dark Lady. If you count in Kit for me, then I suppose, in a wry way, we were even. We always found we had missed each other when we reunited. We were at our best together as friends, writing.

"Would you like to try a new play?" I asked one night, and Will brightened.

"Do you have a topic?"

"No, I was hoping you might."

"Something classical? I could browse through Plutarch."

I agreed, though the ancients were primarily Will's territory—*Titus, Julius Caesar, Troilus and Cressida*—while English history was my preferred terrain. But I owed Will for his recent care of me, and when he proposed the story of Antony and Cleopatra I was glad to have a solid project before us. Though we shifted the emphasis of certain events, our plot kept mainly to Plutarch. I think the strength of our version lies in its portrayal of Antony's and Cleopatra's struggles to possess both love and power. Can you have both in full measure or must one inevitably be sacrificed to achieve the other? If you must choose between them, which is better? Cold-blooded Octavius opts for power and ends victorious. Antony and Cleopatra lose both by refusing to surrender either. The moral: Always keep an asp handy so you may at least die well.

"You see, we haven't lost our touch," said Will when the script was finished.

I smiled, and when *Antony and Cleopatra* was performed at the Globe—with an excellent boy actor as the Egyptian queen—it was moderately successful. But once again the theater was changing, and not, disturbingly, by any innovation of ours.

For one thing, the "city comedies" had become increasingly popular. These were plays like Tom Dekker's *The Shoemaker's Holiday* that portrayed the lives and doings of ordinary Londoners. Often satirical, they exposed city vices and sometimes overlapped the comedies of humors. But however you defined them, the point was that where our common folk in the yard had once thrilled to tales of nobles in love and war, they now desired to see onstage people like themselves. It put lighthearted romances like our *Twelfth Night* out of favor, and I was sad to see them go.

The other rising new genre was tragicomedy, at which Francis Beaumont and John Fletcher soon excelled. A rare example of talented playwrights who actually got along, they formed a partnership and lodged together in Bankside, sharing clothes, possessions and, some said, a mistress. They began writing for the King's Men, and their basic rule for a tragicomedy was that whatever the subject, though some characters might come close to death, no one was allowed to expire. If you preferred light entertainment, I understood the appeal. Even when they richly deserved it, I was sometimes perturbed by the number of characters I had killed.

So, even with a fair profit on *Antony and Cleopatra*, Will and I were beginning to feel like old dogs.

"Beaumont is barely into his twenties, and here I am forty-three," Will lamented on his birthday. "How did it happen?"

"It is all those tomorrows creeping in their petty pace from day to day," I said. "They tend to add up when we are not looking."

Then a letter arrived that simultaneously lifted our spirits and made us feel even older. Our daughter Susanna had received a proposal of marriage from Dr. John Hall, and we were required in Stratford for the wedding.

~

Who would not be proud of a daughter like Susanna?

Charming from head to toe, she was, at twenty-four, a leading young lady of Stratford. She ran New Place with serene authority and admirable efficiency; the servants were devoted to her. She took care of her grandmother and called on sick neighbors with sweets and nose-gays. Gossip and jealousy were beneath her. She never muddied her shoes in the local puddles, always adroitly sidestepping or allowing someone else to spread their cloak in her path. Only once had she put a foot wrong, the previous spring, when she was named recusant for missing the Easter Day service—for what reason, I never knew. Nonetheless, that slight slip reminded her of what she really wanted, to view life from a pedestal, and she was circumspect thereafter.

Now she had found a man worthy of sharing that height. Dr. John Hall—what a catch! A degree from Queens' College, Cambridge. A thriving medical practice. A mature thirty-two and handsome, oh, yes. Esteemed by his colleagues and beloved by his patients, Dr. Hall treated rich and poor alike and rode long distances to attend the frail and bedridden. His father, also a physician, had bequeathed to him a library of medical books, and John employed two apothecaries to prepare the herbal potions he prescribed for his patients. He did not approve of bleeding, which naturally pleased me, and was gaining a reputation for his success in treating that dread disease scurvy. His recipe was a juice made of watercress, brooklime and special grasses. In breeding, temperament and aspirations, he and Susanna were perfectly matched. I think Will, en route to Stratford, had harbored some fatherly notion of inspecting and passing serious judgment upon this suitor for our daughter's hand, but on our arrival the whole effort was preempted by John's sterling qualities. Our future son-in-law showed Will and me much courtesy, inviting us to visit his home and medical office.

"I find I refer most often to Gerard's *The Generall Historie of Plants*," he said, running his finger down the illustrated entries. "He includes many plants from the New World, which, cultivated here, have greatly expanded our usual treatments. But I do not neglect proven ingredients such as bat dung and spiderwebs, and inspecting a patient's water"—he held up a urine bottle—"is essential to a diagnosis."

"We must have the finest wedding Stratford has ever seen," Will announced, and clapping an arm around John—and leaving the details to me—he steered the bridegroom off to the tavern for a toast.

I would have shooed him off anyway. On such occasions, men are about as useful as a three-legged donkey. First, new outfits for everyone: crimson satin for me, a dusty blue silk trimmed in silver for Judith, for old Mary Shakespeare a becoming dove gray. I cleared one of the bedchambers at New Place for a sewing room and began each morning by putting on my thimble. Susanna's gown must be the loveliest of all. I had brought the fabric from London, an exquisite ivory silk so soft and luscious it almost melted on our fingers like whipped cream on the tongue.

"What do you think?" I said, draping the cloth over Susanna's slender figure as she stood patiently before me. We had hired two seamstresses to help us, but I reserved the honor of sewing the bride's dress for myself.

"Is that not a little revealing?" Susanna widened her eyes at the proposed scoop of the neckline.

"In London, it is the latest fashion. Queen Anne herself set the style."

"This is Stratford, Mother, and it is said the London ladies are careless of their morals and reputations. I am not sure I wish to resemble them."

"You won't. You will look lovely." I touched her long blond hair, arranging it to flow loose over her shoulders.

"She will look perfect," said Judith, swooping in to claim her bolt of blue. "She always does. Give me that neckline, Mother. I have no objection to mimicking a court lady—or should that be courtesan?"

Judith draped herself, posturing, and although Susanna smiled benignly, I felt a moment's irritation. We had never been close, Susanna, Judith and I—my fault, of course. But the happy flurry of the occasion offered an opportunity for renewed affection, and I hoped our accord might grow more natural and permanent. Our daughters were warm enough to Will—at least Susanna was. Judith had a standoffish nature that made us both sigh. Or was it only that you never saw Susanna's mind working, for whatever her inward emotions she always presented a smooth countenance to the world. Whereas Judith, oh, dear, could hide nothing. Her feelings were on her face and out of her mouth before her mind could censor. Now she turned her pose on Mary.

"What do you say, Grandma? Shall I flaunt my assets? My, you are a good little mouse with your sewing, aren't you?"

"Judith—"

I raised my tone, but already Judith was sitting innocently beside her grandmother, admiring her handiwork. In decline since her husband's death six years before, Mary had gradually become superfluous in the household as the girls took charge. Even Will's brothers tended to overlook their mother. She had lost much of her hearing, and the conversation around her was a distant commotion she found easier to ignore. When anyone did pause to ask her opinion, she wavered at length and had to be coached to an answer. I had tried to make her welcome in the sewing room, giving her busywork we all knew would come to naught. She must have known it herself—her stiff fingers made for clumsy stitching—but obediently she plodded on.

"Well, then," said Susanna, brightly recalling us to our task, "what about this?" She redraped the ivory fabric below her neck, and naturally the compromise she suggested was just right.

"Perfect," I said.

"As always," echoed Judith.

All of which made me vow to improve relations with my daughters, pay more consideration to my mother-in-law and guard my own health.

~

The fifth of June was the wedding day, and for three Sundays before, the banns were read aloud in church. Does anyone know of any reason why the marriage of Dr. John Hall and Mistress Susanna Shakespeare should not take place? Come forward and declare it!

What, and miss the chance to be invited to the feast?

Indeed, that was the one difficulty about the wedding—too many people wished to attend and thought they had the right. Will was not unanimously the most respected man in town—provincial minds were still inclined to view actors and playwrights as suspect and immoral— but he was one of the wealthiest and certainly the most famous. Moreover, though he hobnobbed with the king, he obviously prized his origins and the honest soil of his birth. That's our Will, he's one of us, and a family, don't forget, that owns a coat of arms. We should have more like them!—a sentiment that surely swelled old John Shakespeare's corpse with righteous vindication in his grave.

Thus, many folk suddenly claimed a long-standing friendship or recalled with utmost clarity some past service they had rendered us. In my wedding errands around town, I was frequently accosted. It was especially intriguing to hear from would-be guests the life I had led in their eyes. Didn't I used to be a wanton woman who tricked a young man into wedlock, then made a shambles of marriage and motherhood to boot? No—come to find out, I was a brave and loyal helpmate who had supported her husband's rise. Why, he would never have made it in London without me. At the same time, I had often been in Stratford, chatting with the wives in the marketplace while my children played happily at my skirts. Really? I wondered how long it would take for my history to be recast when the sought-after invitations failed to arrive.

Will, however, was an easy mark. He spent most afternoons drinking congratulatory toasts with townsmen eager to treat the proud father of the bride. Since he never could say no to an offer of camaraderie and seemed unable to detect those with an ulterior motive, the guest list swelled. A genuine worry arose that the revelers would overrun New Place, so to divert them Will magnanimously ordered ale and cakes to be served to the general public in the town square. It was an admirable solution, for those who had no real acquaintance with the bridal couple were now relieved of the pretense. On the appointed day they could simply head to the square and get straight to the business of becoming falling-down drunk.

And on that day, the wedding went splendidly, the few moments of consternation easily laughed aside. A misplaced brooch while we were dressing, a premature announcement that John and his friends were on their way to collect the bride. "I am not ready!" squeaked Mary. We had forgotten her in the bustle, and there she stood, her gnarled fingers frustrated by the closings of her new dress. "Don't worry, little mouse. I will do it for you," Judith consoled, and laced her up. Will, in umber satin, beamed and tidied his mustache with his forefinger. My dress did not quite fit, binding under the arms, but what a picture Susanna made. When John did arrive, accompanied by a half dozen friends and a trio of musicians to pipe us to church, Susanna stepped out and into the sun.

"Ohh!"

Only the halo was missing as the awed Stratfordians gathered to acclaim the vision of golden hair and ivory silk that alighted amongst them. I felt an odd sensation, as if the air around me had thinned and I could not breathe quite right. Then the musicians struck up a sprightly song, and as our procession wound to church, more people came out to cheer, and a dog trotted along. During the ceremony, while the priest read verses, a spider dropped on Judith's shoulder, and her little shriek was, I thought, too artfully done. Susanna smiled away the interruption. Spiders never dropped on her. Near the end of the ceremony Will reached over and squeezed my hand. He was beaming at something the priest was saying—I confess I had become distracted and lost track of the words—and I started inwardly at the touch. It was gone before I could absorb it, one of those fleeting moments you wish you could call back again.

Outside the church, we were surrounded by well-wishers until my foot began to tap. Yes, yes, beautiful, virtuous, but if you do not let us get on, who will see to the feast? We repaired to the garden at New Place, and now every effort went into feeding our hungry guests. We had nearly bought out the shops in Stratford, and the tables sagged under platters of beef, poultry, fish, venison, oysters, cheese, bread, fruit, compotes, puddings, cakes and tarts along with jugs of wine, ale and cider to keep throats wet. Will sat with his friends beneath the mulberry tree, regaling them with tales of London, a sheen of perspiration and contentment on his face. I talked gaily with Bartholomew and Isabella and their brood from Hewlands. When the dancing and entertainments began, Will was called upon to recite.

"Something fine from one of your plays!" his friends commanded. Unfortunately, the wine had loosened not only Will's tongue but also his brain, and what he uttered was half-doggerel, half-cobbled lines from decade-old sonnets. The crowd applauded uproariously, but then they were mostly drunk too. Passing behind him, I whispered, "Friends, Romans, countrymen," and, properly cued, he orated Mark Antony and received more thunderous applause. No one wanted to give up a minute of celebration. It might be a long time before Stratford enjoyed another such fete.

I kept my head and saw to it that those who overimbibed were eased out and sent home. We had hired extra servants for the day, and I kept them busy running, fetching and cleaning up. By ten o'clock, the sun finally down in the west, I longed for rest. With the last of the guests evicted, we turned to kiss Susanna good night. Though she and John were to move into New Place, they planned for privacy's sake to spend their first few weeks in John's house. I should have had some special counsel to offer her, some fond advice to start off her marriage right. But she needed none from me or anyone else, and she left with a wave, looking as fresh and beautiful as she had at the start.

Will and I went to our room. Woozy Will wanted to sleep and thereby dodge the headache that was bound to afflict him come dawn. I wanted to talk, as a husband and wife ought after such a day, and remembering that touch of his hand, I spoke in the dark.

"Will?"

"Uh?" He fluttered awake.

"It was a fine wedding, don't you think?"

"Mmm."

"Susanna looked beauteous. Did you like the dress?"

"Mmm."

"Mine chafed under the arms, but we were pressed to get them finished, and I did tell the seamstress to concentrate on Judith's gown instead."

"Mmm."

"I worry about Judith, though. Does she not seem to you a little"— I paused—"at odds with herself? Sometimes she acts kindly, like today when she fastened your mother's dress, though her language verged on disrespect. Other times her behavior is sharp when her words are fair."

"Prickly," agreed Will, waking up more than he wanted to, then lapsing back in a yawn.

"Yes, that's it, as if she is always on pins and needles, though as often as not, she turns the jab on herself. I am sure if she smiled more often she would be judged a pleasant young woman. Am I making sense?"

"Mmm."

"They are not friends, Will. I suppose that is what bothers me most. Of course, being sisters is no guarantee of mutual liking, but the world is a hard place, and as parents we want to believe our children will support and succor each other after we are gone. What is there to part Susanna and Judith? It's true Susanna is prettier and the center of attention just now, but we have never favored one daughter over the other. They are so opposite! Judith longs for sunshine, then scorns it when it slants her way. While Susanna—sometimes I want to shake her and say, 'Stop being so mercilessly good!'"

I threw up my hands and gave a chagrined laugh.

Face in his pillow, the great bard of England let out a honking snore.

"Will?"

No answer.

I waited a long moment in the dark.

"Your plays are really stupid, you know."

Nothing.

"Well, not all of them, but definitely *Titus*, *Two Gentlemen* and *All's Well*. Oh, wait. I wrote *All's Well*, didn't I? But I knew it was no good and belonged in the fire."

Silence.

"You drink too much, Will, and you are growing ever balder. Your head shines in the moonlight like a goose egg on your pillow."

Quiet.

"Did you know that in addition to Ben, I slept with Kit Marlowe? It was ecstasy."

A snore.

"Well, I know you don't care, but at least don't say I never told you. Let me see, what else . . ."

I talked for an hour in the unruffled night. A daughter's wedding is a fine time to take stock of your life, to ponder your mistakes and accomplishments, and I wanted to hear what I had to say. I ranged over my childhood, my family. I resurrected my own wedding, though I don't suppose anyone else attending Susanna's nuptials recalled that forlorn ceremony with its single, hasty reading of the banns. I whispered a prayer for Hamnet, who had now been dead the same number of years he had lived, and I rued my distance from my daughters, who ought to be a mother's looking glass wherein we see the spring we once had. I did think there was something worrisome about Judith, inexplicable, unfortunate.

And Susanna, our paragon, our self-sufficient darling. She and John Hall seemed to have all the answers Will and I had stumbled and striven after and learned too late. And isn't it a funny thing about logic, how nimbly it can turn against you where once it argued convincingly on your behalf. All my life I had pointed to Elizabeth Tudor, insisting that if just one woman can do it, the door opens wide. If she could rule a country, so could a queen in Spain or France. If she could write, so could I. But suppose just one woman can be interminably good, virtuous, a model wife and citizen—shouldn't we all be expected to conform to this well-buttered mold?

"I'm sorry I am not what you want me to be," I said to the night. "I never set out to be who I am. But I have made the most of my strange circumstances—I am a great playwright, damn it!—and why should I apologize for that? God save us from perfect women! They will set us back a hundred years."

I looked over at sleeping Will; then I reached for and squeezed his hand.

Chapter 32

$\mathcal{T}$hough Susanna's marriage was a time of celebration for our family, for many others in rural England it was a summer of despair. The chief cause was enclosure, a pernicious practice cloaked in a seemingly innocuous word. What it meant, in true English, was that the rich fenced, hedged and otherwise denied access to common lands that the ordinary folk relied on for tillage and to graze their beasts. With their own ribs as bare as their animals', they rioted, tearing down the hedges and butchering the sheep their betters had pastured on the stolen land. The unrest swept the country from mid-May until the end of July and was most serious in our own Warwickshire and the neighboring counties. But though sympathy was with the rioters, the attempt was desperate, foredoomed. How can pitchforks and starving bellies hope to prevail against unfeeling power and wealth? The uprising was crushed, the leaders executed without delay. Poor men, I hope you have a kinder lot in heaven than in this unjust world.

While Will and I were waiting for the countryside to subside and travel to become safe again, Susanna announced she was with child. You can imagine the universal delight. Susanna was already glowing. Having no new play immediately in mind, I decided to stay in Stratford. Will, however, was needed at the Globe and by the King's Men, and his youngest brother, Edmund, was to accompany him. Now twenty-seven, Edmund had finally summoned the resolve to leave home and pursue an actor's life. Of all the Shakespeare brothers, he was the handsomest, dark haired, dark eyes fringed with thick lashes. Whether he possessed the talent to become a true actor, it was too soon to say, but Will's connections would give him a far better start than we ever had, and it pleased us to think we could further the dreams of another young man from Stratford.

The brothers rode off laughing, and the rest of us settled down to a country autumn. Gilbert and Richard ran their haberdashery. Magpie Joan often stopped by New Place with her three young children and a fund of stories about her husband's hard-to-please customers and their fashion foibles. Then in December our peace was doubly shattered. Joan's middle child, four-year-old Mary, died of a fever, and we were still crying when a terrible letter came from Will: Edmund had succumbed to plague. It was the last thing we had expected, though Will tried to mitigate the shock with assurances that Edmund had not suffered. He had arranged for a costly funeral and burial for his brother at St. Saviour's in Southwark, incense, tolling bells. But all plague victims suffer horribly, and I saw the blotched ink where Will had wept over the paper. I longed to comfort him, certain he took blame upon himself, but the coldest winter in half a century had set in, and the icy, wind-whipped roads discouraged all but the most intrepid travelers.

Meanwhile, Susanna's belly was growing, and in February 1608, Elizabeth, my Lizbeth, was born. Healthy, thank God, and an easy delivery, of course. As for the date, eight and one-half months, hmm. But not a peep was uttered in town. How dared anyone think such a thing of good Mistress Hall? The too fastidious mathematician might have earned a public whipping. Thus, only hearty congratulations flowed to New Place, and while it might have pleased me to discover my daughter was no better than me after all, I agreed with the virtuous judgment. I would stake my last tooth that John and Susanna did not frolic abed before their marriage, and I don't believe they frolicked much after it. They were marble figurines, polished and impenetrable—a half pun, but I'll take it—and after Lizbeth there were no further pregnancies.

They had tried it once, it worked, they saw no reason to repeat the endeavor.

But what a joy was Lizbeth! I sat beside her cradle as she slept, awed by her sweetly puckered face and the tiny movements of her curled fists as she came awake, bright eyed at the world. I stroked the sparse fluff on her scalp and patted her on my shoulder when she fretted for no apparent cause. In the distraught circumstances of my marriage and pregnancies, I had rarely had time to enjoy my own babes. Now I held the beating warmth and breathed the milky scent of this small body and felt blessed.

Will rode back in April to see the baby and found a similar solace. As a member of the King's Men, he had been unable to avoid the yuletide entertainments at court, but given Edmund's death, he participated without heart. In the same forced spirit, he had contributed to a new play, *Pericles*, based on the well-known Roman tale. Though it was to prove popular and the quartos appeared in his name, Will readily confessed it was only half his. He also brought another sad piece of news: Bess of Hardwick had died in February, about the time Lizbeth was born. Though Bess was over eighty, her death offended me. How could that indomitable woman be gone? She was quite likely one of the oldest people in England still in complete possession of her faculties. And what would Hardwick Hall be without her? Ah, but it was her, and I had only to envision her bold initials on the towers to make me chuckle aloud.

Then, just as Will and I were set to return to London, Mary Shakespeare fell ill. John Hall thought it was not serious, but privately we debated our best course.

"Life has felt so precarious of late," Will said as we sat in the blossoming orchard of New Place. "Edmund, our little niece Mary . . ."

". . . Bess."

I sighed and held out my hand to a pair of strolling doves, but they kept on when they saw I had no food. I knew what Will meant. We seemed caught in one of those spells where the reins have slipped from your fingers and the carriage has entered an unfamiliar road, and you must trust to the horses to bring you safely home. A third dove landed beside the first two, and they greeted each other with a soft *coo, coo, coo.*

"You go, I'll stay," I offered. "Your mother's illness may be nothing, and I can soon follow."

Will wavered, but in the end it made sense, and for a while after he left, Mary did improve. I took on her nursing, freeing Susanna to mother Lizbeth. I am sorry to say I did not quite trust Judith to oversee her grandmother's care. But in June, Mary's condition worsened, and she lost control of her bodily functions, frequently soiling her clothes and her bed. It shamed her, and she wept each time I and one of the serving girls had to strip and bathe her. Her hearing failed entirely, and she shook her head at us when we tried to include her in any talk. John Hall prescribed an array of concoctions, but even his skill fell short. At least the potions kept her free of pain, or so it seemed; it may be she suffered in silence. In July I wrote to Will, and he galloped from London. Mary died in her sleep in September, and we buried her next to her husband in the churchyard.

"You have been away from London more than a year," Will observed as we finally rode back.

"Have I missed much?"

He shook his head. "I am writing a new play, *The Life of Timon of Athens.* Plutarch again, but I'm not happy with it. Care to take a look?"

I nodded. More than a year away, during which I myself had written nothing, a disturbing thought. I jutted my chin forward. There had to be something more in me, in us. What was it?

⁓

On our return to London we found the theaters closed again due to plague. They were to remain dark for over a year. Will and the King's Men waited it out by performing at court and private houses. The Burbage brothers had also resurrected the Blackfriars Theatre that had been the financial and perhaps the physical death of their father, and

Will had become a partner in that enterprise. Anxious to be of help, I went over *Timon*, as he had requested, but my efforts were in vain. So, too, when Will invited him to collaborate, were Thomas Middleton's. He was one of the young writers coming hard on our heels, but he had no luck with *Timon*. Misconceived from the start, the play never got beyond a first draft profiling a common type, the raving misanthrope. If you want true madness, see my *King Lear*.

The truth is, none of the plays Will wrote during that period— *Pericles*, *Timon*, the soon-to-come *Coriolanus* and *Cymbeline*—were up to our usual standard, and I don't say that because they were his, not mine. The deaths in our family rudely juxtaposed with the happy events of Susanna's marriage and Lizbeth's birth, our separation and his constant travel back and forth to London, the return of the plague and the playhouse closings—the time was out of joint, and inspiration fell short. I am not even sure why Will started *Coriolanus*, a tale from Plutarch about the downfall of yet another haughty Roman military man. Nobody wanted the classics anymore—lighthearted tragicomedies were the rage—and although Will did work in some astute political observations, the language was unremarkable. I don't believe anyone will be quoting from *Coriolanus* twenty years from now.

"Also"—I handed him back the manuscript with my editing— "you have everyone keep repeating that Coriolanus is 'proud.' Perhaps a few less instances? It is apparent from the way he openly despises the common people he seeks to rule and his inability to control his temper that he is an arrogant man."

"But if something is important, it is best to mention it more than once in case the audience misses it the first time."

"Fine, but after a half dozen reminders, I think even the groundlings will cry, 'Stop! We get it.' "

Will sighed, though he did not take offense. "I just can't seem to muster the enthusiasm I used to have. Anne, what do you think of me publishing my sonnets?"

I hesitated. Everyone has parts of their past they cannot quite put to rest, protean memories that slip in and out of our grasp, and Will must have been chewing over this idea for some time before he spoke. It would mean reliving his whole history with the Earl of Southampton and the Dark Lady and seeing himself at less than his best. But the poetry itself, that was worth saving, and now he could take those youthful verses and burnish them with mature power.

"Will you dedicate the collection to anyone?" I asked. "Are you thinking of another patron?"

He shook his head. "The printer can add something if he chooses. As a member of the King's Men, I have no need to curry favor as I once did. My sole desire is to preserve them in a book." He gave a wry smile. "How much do you think people will pay, five pence?"

He set to, and I did not disturb him during these painful sessions but sat by and read or sewed. Some paths, like death, you must travel alone. In revising, Will did not spare his emotions—he plumbed them—and what had been juvenile and exaggerated sentiments grew into rich and complex revelations. I sometimes think the difference between plays and poetry explains the strengths and weaknesses of my and Will's respective talents. Playwriting is a chameleon art wherein you surrender your identity to inhabit your characters, whereas poetry is the deepest exploration of self. Since I had no identity and Will rarely lost sight of his, it is no mystery where we each excelled.

The volume appeared in May 1609 and contained one hundred fifty-four poems. Almost at the end, I came upon familiar lines.

> *Those lips that Love's own hand did make*
> *Breath'd forth the sound that said, "I hate,"*

My eyes teared. It was our old courtship sonnet, tucked among the Dark Lady sequence, sticking out as immortally and ungracefully as a bandaged thumb. Anyone could see at a glance its eight-syllable line did not match the iambic pentameter of the other poems. That Will would interrupt his story with this awkward tribute to me, to us. I pointed to it, but his only response was a wistful nod, and later, I felt a moment's doubt. Maybe its inclusion was not a tribute but some sort of private joke, a reflection that all his amorous pursuits were in vain, since he was not free to marry anyone else. But I never asked. I would rather stay in the dark and believe what I want—that Will set our sonnet there on purpose, like an anchor in a stormy sea. It is the small triumph of an enduring wife.

I won. I won.

I had needed some occupation while Will worked on his volume and I waited for my own muse to reappear. Thus, I took a bold step and wrote to Arbella Stuart. Though her three-thousand-pound annual income was a fortune to most, at court it hardly sufficed to maintain a household and bestow the endless, expensive gifts required to keep her on everyone's good side. She must also have the latest fashions and in abundance. James had abolished the sumptuary laws entirely, and rampant luxury was the new rule. And whereas other seamstresses often took this as license to use yards of the most expensive fabrics, fringe and lace, I saw it as a challenge to create the most beautiful garments at pinchpenny cost. I could cut a bolt tighter than anyone with no wastage, unpick and remake the same dress thrice over. My economical soul gleamed at the chance to save a shilling and simultaneously fool the world. Moreover, just as at Hardwick and unlike everyone else at court, I was free of ulterior motives and sought neither placement nor favors. Could Arbella use such a seamstress? I received an immediate summons to appear.

At the palace I was shown into a pleasant room where Arbella sat writing, a spaniel at her feet, several ladies seated nearby. What a useless occupation to be a lady-in-waiting, for "waiting" was precisely the nature of the job. You waited to be sent on errands or carry messages, waited to escort your mistress from one room to the next. You waited for her to awaken in the morning so you could dress her, waited for her to yawn at night so you could tuck her into bed. You waited to be called on for a song or amusing conversation or to read aloud from a book. No wonder ladies-in-waiting often fell into intrigues and scandals, for they would die of boredom else. But whatever the inanities of court life, I was happy to see Arbella, to watch her face light up.

"Thank heaven you have come," she said with an airy laugh. "I am in desperate need of gowns."

"I can begin at once, my lady." I hesitated, seeking a polite way to acknowledge Bess's passing, though Arbella had had little contact with her since coming to court. "I am sorry for your grandmother's death and glad to find you so well esteemed by the king and queen."

Arbella flittered her hand. "From one perch to another, that is how a little bird like me must fly. Then I find they have limed the branches, oh, dear."

"If you will have someone show me your wardrobe, I can acquaint myself with your current tastes," I offered. "Are you still as fond of rose satin?"

Arbella blinked, and a wetness sprang to her eyes. "Why, that was my favorite dress when I was a girl. I hadn't thought of it in years."

"I am sure the color becomes you still."

"And I hope I am still becoming to that youthful color." She laughed, and the ladies-in-waiting tittered.

So I went to the palace to sew.

"Today I finished a pair of sleeves in sapphire silk," I might crow to Will in the evening. "You should see them! They are trimmed in black tulle and beaded with pearls."

"I am glad you enjoy it," said Will, sucking his clay pipe, a habit he had acquired during the year I was in Stratford. "But avoid her confidence. She invites trouble, Anne."

"I only offer her my ear. Besides, all is calm save for the usual sniffs and tiffs among her ladies as to who is prettier."

"Who is?"

"What do you care?"

He blew a smoke ring at me, his new trick, and I waved it away. Tobacco was one gift I wished the red Indians had kept to themselves.

But Will was right, and I should have known better, for Arbella soon made me her confidante on more serious matters. I was loath to dissuade her. In the giddy atmosphere of court she needed a levelheaded friend, and I owed it to Bess to look after her. And it started innocently enough, as Arbella let me know in little bursts of her unhappiness. She would speak, then quickly recant, as if afraid of eavesdroppers. Without seeming to, she was asking or at least hoping for my counsel.

"Well, I am in disgrace again," she might say gaily as I tucked and pinned a dress. "I dared to say I ought to have precedence in seating over the princesses when the Spanish ambassador is feasted, and that rude master of ceremonies contradicted me. I shall probably be expelled from court in consequence."

"Oh, no, surely not," I consoled, for that was always my first recourse and the first thing Arbella craved, some reassurance she had not made a fatal error. "His Majesty is far too lenient to take offense at any polite request from you."

"Lenient today, but tomorrow the same scene might provoke him to send me to the Tower."

This was true, for Arbella and the other courtiers as well. James was, to his credit, a forgiving man and often let people take advantage of this quality. More than anything, he desired peace—in his country, in his household—so he could devote himself to his one true passion, hunting. On the other hand, it was his duty as king to get angry when someone offended him, and he strove to do his duty well. Then, feeling bad to have lost a friend, he usually capitulated to make it right. While this might be preferable to the irascible, explosive changes of mood that had marked Elizabeth's final years, at least fear of her temper kept everyone on guard. James's wavering put people off guard, thinking they could press where they had once been forgiven, only to find themselves in peril. Arbella was right to be wary.

She was also bored. When first adopted by her Stuart relatives, she had been grateful to be included as something of an older sister or beloved aunt to the young royals. At thirty-four, however, the allure of being a nursemaid was gone.

"I am set to playing with children," she complained, "in endless games of dolls and bowls."

Here I did sympathize, for despite her sometimes unbalanced behavior, Arbella had a fine mind, and Bess had provided her with an excellent education. She was versed in Latin, Spanish, Italian and French and had been rigorously tutored in the classics. When I conversed with her of the books I had read, she responded with long recitations from memory. Sometimes she seemed to forget I was there and poured out favorite passages like pent-up griefs. Small joy then in enduring the lackluster intellects of the junior Stuarts.

On other days, she berated James and his Privy Council for ignoring her rank.

"When Elizabeth died, I was second to the throne, second after him. Why should I bow to anyone?" she ranted.

"Because James and his family rule now," I replied, and quickly changed the subject. A servant's noggin may roll alongside his master's when treason is the charge.

"If only they would let her marry," I lamented to Will, who shook his head. "Why not? James has enough children to secure the succession."

"Not if they are carried off by sickness or some malcontent seeks to assassinate them and install Arbella as queen. There are still frequent attempts on James's life, and don't forget the Gunpowder Plot."

"But Arbella has everything and nothing. She is the highest lady in England after the queen, yet she has been a prisoner since the day of her birth."

"Perhaps they will let her marry when she is past childbearing and useless."

I wadded up my shawl and threw it at him. Once, he might have been moved to anger or indignation at another human being's plight. Now there was very little fire left; he had mellowed and he liked it. He often joked how old we had become, grandparents, him with a troublesome back, me with my spectacles and a permanently stiff neck from bending over my needle.

"I liked us better when we were young," I said, crossly retrieving my shawl, which he held out to me without rancor.

"You did? But we were poor, and I was unknown. We are comfortable now."

"We are too comfortable. We are complacent. And you"—I did not need to point an accusing finger; my tone was sufficient—"you need to write a new play. Your latest are far from our best."

He spread his hands. "Give me an original idea and I will set to work. I would love to astonish London with something brilliant that shows I haven't lost my touch. But there is only so much one writer can say, Anne, and when it is out you either retire gracefully or spend the rest of your life repeating yourself."

I fell into a troubled silence. Had we dipped our quill for the last time? Tom Dekker was dashing off pamphlets and plays, the latter often in collaboration with Middleton. Beaumont and Fletcher were going strong. Even that slowpoke Ben came up with new plays, composing them alternately with those frivolous masques. His latest with Inigo Jones, *The Masque of Queens*, had presented the spectacle of a dozen impossibly virtuous queens, the jewel of all being one "Bel-Anna." Guess who played that part? The good queens were preceded by twelve hideous witches—my witches, Ben!—just in case the numbskulls in the royal audience missed the point. What a slavering, sycophantic truckling of talent! Ben might try to laugh it off in the tavern, but when you write such stuff over and over and greedily accept payment, your scoffing loses authority. You prostituted yourself like everyone else, Ben, so stop pretending to be God's gift to literature. When we passed occasionally at the palace, he treated me either rudely or guiltily, depending on his mood.

"I am going to bed," said Will, setting down his pipe and rising. "Don't distress yourself, Anne. I have had an excellent run and made my fame. If some of my later plays don't live up, no matter. They will be forgotten, and I will be remembered only for the great ones like *Hamlet*, *Lear* and *Othello*."

"But you didn't write them!" I shouted after him. "I did, I did!" I jumped to my feet, only to see him disappear into the bedchamber with a laughing shake of his head.

I spun about, cursed, looked in vain for something to throw, and cursed again. Then I plunked down in my chair, stuck his still smoldering pipe in my mouth, and sucked a deep breath. *Ack!* I choked violently and spat out a half-burned clump of tobacco while tears stung my eyes and smoke fumed through my nose. Taking the pipe by its stem, I whacked it on the table so hard it broke, then I tossed the pieces in the hearth. What a nasty, disgusting affectation! It would never catch on.

Shortly after the new year 1610 I was in Arbella's dressing room, hemming a gown. It was one of my most beautiful creations, black velvet trimmed in gold ribbon, the bodice and front skirt panel of winter white silk embroidered in a red-and-green holly-berry motif. Arbella stood on a stool while I, on sore knees, circled around the dress with a pincushion tied to my wrist. Whenever I glanced up, she had the smile of a pleased cat. Some worry tickled my brain—that smile was too much for the dress alone.

"My lady?" I began, and she laughed aloud, a burst like an explosion in the small room.

"It is too good to hold in," she cried. "I am to be married at last!"

"To whom?" I asked, bewildered, as she jumped down from the stool and began to prance about. I doubt she would ever have behaved so among her attendants, for they would spread gossip behind her back. But I was trusted, and as I sat back on my heels in amazement and she capered around the room, the story came out.

She had developed an infatuation for William Seymour and he for her, and all was joy and bliss. William Seymour? But he was the younger brother of Edward Seymour, with whom Arbella had tried to elope in 1603, the same episode that some said hastened Queen Elizabeth's death. It had been a complete disaster—the plot revealed, Elizabeth furious, Arbella insane, a Catholic plan to liberate her from Hardwick. If not for Elizabeth's demise, Arbella might have been prosecuted for treason.

Now she thought to reenact that sorry story with Edward's younger brother William? She had taken leave of her senses! And how could William Seymour, though a dreamer by his looks, be so stupid or ill-informed as to ignore those past events? Or did the romantic pair believe the strength of their passion could overcome the king's almost certain wrath? I tried to interject some common sense.

"It is wonderful that Seymour loves you," I agreed, "and please, my lady, forgive my speaking boldly. But I fear you are giving your heart where you may be hurt. James will never allow a marriage that impinges on his family's claim to the throne."

"Aha, this time you are wrong," teased Arbella. "My cousin the king has given me leave to marry any good man in the country."

"He has?"

"Quite so. Now I have chosen William, and he has chosen me. But I must hop back up and let you finish my hem." And she did—she hopped, exuberant as a child.

I worked around the stool behind her, keeping my face hidden while I strove for what to say. "I am very happy for you, my lady, and I confess I barely understand these tangled matters of lineage. I am confused that our late queen forbade you to marry a Seymour, but James has agreed?"

"I told you, he said I may marry any man in the country. I shall have a husband at last." She clasped her hands and swayed on the stool, as if William Seymour were there wooing on bended knee before her. Lineage aside, the groom-to-be was more than a decade younger than she—though who was I to talk?

"And how many people know of your intentions, my lady? Is it a secret or may I share the good news?"

"Oh, don't tell yet, Anne. I have told only my closest friends and you. William and I will make our announcement soon. Our wedding will be the gala event of the season, and you shall create my dress." She giggled. "Rose satin, don't you think?"

I went home and promptly told Will—not the details, only that Arbella was contemplating an engagement I feared could precipitate her downfall.

"I warned you," said Will. "She is addicted to these romantic plots. They are food and drink to her."

"You're right, but this is serious, and she must be convinced to abandon it."

"You can't and you shouldn't try."

"But she trusts me. I am the only one who gives her honest advice. Wouldn't you try to save a friend from self-harm?"

"Of course. But the Lady Arbella is not your friend. She is a royal personage, with all that entails."

"But if I don't stop her, she may be ruined."

"If you do stop her, she will blame you and turn you away, which might be for the best." Will took my hands in his. "These are hardly the old days, Anne, when you had to sew to help keep a roof over our heads. I know you would miss her company and the pleasure of creating beautiful clothes, but any further association with Arbella is dangerous."

"I know. I only thought you could give me some practical advice."

"I have and here it is: Stay out of it."

"But—"

"She is not your daughter. Stay out of it."

I did not stay out of it, but neither did I quite speak up. Instead I kept asking, "Are you sure you have not misunderstood the king or he you?" or some variation thereof until Arbella grew cross and I was forced to seal my lips. In February, the matter erupted. Unable to restrain themselves, Arbella and Seymour held a secret betrothal ceremony, knowledge of which quickly became public. Summoned before the king and Privy Council, Seymour backed down, while Arbella protested that James had given her permission to wed any Englishman of her choice. No, apparently what James had said was any Englishman of *his* choice. The crestfallen couple was excused only after swearing they would not marry without their monarch's consent.

"But he said, he said . . ." Arbella repeated, crying and clinging to me afterward.

"Hush, hush," I soothed, though privately I breathed easier. Whatever James had implied or Arbella misconstrued, the scheme was out, the lovers would be monitored, and if a wedding did take place, it would have the royal blessing.

Then in April Arbella instructed me to commence her wedding gown.

"Has the king granted your desire?" I asked, hardly daring to believe it.

"Not exactly, not yet."

"Then why not wait? You know how fast I can sew. I can stitch it in no time when he does give his consent."

"No! Do not balk me, Anne. Begin now."

I sewed, my thread and my stomach in a twist. This was not good, not wise. If James heard, he was sure to interpret it as a flagrant violation of his orders.

"You will be implicated," said Will when I told him. "You must quit your position. Now, Anne. I order you."

"You order me? That's a good one, Will. Who do you think you are, Petruchio taming his shrew?"

He scowled, hurt, and I apologized; he was only trying to save my neck. Perhaps I did see Arbella too much as a daughter. At least she needed me, where my own two did not. Against Will's wishes and my better judgment, I returned to court. But now I began Penelope's trick, sewing more slowly, finding fault with the fabric or ribbons and sending them back. I skipped days, claiming a recurring headache. But I was no better an actor than Will, and Arbella soon suspected. She threatened to replace me and at the same time humored my excuses as if she were secretly grateful to have them. She was smart enough to be afraid, miserable enough to be reckless. What course others urged upon her when I wasn't there, I cannot tell, but gradually the scale tipped.

"Finish it," she commanded in early June, and I did, but rose satin no longer flattered the agitated wraith she had become. She paced before her mirror as if trying to make her reflection stand still. "Next week the court moves to Greenwich, and we can count on James to go hunting. Then William will come, and we shall be wed."

"Please don't." I clasped her hand and burst into tears of pent-up fright. "I cannot lose you."

"I will," she vowed. "I must. Seven years have I been prisoner here, suffering every manner of neglect and abuse. The time has come to act."

"But—"

"Stop! Cast me into a pit of serpents, chain me with roaring bears or shut me nightly in a charnel house. Bid me lie in a new-made grave beside a dead man in his shroud. All these things that to hear of make me tremble, I will do without fear or doubt to live an unstained wife to my sweet love. Alack, that heaven should practice stratagems upon so soft a subject as myself!"

She threw off my hands and rushed away, leaving me crushed and dumbfounded. She thought—oh, God, she was insane!—she thought she was Juliet. I waited until twilight in the empty dressing room, twisting my hands, but she never came back. The next morning I was denied entrance.

The wedding took place on the summer solstice in Arbella's chambers at Greenwich, performed by a priest and witnessed by a handful of attendants. The date ought to have brought good luck. But within two weeks all was found out, and all was lost. Arbella was imprisoned in a private house south of the city in Lambeth, her husband across the river in the Tower. Her husband—she could say the words at last, and I pray that brief, sweet fortnight of bedding repaid the long years of yearning for a lover's touch.

"I must go to Lambeth and see her," I told Will.

"Are you mad? You won't be allowed anywhere near, and you may be arrested for trying."

"But she is alone and friendless."

"She has brought it upon herself."

"But she is not in her right mind."

"Nor are you to think you can help her. I forbid it, Anne."

"Then you do something. You can talk to the king."

"No, I can't. Thank God the marriage was revealed and pray she is not pregnant."

"Did you reveal it? Did you tell someone?"

"Of course not. How can you imagine it would not be found out? Did they think to stay secretly married forever?"

I dropped my head in my hands, defeated. Of course the marriage would come out. Of course Arbella would be arrested. She had known and admitted it. Foolish, foolish!

But the story was not over, and those who say the plots of plays are fantastic will scarcely believe what happened next. Standing among the crowd at St. Paul's Cross, Will and I followed the bulletins as the drama unfolded.

Despite their imprisonment, Arbella and Seymour contrived to communicate. When this too was exposed, Seymour was condemned to life in the Tower, and Arbella was ordered to pack her belongings. She was to be transferred to the custody of the bishop of Durham, more than two hundred sixty miles to the north. It was the end of the world, and in complete hysteria, she collapsed. She was carried forcibly out of Lambeth on a litter and moved in small stages across London until, at another private house just north of the city, she escaped, disguised in male clothes and a wig and armed with a rapier. Accompanied by a few loyal friends, she fled on horseback to the Thames, where the party hired a boat to take them downriver. Eight hours' hazardous rowing on a moonless night brought them near the open sea, and there Arbella boarded a French ship and awaited her husband's arrival. But Seymour did not come, and though Arbella begged her companions to stay, they overrode her. Her life was at stake if she tarried. Seymour could take another ship and follow. The vessel hoisted sail for Calais, the morning sun shining on the weeping figure at the stern.

Yet the valiant husband was close behind. Disguised in a wig and a false black beard, Seymour had walked out of the Tower behind a tradesman's cart and met a waiting accomplice with whom he riverboated to the sea. Spying a ship offshore that he presumed to be Arbella's, he hired a fisherman to take them out to the vessel. Alas, it was an empty coal ship bound for Newcastle. Seymour immediately offered the captain £40 to alter course for Calais. They were just under way when contrary winds drove them north, and meanwhile at the Tower the alarm had been raised. I think James sent the whole English fleet in pursuit. To him it was a heinous conspiracy to raise foreign support, ally with Catholics, murder him and his family and overthrow his rule. No, no, it was only two people, however misguided, in love.

I would like to think Seymour's ship caught up to Arbella's and they reached arms to each other before the sea drove them apart, but that is not how it went. Unbeknownst to Seymour, Arbella's vessel was captured, and when he landed in Flanders several days later he waited in vain for her to appear. Returned to London, she was committed to the Tower and an official inquiry began. Public sympathy was with the lovers, and it was hoped James would be lenient. But James, rarely resolute about anything in his life, resolutely turned his back on Arbella.

In the Tower, Arbella sank into illness and melancholy. I thought of Ophelia, who lost her wits for love, and of Othello, insane with jealousy. I recalled Lady Macbeth, deranged with guilt, and Lear, delirious on the heath. And what of Kit's wild delusion that he could live forever, and Will's strange spell when he could not write? What of my whole crazed brain wherein imaginary worlds seemed so real? I think we are all mad to some degree, that it lurks inside us like a pale white shoot in the dank earth, awaiting its moment to sprout. Now Arbella's madness pushed up, tender and shivering, growing into the light.

I do not blame William Seymour. Whether he truly loved Arbella or only his chances for the throne, he took the risk and was to suffer a long exile in France. But I bear a mighty hatred for James Stuart for his treatment of Arbella, and when his eldest son, Henry, Prince of Wales, died in 1612 at the age of eighteen, I was cruel enough to think it no less than the king deserved.

For months, each time I walked past the Tower, I searched every high window in hope of glimpsing a waving hand. Then for weeks, I looked down. After a while, I looked straight ahead and walked on.

Chapter 33

With Arbella gone, my life came up short. I twisted and turned; everywhere I bumped into a wall. Though the playhouses had re-opened, my muse remained silent, and I began to fear she had flitted away for good. My pleasure in sewing deserted me also. My fingers were tired—how many hundreds of thousands of stitches had I done over the years?—and even when I wore my spectacles, the fine details of embroidery required many hours' squinting to make the design come out right. Arbella's wedding gown was the last beautiful thing I ever sewed. But to surrender that occupation felt as though a chunk had been cut out of my life, and I had a horror of becoming useless. What would I do for employment? An old wife is of no interest to anyone.

While I had been agitating over Arbella, Will had composed *Cymbeline*. By the results, he too was struggling. He plucked the ancient Celtic king from Holinshed, dropped him as a minor character into a popular plot from Boccaccio, stirred in a wicked stepmother and other fairy-tale elements, and flavored the mix with tragicomedic aspects in the style of Beaumont and Fletcher. It reminded me of a beleaguered apothecary pulling bottles from the shelf in the hope of concocting a miraculous new elixir. When I handed back the manuscript with a puzzled shake of my head, Will let out a groan.

"I thought I had it. Audiences want lighthearted fare, Anne, and I am trying to oblige them."

"I know, and *Cymbeline* does offer many delightful surprises. Perhaps you should go further and play it up? It doesn't yet have a ghost."

Will gave a second groan and went back to work, leaving me sorry not to have been more helpful. For years I especially had labored to develop complicated characters that drew from deep emotional wells. I had thought it the pinnacle of my art. But in the new genres of romance and tragicomedy, Hamlet and Lear had no place, and the characters in *Cymbeline* were caught halfway. I pictured them scratching their heads and querying one another: Should I project utter despair here or just morose melancholy? What are the ramifications of my mood on this convoluted plot? Am I supposed to be real or do I represent the ideal? What is my motivation? In hindsight, *Cymbeline* was a bridging exercise, and when it was performed, the actors overcame most of its flaws. But at the time what Will and I saw was a less than wonderful play.

"I used to pour forth poetry like a golden ewer," he grumbled. "Now I am a rusty pot upon a shelf."

"Nonsense. Stop pitying yourself and get back to work. What would your partners say, what would the other playwrights say, if they saw you dragging like this?"

"Dragging? I have only just finished *Cymbeline*. Can't I enjoy a respite until the next idea comes along?"

"No, you can't."

"Why not? You ought to have some sympathy for me. I am only human."

"You are, but William Shakespeare is not."

"And he is wearing me out. Why are you pestering? What is the matter with you, Anne?"

Will glared, and I exhaled a sorry breath, for I deserved the rebuke. Well, what do men expect? We women are as ambitious as they are, and when we are denied any outlet for our God-given talents, when we have no status of our own but only that which we derive through

our husbands' rank and accomplishments, then the only reasonable occupation left to us is to encourage, exhort and if necessary browbeat
them until they achieve success. Whereas if you let us rise or fall on our
own skills and industry, all nagging would stop. There, I have solved it,
the age-old moan, and so long as men deny the sense of this, they have
no one else to blame when their meek dove wife turns into a scolding
jackdaw.

But of course it wasn't really that simple—nothing between Will
and me ever was—and the true cause of my bad temper was my own
guilt. I hadn't penned anything since we wrote *Antony and Cleopatra*,
only edited and copied for him. *Please, muse, where are you? Do not
leave me like this.*

"Forgive me," I said to Will. "I am in the wrong and had no
grounds to be cross. But I am loath to see *Cymbeline* stand as your final
effort."

He winced.

"It is not a bad play," I added hastily.

"It is not a good one."

"Then what we need is a challenge. What we need . . ." I hesitated,
then pushed on. "What we need is the fear of death. Suppose we have
only one play left in us, Will. What do you want to say? What is your
final message?"

He looked away, troubled, and suddenly I too felt a shadow creep
over me. We were already older than most people lived to be. How
long before the sands ran out?

"I would like to ask forgiveness," said Will. "If I have hurt anyone,
I would like to be reconciled before I depart."

"You did write of reconciliation in *Cymbeline*."

"But not very well."

"Then let's try again. One more great play, Will. You must summon
all your powers, your vision of poetry, your command of stagecraft,
characters, plot. You must write something to seal your reputation
forever."

Throughout that winter of 1610 we traipsed back and forth to the booksellers in search of a subject, reading and rejecting, until one day a pamphlet snagged my eye. Or rather a corner of it did, for that was all that peeked out from beneath the larger volume an inconsiderate customer had deposited at an angle atop it. A mysterious corner—I teased out the suspense for a moment; might this be the treasure I sought? No, but I was pleased nonetheless at what I uncovered: an account of the amazing Bermudas shipwreck. I had been wanting to read about it, for the recent true events had astounded all London, and since Will and the King's Men were at court that evening, I now had fine company to join me at the hearth. I grabbed my mug and settled down for a bold seafaring tale.

In 1606 King James had granted a charter to the Virginia Company to explore and settle the New World. They sent Captain John Smith, who, along with his crew, founded the colony of Jamestown in the territory of the fierce red Indians. Captured by these terrifying natives, Smith was saved from death at their hands only by the intervention of an Indian princess called Pocahontas. Much later, she came to London with her English husband, John Rolfe, and here she sickened and died in our strange land. But back to Virginia—the colonists were soon starving and in desperate need of relief, so in 1609 the Virginia Company sent eight ships to resupply them. A violent storm scattered the small fleet—howling winds, tossing seas. Seven of the vessels eventually made it to Virginia; the eighth was last seen sinking in the waves.

On that ship the men bailed until they were spent. Then, sinking down on the deck, they yielded themselves to the sea's mercy. At this utmost extremity, the captain spied land, the dreadful coast of the Bermudas, known to be inhabited by witches and devils drawn to the island by its monstrous thunderstorms. Choosing the lesser of two evils, the crew drove the ship toward the rocky coast, where by God's grace it ran ashore between two rocks and stuck fast without breaking. The men scrambled off the boat, and there, instead of a hell on earth, they found a fertile paradise of fruit and fowl, fish and wild swine. They stayed almost a year, salvaging from their shipwreck sufficient timber and tackle to build two smaller vessels on which they finally made their way to Virginia. What astonishment and rejoicing, for all had believed them to be utterly cast away.

I clapped my hands. O, marvelous tale! Then I sighed. Tomorrow, another trip to the booksellers to find something worthwhile.

~

"I think I have it," said Will a few days later, dangling a small book between his thumb and forefinger.

"You have found our topic?" I held out my palm. As long as it was something he loved, I was content.

Will pulled the book back, grinning. "First, let me tell you the story. A king of Bohemia suspects his wife of an affair with his good friend, the king of Sicily, so he imprisons the queen, who in jail gives birth to a daughter. The king has the poor infant set adrift in an open boat and puts the queen on trial. Then word comes from the oracle of Apollo that the queen is innocent and the daughter is the king's own child. Meanwhile, their young son dies and the queen falls down dead in grief, never knowing her little daughter has been washed ashore and adopted by a poor shepherd. Sixteen years later, the beautiful shepherd girl falls in love with the son of her father's former friend, the king of Sicily. . . ."

The smile had slipped off my face. "Will? Isn't that *Pandosto*?"

"Of course." He handed me the book. "Why not?"

I opened the novel. *Pandosto* by Robert Greene, one of his most popular works. Everyone would recognize the story instantly. It had been printed some four or five times. And to choose for our final play a piece by the man who had sought to ruin us, the upstart crow? This would never do.

"Why not?" Will repeated, though I hadn't said a word. "I won't kill the queen, as Greene does, or have the king commit suicide from remorse, though I believe the young prince has to go. For a title, I was thinking *The Winter's Tale*."

I sighed. I did like the title, most apt as we retired into the winter of our lives.

"Well?"

"It is just not very original," I said, seizing the most obvious objection while I strove to sort out my feelings.

"Few plays are. You know nothing is sacred among writers. We all gnaw one another's bones to suck our mouthful of marrow."

"Yes, but if this does turn out to be our last, I want it to be something special. *Love's Labor's Lost* and *A Midsummer Night's Dream*—those were our own invention. Oh, Will. Robert Greene, of all people!"

I thumped down the book and made sputtering noises, and he shook his head at me.

"Women," he said. "Do you never in your lives forget or forgive the tiniest detail?"

No, we don't. Sad—because I had hoped to end our career as we had begun, writing together. But since I could not be content with Will's choice after all, there was nothing for it but to write my own last play. Send me an idea, I ordered the muse, and to smooth my prickled mind, I reread my Bermudas pamphlet meanwhile.

A tempest, a sinking ship, and in the distance an enchanted island capped by a black thundercloud. A magician, his daughter, a cannibal, an airy sprite. It has often seemed sorcery to me how a play arises in the brain, a mist swirling into shape, a spell gathering force. From there, the magic took sway, and I saw this play happening as I had never quite seen a play before, the ship moving, waves tossing, rocks and caves. Presented at court by the King's Men, it could resemble a masque. They could create a whole ship if necessary and a forest of trees for my sprite to caper in the branches. There might be leftover sets from previous productions we could employ. I would coerce Ben to help me, and if he balked I would box his ears. But unlike the amateur theatricals created for our silly royal family, mine would be a real play with a full-bodied plot, shimmering poetry and a cast of consummate actors. This was it, the way to move the whole art of playwriting forward.

Oh, my fingers, what cramps I gave them, what pain to my eyes. I should have taken it more slowly, but I feared to rest. What if I died before I finished? What if tomorrow I fell deathly ill or was run over by a cart? Once when I was forced to go out to procure food, I nearly did get trampled. My head was so full of Prospero, Miranda, Caliban and Ariel that I walked into the path of a galloping horse.

"Look out, you crazy old woman!" the rider yelled, and catching my balance I glimpsed the departing livery of a royal messenger on urgent business and around me the raised eyebrows of the crowd.

Crazy old woman? If only they knew.

At the end of that day, I prayed.

"I have never asked for much, God," I began, then halted. I had asked, or at least hoped, for much—health and prosperity for my family, happiness for Will and myself. And I got it, mostly, though I was not always sure from what source. To now put in a special request that God spare me until I completed my play might be considered supremely impertinent. Besides, did I really want to draw God's attention to what I was about? Better to keep my dark arts to myself.

Well, I do not say every aspect of *The Tempest* came out perfectly. Like a bricklayer setting a wall, I mortared and nudged and realigned. Rather a down-to-earth image for such a creative process, but I am running out of flowery ones, and if you can do better, go write poetry yourself. Of the characters in the play, Miranda was easy. The same excellent boy who had acted Cleopatra and the girlish roles in *Pericles* and *Cymbeline* put her voice in my head. But Caliban gave me exceeding trouble, for though Monsieur Montaigne argues in his *Essays* that savages are noble beings uncorrupted by the vices of civilization, mine proved crude and lewd. He hissed and spat at me and hopped about the room. *Give me liquor*, he cajoled, so I let him imbibe with the jester Trinculo and the drunken butler Stephano. Then, to repay me, the beastly ingrate persuaded Stephano to attempt to kill Prospero. Of course, I could not let them succeed, and Caliban's low nature did provide a helpful contrast to airy Ariel. But I suggest Monsieur Montaigne go live a while amongst the savages before issuing further glowing opinions of them.

I also followed Will's example for my play's apparent theme, the reconciliation of the older generation through the union of their children. Hardly original, after all—I did it in my first great work, except the children die. *Romeo and Juliet*, sixteen years past—how time runs away from us like a taunting child. But the real theme of *The Tempest*, the long study, masterful wielding and eventual surrender of art, is what I like to think gives my play its exquisite poetry and power. Badly acted, Prospero will appear a cheap conjuror or a once-mighty man fixed on a cold revenge. Played with every nuance with which I endowed him, he compels you to look deeper, to peer into the dark glass. Can you see the face, the reflection? All my life I had been cast away on an island in the very midst of the world, a lonely existence consoled by playwriting, in secret practice of a magical craft. More than any other, this play holds my soul.

At the end, Prospero did not really want to break his staff and drown his book.

"But if you do not," I whispered, "then as you grow old, others will inevitably wrest them from you. If not by outright theft and violence, then by seduction and stealth. Even with magic, you cannot live forever. If you are to avoid a pathetic end, best to do it yourself."

Prospero regarded me but made no reply. I composed him a majestic farewell speech and hoped he would obey.

> *I have bedimmed*
> *The noontide sun, called forth the mutinous winds,*
> *And 'twixt the green sea and the azured vault*
> *Set roaring war. To the dread rattling thunder*
> *Have I given fire, and rifted Jove's stout oak*
> *With his own bolt. The strong-based promontory*
> *Have I made shake, and by the spurs plucked up*
> *The pine and cedar. Graves at my command*
> *Have waked their sleepers, oped, and let 'em forth*
> *By my so potent art. But this rough magic*
> *I here abjure—*

Eyes glittering, he slowly tore a page from his book, crumpled it and put it in his mouth. Then he dissolved back into the mist of my brain, and I never saw him more.

⁓

Will likewise got *The Winter's Tale* admirably right, though it strikes me that in both this play and *Pericles* we have wives who seem to die and then are miraculously resurrected and reunited with their husbands many years later. Coincidence? Are we all forgiven, Will? Does it make up for the absent wives and mothers in so many of the plays, yours, mine and ours? On the other hand, if Lear had had a wife, she would have prevented his knuckleheaded estrangement from his daughters. Prospero's wife would have hauled him out of his study to confront his usurping brother, and he would not have been deposed. Besides, plays are always short on female characters. Why waste an actor in an unnecessary female role? It is not always wise to read too much into things, you know.

Will did like *The Tempest*—why not, he wrote it, didn't he?—and the King's Men enacted it for James at Whitehall on Hallowmas Night, 1611. I stood in the background, critiquing the production. On second thought, the masque elements may have been a bit overdone. The story would have gained even more depth and mystery had it been performed outdoors in a real forest with a rocky outcrop or two, preferably under a threatening sky. Nonetheless, Dick Burbage did justice to Prospero, and the boy actor made me think back to young Christopher, who had once played our girls' roles. Poor Christopher—he had married and gone into his father's candle-making business and died of a tumor before his twenty-fifth birthday.

"Not a bad play," said a voice in my ear, and I turned to see the leering grin of Ben Jonson.

"What are you doing here?" I asked, only slightly nettled, for he had every reason to be at court.

"Spying on the competition." He tipped his head toward the stage. "I see you have made use of some of our scenery from the masques?"

"Yes. How are you and Inigo Jones getting along these days?"

"Mr. Jones, Mr. Jones, Mr. Inigo Jones. How I would like to break all his bones." Ben started on a singsong and ended in a ferocious scowl accompanied by a stick-snapping motion of his hands. "The man will drive me mad. He is a conceited, loudmouthed know-it-all."

I laughed. "And you are not?"

"Me? I am sunshine and sweetness incarnate."

"And a good writer. I saw *The Alchemist*."

Ben nodded. "It seems we both had magic on our minds, though I debunk it and you prefer to believe." His gaze went back to the play, and we watched for several minutes in silence. It was the farewell scene, and when I glanced at him again, I started.

"Ben?" I offered him my handkerchief.

He used it, cursing in a low voice. "I could rush forward this minute, Anne, and swear before all the court I know the true author."

"Then you and I will be laughed out together. Listen, Ben, just listen."

When the performance ended, Will stayed to be feted. I could have stayed also, but I walked home alone, not wanting any babble and backslapping to disturb me. That night was excellent! At times, the careworn face of the king even lit—think of it, with my poetry I could make a king forget for a few hours the worries of the world. And I was carrying a sensation that would have to last me the rest of my life—the sound of applause.

If I had the strength, I would tear a page from the folio now, stuff it in my mouth and take it with me to heaven—or to the devil, where I will dance with my singed feet on the hot coals.

Chapter 34

$\mathcal{E}$arly in the new year 1612, Will and I paid an extended visit to Stratford. A lull in the winter weather made for an unexpectedly pleasant journey, but we were there less than a week when Gilbert died.

Oh, sad, sad. There he was, standing by the table at New Place as Judith and I sorted through the apple bin to uncover any that might be bruised and rotting. We planned to bake them up with cinnamon in pies.

"One for me," cried Gilbert, snatching a plump fruit that threatened to roll off the table. He chomped it between his teeth so the juice ran down his chin and turned his head in profile as if to portray a grinning roast pig on a platter. Then he paused, took the apple from his mouth and appraised it. "That's odd," he said. The fruit popped from his hand, and he clutched at the air, Judith and I laughing at his foolery. The next instant, he let out a cry and jerked as if a string had snapped inside him and bent him askew. Falling, he hit the table, and apples tumbled and bounced across the floor. He lingered a day with the right half of his body paralyzed, trying to talk from his twisted mouth. In the middle of the night, while Will and I kept vigil, his body gave a final spasm, and his face froze in death.

Will settled his brother's modest estate and passed out little remembrances to Gilbert's chums, there having been no time to draw up a legal will. Ten years younger than me, Gilbert was. Aside from the natural sorrow I felt at his passing, at the memory of our brief love, I was forced to assess how the years had crept over me. My hair was graying, and look at my skin. What was that brown splotch on my forehead that had not been there before? My cheeks had begun to sag; was I developing jowls? I pushed and patted at them in alarm and to no avail. And my legs—a nasty blue vein that popped and curdled on my calf. Well, who was going to look under my skirt anyway? I harrumphed at my reflection, which was in itself a dismal, old person's noise.

Yet the arrival of spring brought consolations, and Will and I often went for walks in the countryside or to the market. We doted on our little granddaughter, Lizbeth; four years is a fine age to be. You can talk and eat with good manners. You are brave enough to pick up a toad and cup it in your hands. You are silly enough to pinch your nose and giggle, "Eyeuw!" when your grandfather steps in a dog pile, and smart enough to observe how your antics have the power to turn his half-uttered curse into a hearty guffaw. Each time one of us proposed returning to London, the idea would lose its allure as soon as Lizbeth skipped into the room.

"I don't know what is next, Anne," said Will. "Some days I am ready to quit and idle out my remaining years in Stratford. Other days, I wonder if the success of *The Winter's Tale* and *The Tempest* are not the end of my career but a new phase, a sign that I am meant to continue."

I murmured, avoiding a direct answer. I knew *The Tempest* was my last play. But what if Will, back in stride, had some future great work ahead of him? He was also still a member of the King's Men and expected to participate in the company. So once again we went to London, where he and his colleagues were soon busy preparing for the marriage of Princess Elizabeth in February 1613 to the elector Palatine of Bohemia, an event that caused the perpetually empty royal treasury to become even emptier. Will's contribution was *The Famous History of the Life of King Henry VIII*, which he cranked out with help from John Fletcher. Unfortunately, he should have taken his cue from Prospero or from any good actor who knows when to exit the stage. *Henry VIII* is less a play than a blatant tribute to the Tudors, not a portrayal of history but a shameless polishing of it. Will cut it off at the christening of Princess Elizabeth, a smart choice, for how was he going to explain the beheading of her mother and whoring Henry's subsequent wives? In addition to *Henry VIII,* the King's Men performed more than a dozen of our plays, along with Ben's *The Alchemist* and the latest works by Beaumont and Fletcher.

Will offered to take me to the festivities, but I declined. The royal wedding only stirred sad memories of another, thwarted nuptial and of Arbella still languishing in the Tower. Moreover, I had caught a chill shortly after Twelfth Night and spent most of January and February shivering in bed, a goatskin flask filled with hot water tucked to my stomach. How miserable! I detest being sick and secretly feared I would be the next of the family to go. Instead, only a year after Gilbert's death, it was younger brother Richard who followed him to the cemetery. A month shy of his thirty-ninth birthday, he took ill with a sweating fever that raged and devoured him. The shock was even greater than at Gilbert's passing, for after years of bachelorhood Richard had begun courting an amiable young widow, and we had anticipated a spring wedding.

"It can't be," said Will, ashen faced as we read the letter. He had caught my illness, though not as severe a case, and we both sat shawled before the hearth. "Now I am the only one left. Four brothers and no son or grandson among us. Not a single male descendant to carry on our name."

"Is it so important?" I asked, rubbing my head against his shoulder in consolation. "We have Lizbeth and the prospect that Judith might marry or Susanna and John produce more grandchildren, even if their surname is not Shakespeare. Besides, what's in a name? A rose by any other . . ." I took it as a sign of my lingering illness that I would so tritely quote myself.

"But what have we done it all for, if not our family and heirs?"

"We did it because we were selfish. We did it for ourselves." I laid my hand on his as he hung his head. "I don't mean that badly. It has profited everyone far more than had you become a glover. You can look back and be proud."

Spring came—didn't we just have one?—and Will bought a house over the great gate of Blackfriars. At this stage in our lives, it was the last thing we needed, but I put it down to his usual urge to invest and bit my tongue. At least I could spend long afternoons sitting in the adjacent garden, soaking up the sun—ha, sun in England? Still, I turned my face to every pallid beam. I watched the daffodils push up. I heard the bees begin to buzz and the birds sing. One morning I observed five little sparrows in a rain puddle in the garden, comical creatures, ruffling and fussing their feathers in the makeshift bath. On completing their ablutions, they hopped out of the puddle, squatted in the dirt and proceeded to give themselves a vigorous dusting. No wonder they are called birdbrains. I laughed, a pale sound, but at long last my health was returning.

On a June day I was reading in the garden, that revolutionary volume of poetry by Aemelia Lanyer published two years before. The wife of a court musician, Lanyer argued through her poetry that women deserved equality with men and that Adam was more guilty of sin than Eve. It had occurred to me she might have been the Dark Lady of Will's sonnets. She was of Italian extraction, she had once been mistress to the Lord Chamberlain, the patron of Will's old company, and Will could have met her at court. But when I had casually shown him the volume, he had given no sign of recognition, and since I hadn't particularly cared at the time, it hardly mattered now. Finally, a book in a woman's own name! I was relishing the section entitled "Eve's Apology in Defense of Women" and thumping my fist to Lanyer's call for female equality when Will came to find me.

"They are playing *Henry VIII* at the Globe this afternoon," he said. "Do you feel like going?"

"Only if we pamper our bettermost bums with a seat in the gallery. My groundling days are behind me."

"Behind you indeed," Will teased, patting my posterior, "but never fear. We will even get cushions."

We strolled across London Bridge and were waved in by the money collector at the Globe, for of course the famous playwright and his sister might sit wherever they chose. We wedged through the crowd to the upper gallery and found a spot along a bench. I gazed down at the stage, furnished with banners, a canopied throne and a small cannon. "Remember when—" I began, then stopped before the flood of memories could overtake me. Instead I peered around the packed yard. Though Will had recently dabbled on *The Two Noble Kinsmen* with John Fletcher, no final masterpiece had sprung forth, and as if reading my thoughts, he joined me in looking down. Which one of them would be the next Shakespeare? That eager boy with his elbows propped on the stage, the young woman gazing starstruck at the painted heavens?

The actor designated to speak the prologue strode to the front of the boards. "I come no more to make you laugh . . ."

If only he had, if only they had picked a different play. The beautiful day called for a romantic comedy, not Tudor politics and wrangling lords. Near the end of Act I, to announce the arrival of King Henry at Cardinal Wolsey's house, the cannon was discharged.

"Will!" I remonstrated, clapping my hands to my ears too late to avoid the thundering boom. We had both ducked as something flew over our heads, likewise most of the audience.

"Special effects," he said, grinning.

Nettled, I returned my attention to the play. King Henry and his companions had entered disguised as masquers, and he and Anne Boleyn commenced dancing. Flirting already, Henry. Have you forgotten you are married to Catherine of Aragon?

"Look!" cried a man in the yard, but instead of pointing to the stage, his finger aimed toward the section of roof above us. Heads swiveled, and the actors stopped speaking and gaped upward.

"What is it?" I asked Will, as those near us glanced around in similar confusion. Then with a sinister crackle, a small clump of flaming thatch dropped out of the roof onto the lap of a short man behind us.

"Fire! Fire! Run!"

"No!" Will cried, as people jumped up shrieking. "Stay and help put it out!" Already someone was spraying a bottle of ale on the short man's lap to douse the flame, and except for his burned breeches, he seemed unharmed. But a panic had begun, and though I added my voice to Will's, no one listened above the yelling. We were pushed and half trampled, as from the stage, yard and lower galleries, actors and audience fled for the exits.

"Anne, Anne!" Will caught my hand as another chunk of burning straw dropped and the stampede threatened to separate us. Hot smoke puffed downward, and we were pummeled toward the stairs by a gasping, coughing mass of elbows and arms. "Out of my way, peasant scum!" a man shouted, and women shrilled as sparks landed on them. As more lumps of roof fell, a frightful squealing added to the din—rats tumbling from the fiery thatch and wildly clawing their way over the mob. I choked and squeezed my eyes to keep them from burning and held with all my might to Will's hand. Behind us, the benches had caught fire, and the boards cracked and popped like logs on a hearth. The press of bodies surged down the stairs and spilled out the door, and we landed on our knees, soot streaked and panting.

"Get water!" Will shouted, rising, as Dick and Cuthbert Burbage, Robert Armin and the other actors joined us, but there was no water, no buckets—what could we do, run dip mugs in the Thames? I pulled myself up, and we watched in helpless agony as the halo of fire around the roof collapsed into the top gallery and that gallery into the one below. It was still a beautiful day, and as the licks of flame danced upward against the bright blue sky, the seared air waved before our eyes and a few puffy white clouds looked down unconcerned. In less than an hour, the Globe was a black circle on the ground.

"It was a piece of wadding from the cannon," said Dick dumbly, and Cuthbert began swearing, though no one paid him any attention.

The Globe, our Globe, gone. We had built it with our own hands, or so it had felt that freezing December night of 1598 when we dismantled the old Theatre to save its timbers, that night my cloak caught fire and Will got the splinter in his palm. Tears stung my eyes, but Will beat me to it. To my amazement, he burst into sobs and sat on the ground, and I dropped down beside him and mewled along. We rocked and clutched each other, wailing.

"Take heart," said Armin, patting Will's shoulder, though his own eyes were wet. "The Globe can be rebuilt."

"And no one was hurt, thank God," Dick added. "A few bruised and some lost their cloaks."

Will mastered himself and got to his feet, brushing his clothes to shake off his embarrassment. "They're right. Come, Anne." He extended a hand, but I pushed it away. If he was too cowardly to let his tears be seen, I would take up wailing for him and not leave off until it was good and done. I hugged my knees, bowed my forehead to my skirt and howled. "Come, Anne," Will tried again. "The Globe can be rebuilt. Don't cry."

"All right," I said, sniffling myself into a semblance of recovery. But when the other actors trailed away, Will rejoined me on the ground.

"Do you remember?" he began, drawing me to him, and now the memories poured out, while we took turns murmuring, "I know, I know."

Why, God? Yes, it was only a building, but weren't there plenty of others in London to burn? Or are the Puritans right and you deliberately targeted our sinful doings with a well-aimed spark into our sticks and straw? Or was it a judgment on that old whoremonger Henry VIII, or maybe you just didn't like the play? But of course what I was really crying for was us—all pity is self-pity in the end. As Will said, a new theater would arise, and one soon did. But we were too old to be part of it. William Shakespeare was done.

Chapter 35

$\mathcal{I}$n the autumn of 1613 Will left the King's Men, and we retired permanently to Stratford. Occasionally, we heard news from London. Tom Dekker was in prison—he never had been more than a step ahead of his creditors—but continued writing pamphlets in jail. Francis Beaumont married an heiress and gave up writing, leaving John Fletcher to carry on alone. Ben continued to quarrel with Inigo Jones and had a new play, *Bartholomew Fair*. In 1615, Robert Armin died, as did Arbella Stuart, sick and insane in the Tower. They said that over long months she refused medical treatment and starved herself until the flesh wasted from her body. I mourned Armin's death but gave thanks for Arbella's. Finally, she was delivered from the tragic life in which she had been imprisoned. She was buried in the tomb of her ill-fated cousin Mary, Queen of Scots, in Westminster Abbey. On the table beside her bed in the Tower, they found a well-thumbed copy of *Romeo and Juliet*.

Our return to Stratford prompted John and Susanna to move out of New Place and build their own home, Hall's Croft. I took command of New Place, much to Judith's displeasure. Too bad, daughter. If you want a home of your own, get busy and secure yourself a husband. Seduce one if you must; it worked for me. But in truth, I had no experience running a large household, and at first my confidence was shaky as I assigned the servants' duties and conferred with the gardener about my preferences for flowers and herbs. I called often upon my memories of Bess building Hardwick Hall. Although New Place was obviously much smaller, the same principles of managing your workers and getting results applied.

Above all, I could not risk letting Judith butt in or Susanna dispense too much advice or it might appear that I, like Mary Shakespeare before me, had become superfluous. Once I overheard my daughters chiding together, unaware I had stopped on the other side of the half-open door.

"She ought to rest. She was ill all last winter in London. My only desire is to take care of her." This, righteously, from Judith.

Susanna, solicitous: "And the commotion displaces Father. He spends more and more time in the tavern to escape the hubbub in the house."

Judith, generously: "Why don't you invite her to Hall's Croft more often to see Lizbeth? That would keep her occupied and give you some respite from the child."

Susanna, adroitly: "But I do not desire any respite from my precious child and have servants to tend her when I do. Why don't you encourage her to visit her brother in Shottery? It is an easy stroll, and she could spend all day there."

You see how I was valued in my own home. But it was my home, and I rather enjoyed outfoxing my daughters in these little domestic wars and could not fail to win as long as Will was on my side. Which he was, because like most men he never guessed at the minor campaign that was being waged. He was living out the sunset he had long envisioned, and his daily stop at the tavern was the high point of his routine. He often put his arm around me when we paused to converse with friends or neighbors in the market.

"Anne and I," he would begin, and there would come his arm around my waist and a beam upon his face as he described some new furnishing or wall painting we had purchased or our progress in re-thatching the roof. He was fifty, bald and potbellied, and I may have been falling in love with him once again.

~◦

"If only we could find Judith a husband."

Sitting in the garden on an autumn eve, I handed Will a glass of wine. We were now two years in Stratford, and it had been another pleasant day. A market day, and after calling at Hall's Croft for Lizbeth, we had strolled among the vendors and to the bakery for a sweet, then on to the blacksmith's shop to watch the snorting horses being shod. For her seventh birthday, we had bought Lizbeth a canary in a wire cage, and she insisted on bringing the pretty yellow bird on our walks. People smiled at the sight of us, and I suppose it was that fond family image that made me wish for a like contentment for Judith, for although I rarely forbade her anything, she continued to chafe under my man-agement. How she would do things differently when mistress of her own home was a frequent remark.

"Yet she rejects everyone we suggest," Will reminded me, sucking his pipe.

"I know, but she is nearly thirty-one," I prodded. "Can't we do anything?"

"Who else is a likely candidate?"

I named a few men, and we mulled their qualifications and tried to predict Judith's reaction—sheer guesswork, given her fickle nature. Poor child, she was one of those who could never seem to find true contentment. If life were a brimming treasure chest set in her lap, she would still manage to find the lone chipped stone. But unbeknownst to us, Susanna had also taken up the matter. No doubt she felt it reflected badly upon her and John to have an unmarried relation at an age when proper folk were finally wed. Fortunately, she had a suitor at hand.

Thomas Quiney came of a respectable family and had much to rec-ommend him. His late father had been an acquaintance of Will's, his grandfather a friend of John Shakespeare's. Though four years younger than Judith, he was no green boy come a-wooing but a solid business-man, a vintner and the owner of a tavern. But something bothered me. I could see why John Hall or any man would love Susanna—she made it easy. I could understand why Will had fallen in love with me—I am an enchanting woman. It made perfect sense why my father had cher-ished Duck and even why quiet William Hart had paired with Magpie Joan; if you are shy, it can be a blessing to have someone do your talk-ing. But I could not see how any man could love Judith when she did not love herself and did not think highly of anyone who did.

Yet Judith now became ardent toward Quiney, and he professed to love her. Though I was sure his sentiment included a private rubbing of his hands to think how marriage to Will Shakespeare's daughter would improve his fortunes, I did not fault him for this. It is the way of the world. Marry up, Bess of Hardwick would have said, always marry up. Except that Quiney's loud declarations of affection made me think the gentleman did protest too much. There was something bristly about their entire courtship, and I tried to speak to Judith about it, to ascer-tain whether she was truly satisfied with her choice.

"Of course I am."

"Happy enough to forgo all others?"

"Why not, when I have forgone everything else until now? Don't you like Thomas?"

"Most assuredly. I only want your happiness."

"Then I will take what happiness I can get."

"But do you feel you know the man well enough?"

"Did you?"

The words stung, as intended, as deserved. "One can never know a person's whole character until you have lived with him for a lifetime," I replied evenly, and let the matter drop.

But the real trouble was that none of us knew Quiney, and the more I tried to engage him, the less I succeeded. Though honesty sat on the front of his face, he had a smooth way of answering a different question than you had asked. At the same time he was jocular, presum-ing himself to be already a member of the family. Now, a writer is nothing if not an astute observer of human nature, and I believe I had proven myself better than most. Yet there was something evasive about Thomas Quiney, and he kept me at a distance, even as he sat down to a meal under our roof. Judith fussed about him, playing the giddy sweetheart, a role that did not become her years. What was wrong? What was wrong?

"Is there no one else for Judith?" I said to Will, twisting my hands.

"Why, what objection can you have to Quiney?" he replied. "I'll have one son-in-law a tavern keeper to supply me with ale, the other a doctor to cure my headache when I have imbibed too much of it."

"Don't joke. I know people, Will, and it is precisely because I can't pin down my worry about Quiney that I am sure something is not right."

"The only thing that is not right is my stomach. Did that sauce at supper sit ill with you?"

I clucked and waved him on to bed. If he continued to ignore my admonitions about his pipe and ale and too much rich food, it was no surprise his innards rebelled.

Judith's wedding date was set for February 10. In January, to my consternation, Will began to draft his will. He assured me it was only prudent. With his last child about to marry, he must see to both his daughters' futures. Oh, do not tempt fate. Do not call attention to yourself. Mere days after he began composing the document, he took to bed with another upset stomach.

"It feels bad," he said with a grunt.

"Nonsense, you only want to lie abed to escape the wedding preparations." I plumped his pillow and handed him a cup of broth, the most John Hall would allow him to consume. "Leave that alone"—I gestured at the latest draft of his will—"and get better. We must not do less for Judith's nuptials than we did for Susanna's."

"I want to finish it." He nodded to the paper. "What shall I leave you?"

"A pot of gold. Now sip your broth and stop malingering."

Will recovered, and the wedding of Judith and Quiney took place as planned. It was not as good as Susanna's. I don't know; it seemed less beautiful somehow. Maybe it was the weather, a sloppy winter day, whereas Susanna's June walk to church had been sunny and bright. But Susanna could make any day sunny, whereas Judith, even on a midsummer's morn, had a cloud above her life. I sat in the front pew with a sense of foreboding, and Judith was a case of nerves, not relaxing even when the ceremony was over and the feasting began. I had hired in a small army of cooks and servants, and there was no fault with the quantity and quality of the food. The partying went on until nearly midnight, though the newlyweds had left earlier for Quiney's house.

"All's well that ends well," said Will.

"Oh, stop it," I said.

Three weeks after the wedding, Will had another attack of bad stomach, and this time he had not cheated on rich food. He cringed in bed, moaning until he found a comfortable position; then he demanded pen and paper.

"Not that again," I begged. "You must rest."

"I must finish my will. What do you want me to leave you, Anne?"

"Diamonds and rubies. You will make yourself worse if you hunch up like that."

"It is the only way I can lie without pain."

"I will get you another pillow and more blankets. This room is too cold."

"What do you want me to leave you, Anne?"

"I want you to leave off this nonsense. You are not dying."

I bundled him in blankets, then hurried to Hall's Croft. Both John and Susanna returned with me, but while John went upstairs to attend Will, Susanna drew me aside.

"John and I have just heard disturbing gossip, and though surely false, it must be stilled."

"Gossip about what?"

Susanna pressed her hand to her brow and sighed. "They say Thomas Quiney has brought shame to a young woman named Margaret Wheeler, and she is seven months gone with his child."

"God, no!"

I lost my breath, and Susanna helped me to a chair.

"Does Judith know?" I demanded. "Is it proven? Has Quiney confessed?"

"I don't know. I pray it is only rumor. We must go to Judith and someone must confront Quiney. We will take his side until we determine the truth."

But I knew. That was it, the clue we had all overlooked, the one thing absent from Quiney's courtship of Judith: despite his avowals of love, not a single wink or jest from the bridegroom hinting at the carnal pleasures of the wedding night to come. Even porcelain John and Susanna had blushed a little together. The reason for Quiney's lack of interest was now obvious. He must have been satisfying himself regularly with Margaret Wheeler even as he wooed our daughter.

When John came down from examining Will—an irritable stomach, more herbal potions to be administered—we three conferred. John would approach Quiney at his tavern. Susanna and I went to deal with Judith, who nearly scratched out our eyes. She loved Thomas, he loved her, the Wheeler girl was lying and it was somebody else's bastard she was trying to foist upon him. Then in the next instant she collapsed and cried that she was not loved, never had been, that Quiney and everyone else had deceived her. She blamed Susanna for promoting the match, and Susanna, shaken to the core that something she had undertaken had turned out so badly, became flustered and tried to excuse and exonerate herself. Meanwhile, at the tavern, Quiney was denying the affair. Perhaps he hoped to brazen it out and discredit Margaret Wheeler. But she had her supporters, and they swore Quiney had promised marriage, a serious charge. Quiney then buckled and confessed all.

If the scandal had happened to anyone else, what a comedy I could have penned! Midnight assignations and bawdy beddings, a respectable daughter and an ignorant country girl both deceived by an unscrupulous vintner. Toss in a well-meaning sister and her upright physician husband and the aged parents wringing their hands. Add some low scenes featuring the buffoonish townspeople, then wrap it up with the last-minute revelation that the elderly parents were actually the foremost writer in England. It could have been my best ever, but it is not so funny when it happens to you. It's not a comedy, it's a tragedy, and as the scandal burned through Stratford, each telling added another faggot to the fire until all ears were ablaze. Judith was pitied, Quiney castigated. We were mortified.

We tried to keep the news from Will, but it was impossible. He got out of bed, swearing against Quiney, and yanked himself into his clothes. He made it halfway down the stairs, bracing himself along the wall, before a pain doubled him and he fell. Horrified, I half carried, half dragged him back to his mattress. He fought me with his fists, punching in useless frustration as I tried to wrap the blanket around his flailing arms.

"I will murder him!"

"No, Will, you must let us take care of it."

"But it is not supposed to end like this, not after I have worked so hard to restore our good name!"

"Hush, Will, hush."

"Our daughter betrayed. Our son-in-law a scoundrel. A bastard child living openly in the same town."

"Perhaps the marriage can be annulled, Judith's reputation saved."

"Damn him!" Will gave up fighting and clutched his gut. "I will have John concoct some poison."

"What good would that do but make us murderers besides?"

I soothed and patted, though I was near despair for both Judith and Will. For a moment, my brain lighted with a vision of poisoning Quiney myself. Having made recent visits to Hall's Croft for medicines for Will, I knew exactly where John kept the fatal substances. Why, good father that he was, he had pointed out how the shelf, high on the wall, was out of Lizbeth's reach. I would mix the lot of them, arsenic, nightshade, foxglove, and pour it down Quiney's throat. Then Will would rest easy and get better. Oh, God, why did you invest us with conscience when the blood cries out for revenge?

"Hush, Will, rest. It may not be so bad as it seems. We will take legal advice, and perhaps the girl can be paid to go elsewhere."

I hated myself for the words as I spoke them. Margaret Wheeler's witnesses had confirmed that Quiney promised marriage. I had gotten pregnant by Will without even that much to go on. And what had been her devastation when she heard of his marriage to another woman? Quiney had kept both her and Judith in the dark. Yet she must go away, she must leave Stratford. To think of her parading in town, carrying in her arms a child with Quiney's features—

"It is awful, Will, but we can surmount this. Margaret Wheeler shall be bought off, and generously. Judith will hold her head up. Quiney will bow his down. We will walk to church on Sunday and sit in the front pew like good citizens. And you will rest, take your medicine, give up that malodorous pipe and get better. There, I have spoken."

"So you have. And are you God to make such decrees?" A smile cracked Will's face, though he still huddled on his side beneath the blanket.

"Yes, I am. Don't argue. I have decided."

It turned out that on almost every count I was wrong.

Chapter 36

*O*h, God, you are brutal.

Only days after I had spoken of buying off Margaret Wheeler, she died in childbirth and the babe with her. Too anguished and ashamed to send for help when the pangs came upon her, she died alone in an outbuilding of a neighbor's farm, having been driven away by her family for her sin. She had just enough strength to wrap the infant in her skirt and cradle it in her arms; then she turned on her side with the little blue-faced corpse tucked to her breast. When the farmer stepped in at daylight to fetch his scythe, he scattered the rats crawling over them. It was a boy, and he had Quiney's dimpled chin.

I think I alone cried for Margaret Wheeler, though John and Susanna were not uncompassionate. Will, weak abed, was given only the barest report. Judith said, "It serves her right," and to my anger, many townspeople soon said the same. A slut, a wench, to open her thighs to a man before marriage, though a few goodwives lowered their eyes and mumbled that perhaps Margaret ought to be more pitied than blamed. I wondered if Judith and Quiney—he would never be Thomas to me— had prayed for this very outcome. How conveniently the slate had been wiped clean. Quiney almost strutted about town afterward, when he should have been ashamed to step out-of-doors. But if God did kill

Margaret and her child, it was not to spare the Shakespeares. In that cruel spring of 1616, he had other surprises in store.

Hard upon Margaret's death, we learned that Quiney had never received the special license needed to marry Judith during Lent. He claimed an innocent oversight—he had forgotten—and I almost believe it. How can you remember to acquire a trivial piece of paper when you are about to be exposed as a liar, deceiver and begetter of a bastard? And why didn't we think of it? I suppose because Will was unwell and I was too busy with the wedding preparations, though it is also true that it is easy to overlook customs you no longer regard as significant. The church took a different view and swift retribution, and Judith and Quiney were excommunicated. In London, none of our friends would have paid it a moment's notice. But in Stratford, this second hiss of scandal was even harsher than the first, slithering through town like a viper flicking its tongue.

"We must go to church. We must throw up a front." Susanna punched her fist into her palm. "It is imperative we do not cede our position."

"Lower your voice," I begged, jerking my gaze toward the ceiling. Will had just begun to recover when the news prostrated him. "Your father is too sick to rise, and I will not leave him."

"It is for his very sake that you must, Mother. We at least have no reason to feel guilty." She gestured from John to me and back to herself. "If we are seen to be faithful and humble and render our trust in God, the more quickly our reputation will mend."

So we sat in the front pew, scandal coiled at our backs. I could almost hear Kit laughing.

Excommunicated? Ho, ho, that's rich! If there is no God, what are you excommunicated from? From a church, a building, a flock of bleating sheep who believe in a fairy tale of salvation. They will soon be sheared of their illusions and run around nicked and naked. We are all damned anyway, don't you know?

But it does not matter whether a thing is true, I retorted, *only whether everyone believes it. Then it gives them the power to make your life miserable.*

When the ordeal of church was over, I went to Quiney's house.

"I will speak privately with my daughter," I ordered before he could get out a fawning word of welcome. He dropped the pretense, knifed me with an angry look and turned on his heel to fetch her.

"Listen to me," I said when Judith entered, resentment burning in her eyes. "You have made a mess of it, the two of you, and you must perform whatever penance is ordered and set matters straight. That Margaret Wheeler and the child are dead should sear Quiney's soul, not incite him to swagger about the streets. That you are excommunicated is sheer stupidity. A piece of paper, Judith, that's all it would have taken. Now you are defiant when you should be penitent, cold-shouldering those who would stand by you while others condemn you behind your back. Don't you realize the extent of your offense? Your father is gravely ill, and you have hurt us to the core."

Listen to me. How often I have used that phrase, how often I begged, commanded, insisted on being heard. But no one listened to me. Hard as stones were Judith's eyes, deaf her ears, immune her heart. I may be miserable, her look said, but it is my own misery, and I take pride in it.

"Why?" The word twisted itself out of her mouth. "Why should I care what you or anyone else thinks of us? Margaret Wheeler and her little imp got exactly what she deserved. I bear no guilt. I was virtuous." She scanned a look up and down me, no mistaking what she meant. "If the whole town shuns us, so what? Your feelings are nothing to me, as I am nothing to you. You wish I was the one who had died."

We regarded each other, me in bewilderment, on Judith's face a triumphant sneer. She could not mean I wished she had taken Margaret Wheeler's place?

"You don't hide it well even now, Mother. And you're right, everyone is right. I am ugly and disagreeable, and I should have died in his place. But I don't forget him. I loved him. I am not afraid to look at his grave!"

Hamnet. Oh, God, my daughter was deranged. Indeed, at that moment Judith appeared so wild that her shoulders shook with the effort of not bursting into—what? Tears? Rage? Yet however genuine her distress, there was also something pathetic in it and a desire to be seen as pathetic, which infuriated me. Do not blame this on the dead, Judith. I forgive you your anguish and can see how it is misdirected from your present plight to a loss we all felt twenty years ago. But to have harbored and brooded and nursed it so long? Were you two so inextricably bound that you never broke free? Oh, child, I would still do anything I could to help, if only you would let me. But you won't, and you never have.

"Your father and I love you," I said; then I left. At home, I found Will had struggled up onto his pillows and was holding a paper in his hand.

"Send for the lawyer," he said. "I haven't much time, Anne."

⁓

For the next few days Will deliberated with the lawyer. All the river of language that had flowed off his pen, sparkling, leaping, splashing— now it came down to this last stiff trickle, these dull legal lines. I kept him fed, bringing broth and a soft-baked apple or custard to tempt him. He nibbled a spoonful or two to appease me.

"It is almost finished," he said. "I am leaving Judith an inheritance of three hundred pounds." He nodded toward the latest draft on his bedside table. What a mess—I would have to copy it over for him. "Whatever happens with Quiney, she will have money of her own."

"A wise provision," I conceded, "though unnecessary, as you are going to live many years yet."

"New Place, the Henley Street house and all our other lands I leave to Susanna. We can trust John."

"Are you sure? Perhaps you had better stick around."

"Of course, you shall have your one-third share as my widow."

"Very well. If you insist, I will take it."

My pertness amused him, and he smiled. "But you must have

something else. See where I have bequeathed twenty pounds to Joan and money to Dick Burbage, John Heminge and Henry Condell to buy memorial rings?" He poked the paper, serious again. "It will seem indifferent of me if I do not make an extra gift to you. Promise me you will think about it?" He sighed, his mouth slackened, and, frightened, I took his hand. After a while he fell asleep, and I left the room.

What to do? If a person believes he is dying, is it better to agree and make his last days as easeful as possible by approving whatever he says? Or does that only encourage him to sink lower and mistakenly release his hold on life? If you humor him and he does not die, what if you have made promises you cannot keep? Or should you forbid him to surrender, bully him to survive? If you browbeat him and he does die, did you hasten or even cause his end? How do you talk to a man you are trying to trick into recovery?

Sometimes I exhausted all my tactics in the course of an afternoon. Then, alone as the sunlight faded from the sky, I sat and cried. I was angry at Will for not getting better, at Judith for marrying the wrong man. I tried to pray; how weary, stale, flat and unprofitable the words sat on my tongue.

And on the morrow—

"What special gift do you want me to leave you, Anne?"

"A porridge pot."

"Not good enough. I have left Lizbeth a substantial amount of silver plate."

"Throw in a chamber pot for me then."

"Be serious. What about money? What about a hundred pounds?"

"Is that what I am worth?"

"It is not a question of worth. It is a financial provision so you may have whatever you need."

"I need *you*. I want"—my eyes teared—"I want what I had in the very beginning, your love."

A tinge of regret played across his face. "You have always had it," he said softly, "though never as much as you deserved."

I crawled in beside him, and for a long while, lying close, we said nothing more. "Bequeath me this bed," I said, patting the mattress on which we lay.

"This bed?" He had been stroking my hair, and he paused to give me a puzzled look. "The one in the guest room is better."

"But this may be the last place we will ever be together. . . ." I brushed my eyes and reached for the paper on his table. "Be specific so there is no mistake. 'I, William Shakespeare, do bequeath to my wife, Anne, my second-best bed. . . .' "

He wrote the words, I summoned the lawyer and on March 25 the final document was signed. The very next day Quiney pleaded guilty to carnal copulation with Margaret Wheeler and was sentenced to public penance, and we girded ourselves for the humiliating spectacle of our son-in-law appearing in church in a white sheet for three successive Sundays. But after subtle pressure by John and Susanna, the penalty was reduced to private penance and a five-shilling fine. A dead mother and baby. Five shillings.

I reported the decision to Will.

"But Judith is still married to a scoundrel who will make her un-happy." He sighed. "And what are we to do about the excommuni-cation?"

"Nothing. It will wear off in time."

And here I was right, for within two weeks the scandal was waning, and like greedy pigs nosing for truffles, the town gossips were busy root-ing for fresh notoriety to take its place. Judith and Quiney were still ostra-cized, but less vehemently. They were Shakespeares, after all, and while no one was sure they should be the first to forgive our family's transgressions, no one wanted to be the last either. The news brought fresh color to Will's face, and I began to hope we had scenes yet to be written.

Then someone grabbed the pen out of our hands.

⌒

On April 17, Magpie Joan's husband, kind and unassuming William Hart, died. Caught up in Judith's misfortunes, we had not noticed he looked unwell, and perhaps to spare us another worry, he and Magpie both ignored what proved to be serious symptoms of a disease of the blood. Magpie was inconsolable, and as she cried on my shoulder at her kitchen table, I fought my own flood of tears.

Only a few days later, Will betrayed me. He had recovered sufficiently to sit in the garden beneath the mulberry tree, and when two friends ambled by and hailed him—my back being turned—he slipped out with them to the tavern. They drank and ate a plate of oysters and drank some more. And there Will was, young again, ready to take on London and romp and roister and write himself a reputation. He was laughing, eyes ale-bright, cheeks flushed, caught up in bonhomie. Were the oysters bad? No one else got sick. A frightened, breathless boy came running to fetch me.

"Mistress Shakespeare! Mistress Shakespeare!"

I did not waste time asking questions. I ran, gasping, my bad hip wincing, my gait lopsided like a person with one shorter leg.

"It's not good," Will said, grinning weakly at me from the chair where his comrades were trying to minister to him. Then he doubled and torqued in pain.

They carried him home and upstairs, and John Hall quickly arrived. When he emerged from the bedroom, his usual confidence had deserted him.

All that night I sat by Will's bed. I thought everything it is possible to think of at such a time and made sense of nothing. If only he had stayed with me! But then, he had never stayed with me anywhere for long. I was second-best to all his other loves: the theater, his comrades, his business ventures, his poems and plays.

The end came the next morning, his fifty-second birthday.

He said to John and Susanna, "Look after your mother and Judith." Two women obviously incapable of taking care of themselves.

To Judith, he said, "I'm sorry." For what? For Hamnet? For not protecting her from Quiney? He didn't have the strength to explain.

And to me? Last words, Will, to me, your wife? I leaned close, and he breathed in my ear.

"I'm cold, Anne," he whispered. "I'm afraid."

"I'm here," I whispered back, clutching his hands. "Hold tight."

He gave a wistful smile; then his eyes turned to glass and his fingers slipped from mine.

Chapter 37

It is a foggy state you live in those first days and weeks after a burial, when the physical absence of the once-corporeal person seems unreal and unfair. Where has he gotten to? He should be here. I wandered from room to room, touching Will's clothes, his books, his chair by the hearth. More than once, I thought I heard his voice. Even standing in the church before his grave, I was half convinced it was a mistake and he would be there when I got home.

Then it did sink in, and there were days my hair went uncombed and shadows haunted my eyes from the hours I walked the night, un-visited by sleep.

"You cannot live in this huge house alone, Mother." Susanna *tsk*ed, looking around New Place.

"I don't. I have servants. They cook and clean and launder."

"But they are not family. Who will care for you in your old age?"

"I will let you know when I get there."

"But you must be lonely. Wouldn't you like to have your little granddaughter here to keep you company?"

All of which was Susanna's polite way of claiming her inheritance of New Place. What's the matter, daughter? Hall's Croft not big enough? But why shouldn't she and John have what was theirs, and besides, I *was* lonely. So Hall's Croft was sold, and Susanna, John, Lizbeth and their servants moved in with me and mine. New Place was large enough for all, and it was perfectly understood that as widow I retained the right to live there as long as I pleased. But I did have to shape up. Susanna could not allow her mother to be seen about town in a woebegone state, and eventually I emerged from my grief. I kept busy keeping busy, supervising the flower beds and the bread baking. I spent many mornings tutoring Lizbeth, an ever-curious mind. Did anyone care what I thought and felt about these things? Was anyone still listening?

In November 1616, exactly nine months after her wedding, Judith gave birth to a boy whom they christened Shakespeare Quiney. Susanna may have urged the name upon them; no one asked my opinion. Judith and her husband seemed both proud and defiant at the choice. *Non Sanz Droict*, they probably told themselves, to use the Shakespeare name after having caused us such shame. But it had the desired effect, for who in Stratford could continue to shun the couple who had produced Will's first grandson? Judith did grudgingly acknowledge me at the baptism, and we settled into the careful distance we would maintain from then on. The little boy died the following May at six months of age, and I was glad Will was not alive to endure yet another loss. I would have given anything to trade my life for that child's.

But it seems I had one more task to perform. For just when I thought myself a dwindling player, reenter Ben Jonson.

In the same year Will died, that boaster, that barrel of bombast, that bottomless braggart Ben published a folio of his own works as a tribute to himself. Damn! Why didn't Will and I think of it? But there it was right in the Stratford market, a handsome, hefty volume bound in brown calf's leather. The title page featured an elaborate engraving of a classical monument decorated with allegorical figures representing the various literary genres, and the collection comprised some thirty of Ben's plays, masques, poems and court entertainments. Do you suppose he deliberately waited to publish until Will was dead and thus usurp him? We would see about that!

I inventoried the plays in my possession. The most popular—the various *Henrys*, the two *Richards*, *Romeo and Juliet*, *Hamlet*—had appeared as quartos over the years, though some versions were extremely garbled. So many hands had intervened, the actors improvising speeches, inserts and deletions to please a select audience or the authorities, careless mistakes injected by hasty printers or their sloppy apprentices. Of some plays, like *The Two Gentlemen of Verona* written by Will for the Earl of Southampton, I had no copy at all. And what of the collaborations like *Titus*, *Pericles* and *Henry VIII*, which were only half Will's work and certainly none of mine? Should they be included? Difficulties poked at me, my worsening eyesight impeded and after a few months I put the project aside. Ah, well, did it really matter? Wasn't it enough that I kept them dusted on a shelf?

Then in the summer of 1619 Ben turned up in Stratford. Turned up, ha. Strutted, sauntered, swaggered. He was returning from a year-long visit to Scotland when it struck him that he ought to detour by Will's grave and pay him homage. Kick dust on his bones, more likely. Or maybe Ben really did feel magnanimous; Will's departure from London had left him the undisputed head of our English men of letters. He sent a boy running ahead to announce him.

"Great citizens of Stratford!" cried the breathless child. "The good—" His face fell in confusion; then he proudly recovered his line. "Good citizens of Stratford, the great Ben Jonson arrives!"

"Bring him here!" I commanded from the upstairs window; then I hastened to change my workaday dress. Even at sixty-three—good God, was I that old?—I had enough vanity to want a former lover to see me at my best. Though Ben probably gave even less thought to me than he did to his long-forgotten wife, his visit would elevate my standing in town for a spell, and the older one grows, the more one puffs at small notice. Too bad Susanna, John and Lizbeth were out visiting for the day— Wait. Maybe it was just as well. Ben was the one person who, unwittingly, might expose my past identity as Will's sister. I gave a last glance in my mirror and hurried down to meet him.

"Anne, here I am! What a quaint village, Stratford, perfectly in keeping with the scope of Will's ambitions."

He strode in and bounced a look around New Place, no doubt counting up the value of the plate and furnishings. A crowd of neighbors hovered behind him in the doorway, hoping to be invited inside. I smiled at them and cast the servants a look that said kindly close the door. The perfect picture of a court lady receiving an important visitor, and I was gratified to see disappointment and a tinge of envy on my neighbors' faces as I gently shut them out.

"Mr. Jonson and I will take refreshments in the garden," I informed the servants. It never hurt to remind them I was a person of consequence. I led Ben out, and we settled in chairs beneath the mulberry tree. "Tell me about your trip to Scotland."

Ben stretched his legs. "The long and short of it is that Scotland is a brawny place, by which I mean the kilted inhabitants have as much muscle between their ears as they do on their hairy calves. I was right to mock them in my great play *Eastward Ho*."

"Your great play? As I recall, John Marston and George Chapman had an equal hand in it."

"No, no, a small hand, a finger's worth. They may have spilled a drop of ink on the paper." He paused to sample the ale and cakes that had arrived before us. "A decent brew. It is thirsty work walking to Scotland and back. I stayed awhile with William Drummond of Hawthornden, poor soul. He aspires to be a poet, from which I vigorously discouraged him."

"Why? Do you fear the competition?"

"Me? The king's own poet? No, I told Drummond he were better off to be a rich lawyer, physician or merchant, for Dame Poetry would beggar him as she had beggared me."

"But as the king's poet, you surely receive a royal pension. To all appearances you do well." I eyed his ample belly and fine clothes.

Ben patted his stomach. "Yes, thanks to old James, I can count on a hundred marks a year. I have abandoned the public stage and am writing mostly masques now, you know."

"Still getting along splendidly with Inigo Jones?"

Ben's face blackened. "The man is an arrogant ape, but I shall trump and outface him. I am about to be awarded an honorary master of arts degree from Oxford. Does Jones have a degree? Does he? No. And I have something even better, Anne. I have posterity at my beck and call."

"Posterity?"

"The future, Anne. It is all mine. I have begun to gather about me—no, no, I must be honest; they come to prostrate themselves at my feet—I say, I am surrounded by admirers, young poets, the up-and-coming crowd. In London they sit awestruck before me as I bestow upon them the manna of my wisdom. I call my loyal disciples 'the Tribe of Ben,' and I shall disperse them into the desert to spread my fame to every corner of the earth. Everyone will write like me from now on."

It was all I could do not to laugh, in between wanting to throttle him, of course. But over the years I had found it best when confronted with a bubbling pot simply to lift the lid and let the steam blow off. In Ben's case it took a good two hours, during the course of which I gave him a fine lunch of oysters, roast chicken and a cucumber salad, finished off with an apple tart. He had undertaken his Scottish journey on foot to lose weight and was disgruntled it had not worked. Observing his appetite, I suspect he sat down after every leg of his travels and ate double. Despite his disdain for the Scots, he boasted of having been made an honorary citizen of Edinburgh. He had also criticized poor Drummond's verses—was that any way to treat his host?—and regaled him with his opinion of every other poet in England. Drummond had been so grateful for the insights that he faithfully recorded their conversations in his diary to preserve Ben's judgments for the benefit of scholars. I listened, rapt. Ben could never have written *Hamlet*. How could he penetrate the soul of another when he was afraid to look too deeply into himself?

At last the steam fizzled out. "I suppose I ought to go to the church and take a look at Will's monument," he offered.

"Let me accompany you." I would not have missed this for the world.

I called the servants to clear the dishes, and Ben and I went out the door. To my relief, the neighbors had grown tired of hanging around. The church was empty on our arrival, and I led Ben to the chancel, where Will was buried beneath the floor in front of the altar. It had taken some time after his death to come up with a suitable memorial, a bust in a niche on the wall. I didn't much care for the sculpture, but Susanna approved it so I did not argue. I awaited Ben's verdict.

"He looks a little swarthy."

"Yes."

"Thinner than I recall."

"He lost weight at the end."

"Was he that bald?"

"Quite."

Ben fidgeted for something nice to say. "He has a quill in his hand."

"Hmm."

"I suppose it comforts your family to pay him regular visits." Spoken with a touch of jollity. "Good old Will, gentle Will."

How long should I keep him discomfited? Ben had always shied from contemplating illness or death. Remember the time I was so sick and he held me down while the doctor bled me? He never looked on me the same again. Go ahead, torture him a little then.

"It does indeed give me great comfort"—I sighed—"to stand here gazing upon him. Sometimes I fix myself here for hours on end."

Ben gulped. "Well, I am glad I could pay him a visit, however brief." He made a move to go.

"Oh, but you haven't read the inscription on his grave. Look." I pointed to the floor. "Read it with me for old times' sake, won't you, Ben? 'Good frend for Jesus' sake forbeare, To digg the dust encloased heare . . .'"

Ben stumbled along.

"What do you propose to have inscribed on your grave someday, Ben? And where will it be? I suppose there are plenty of churches in London that would gladly make room for your esteemed corpse in their yard. Of course, after a while all the bodies are dug up and piled willy-nilly in the charnel house to make room for new burials. Would you like to see our charnel house? It is right through this doorway."

"No, no, thank you." Ben shuddered. "Besides, a great writer like me won't end up in a charnel house. London will hardly do less for the king's poet than Stratford has done for Will."

"Oh, but did I not make myself clear? It isn't for any reverence as a poet that Will is buried here."

"It's not?"

"No. It is because years ago Will purchased a share in the parish tithes, which gave him the right of burial inside the church. As you can see from that warning not to move his bones, the mere thought of being unearthed and tossed in with the rabble made him shiver."

Ben shivered.

"That right now passes to our family," I continued. "So I will be buried here beside him—no soggy plot of dirt and squiggling, squirm-ing worms for me." I laughed and wriggled my fingers at him. "How has your health been, by the way?"

"I would welcome a little air even now."

"Would you? In a minute. Do you know, I have been thinking about that folio you produced of your collected works—a handsome endeavor. I would like to see the same done for Will." I linked my arm through Ben's and drew him closer to the grave. "He cursed any that might move his bones, but he never said don't step on them, did he?"

I dabbled my foot this way and that on the stone, and Ben's face went green.

"I think William Shakespeare should have a folio of his collected works, don't you, Ben?"

"Yes, of course, if we could just—"

"I am delighted you agree, for you are precisely the person to assist me." I hadn't known I was going to do that, revive the idea of a folio. It just happened, an inspiration, but then, I am half a genius.

"Yes, of course, anything for my good friend Will. Some fresh air—"

"In a minute. So you promise, you swear by God almighty here in this holy church—by the way, what are you these days, a Protestant, a Roman Catholic? Or does it matter, since God sees and hears all, and you do promise to help me, don't you?" I grabbed his hand; he had been edging toward the door. "Couldn't you just stay here contemplating this sacred place forever?"

"All right, I will help you!"

"You swear it? A solemn oath?"

"Yes, I swear. I don't think those oysters you gave me for lunch are agreeing with me, Anne."

I patted his belly. "What a coincidence. Some say it was a surfeit of oysters and ale that did Will in. Do you suppose his ghost is hovering here, hoping to greet you? Or maybe to thank you for your promise. You know how ghosts can be when people break their word to the dead."

Ben's face went white, and I released him from his torment and led him back outside. He sucked in a welcome breath and began to recover his wits.

"Wait a minute. Why do you want a folio for Will when you wrote the plays, or at least some of them?"

"Did I?"

"You know you did. I threatened to expose you."

"But you didn't. You liked the joke, and now it is too late. No one will believe you. So let me have my way on this. I am content to die anonymous."

Ben's forehead creased, and we stopped walking, and for a moment, perhaps the only moment in his life, I think he did try to peer into someone else. "Why?"

"Because I know." I pressed my fist to my heart. "I know the truth and that I have done something glorious." And in that instant, tears came to my eyes, and all the joy of it rushed back over me.

"Well," said Ben, "if that is what you want."

We returned to New Place, where I dug out my list of missing plays.

"Your task is to find them and send them to me," I ordered. "Somewhere at the theater or in the belongings of the King's Men, there must be copies."

Ben nodded and set out, and I waved from the doorway. I was not hopeful he would keep his word. When had any man ever kept a promise to me? But his visit had stuck a pin in me, and once more I took the plays down from the shelf.

~

"What are you so busy at, Mother?" asked Susanna, not bothering to knock before entering my room.

I quickly pulled a blank paper over my work and tried not to look guilty. An old habit, covering up for myself. Why? Two decades into the seventeenth century, more female writers had emerged to join Aemelia Lanyer. Elizabeth Cary's *The Tragedy of Miriam* in 1613 was acknowledged the first original drama by an English woman. In 1617 Rachel Speght published a tract reinterpreting the Bible in terms favorable to our sex. We should be used to the idea that women could write. Besides, Susanna was a modern wife married to a modern doctor who espoused the latest medical advancements. Who better to confide in than my enlightened daughter? I removed the paper to reveal a quarto of *Richard III*.

"I am editing your father's plays. If Ben Jonson can have a folio published, why not William Shakespeare?"

"And you are correcting his work?"

"Yes."

A moment of silence followed, during which Susanna apparently expected me to recognize and retreat from my presumption. I did, unsettled, but for an entirely different reason. I had every right to edit the plays, but what if I overdid it? Kit's voice was there in *Richard III*, and did I really want to lose those last precious traces of him? When I composed *Romeo and Juliet* at Hardwick, my tale was inspired by Arbella's headstrong romantic longing. How dare I, an unloved old widow, presume to reconfigure those youthful passions? Perhaps it was better to let the plays stand, warts and all, as a testament to what we believed we knew then. Damn, now I would have to go back, unedit my edits, uncut, uninsert, recopy. Meanwhile, three months after his visit, I still had nothing from that irresponsible, untrustworthy, infuriating promise breaker Ben Jonson.

Susanna glanced around the room. The bed made, the windowpanes sparkling, a vase of lavender to freshen the air. No visible sign of insanity. She relented.

"Of course, Mother. Whatever you like. But do not sit overlong or your hip is bound to aggravate you, and you really should have a better light." She opened the curtain wider and pushed my ink bottle closer. "Don't forget to take your medicine and get out for a little walk. You know how John feels about exercise."

She patted me and left, having found the tack that would do her the most credit. Is it possible to drown in your own goodness like a fly in molasses? At times like this I wanted to march straight to Judith's house, plop myself down and say, "Your sister is driving me crazy. Let's seal her up in a barrel and drop her into a pond." But Judith would have no more sympathy for my project. My chickens were roosting—this is what I got for running away from Stratford and abandoning my daughters' education.

And now, increasingly, infirmities slowed my progress and tried my temper. I lost another tooth—that made three in the last year—this one so painful it had to be yanked. Even with a new, stronger pair of spectacles the words swam and darted before my eyes like a school of fish chasing itself over the page. When I arose after a long session I had to brace my hands on the table and stand on my left foot until I could rotate my reluctant right hip securely into its socket. I took up muttering, for the project grew ever more complicated. Every time I set a rule—I will not add new lines, only improve existing ones—I was forced to make exceptions. When Susanna sent a servant to summon me for meals, I got cranky.

"Can't you see I am absorbed in a matter of vital importance? Set my plate aside until I come down."

So there I was, my plans for a folio trailing to an ignominious end. Then out of the aerial blue, a package arrived.

$$\sim$$

Ben, you exasperation!

It was January 1621, more than a twelvemonth since he had pledged his assistance, and now he decided to make good? I tore open the wrapping. Musty rolls of *I Henry VI*, *King John* and *The Two Gentlemen of Verona*. Clean copies of *Julius Caesar* and *Twelfth Night*—I loved that play! *The Taming of the Shrew*, *As You Like It*, *All's Well That Ends Well* and a half dozen more. He had sent everything I was missing plus a jumble of others, perhaps in penance for his tardiness. Exactly how or where he obtained them, Ben did not explain. His letter boasted only of the "exhausting searches and endeavors" he had undertaken, his "unyielding travails" and "mighty scourings and investigations." He was gratified he could repay his solemn promise to me, and, his debt being discharged, his conscience was clear.

What conscience? What "exhausting searches"? From the mildew on the papers, he had had no farther to look than the storage trunks at the rebuilt Globe. More likely, he hadn't looked at all. He had dropped his obligation by the wayside the minute he departed Stratford and did not think of it again until, during a chance visit backstage, the plays popped into his hands. Did he even ask anyone's permission to take them? Dick Burbage had died in 1619, leaving hardheaded Cuthbert in charge. Rather than observe any niceties of the scripts' ownership, Ben probably just swiped them.

Once more I set to work. Please, God, spare me a little longer. Give me the strength to finish what I have begun. I knew not all our plays were worthy; more than I cared to admit were below our best. But I took the package as a sign. These fragile rolls wanted to be found, perhaps the worst of them most of all. They had lain there in the airless dark, mute and helpless, until nosy Ben Jonson poked into that trunk.

It was how I had found *Hamlet*, searching for velvet ribbon, acorn brown. Think how many plays by Kit, Tom Kyd, Robert Greene, Nashe, Peele and a dozen others had already been lost, the amazingly awful along with the astoundingly good. And who knew but that critical judgment of them might be completely reversed in centuries to come? This was the start of our English theater, the foundation on which future playwrights would build, and the fate of the cornerstone rested in my hands.

It took another year to complete the laborious job of editing and rearranging. Errors, inconsistencies and bad writing remained. I was running out of both eyesight and time. But what of the next step? I hadn't the strength to journey to London and negotiate with a publisher. Should I ask John and Susanna? John was too busy, and Susanna, when I hinted, disabused me of any last shred of faith in my children.

"We are very glad you have enjoyed your little pastime, Mother. Now you really must have a long rest. I am to blame for allowing you to overexert yourself." She tried to shepherd me upstairs to bed, and when I threw off her hands she lost a degree of patience. "Mother, John and I have been as tolerant as we can, but it ill beseems our family's reputation to have an addled grandam muttering away in the attic and appearing in public with ink stains on her sleeves."

What? This was how I was perceived in Stratford? I sank into a chair, stunned.

"Now, if you take your medicine, you may go sit in the garden," said Susanna. "I will fetch a servant to keep you company."

For the next few days I feigned submission, until one morning Lizbeth and I were alone in my room.

"Lizbeth, I need your help."

"Of course, Gran. What is it?"

"I must send a package to London, and my stiff fingers cannot manage the wrapping and string."

"What is it we are sending?"

For a wishful instant, I debated spilling the whole story. But it was too much weight to lay on her fourteen-year-old shoulders when the outcome was still uncertain.

"A package of papers."

Lizbeth frowned toward my table. "Grandpapa's papers that you have been scribbling on? Mother says you are not to tire yourself with them any longer."

"I won't. As soon as we send them to London, they will be gone."

"Well, I guess that is all right then."

She went to find wrapping, and I reread the cover letter I had composed.

Dear Ben . . .

Yes, Ben, damn it. As far as I knew he was still writing masques for the court and probably quarreling more violently than ever with Inigo Jones. Speaking of court, wasn't it high time for people to start asking of James, as they had of Elizabeth, Is he dead yet? But to my letter— Ben had come through for me once, albeit belatedly, and might do so again. His own folio had been a brave assertion that plays were the equal of poetry, true literature deserving of preservation and respect.

Now here is the complete manuscript, I wrote him. He had only to take it to the King's Men and insist on publication. I did not trust sending it to Cuthbert directly; he had no regard for me and probably assumed I was long dead. But since new quartos of our plays were still being issued, that proved there was money to be made by Will's name, and I instructed Ben to make that argument to the company. Think of the profits they would reap from sales of William Shakespeare's complete oeuvre and how it would permanently enshrine his reputation. Wait—I struck the second half. Lauding Will was the last thing to say to motivate Ben.

You promised, my letter concluded, and as a carrot, I had suggested he write the introduction. A risky move, but how could he refuse this golden chance to have the last word on his rival, to condemn or extol him for all time?

Lizbeth's voice sang up the stairs, "Gra-ann, here I co-omme!"

We stacked and bundled the papers, and Lizbeth tied the string, humming with the simple pleasure of a job well-done. I sent her out to the carrier and lay back on my bed, tears squeezing from my closed eyes.

Two months later a note from Ben advised that he had done his part, and the project rested with the King's Men.

Please, God, I beg you.

Nothing happened.

⁓

I spent the next year and a half keeping death and my elder daughter at bay. I dissembled when I was sick, marched bravely about town in spite of my limp, held a book in front of my eyes as if I were still reading. But then I fell; I do not know how it happened. One moment I was on the stairs, the next pitching headlong. The pain cut through my hip like a blade.

"You are not to rise from your bed again, Mother," said Susanna, and this time there was no smile, no tenderness, no saintly pretense. I made a feint of resisting, hoping to bluff her, but found I could barely move. Damn! I twisted in my sheets when she left the room. Trapped, imprisoned, at their mercy. What if John and Susanna decided to poison me? He had all those concoctions—who would know? I must stay alert, keep a sly eye on the servants, their minions. I sent for Judith and her boys—she had had two more since the death of little Shakespeare Quiney—and perhaps it was not too late to make an ally of my second-best daughter? But I saw it was a mistake the moment they arrived. Judith regarded me gloatingly, and the little boys were affrighted, my first real clue to how terrible I looked. I quickly patted my hands to my hair—but what was this that met my fingers, this shorn mat? I screamed, and Judith, affronted, hustled the children out of the room.

"My hair! What have you done to my hair?" I wept as Susanna appeared.

"Hush, Mother," she said, fighting to capture my hands as I tore at my scalp. "You had a fever last week, don't you remember? Your hair began to fall out so we cut the rest."

I buried my face in the pillow and racked myself with sobs. No, I did not remember. My hair, my beautiful hair!

"How dare you have me bring the boys here, to the bed of a madwoman," Judith scolded Susanna, her voice deliberately loud, intending me to hear. "She will give them nightmares. I am astounded you let Lizbeth in."

"She is our mother." Susanna clenched her jaw; I could hear it in her voice. "We will pay her the proper respect until the day she is buried."

The two of them began squabbling. It was almost worth my humiliation to throw strife between them. I hoped Judith would take her bad mood home to Quiney and make him miserable too. And I was glad I had not made a will of my own, just left a few trinkets for them to fight over, a final joke, ha, ha.

A hand squeezed mine.

"Don't worry, Gran," whispered Lizbeth. "I'm here."

Epilogue

"*G*ran? Do you swear? Is it true?"

Is what true?

"Granny? Gran, can you hear me?"

Yes.

"Answer me, Gran! Open your eyes!"

A hand squeezes mine, and I blink up my lids. How long have they
been closed? Ah, but what does it matter when clouds sit on my sight?
I'll lower them again, more comfortable.

"Gran, don't die!"

Lizbeth's voice pitches up in fright. Die? Who? Who is dying? I
toss my head, searching around the troubled gray room, groping toward my granddaughter's voice. It should be right in front of me, but
the distance plays tricks on my ears. "There, there, shh," I murmur. I'll
not let anyone, not Death himself, distress my sweet girl.

"What did you say, Gran?"

I said, *There, shh, don't worry* . . . didn't I?

"I don't understand. Maybe I should run and fetch Mother from
the market, but I don't want to leave you alone."

Her fingers start to slip indecisively from mine, and I clamp them
hard. "Stay."

"Yes, yes, I'll stay, Gran. I won't leave you."

Relief floods Lizbeth's voice. I must have spoken clearly that time. But it is a bad joke to pull on her, for suddenly I know the end is coming. Do you know how I can tell? No more pain. It's gone. I feel through my body. The broken hip—not there. The stiff fingers—Lizbeth is chafing them to warmth in her hands. I run my tongue over my gums, poke it snakelike into the holes of missing teeth—free of ache, every one. Am I supposed to be grateful, God, that at this last hour you have seen fit to ease me? You could have done it long before.

"Don't try to talk, Gran. I will read you some more of Grandpapa's folio."

I nod and *hmm*, and Lizbeth pats my hand and lets it go. I hear the hefting of the volume, the turning of a page. What a lovely sound, a page turning. Do you remember the booksellers' stalls at St. Paul's? Do you remember those treacled sonnets Will and I used to dash off to be sold to amorous swains? Wait, wait, whatever happened to that first sonnet Will wrote for me, the one he presented me by Shottery Brook, the one on which I learned to read? *Those lips that Love's own hand did make* . . . Where is it? Think, Anne. My whole body struggles, but I must not be moving, since Lizbeth senses nothing amiss. Ah, that's right; it is safe. He published it in his sonnet collection.

Lizbeth is skimming *I Henry IV*. "Don't you adore Falstaff, Gran? He is so fat and amusing!"

Will Kempe, you old scoundrel, have you danced your way around heaven yet?

"Listen to the names he calls Prince Hal to tease his thinness. 'You starveling, you elf skin, you dried neat's tongue, you bull's pizzle, you stockfish.' "

Lizbeth laughs, and my brow crinkles. I don't recall myself being that funny. There was often little in my life to be funny about. But look, Will, I have done it, though I am not entirely sure how it came to pass. Ben delivered the manuscript to the King's Men, but whether Cuthbert then assigned the project to John Heminge and Henry Condell or they took it upon themselves, I cannot tell. Someone, on perusing the packet, must have gleamed at the potential profits therein. I am grateful anyone could read my script; it was so crabbed toward the end. Or did they? Did they use my edits or merely steal my idea and revert to earlier quartos, bad versions? How can I tell? Damn, oh, damn! Has even my final effort come to naught? I shake my bed in fury as Lizbeth laughingly reads on.

I know, I will write to Ben and insist he oversee a revised printing. While I'm at it, I will tell him what I think of his introduction, namely, that it is better than I expected. What was it he said in the tribute? That Will outshines Kit, Lyly and Kyd, and that Nature will disown her former favorites among the writers of ancient Greece to revere Shakespeare. Very nice, though I hope such lavish praise will not produce the opposite effect and prompt readers to say, "Oh, come now, he can't have been that good." Yes, he, we, were. But I don't want to see Will so overshadow Kit and the others that no one ever reads them. The wonder of our stage! No, it is the stage that is the wonder, for without it where would Will's talent have found its outpouring? He would have lived and died a frustrated glover in Stratford; you, Ben, a bad bricklayer; me, a cackling, addled grandam.

Lizbeth has turned to *Henry V*, and I begin to recite along with her. " 'O, for a Muse of fire, that would ascend the brightest heaven of invention . . .' " My voice must have recovered sufficiently, for after a minute or two hers trails off, and she lets me finish alone.

"Your memory is awfully good, Gran. Shall we do Juliet?"

I nod, and there is that miraculous sound of turning pages, and we are off to fair Verona in search of true love. " 'Wilt thou be gone? It is not yet near day. It was the nightingale, and not the lark, that pierced the fearful hollow of thine ear.' " Stay, Romeo, stay.

"Julius Caesar?" says Lizbeth. "Mark Antony's speech?"

"No, I did not write that one."

A halt. "You didn't?"

No, I told you. I don't take credit for what's not mine.

" 'To be or not to be'?"

I smile. Everyone knows that one.

"Something from *Titus Andronicus*?"

Ugh! That monstrosity! I am too faithful; I should have burned it. Lizbeth isn't turning pages anymore, just waiting for me to start. I indulge her and begin murmuring.

" 'The lunatic, the lover, and the poet are of imagination all compact . . .' "

"Gran?" Lizbeth's voice filters toward me. "Gran, how do you know that?"

I wrote it, insolent child. *A Midsummer Night's Dream*. Half mine—weren't you listening? Now give me a kiss good night. I want to sleep.

"Gran, wait, what about *Twelfth Night*? What about *Antony and Cleopatra*?"

All right, all right. Don't be so importunate. Just one more and then I must shut my eyes.

" 'Give me my robe, put on my crown. I have immortal longings in me.' "

Lizbeth gasps. "You did write them! You did!" She shakes my shoulders as if to convince me.

Well, of course, for the hundredth time I told you so.

Lizbeth jumps up and paces to the window. "I must get Mother and Father. They must hear what you have told me."

Don't bother; they won't believe you. No one will. The ramblings of a demented widow on her deathbed. Yes, she spent some time in London with your grandfather, but that was only to keep house for him as a good wife ought. With the folio published, Will's fame is so gloriously sewn up, I cannot unpick what I helped stitch. And here is the final thing I will say about the plays of William Shakespeare. Whether they are his, mine or ours, the test of true art is that it is greater than the artist. It lifts you to ecstasy, then brings you to your knees, and by God, I am humbled by these plays!

I sink deeper into my body. No pain, that's nice. Do you know that on the last walk I took—it must have been in the spring—I made it as far as the church to stand before Will's grave. Any worms down there, Will? I'll be lying beside you soon. I'll bring you word on what everyone in Stratford is doing. I'm looking forward to it. I miss you. But

maybe you won't want me. I am even older now. Then a voice interrupted, and, turning, I saw the priest had entered the chancel—
probably to make sure I wasn't stealing the candlesticks off the altar.

"Good day, Mistress Shakespeare," he said. "Have you come to
pray for your late husband's soul?"

"I am sure his soul is fine," I said curtly, ignoring his insulted look.
Well, he was a conceited sort, and I never liked him. I gestured toward
the volume he was carrying. "Is there some recent birth or death to be
entered in the parish record?"

"A baptism, a baby girl, done this very morning."

"Ah. May I see?" I limped closer. A book of any kind is an invitation, and what could be more intriguing than this fatal compression of
lives? I wondered that I had never heeded it before. "I should like to
see the entry for my husband's burial."

"Very well." He gave me an appraising look and decided to humor
me. "Here it is. I will read it to you. "

"I can read it myself."

A huff of air left his throat, but whether it was disbelief of my literacy or indignation at my temerity in correcting him, I did not care. I
fished my spectacles from my bag and peered and squinted, while he
smugly let me suffer. Ah, there it was: *1616 April 25: Will. Shakspere,
gent.*

"Let me see the entry for our marriage," I began, then caught my
tongue. Thanks to our indiscretion, Will and I had been forced to a
hasty wedding in Temple Grafton, remember? There would be no record of our union in Stratford. "My children," I corrected. "Let me see
their baptisms."

Another huff, but he turned back the pages. "I will read it to you,"
he said again. No doubt he thought my previous remark meant only
that I could recognize my husband's name on a page. I kept silent and
let him think it, though by luck my eyes beat him to both entries.

1583 May 26: Susanna, daughter to William Shakspere.

*1585 February 2: Hamnet & Judeth, sonne and daughter to William
Shakspere.*

"And Hamnet's death?"

More slowly, the priest turned the pages forward. If seeing the entry for Will's burial had so upset me that I imagined I could read, what might I do upon revisiting the death of my only son? He pointed to the line but refrained from uttering a word.

1596 August 11: Hamnet filius William Shakspere.

"Thank you," I said sharply.

I pivoted and stumped out, shaking with rage. Where was I in this book? Where was my name? I had told Ben I was content never to be acknowledged for my plays, but to have my life go completely unrecorded . . . Did Will have no wife, our children no mother? Were they born out of midair and suckled by fairies? *Anne Shakespeare* would appear in the register at my death, no mistaking a corpse. They would be glad to get rid of me, want proof I had died. But my life had vanished as if I never existed. By God, where was I?

I held my sobs that day until I reached home. But I do not cry now. I have lived an extraordinary life, and though history will get it wrong, *I* know. If you owe me anything, God, you will have plays in heaven, and I will write them and sew magnificent costumes with my old friend Mr. Phipps. I will stitch robes for your angels, my Hamnet among them. And I'll ask Will to write me another sonnet, a new one, that vows he will love me to the end. If I had only known where my life was to lead, there is so much I would have done differently. But most of my path was without signposts; I had to get there before I knew where I was going. Now peace is descending—Lizbeth, come back from the window! Give me your hand!

"Gran! Gran! What is wrong?"

Nothing, child. Nothing at all.

Afterword

$\mathscr{I}$ first became interested in the Shakespeare authorship question more than a decade ago. Never mind which theory you espouse—just asking the question is a golden key to unlock the treasure chest of Elizabethan history and literature. It gave me the perfect excuse to read, reread, absorb and be enthralled by the poems and plays of William Shakespeare, Christopher Marlowe and their contemporaries. It allowed me to explore aspects of history of which I had only surface knowledge and to make the acquaintance of fascinating characters like Bess of Hardwick. I learned far more than I ever expected, and that in itself is richness beyond compare.

But in reading the theories and opinions of various Shakespeare experts, I soon became aware that no matter how divergent their claims on every other issue, on one matter, almost without exception, they were agreed: Shakespeare's marriage to Anne Hathaway was a youthful mistake in an otherwise glorious career. At best, they said, she was unimportant and we can forget about her. At worst, they declared, she was a homely, coarse, illiterate, immoral country wench who seduced an innocent boy and made him miserable thereafter.

How do they know? Other than some basic facts about her parentage, we have perilously little information about Anne Hathaway Shakespeare. She was the daughter of Richard Hathaway, a yeoman farmer of Shottery, and his first wife. She was three months pregnant at the time of her marriage to William Shakespeare, and they had three children altogether. She is buried beside him in Holy Trinity Church in Stratford. That's it. No authenticated portrait of Anne exists, no description of her character. Yet many experts have no hesitation in making bold assumptions about her temperament, her appearance and her negative influence on the Bard. If they can make such confident judgments based on absolutely no evidence, why should anyone trust their other claims about Shakespeare?

This novel lets Anne tell her side of the story. Even as a work of fiction, it has involved extensive research. The range of disagreement among historians and Shakespeare scholars covers virtually every aspect of his life and work, and even seemingly simple questions often lack a definitive answer. Was the sixteenth-century Thames clear and silver, or brown and polluted? What was the audience capacity of the original Globe? Did the dismantling of the Theatre take place in the dark of night or the broad light of day? Every time I thought I had pinned down some fact, I would come across another authority tipping the scales in the opposite direction. Dating the plays is a matter of particular contention, and as for the identity of the mysterious Mr. W. H. of the sonnets, I'm not sure we will ever know.

In the end, though I have tried to stick as closely as possible to what we think we know about Shakespeare, I have also taken a few minor liberties with history and simplified complex events that deserve a volume in themselves. For this I make no apology. My goal—my duty as a writer—is to tell a gripping story, and when faced with alternative scenarios I chose the one that best advanced my tale. Nevertheless, I am sure that in the course of writing the book, unintended errors have crept in. For these, I do humbly beg pardon.

Anne has been pouring her story into my ear for five years now, and I shall be sorry to let such fascinating company go. I hope she also enjoyed our collaboration and is satisfied with the result. As to who really wrote Shakespeare, I would be happy to have my novel add fuel to the fire and encourage others to read, study and form conclusions of their own. Of course, my book is fiction.

Or is it?

Arliss Ryan

Acknowledgments

It is a pleasure to thank those who have helped make this novel a reality.

My agent, Robert E. Guinsler of Sterling Lord Literistic, Inc., represented the book with unbounded energy and enthusiasm. Ellen Edwards, executive editor of New American Library, approached the manuscript with great care and thoughtfulness and made many excellent suggestions. I am extremely grateful to both of them for taking on the project and helping me bring it to completion.

For their fellowship, feedback and criticism, I thank my writers' group: R. J. Feliciano, C. J. Godwin, Jim James, Mel Minson, Rosalinda Sanquiche, Drew Sappington, Claire M. Sloane and Marie Vernon.

I am particularly indebted to Dr. Arvid F. Sponberg of Valparaiso University and his wife, Bonnie B. Sponberg, and to Dr. Elizabeth Burow-Flak, also of Valparaiso University, for reading and critiquing the manuscript. Their in-depth comments and insights on Shakespeare and his times added dimension to the book.

During a research trip to England, I garnered a tremendous amount of information from the tour guides and staff at various historic locations, including the Shakespeare Birthplace Trust in Stratford-upon-Avon, the Globe and Rose theaters in London, Kenilworth Castle and Hardwick Hall. I thank them all for their knowledge and their passion.

Most important, I once again thank my husband, Eric, and our children, Kira and Dane. From critiquing the manuscript to trekking with me around England to developing concepts for cover art, their contributions are immeasurable, as are their love and support.

Arliss Ryan is the author of two previous novels, *The Kingsley House* and *How (Not) to Have a Perfect Wedding*. She lives in St. Augustine, Florida, where she works as a writer and professional storyteller. She is married and has two children. Visit her Web site at arlissryan.com.